P.D. HAYNIE

Fiddler's Rose

First published by Spiral Path Publications 2019

(Iteration 112019)

First edition

ISBN: 978-1-950237-03-6

This book was professionally typeset on Reedsy.
Find out more at reedsy.com

For Julia, who never stopped believing that she was married to a writer, in spite of the nearly overwhelming evidence to the contrary.

Contents

Preface

The long version of the story behind this book begins with a bit of fiction I wrote when I was nine years old that impressed the hell out of my fourth grade teacher, continues though decades of acquiring and honing my tools as a writer, and the bitter realization that the ability to create on demand, which I utterly lacked, was necessary to make a career out of writing. Along the way, I stacked up large portions of at least four novels, and a thin portfolio of solid short stories. I even tried to quit completely in 2009, but that didn't take, either, so in addition to be being a failed novelist, I was also a failed former novelist. But then...

The short version of the same story begins with a tiny bit of nearly random prose that I posted to Facebook on December 30, 2017: "She was born to fisherfolk in a small coastal village. Her parents had named her, "Emerald", for her eyes, but she had never really taken to the name. It had always struck her as a name that evoked silk and porcelain, and she had known, from the time she was very young, that she was a creature of leather and steel." About six weeks later, my wife mentioned to me that she wasn't fond of most of my recent output, and that she enjoyed my earlier work more. This led to a conversation about what she liked best about my writing, which led me to examine what I liked best about my writing. This, in turn, led to an inventory of my writing tool kit, or rather two inventories. First, to determine what I was best at, and second, to determine what I enjoyed most. I cross referenced the two lists, and asked myself what a story that was built around the things that were high on both lists would be like.

For decades, my process was to conceive an idea, and then figure out how best to tell it, and then actually do the writing. Now, for the first time, I was looking at a toolbox, and a pile of random parts, and I asked myself, What can I build out of this? This book is the answer.

P.D. Haynie
December, 2018

Acknowledgement

To all of the authors, living and dead, who taught me how to write;

To all of the game designers, living and dead, and their minions, who taught me how to build worlds;

To two generations of aunts, whose love of language was infectious;

To Kurt, Steve, and Tom, who should have lived to see this day, and to Bob, who did;

To the readership of "Stygian Circlet", and the denizens of LiveJournal, for support and encouragement;

To my several adopted nieces and nephews, for encouragement and inspiration;

To the Facebook gang, for whose advice I often asked and almost never took;

To the stalwart few who read this book as a chapter by chapter serial;

I offer my heartfelt thanks. This book would not have been what it is without you.

1: Sufferance

Beauty has no need for goodness, and Charm can count on being forgiven.
—*The Book of the Blind King's Wisdom*

==)»> 1:1: Endless Plains

"You're a unicorn, aren't you?" Rose asked.

The centaur looked startled. "I'm a centaur," he said.

"Of course you are," Rose answered. "Two nights ago, I had a dream about being a horse. I've never had a dream like that before, have never been on a horse, have never even given them much thought. But there I was, running across an open plain like this one at an amazing speed, and it felt GREAT. And then this unicorn showed up, and we had sex, and that was pretty great too. And then the dream ended."

The centaur looked nervous; Rose continued. "And then LAST night, I had a dream about being a centaur, and I have REALLY never given any thought at all to centaurs, but it was still really interesting..." She cupped her breasts with her hands. "But let me tell you, galloping is not NEARLY as much fun when you're a centaur as when you're a mare. You should remember that. But anyway, the unicorn showed up again, and we had sex again, and it was still pretty great."

The centaur was beyond nervous now; Rose smiled. "So tonight, I have ANOTHER dream about being a centaur, in pretty much exactly the same open plain, and along comes a centaur who has exactly the same coloring as the unicorn, and even has some kind of weird white bone thing in the middle of his forehead, and you expect me to NOT know that you're the unicorn again?"

The centaur dropped his eyes, sighed, then looked back at Rose and shrugged. "I like variety..."

"Would you at least tell me your name?"

"Fiddler. My name is Fiddler."

"I'm pleased to meet you, Fiddler. My name is Rose."

"Pleased to meet you, Rose. Can we get on with the sex now?"

Rose shrugged and said, "Oh, what the hell."

==)»> 1:2: Waterfall Meadow

"What in hell are you supposed to be?" Rose asked.

"I'm a faun," Fiddler answered. He did a quick full turn.

"The lamb's tail is charming, but... Why?"

"Because you wanted your own body, and unicorns and humans don't... mesh... well."

"Oh. Right. But why not just be human?"

Fiddler shrugged. “Once you’ve gone goat, you’ll never go back.”

“Gods.”

==)»> 1:3: Waterfall Meadow

“This is a really beautiful place,” Rose said.

“I thought you’d like it. Open plains are kind of pointless for human legs.”

Rose nodded. “Is this place real? Does it exist in the real world?”

Fiddler shrugged. “The waterfall isn’t as high, or as full; the water isn’t as clear, and is a lot colder; there’s more mud, and less sand; the lawn isn’t as nice... It’s a real place, I’ve been there, but I’ve been dressing it up, over the years.”

“Well, it’s gorgeous. And... Could we talk for a while first? Or... All right, after. Promise me we’ll actually have a conversation, after.”

Fiddler nodded. “After. Or maybe between.”

==)»> 1:4: Waterfall Meadow

“Corrosive flower?” Fiddler asked. “Why does your belly say, ‘Corrosive flower’?”

Rose propped herself on her elbows and looked down at the tattoo between her hip bones. “Corrosion Flower. It’s supposed to be ‘Corrosion.’”

Fiddler shrugged. "Maybe. I'm not an expert at reading dragon runes. But... Why?"

"It's my name?"

"Didn't your parents like you?"

Rose grinned. "My parents liked me well enough, but they named me, 'Emerald', because of my eyes. The tattoo is an anti-pregnancy charm; the... um... magician who did the spell helped me pick out the name."

"Corrosion Flower? Did HE not like you?"

"She. Auntie Moss. She had a little house in the woods not far from town where she had lived for more than a hundred years, if the stories were true. She helped the local women with things like getting pregnant, giving birth, not getting pregnant, not giving birth..."

"NOT giving birth?" Fiddler asked; Rose just stared at him. "Oh. Right. So she wasn't human?"

"Probably not, if the stories were at all true."

Fiddler nodded. "That explains why the charm is so strong."

"Say what?"

Fiddler tapped the tattoo with his finger. "It's a real part of who you are. As a horse, or a centaur, or anything else I might have you manifest as, that tattoo will always be there. I can shape the body underneath it, but I can't blank it out."

"Interesting. So... I knew that getting involved with one of the local boys was a trap, so my first time was with a sailor off of one of the coasters, and the dice fell badly, and I went to Auntie Moss for help. And she did help, but she also told me that the service was one to a customer, and that she COULD take me off of the path of motherhood permanently, but I had to decide SOON..."

"Or the choice would be made for you..."

Rose nodded. "Yeah. It wasn't hard. I didn't know of a single woman who had been born in that village, and had a child there, who didn't stay in the village until she died. So I started asking questions at the docks, and found out about Osprey and 'Sea Queen's Sufferance', and after a couple of tries I talked her into taking me aboard the next time she came through..."

"Why did Osprey matter?" Fiddler asked.

"Because she was a female captain. With a male captain, I would have tried to pass myself off as a boy; that had been my plan all along. But when I saw that Osprey had her own ship, and had a few women serving under her, that just made everything easier."

Fiddler nodded. "And then you went to see Auntie Moss again..."

"And got the tattoo. Right. She told me that since I was moving onto a new path, I needed to take a new name, and I asked for 'Rust'. Not 'Rusty', which is what my sailor had called me, because of my hair, I guess. But 'Rust' is a thing, and 'Rusty' is a condition, and that difference mattered to me."

Fiddler smiled. "You're picky for an illiterate fisher-folk brat."

"Damned straight. So I told all of this to Auntie Moss, and she did a rune casting, and then a bigger rune casting, and then she added a bunch of special runestones to the mix and did a few more rune castings, and then she drew a rune for me, and said that it wasn't 'Rust', it was 'Corrosion'. And then she drew another, simpler rune that she said was, 'Rose', and that together they added up to 'Corrosion Flower'. She suggested that as my new name, and said that 'Rose' was indicated in the pattern as the short form, and I fell in love with it right there."

Fiddler nodded. "I can see that. Or at least feel it."

"So then she did another rune casting, and gathered some ingredients, and did another casting, and more ingredients, and another casting, and then she showed me this little bottle of something, and told me to memorize the runes on the label."

"Did you?"

"I think so." She rolled onto her stomach and started to draw elaborate symbols in the sand. "She told me that someday I would earn a way to translate the runes, and that I would eventually need to know what they said, because the stuff in the bottle was the most important thing in my particular charm, even though she had never used it for anyone else before."

Fiddler stared at the runes Rose had drawn. "That's ominous."

"The story, or the runes?"

"Both, actually."

Rose sat up and looked Fiddler in the eyes. "But you can read the runes?" Fiddler nodded. "And they say?"

Fiddler grinned. “Have you earned it?”

==)»> 1:5: Osprey’s Cabin

“Hello, Fiddler. Guess where I am.”

==)»> 1:6: Waterfall Meadow

“You talked to Osprey,” Fiddler said.

Rose shrugged. “I talked to Lyssa, first, and she brought me to Osprey.” She sighed. “There are four women on this ship, Fid, and you’ve been doing this dream sex thing with all four of us.”

“You seem to think that that’s a problem...”

Rose glared at him. “OF COURSE it’s... Damn. I was angry. I was furious. And now I just want to have more sex.”

“That’s fine with me.”

==)»> 1:7: Waterfall Meadow

“You still owe me a story,” Rose said.

“Do I?”

Rose sighed. “Osprey told me some of it, and offered to tell me more, but I said I would give you a chance to tell me your version, and she said I could come back to her if you didn’t co-operate.”

Fiddler winced. "It sounds like I'm trapped."

"Only if you want to see it that way."

Fiddler shrugged. "I used to be a unicorn. I was a unicorn for hundreds of years. And then one day a wizard decided that he wanted a unicorn horn dagger to add to his collection of magical items, and he killed me, and my spirit retreated into my horn, and he re-shaped the horn into a dagger, and then I killed him. And now I'm a ghost bound to a dagger that used to be part of my body."

Rose scowled. "Someday, I'm going to figure out a way to get you to tell that story properly."

Fiddler snorted. "I'll bet I can make you forget your own name before that day ever comes."

Rose rolled her eyes. "You make me forget my own name on a regular basis. But it always comes back."

==)»> 1:8: Waterfall Meadow

"I think I like being a faun," Rose said. "It's... comfortable."

"I thought you'd like it," Fiddler answered. "I certainly like it on you. You're... delicious."

"It's too bad there are no mirrors here. I'd like to see."

"No mirrors? You mean like that one behind the tree over there?" Fiddler laughed as he pointed.

"I think I understand 'delicious'," Rose said a few moments later. "This mirror... these mirrors are amazing."

"Of course, being magical, there's no reason to believe they're telling the truth."

Rose glared at him. "There are SO many reasons I should hate you."

==)»> 1:9: Waterfall Meadow

"I understand that you're a hero."

Rose scowled. "I killed someone, if that's what you mean. I think that 'hero' takes a bit more than that."

"But the story?"

"Lyssa and Dzee and I were in a tavern; we stick together shore-side, mostly. And yes, we were talking about you, at least some of the time, and yes, you should be worried about that. But there was this drunk who wouldn't leave Dzee alone; I think he just wanted her to follow him into the alley so he could rape her. So I got him to challenge me to a duel."

"Got him to?"

Rose grinned. "When a woman starts needling a lustful drunk who outweighs her about his virility, he's going to want to get violent."

"And you were sober?"

"More sober than he was, anyway. If I'd really been sober, I would have found another way. But he made the challenge, and I accepted and called knives, and they cleared us a circle, and I stripped to the waist..."

"Because?"

"Because he was a lustful drunk and I thought that the jiggle would distract him, and because I was drunk enough to think that it was a good idea. And it probably was. And then someone called, 'Go!' and I dodged his first lunge and put a knife through his throat into his spine. I got a pretty decent scar on my gut out of it, though."

Fiddler shook his head. "That was really stupid."

"Probably. But no one got raped, and someone else paid our bar bill, and someone had sewn up my stomach and I had gone through a pitcher of beer before I remembered to put my shirt back on."

"You're going to get a reputation."

Rose shrugged. "I protect my friends, I can fight, and I have pretty nice breasts for being so skinny. I could do worse."

"I can't argue with any of that."

==)»> 1:10: Waterfall Meadow

"Tell me about unicorns," Rose said.

"You first."

"What?"

Fiddler rolled his eyes. "Tell me what you know about unicorns, and after

I've stopped laughing, I'll consider correcting you."

"And you call ME a brat. All right, they're rare, and when they do show up, they tend to kill stallions and bulls and rams and stags, and sometimes they carry away innocent young girls who are never seen again."

"Humph. We only kill when we have to, and the girls we kidnap aren't all that young or innocent. At least mine never were."

Rose laughed. "There is no way I am going to let you stop there."

Fiddler sighed. "Unicorns are... fertility creatures. Sort of really minor fertility gods. We come on a herd of appropriate creatures — that usually means horses or cows or deer or sheep — and we impregnate every female in the herd that isn't too old or too young or already pregnant. If the males insist on being killed before we finish, we kill them."

"They're animals, Fid. They don't know any better."

"I know. It always made me sad."

"But you never left the herds alone."

"Can you stop breathing? As far as I know, that was what unicorns were built for. I don't think I was able to think about not doing it, when I was still alive."

Rose was quiet for a while while she thought about that, then asked, "What about the girls?"

"I had more choice, there. But imagine. You're an intelligent being, able to read and understand language, and you're compelled to seek out and mount cows and horses and sheep and deer wherever you can find them.

It gets LONELY. And it's really nice to have someone to comb out your mane and tail, and pick off the burrs. So we dream walk, and we look for unhappy young women, and we offer them a deal: Life as our servants, instead of whatever local hell they are living in."

"And they would come?"

"Don't be surprised. It was quite a pitch." Fiddler's voice took on a theatrical edge. "Come with me; you will probably never again sleep under a roof, or in a bed. You will often be cold and hungry and exhausted. You will work hard, and you may not live long. But you will see more of the world than most have ever dreamed of, and you will never be alone."

"And they would come."

"You probably would have."

Rose blinked at that. "Do you think so?"

Fiddler shrugged. "I know that the Corrosion Flower was born with the horizon in her eyes."

"That may be the nicest thing anyone has ever said to me."

Fiddler grinned. "No one else has ever known you as well as I do."

==)»> 1:11: Waterfall Meadow

"Why do you call yourself 'Fiddler'?" Rose asked.

"Because I am one."

“But... You’ve never had hands, other than in here, have you? So you just make it up?”

“I am deeply offended by the implication that I would in any way cheat at so sacred an art.”

Rose rolled her eyes. “I doubt that you’re capable of being deeply offended by anything.”

Fiddler stood, and indicated two fiddles that were suddenly at his feet. “May I introduce the Ogre, and the Princess. If the action on the Ogre were any worse, I would smash it to bits, and if the tone were any more suspect, I would throw it on the fire. The Princess has as fine an action as any fiddle that has ever existed, and a tone to match. When I learn a song, I beat it into submission on the Ogre, and when I am satisfied with it, I play it on the Princess, and the rocks themselves weep.”

“That’s quite a claim.”

“I am prepared to demonstrate. Name a tune.”

“‘Chasing the Luck’.”

“The Lady has good taste,” Fiddler said, then picked up the Princess, checked the tuning, and began to play.

When he had finished, Rose took a ragged breath and said, “Gods and Monsters, Fid, that’s better than sex.”

Fiddler bowed and said, “The Lady flatters me, but I beg to differ.”

“And you’re prepared to demonstrate?”

"Always."

==)»> 1:12: Waterfall Meadow

"So how did you learn to play the fiddle? Did one of your servants teach you in here?" Rose asked.

Fiddler did not answer for some time, then said, "I learned before I became a unicorn."

"WHAT?!?"

Fiddler shrugged. "Unicorns aren't born unicorns. When a unicorn impregnates a herd, almost all of the offspring are female. Extremely healthy and beautiful females, as it happens, but females. But every now and then, maybe one in a thousand, there's a male. And that male is a healthy and beautiful member of his mother's species until late in his adolescence, and then one morning he wakes up, and he has become a unicorn, and his head is full of language and intelligence and more information than he had ever suspected existed in the world, and he runs away as fast as he can. After a day or two the terror wears off, and he goes looking for other unicorns, and once he finds one, he usually learns a few more things he needs to know, and then goes on his way. Unless the first unicorn he meets is one of the foul tempered jealous ones, in which case he'll probably just be dead."

"You went through that?"

"More or less."

"But you learned to fiddle first."

"Yes. It's something of a riddle."

"Stop that. I'm trying to think."

"And I'm trying to prevent you from thinking, and I'm going to win."

==)»> 1:13: Waterfall Meadow

"You were right about me getting a reputation," Rose said.

Fiddler blinked a few times, then said, "From the fight?"

"Yep. The story has spread along the coast. Most versions are pretty accurate, but some say I stripped completely naked, and a few say that I castrated the fellow before I killed him. And since I'm the only tall, female, red-haired sailor on the coast, I'm easy to identify."

"Do you like it?"

"I think so. I get a lot of free drinks out of it."

"That never hurts."

"No, but there's more to it than that. It's as if... They still see me as a woman, but they don't see me as a woman FIRST. I'm a fighter, and a sailor, and THEN a woman. It's a big difference. Makes me wish I had killed someone sooner."

"Really?"

"No. I still see the light go out of his eyes as his blood flows over my hand almost every night."

"I have a cure for that."

"I've noticed. But it wears off."

==)»> 1:14: Waterfall Meadow

"You were born a centaur, weren't you? That was how you learned to play the fiddle," Rose said.

"Yes," Fiddler said quietly.

"I would very much like to hear the story," Rose said, just as quietly.

Fiddler blinked a few times, then nodded. "As my Lady wishes." He laid back, put his hands behind his head, and talked to the air. "Centaurs hate unicorns. Centaurs are physically compatible, and have enough horse in them that they are utterly susceptible to unicorn magic. So a female centaur who finds herself alone with a unicorn WILL become pregnant, and, as the magic goes, will be happy about it, at least until the birth takes place. And then she will be angry that she was ensorcelled and raped, but she will have a beautiful new daughter, and life will go on."

Fiddler took a deep breath and let it out slowly. "Everything is different with centaurs. With horses, it's one stallion and thirty mares, and if the stallion causes trouble, he can be killed in short order. But with centaurs, there are about as many stallions as mares, and they have spears and bows, and the unicorn needs to either run or die. But some unicorns are crazy, and like the challenge."

Fiddler rolled onto his side, mirroring Rose's position, and looked into her eyes, briefly. "My mother was different. She got it into her head that she wanted to bear a unicorn's child, and when she heard a rumor of a unicorn in the area, she went out looking for him. And they had sex, and then, since she was sure she was already pregnant, she went back to her village and had sex with every male who had a little time to spare."

"And no one thought that was odd?"

"Not really. Centaurs are kind of anti-monogamous."

"And the why of that?"

"She was hoping for, and expecting, a female child, but if the child was male, and the village knew it was the child of a unicorn, it would have been killed at birth."

"And then you were born."

"And then I was born, but the only one who knew I was under a death sentence was my mother, and she wasn't going to tell anyone. When I was eleven years old, my mother took me off to a little cabin in the middle of nowhere, and then she told me what I was, and why we were there. And we lived there until I was fourteen, and I changed. I played the fiddle a LOT during those three years."

"Because you thought you were going to lose the ability."

"And my hands, and my face, and my ability to speak... I was not a happy child, in those days."

"I am so sorry you had to go through that, Fid."

Fiddler shrugged. "There have been compensations."

==)»> 1:15: Waterfall Meadow

Rose said, "I'm looking for another berth, Fid."

"What?!?"

"I've been looking into going to another ship. I've gotten offers from a couple of different pirate chasers; they're always interested in topmast monkeys who can fight. I've been everywhere that the 'Sufferance' is ever going to go, and it's time to move on."

"But I might never see you again..."

"Don't do that, Fid. Don't reach inside my head and make me feel like I can't live without you. We both know that that fades away as soon as I wake up, anyway, and then I'm just twice as unhappy or angry as I was before. And that's part of the problem. I enjoy being with you, but I never know, the next morning, if what I feel is real, or just the result of you messing around in my skull."

"You're my friend."

"I think so. Sometimes I even think I could fall in love with you, but that just makes it worse. Because not only do I not know if it's real, I know for certain that you will always belong to Osprey. You might even be able to make me content with that, confuse me so much that I didn't mind being the spare woman. But I would never agree to that if you didn't mess with my head." She stopped for breath. "Gods, Fid, I'm not even the ONLY spare woman; you have Lyssa and Dzee too, and any other girl that comes on board."

"How soon?"

“I don’t know. Whenever I get an offer I like. Probably the next time we raise Ironbridge.”

Fiddler stared at her for a long moment, and then smiled. “I don’t suppose we should waste time, then.”

“Fid, wait. Would you play ‘Chasing the Luck’ again for me, first?”

Fiddler smiled more broadly. “As my Lady wishes.”

==)»> 1:16: Osprey’s Cabin

“This is it, Fid. It’s been a lot of fun.”

“May the gods smile on you, Rose. Think of me from time to time.”

“Every time I hear a fiddle. Every damned time.”

2: Losthaven

No need to search, it's time to mourn;
Your bride's gone off with a unicorn.
—Kzanti children's song

==)»> 2:1: Darkness

"Rose?"

"Fiddler?!?"

"Rose! Is that really you? Gods, please let it be you..."

"Fid? What's wrong? Why is it so dark?"

"I'm... I think I'm on the bottom of the ocean. You're very far away, and I don't have much energy."

"You're... Did something happen to Osprey?"

"She drowned. She... We were on deck during a storm, and she was swept overboard, and she drowned. I tried to help her, but then her ribs started to break, and she's dead now."

"When did this happen? Is the 'Sufferance' all right?"

"A while ago. I don't know. I don't know anything. You're the first person I've talked to since then."

"Fid... How long was it, after I left the 'Sufferance', that this happened?"

"I don't... A year?"

"I left five years ago, Fid. You've been alone on the bottom of the ocean for four years?"

"I guess so. I don't know. Probably?"

"Fid, how did you find me?"

"There are lights that I can see when I look for them, off in the distance; sorcerers and dragons and strange things. I can tell what they are if I try hard. And then I found YOU, and you're a sorcerer now, too, aren't you, and I'm so lonely..."

"Can you find me again, Fid? Tomorrow, when I'm asleep again?"

"Yeah, I think so. I hope so. I know what your light looks like, and sort of where it is. I can find you."

"That's good, Fid. Morning is going to come, and I'm going to wake up, but at night, when I'm asleep, I'll always want you to find me. Always. Remember that."

"Right. Rose always wants to talk to me."

"I think that that's very important, Fid. Never forget it. Never doubt it. Do you have any idea where you are?"

"No."

"I'm going to find you, Fid. I'm going to bring you back."

"That would be really good."

==)»> 2:2: Darkness

"Rose?"

"Right where you left me, Fid. How are you today?"

"Really glad I found you again. I couldn't touch you when you were awake, but you're back, now."

"I will always... I'll do everything in my power to always be here, Fid. And I'll come for you as soon as I can, but it may be a while."

"I can wait. I don't have much choice. But it really helps knowing you are there, and trying."

"I went down to the docks today, and put out a reward, looking for anyone who can give me a date and location for Osprey's death. That should help."

"It should. Any idea of when you'll come?"

"First where, then how, because the where will influence the how, and THEN when."

"So a while."

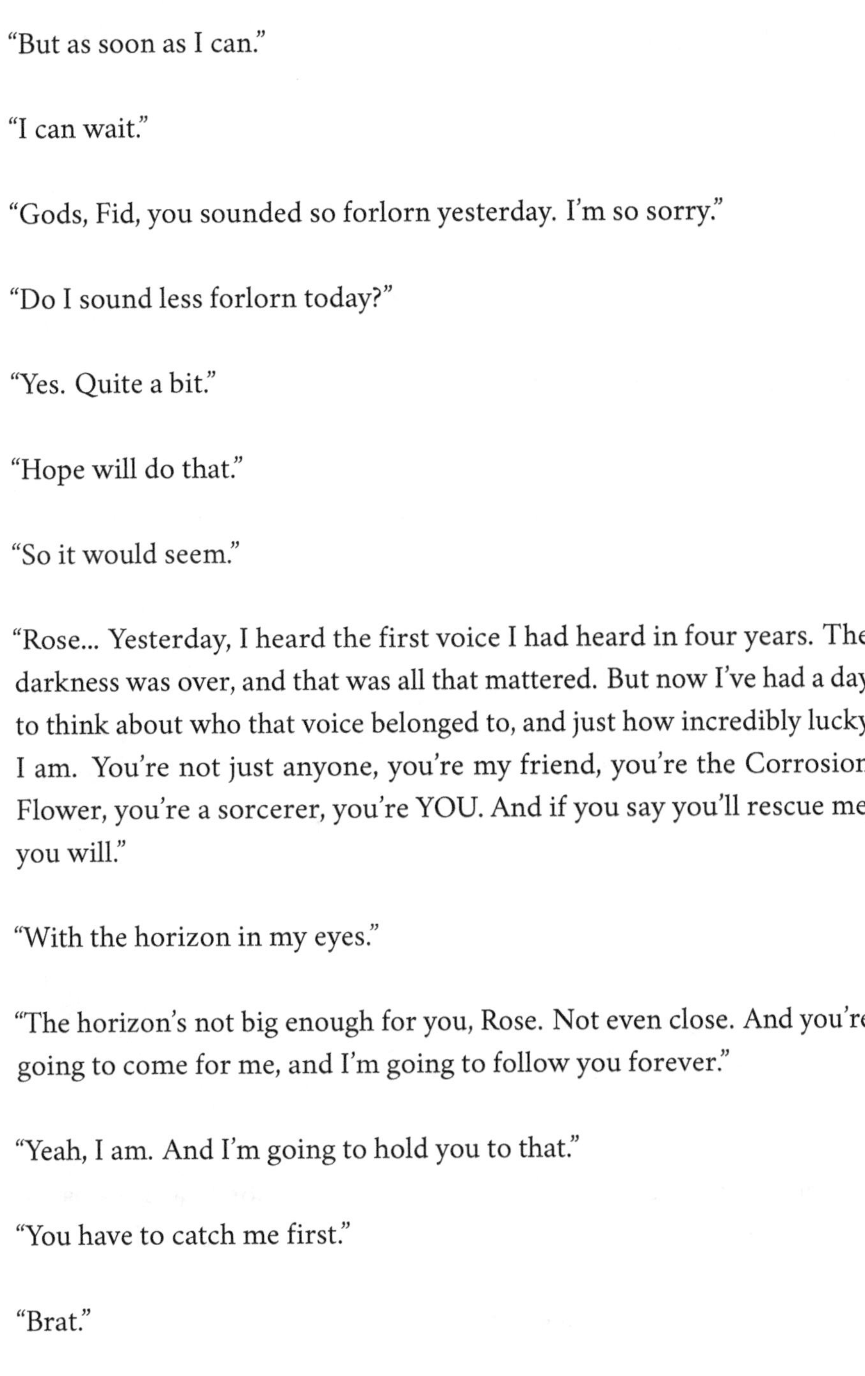

"But as soon as I can."

"I can wait."

"Gods, Fid, you sounded so forlorn yesterday. I'm so sorry."

"Do I sound less forlorn today?"

"Yes. Quite a bit."

"Hope will do that."

"So it would seem."

"Rose... Yesterday, I heard the first voice I had heard in four years. The darkness was over, and that was all that mattered. But now I've had a day to think about who that voice belonged to, and just how incredibly lucky I am. You're not just anyone, you're my friend, you're the Corrosion Flower, you're a sorcerer, you're YOU. And if you say you'll rescue me, you will."

"With the horizon in my eyes."

"The horizon's not big enough for you, Rose. Not even close. And you're going to come for me, and I'm going to follow you forever."

"Yeah, I am. And I'm going to hold you to that."

"You have to catch me first."

"Brat."

==)»> 2:3: Darkness

“Hello, Rose.”

“Hello, Fid. How are you today?”

“Very much the same, thank you. How else would I be?”

“How do you do it, Fid? Why are you sane?”

“I'm not IN the dark, Rose, I'm just surrounded by it. I have my dreamspace; I have my music, and I can run, and swim. And I started doing sculpture, of all the lovers I could remember.”

“I thought you were short of energy.”

“I am; I used to draw on Osprey, or my other partners, whenever I would reach out. But the dagger stores some, and recharges itself, slowly. And the dreamspace is really all inside the dagger, so it doesn't take much, or any.”

“Hmm. Fine. Have you made a sculpture of me?”

“Three of them. As a human, as a faun, and as a mermaid.”

“A mermaid?”

“It seemed right. And if the faun was delicious... I don't have words for the mermaid.”

“You'll have to show it to me sometime.”

“As soon as I can.”

==)»> 2:4: Darkness

"And how is her Luminosity this evening?"

"Restless, Fid. And frustrated. Nothing went right today."

"I'm sorry to hear it."

"Why 'Luminosity'?"

"Because you ARE, Rose. Before, you were fairly ordinary, magically speaking. And now you're big and bright."

"I was a sixteen year old girl, Fid. And now... I'm a lot different."

"And the story behind that is?"

"YOU want ME to tell YOU stories? After all the dodging you used to do?"

"I'm sorry, Rose. I'll try to make it up to you. And soon enough I'll never be able to say 'No' to you ever again."

"What was that?"

"If you recover the dagger, and bond with it— which I want you to do— I'll be your slave as long as you draw breath. It's the nature of the magic."

"That's awful, Fid."

"It is the way of things. I'm a ghost, and I've just spent four years with no company at all. I'm fond of you, I think you're fond of me, and it will be my honor to serve you."

"So you were Osprey's slave, before."

"Yes."

"And she didn't care that you went dream walking with me and the other girls?"

"Well... She saw no point in objecting. I can't refuse an affirmative command, but 'Don't' is not affirmative. Not when the person who gives the order has to sleep."

"You devil!"

"No, I'm a ghost. A charming and elusive ghost. Also a persistent one. The story?"

"Tomorrow. You deserve to have the need to sleep played against you."

"Well played, my Lady. Until tomorrow, then."

==)»> 2:5: Darkness

"Good evening, Madam Storyteller."

"Remind me again why I don't hate you."

"Because I am a paragon of moral rectitude?"

"Para... That may be the most absurd thing I've ever heard anyone say."

"I exist for your amusement. But you still promised."

“I’m not sure I did, but I’ll tell it anyway. And I can feel that grin.”

“I have never grinned in my life.”

“You’re dead.”

“There is that. The story?”

“The story. Fine. I left ‘Sufferance’ and shipped out on the ‘Storm Turtle’, a pirate chaser. They rated me as an Able Seaman, and an apprentice at arms. They worked me hard, and I earned my keep. I learned how to use a lot of weapons, and fought in several actions. My tally got up to nine kills...”

“Including that first duel?”

“Yes. The deed gets easier. And the ghosts get smaller, eventually. Eventually. They promoted me, called me an Able Seaman at Arms. I felt like I belonged, it was good. And then one day, after I had been on the ‘Turtle’ for about two years, there was a situation where I got myself isolated against two opponents. Some of my crewmates saw the situation, rushed to help me, and when they got there I was still standing and my enemies were dead. And then they started doing tallies, and decided that I had killed someone else earlier, making three in one day.”

“That sounds impressive.”

“My crew mates thought so. The next time we made port, they wouldn’t let me buy a drink, and I took advantage. There was a man in the bar; he had red hair and green eyes, and he started calling me cousin because we matched. And then I started calling him cousin, and we ended up in bed together.”

"And you promised me you would be faithful."

"You have a sick sense of humor. I woke up sick the next morning, fevered and delirious. I stayed that way for several days. The 'Turtle' waited an extra day for me, but eventually they had to sail, and left me and all of my things with the local healers. Healers who didn't actually have any idea what was wrong with me, as it happened."

"But you recovered anyway."

"But I recovered, eventually. I woke up with a head full of a language I didn't know, and the ability to cast a handful of minor spells. I think that I've learned what it felt like when all of the unicorn knowledge landed on you."

"It sounds like it."

"Do you remember the runes I showed you, that Auntie Moss had taught me?"

"Yes. They said, 'Sea dragon blood'."

"Just like that? No torment before you told me?"

"You already knew. What would be the point?"

"Spoilsport. So, yes, the mystery language was Dragontongue, and I got fine scales over most of my body to go with it."

"Scales?"

"Yup. The redhead had them too, but he had some kind of illusion over them. I only know they were there from my fingertips, and by the time I had my hands on him, I was too drunk and too involved to care."

"Really? Scales? I know you get really involved but... Scales?"

"Do you want me to tell the story or not?"

"Forgive me, your Reptilian Majesty. Please continue."

"Do you WANT me to leave you on the bottom of the ocean?"

"No. Sorry."

"So... I took my scales down to the local sorcerer, and he did some magical examination, and he decided that I must have had a sea dragon in my ancestry. So that, plus the sea dragon blood in my tattoo, combined with another injection of... material from my scaly red headed friend. who apparently was a sea dragon at some level..."

"You're kidding."

"No. I blush every time I think about it."

"And?"

"And those three things combined to trigger a metamorphosis. Which made me a dragonmage, mostly a hedge wizard. And then I talked Drellan, the local sorcerer, into taking me on as an apprentice, and then a few weeks ago, I broke the Second Circle and I became an honest-to-brimstone sorcerer."

"With scales."

"You're not going to let that go, are you?"

"I kind of want to take them for a test ride."

"Good night, Fid."

"Until tomorrow, Rose."

==)»> 2:6: Darkness

"Hello, Rose."

"Hello, Fid. It's your turn, tonight."

"As my Lady wishes. If only I had a story to tell."

"Tell me how you died. Full orchestration, four part harmony."

"It's a long story."

"I thought you were going to follow me forever."

"But I'm an incorrigible liar."

"Which means you should have no trouble making something up. Tell the story."

"But to tell that story, I have to tell you about Salsi, and to tell you about Salsi, I have to tell you about Kellath..."

"Sooner started, sooner finished, Fid."

"And that means I have to start with more about unicorns, and how they interact with humans."

"Impatiently, I should think."

"Indeed. Let's start with the dreamspace. A sleeping unicorn, or a dead one, as it turns out, can usurp the dreams of any creature that CAN dream, and pull that creature into his dreamspace."

"Any creature?"

"Any creature that dreams, though there isn't much point if that creature doesn't have language. Inside the dreamspace, we, the unicorns, have a great deal of power, though there are limits. We can shape earth and rock and plants as we wish, but we can't create animals; we can shape our guests in any way that we wish, and we can shape ourselves within certain odd limits. Our own forms always have cloven hooves, pointed ears, a tail of some kind, some kind of single horn, and our hair is always silver-white."

"So the faun shape you wore was the closest you could get to being human."

"Exactly. We can't actually compel our guests to move the bodies we make for them against their wills, but we can manipulate their desires to an extent that's almost the same thing."

"There's a difference?"

"It's deception rather than coercion. Suppose there was a coffin in front of you, and someone wanted you to get into it. He could physically overpower you, and force you into the coffin, or he could offer you some absurd amount of gold to climb in on your own. Assuming there's no gold..."

"And there almost certainly isn't..."

"...The first example is coercion, the second is deception. You could do either with magic, and no physical contact, but they're different things. Unicorns can't do magical coercion in the dreamspace. They can do physical coercion; a unicorn can commit significant acts of physical violence on his guests if he wishes to. Some of my cousins are sick and evil creatures."

"But not you."

"I have tried very hard to avoid evil, but I have been extremely careless and stupid on occasion."

"Careless AND stupid. That's an exit line if I ever heard one. Goodnight, Fid."

==)»> 2:7: Darkness

"Good evening, Rose."

"Good evening, Fid. Where were we?"

"You were regaling me with stories of your childhood."

"You should be ashamed. You're capable of much better lies. And we were discussing coercion and dreamspace."

"Ah. That."

"So. A unicorn can pull anyone into his dreamspace, and do anything he wants."

"Almost. Some people are too strong. You, for instance."

“I seem to recall otherwise.”

“That was then. Osprey was stronger than you were, and I drew my strength from her. When I was alive, I was stronger than Osprey was. But you, now, are much stronger than that.”

“Good to know. Wasn’t there a story in here somewhere?”

“Eventually. Maybe. Other than recreation, the USEFUL thing that unicorns do while dreamwalking is find and recruit servants.”

“And just how is a a ‘servant’ different from another guest?”

“A servant has been bound to the unicorn with a blood oath, and can communicate with the unicorn while conscious without physical contact with the unicorn’s horn.”

“Which is otherwise necessary, even if the unicorn is dead?”

“Even when the unicorn is dead. The difference is that the living unicorn is stronger than the servant, and able to control her emotions, and the dead unicorn draws strength from the partner, so the living partner is dominant.”

“Again, good to know. But that seems to be a pretty minor difference.”

“The communication includes the same level of emotional control that the unicorn has in dreamspace.”

“So a servant is really a slave, who can be made to want to do anything the unicorn wants.”

“Yes.”

"And you think I would have made that deal?"

"Sixteen-year-old you, maybe. Not who you are today; you're too scary."

"I'll take that as a compliment."

"I'll take that as an exit line."

"Weasel."

"No, unicorn. Though I admit to occasional similarities."

==)»> 2:8: Darkness

"Good evening, Rose."

"Good evening, Fid. Still waiting for the story."

"I am vanquished; my subterfuges are defeated, I surrender."

"I'm rolling my eyes extravagantly."

"Even so. Well, then... After I changed, after I became a unicorn, I followed the... Instinct? Compulsion? Whatever-it-was, and went looking for another unicorn. The one I found was mostly crazy, and tried to kill me, but he had never been anything but a unicorn, really, and I had been a centaur, and I understood things about fighting that he had never had to learn. And he was used to fighting creatures that were not nearly as fast as he was, and he didn't have that advantage against me, and eventually I killed him. I was REALLY unhappy about that, but I kept looking for other unicorns, and eventually I found one."

"And this one wasn't crazy?"

"No, he was really nice, and he had a healthy and very friendly servant, too. And he told me some things about dreamspace, and a LOT about taking care of servants, and his servant taught me some things about having sex as a biped..."

"Wait a moment. I need to... I think I need to forget that last line, but... Taking care of servants?"

"Humans can't live by grazing, and need clothing under most circumstances, and are really easy to kill if you do something like tell them to stop complaining."

"I would imagine."

"So I went on my way, and when I got lonely, I went looking for a servant. I went through the first few pretty quickly, in spite of the coaching, until I figured out what to look for when I was recruiting, and learned the necessary survival skills myself. Farm girls, even on remote farms, don't often have the hunting and tracking skills that life with a unicorn required, so I had to be able to teach them."

"That makes sense."

"I learned to look for battered wives with no children, or perhaps a single child that made her unhappy that she was willing to abandon. Sometimes they killed their husbands as they left; sometimes I killed their husbands. One killed her husband AND her infant child; I didn't know she was planning that until it was done. She killed herself not too long afterwards, and I didn't regret her death. I felt pretty awful about the whole situation, though."

"So you were a monster with a guilty conscience?"

"If you like. I never just turned around and recruited a new servant, though; it was usually at least a year, and sometimes several years, after each loss, before I went looking for a new servant. And that, finally, brings us to Kellath."

"Who you mentioned at the start of this?"

"Yes. He was my next-to-last servant."

"HE?!?"

"Yes, he. My worst mistake in a long string of them. I'd been alone for a long time, and had wandered far north. I didn't think about it at the time, but I guess that one of the reasons was that there were fewer herds up that way, and fewer herds meant fewer compulsions. But I got really lonely, and started wandering to the edge of settlements and doing dream walks. And I found Kellath, who was a middle-aged slave from the south who hated his life, but knew he would die in the wild if he tried to run. So I offered him a chance to go south again."

"This can not end well."

"It doesn't. After a few weeks, I got stupid, and put it in his head to wonder what it was like to be a woman, and it went from there. I was happy, he was happy because I forced him to be happy, and then one day while we were on a mountain trail along the edge of a cliff, he jumped off of my back and over the edge."

"So not EXACTLY evil, but REALLY careless and stupid."

"Yes."

“I need to think about that for a while.”

“I’ll be here.”

==)»> 2:9: Darkness

“Good evening, Rose.”

“Good evening, Fid. Please tell me that last night was the worst bit.”

“Well, I’m going to die, but yes, that was the worst thing I’ve ever done.”

“Onward and upward, then.”

“Indeed. After Kellath, I was alone for a LONG time. More than a decade. But as always, I got lonely, and started to dreamwalk again, and eventually I met Salsi, who was intelligent and personable and the most miserable person I had ever met. She was married to a brute who beat her regularly; when I first started talking to her, she was on her third pregnancy, having lost the first two to her husband’s fists. I offered to kill him more than once, but she told me that she wanted to persevere. And then the brute came home drunk, and she lost this pregnancy too, and I kicked down the door and pinned her husband to the wall and watched him bleed out. Then I healed Salsi, and asked her to be my servant, and she accepted.”

“How did you know what had happened? How did you find her?”

“Because I was waiting for her in dreamspace, and she turned up unconscious. I knew where she was physically because I had been looking for her, and asking her questions. She took the oath, climbed on my back, and we ran. I had learned a LOT about the care and feeding of servants, by that time, and I kept her alive for nearly a hundred years. We worked out a deal where we would actually get paid for servicing the herds. Life was really good for many years."

"And then someone killed you."

"And then a thrice damned sorcerer named Belkith Norr decided he wanted a unicorn horn dagger, and eventually he found me. For a few years he just sent servants; they tried to kill me, and I killed them instead, and they tried to capture Salsi, and I killed them instead, and then finally Norr got bored, and came in person, and blasted me. I don't know what happened to Salsi. That's kind of worse than being dead."

"I don't have words, Fid."

"There aren't any. I appreciate the thought, though. But to continue: When a unicorn dies, its essence retreats into its horn. The unicorn can give up existence if it wants to, but life as a ghost in a unicorn's horn isn't that bad. And the horn is anchored to the skull unless the unicorn lets go of it. So Norr threw a domination spell on me, and made me let go of the skull, and then he used magic to reshape the horn into the dagger you know. And then he used another compulsion spell to force me to create a blood bond with him, and then I was his slave."

"Except..."

"Except that he was such an arrogant bastard that he never actually learned the rules. 'Never attempt to harm me in any way,' is not an affirmative command. He opened the bond between us, which gave me access to his power, and then he tested the edge of his pretty new toy against his thumb, and I turned the full force of his will, which was significant, against his body, which was pretty ordinary, and he died."

"Which left you where?"

“Which left me locked in a sorcerer’s workshop, waiting for some enterprising thief to break in and let me get on with my existence.”

“Why do I get the feeling that this isn’t something else that I should feel sorry for you for?”

“Norr had a dragon bone staff, that was also left behind in the lab when he died.”

“And...?”

“When a unicorn dies, its essence retreats into its horn. When a dragon dies, its essence is fragmented throughout its entire skeleton, and under the right circumstances, each of those fragments can develop into a complete personality. So Norr’s staff actually had a dragon spirit that hated Norr as much as I did.”

“You are NOT going to tell me...”

“Yes, she was female. Sulissa and I became very good friends before the helpful thief finally made his entrance.”

“Why do I think that if I leave you where you are, you’ll find a new species of mermaid?”

“I’d really rather have you, Rose.”

“And on that note, good night.”

3: Ironbridge

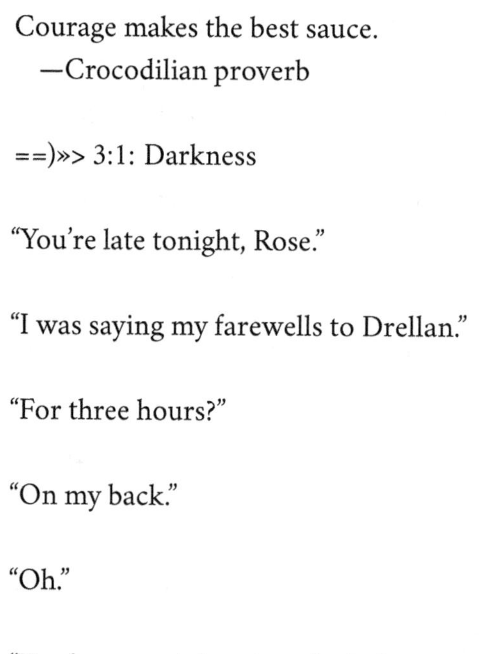

Courage makes the best sauce.
—Crocodilian proverb

==)»> 3:1: Darkness

"You're late tonight, Rose."

"I was saying my farewells to Drellan."

"For three hours?"

"On my back."

"Oh."

"You have no right to ever be jealous over anything, and you know it. And Drellan has been a perfect gentleman for three years, and I don't think he has had sex since I've been studying with him, and I KNOW that I haven't, and I may not see him in a long time, if ever."

"You've been practicing that speech."

"Maybe a little."

“Convincing yourself?”

“Preparing myself for the inevitable caprine interrogation.”

“Was it worth it?”

“It’s been three years, Fid. What do you think?”

“I think that I’ve been on the bottom of the ocean for four years, and I might hate you.”

“I’m going to rescue you anyway.”

“Well, then.”

==)»> 3:2: Darkness

“You’ve moved since last night, Rose.”

“I’m heading west to Ironbridge. After three years in Losthaven, it was time to move on. Am I closer to you? Can you tell?”

“I don’t think you’re closer or farther away, just in a different place. What’s in Ironbridge?”

“Other than a big city? Mostly, it’s the first leg of the trip to Sweetwater. I think I need to go home and have a talk with Auntie Moss. And if that helps figure out where you are, all the better.”

“Because finding me is the first step in bringing me home.”

“Something like that. You said something the other night about me being three hours late. Do you have some way to tell time?"

"I built a day long sand clock, right after I found you. I was making myself crazy checking to see if you were asleep, so that I could talk to you again, so I built a clock. It took a few days to get it calibrated, and it probably isn't very accurate, but it does what I need it to do."

"I'm impressed, Fid. I didn't know you were such an inventor."

"You remember those fiddles I built?"

"Those... I didn't realize, Fid. I just thought... I took them for granted."

"I built a better-than-sex fiddle, and you just assumed I had picked it up in a store somewhere. Inside the dreamspace. Where there are lots of stores, after all."

"I get the point, Fid, and I'm sorry. But the reason I asked about the clock is that I've been working on a meditation technique that might let you contact me when I wasn't asleep, but you would need to come looking for me while I was meditating. Want to try for noon today?"

"That... would be good, I guess, but what would be the point? I only have so much energy."

"But if I were actually looking for you, trying to get close enough to you to find you by sight or spell, I might want to check in with you and get a bearing more often than every 24 hours."

"You've been putting a lot of thought into this. I might even forgive you for taking my Princess for granted. Someday."

"See you at noon, Fid."

==)»> 3:3: The deck of the "Wandering Star"

"Hello, Rose. Been waiting long?"

"Almost two hours, but I started an hour before noon. Your clock is about an hour slow."

"I'll fix that. What else is going on? It feels like you're grinning like a fool."

"I earned a refund on my passage this morning. And a bonus."

"That's impressive. How?"

"Chicanery."

"Without consulting me?"

"You weren't available."

"What happened?"

"We were becalmed sometime after midnight, and started to drift toward shore. Almost all of the land between Losthaven and Ironbridge is marsh, about 500 miles of it. It's all crocodilian country. When dawn came, we still had no wind, and there were a couple of longboats full of crocs headed for us."

"You did NOT lead the crew in a defense against croc pirates."

"No, I swindled them. I hailed them in Dragontongue, and told them that I was the servant of a major dragonmage, and that if they forced me to wake up my master, he would kill them all. They hesitated, and I told them that if we had to kill them, we'd use their bodies for fish bait, and they turned around and went back to shore. And then the crew put out the longboat and kedged us back to deep water, and the captain gave me back my passage fee and offered me a share of the ship."

"For running a scam on some crocs?"

"He didn't know what I'd done. I'm the only one on the ship who can speak Dragontongue. All anyone other than you and I know is that I told the crocs to go away, and they went. The crew is terrified of me, but grateful."

"I'm missing something here."

"Crocs aren't used to people knowing their language, so when I did, and sounded well educated, they knew I was a sorcerer. And when I threatened them with a bigger sorcerer, they were inclined to believe me."

"And the fish bait line?"

"Cannibalism is a big thing with crocs. You show respect for an enemy by eating him. Being used for bait is the most horrible thing that can happen to a dead croc; it's a passport into crocodilian hell."

"So they decided not to take the chance."

"Yes."

"That's kind of evil. I'm impressed. How'd you learn so much about crocs?"

"Tonight. I need to get out of this trance before my my feet develop gangrene."

“Until then, Rose.”

==)»> 3:4: Darkness

“More comfortable now, Rose?”

“Wrapped up in my old hammock, which is cleaner that it ever used to be, and slightly drunk. The captain insisted on expressing his gratitude with brandy. Pretty good brandy, too.”

“Someday you can share the memory with me.”

“Maybe. If I don’t find some better brandy in the meantime.”

“That would be good, too. You were going to tell me about crocs?”

“It starts with kobolds. Do you know anything about them?”

“Small, look like crocs, but aren’t swimmers. Dangerous in packs, nuisances otherwise.”

“You can add to that that they’re kind of dumb, and really enjoy cruelty; they’re fond of food that screams while it’s being eaten. And then the thing that everyone seems to miss: They’re amazingly loyal. A kobold who feels an honest debt to you will die for you.”

“Which implies you have first hand experience of this.”

“Yeah, I saved a kobold beggar from a beating that might have killed him. Had to kill the drunk responsible, though.”

“That was hardly full orchestration and four part harmony.”

"No, it wasn't, was it? Well enough... There was a kobold beggar that I saw almost every day; he had a threadbare, faded blue cloak to help him hide from the sun; I would greet him when I saw him, and call him, 'Mister Blue'. He responded by calling me,'Dutchess', because I spoke Dragontongue with an educated accent. Most kobs can speak some Kzanti, usually pretty badly, but they speak Dragontongue among themselves. Drellan and I were probably the only people in Losthaven who spoke Dragontongue, and Drellan was always too self-conscious of his accent to try to speak it conversationally."

"Drellan isn't fluent?"

"Drellan isn't a dragonmage; he learned almost all of his magic in Kzanti, just had a few necessary words and phrases in Dragontongue. But he was pretty much topped out as a sorcerer without leaning Dragontongue properly, so when I came along and offered to teach him the language in exchange for magic lessons, he jumped on the chance."

"And then there was a kobold named Blue..."

"And one night I happened to be nearby when a drunk tripped slightly over Blue's feet, and got angry and kicked Blue in the face. He was setting up for another kick when I pushed him away; he turned on me and drew a knife. I backed off, he turned back to Blue, and I pushed him away again. He charged me, I dodged and gave him a bit of a push, and he sprawled head first into a wall. He didn't get up. I gathered up Blue and took him off to the local healers, who wanted a bribe I could barely afford to patch him up. And I thought that was the end of the matter."

"But Blue didn't see it that way?"

"Very much not. He showed up at Drellan's doing his best to pay me back with all the resources a kobold beggar could muster."

"Ah. The wealth of empires."

"Very, very small empires. But we started having real conversations, and I started finding odd jobs for him."

"If you feed them, you can never get rid of them."

"Probably not. Until tomorrow, Fid."

"Until tomorrow, Rose."

==)»> 3:5: The deck of the "Wandering Star"

"So how long until noon, Rose?"

"A quarter hour, maybe. You're close."

"I do my best."

"I'm having trouble understanding how your clock works at all. Isn't the dreamspace all in your head?"

"I used to think so, when I had a head. Now I'm a disembodied personality bound to a piece of my former body which is almost immutable and indestructable, and the dreamspace hasn't changed. Whatever and wherever it is, I was able to get a two hour error down to a quarter hour, so something works."

"I guess so. Mark."

"Done. Tomorrow will nail it down hard. See you tonight."

"Until tonight, Fid."

==)»> 3:6: Darkness

"Safe in your hammock again, Rose?"

"And sober, tonight. Where were we?"

"Kobolds. Specifically one in a blue cloak."

"Ah. I found out that kobolds are not only loyal, they're utterly honest. Enthusiastically sadistic, and unbelievably vengeful if crossed, but utterly honest and terrifyingly loyal. It takes four kobolds to do as much raw work as a man can do, but you can hire a dozen kobs for the price of a poor man."

"And ten men to match one horse. But I see where this is going."

"Blue introduced me to his village. I started making deals, providing kobs to do work in Losthaven. It spread from Blue's village to other villages. And all of this was in my spare time; I was still studying with Drellan full time. And then one day Blue came to me and asked my help; the kobolds were having a problem with crocs, and thought maybe I could accomplish something."

"The kobolds appointed you as their ambassador to the crocodilians? That would be hilarious, except it was probably life threatening."

"You've been reading ahead. I went looking for the croc village, and was met by a war party that told me I wasn't worth their time, and that if I didn't go away they would fill me with spears. I did the 'How dare you?' thing, and claimed a right to prove my worthiness."

"Which entailed what?"

"I had no clue. But it got me an interview with the village shaman, who informed me that I had volunteered for a duel to the death with a champion of his choosing."

"And you didn't run? You shouldn't take chances like that; you have a ghost to rescue."

"I didn't know you were lost, at that point. And I didn't see any alternative; my kobold escort was long gone, and I was alone in a croc village. I realized that if I didn't fight and win, I was going to be the occupant of the roasting pit they were preparing. I said as much to the shaman, who said that that would only happen if I fought and lost. If I refused to fight, they would cut me up and use me for bait."

"Which is how you know about that."

"Which was the first time I had heard about it. The shaman was talkative, and I've spent a fair amount of time with him since then. He told me that he hoped that I won, because I was skinny and looked kind of stringy, and my opponent had meat to spare. Also he was a loud mouthed dimwit that the tribe would be better off without. Then he pointed my opponent out to me, and made sure I noticed that he was celebrating in advance with some kind of fermented stuff. NASTY fermented stuff, but I didn't find that out until later."

"You can keep that memory to yourself, if you don't mind."

"Spoilsport. So they drew a circle, and we took our places. My opponent was a LOT bigger than I was, and he had a spear and a round shield. I had my rapier, and I had found a buckler that they let me borrow. He was a hunter, mostly, and had fought some mock duels; I had learned to fight from pirate hunters, and trained with the Losthaven militia whenever they could be bothered to meet. And I was faster than he was. He charged, I dodged, and gave him a small cut as we separated. And again, and again. He was losing blood, and slowing down, and I started to go on the offensive. During one disengagement, he asked me to promise him that I would eat his heart."

"WHAT?!?"

"That was my reaction, though I was breathing hard enough that it wasn't quite that emphatic. He repeated the request, and I told him that I would if I were allowed to. Then he said, 'Thank you', spread his arms wide to expose his chest, and looked straight up into the sky."

"And you killed him."

"And I slammed my sword into his heart as hard as I could."

"Do you eat the heart?"

"Yup. Well, half of it. The thing was huge, and I asked the shaman if it would be disrespectful to offer part of it to someone else, and he said no, and licked his teeth. And when we were done eating, we did our negotiation over too much of that nasty fermented green stuff. I spent the night in the village, and in the morning they gave me all four of my opponent's fangs, and I went home."

"And you're wearing his fangs around your neck right now, aren't you?"

"Yup."

"Do you know his name?"

"Lostclaw Bonecarver. Or the equivalent in Dragontongue. His friends called him something like 'Losty'."

"Exit line?"

"Twice. Noon again tomorrow?"

"Absolutely."

==)»> 3:7: The deck of the "Wandering Star"

"Boo!"

"Dammit, Fid, you almost missed it."

"But I didn't, did I?"

"You mean you delayed on purpose?"

"If one must do a thing, one should do it with as much style as possible."

"You... Damn. Mark."

"Done and documented. See you tonight!"

"You...!"

==)»> 3:8: Darkness

"Something feels different tonight."

"I'm sleeping in a bed on dry land, after seven nights in a hammock at sea. I'm surprised you can tell the difference, though. I didn't know you got that much information."

"I just know there's a difference. I didn't know what it was."

"Ah."

"So what now?"

"I'm going to spend a few days on the docks, trying to find information about the 'Sufferance', and then I'm going to go looking for a ship that will take me to Sweetwater."

"You never heard anything in Losthaven?"

"No, but that was always a long shot. 'Sufferance' really only traveled between Ironbridge and Turtle Bay, unless something special and lucrative came up."

"And if you don't find anything?"

"Then she never made port after Osprey died. Which would be several kinds of bad news. If she made port, even if she had to be scrapped afterwards, there'll be something."

"Do you think she's still sailing?"

"It depends on how much she was damaged, and how much legal trouble there was. I THINK Osprey owned her, but there may have been loans, or partners, or heirs. Or maybe old Kyle, the purser, had the presence of mind to forge her new papers, and sail away under a new name."

“Wouldn’t that be piracy?”

“Technically, but if Osprey owned her free and clear, and had no heirs, that would keep her sailing, and out of the hands of whatever harbor authority decided to snatch her. It would keep the crew working honestly, more or less.”

“Are all sailors thieves at heart?”

“No. Absolutely not. I definitely heard about an honest one, somewhere. Far away. Never actually met him, though.”

“That’s an Osprey line.”

“It is, isn’t it? I had forgotten.”

“I miss her, Rose. She deserved better.”

“We all do, in the end, Fid. Or maybe not. She died doing something she loved, with someone who loved her holding her hand.”

“Metaphorically.”

“Metaphorically, with benefits. Good night, Fid.”

==)»> 3:9: Darkness

“Good evening, Rose.”

“Hello, Fid. I’ve got news on the ‘Sufferance’. She landed here in Ironbridge after Osprey died.”

"And?"

"She had come all the way across the bay from Silverport, nearly a thousand miles. The crew got salvage rights, sold the ship and cargo, and shared out the proceeds. 'Sufferance' was refitted and renamed, and is who-knows-where now. So I'm headed for Sweetwater as soon as I can find a ship, but I'll keep looking for old crew mates in the meantime."

"Is this worse news than I understand?"

"It's... Fid, the whole time I was on the 'Sufferance', we never went east of Ironbridge, and almost never went south of Turtle Bay. 900 miles of coastline at the most. I thought I could just sail along that route until I sailed over your head, and then I would be able to start working on how get to you. You were supposed to be within a day's sail of dry land, in water that was no more than a few hundred feet deep. That was bad enough, but I was ready for it. There's 900 miles of open water between Ironbridge and Silverport, and I have no idea how deep it might be. Rescuing you might not be possible."

"Are you quitting?"

"What? No. Of course not. I used to be able to see the top of the mountain, and now I can't anymore. That's discouraging. But the job has always been to climb and keep climbing, and I will."

"Even if you never see the top of the mountain again?"

"Even so."

"Why?"

"Because you're my friend, and you need help, and I'm in a position to try. If I manage to prove that the task is really and truly impossible, well... We'll see. I just need to get used to the idea that we may be working on this for a LONG time."

"Sorry."

"Don't be. It's not your fault you're where you are. It's only slightly Osprey's, and I don't hold it against her. If she hadn't gotten herself killed, I couldn't dream of having you all to myself."

"Do you?"

"Not really. Maybe a little. People confuse me."

"You want some advice? Advice born of several hundred years of dealing with people?"

"Sure."

"I don't have any. People confuse me, too."

"Brat. And here I was feeling all weepy and apologetic because you're the one who's trapped.

"But I have a lifeline, Rose. I'm not allowed to give up hope unless you do."

"Not allowed?"

"You're a gift from the universe, and I'd be a fool to not be grateful."

"And thus, with words of honey, was the maiden's heart won."

"Maidens are small beer. You are a killer and a child of dragons and a weaver of magic. "

"You're utterly shameless and incorrigible and I am GOING to find a way to rescue you."

"I'm certain of it."

==)»> 3:10: Darkness

"Good evening, Rose."

"And to you. Fid, why did you contact me when you did? I'd been sleeping in that same bed for three years."

"I hadn't seen you before that. When Osprey first died, I spent a lot of time looking at the world around me, wondering who or what I could see. There are a lot of sorcerers, a few dragons, Maelstrom the turtle..."

"You can see Maelstrom?"

"Oh, yes. It's hard to NOT see him. He's the biggest, brightest light I can see. He never seems to sleep, and he's almost constantly in motion. He's... His mind is really alien, even for a dragon. He gives me a really strong impression that if I get too close I'll get pulled in, and not be able to escape."

"I've only seen him once, in the distance. He's amazing."

"He is. But you... I had found Drellan. I didn't know his name, but I knew there was a single sorcerer there, just a bit to the right of the big forest dragon."

"The Jade Empress?"

"I wouldn't know what she calls herself. But she's BIG."

"She claims all of the marshland between the Lost River and the Iron River, and no one argues with her."

"Ah. Well, after a while, I got to know who was where, and there was no one I willing to risk talking to, so I didn't check very often. Of course, since it was the only thing in my existence that ever changed AT ALL, I couldn't stay away completely. And then one day a light popped up next to Drellan, and I realized that I recognized it, and here we are."

"I had just broken Second Circle. That must be it. Interesting."

"So you would have been leaving Drellan anyway, even if I hadn't turned up."

"Yes. And I was still going to go have a talk with Auntie Moss. But everything has more purpose, now."

"I'm flattered."

"Yes, I have to rescue my idiot unicorn friend."

"Ouch. And on that note..."

==)»> 3:11: Darkness

"Good news?"

"I found a ship, Fid. I'll be back in my hammock, and on the move, tomorrow night."

"On the way to Sweetwater?"

"Yes. My ship won't bother to make port; it's too big. But it'll anchor out, and the locals will come out to trade barrels full of water, and barrels full of salt fish, for empty barrels and silver. I'll have to talk my way onto one of the local boats, but it shouldn't be too hard; I know most of the boatmen. Or I did, six years ago."

"Will they be glad to see you?"

"I hope so. If my parents were REALLY angry about me leaving, there might be some hard feelings. I'll find out soon enough."

"That you will. How far is it?"

"Five hundred miles, more or less. At least fifteen days."

"Why so slow?"

"We'll be stopping along the way, and about a third of that distance will be to windward. That reminds me. You said that the Jade Empress was to the left of Drellan."

"Yes?"

"And I'm currently to the left of the Jade Empress?"

"Also yes."

"Can you draw a map? Or at least, a plan of the angles. If you look straight at Drellan, the place I am now is some fraction of a circle to the left of your current position. And before long, we'll know how much of a circle separates Drellan from Sweetwater. Bearings from two fixed points gives you an arc of possible positions; bearings from three fixed points gives you an exact location."

"Exact?"

"To the limit of the accuracy of the measurements."

"Ah."

"It's something. The smaller the search area, the shorter the search."

"I think I need to go work on map making, then, given that you'll be on the move in the morning. I... I am very glad that you are you, Rose."

"I go well with myself. And thank you."

4: Sweetwater

The gods of chance are at least as likely to reward audacity as they are to reward brilliance.

—Perrin Ironhand, *Armor and Hob-nailed Boots*

==)»> 4:1: The deck of the "Sea King's Plaything"

"You're not sleeping, Rose."

"No, it's too beautiful a night. The weather is good and the air is warm and the sky is clear and we're sailing along the same stretch of coast that the 'Sufferance' covered when I first signed onto her, and I just had to try to share it with you. I'm tucked up under the bowsprit where no one is likely to trip over me."

"You feel happy."

"I am happy, or as happy as I'll let myself be with my best friend on the bottom of the ocean. Which is actually pretty damned happy."

"I'm glad. It feels good."

"Does it? Then I'll have to try to cultivate the experience more often."

"I'd like that."

“If you were here... If you were a living person, this would be a moment that was just too sweet to spoil with conversation.”

“Then don’t try to talk. The link will remain, and I’m glad of it.”

“You’re amazingly sweet for an incorrigible lust-monster.”

“You’re amazingly sweet for dragon-blooded killer.”

“Shhhh.”

“As my Lady wishes.”

==)»> 4:2: A cabin on the “Sea King’s Plaything”

“Rose? Are you all right?”

“Fid! I feel like I could explode. There’s no way I could sleep; I can barely stay calm enough to hold this trance.”

“Because...?”

“I saw Maelstrom today, Fid! I TALKED to Maelstrom today.”

“You... talked... to the Great Monster Turtle.”

“It was just so amazing he’s...”

“ROSE!”

“Huh?”

"You need to calm down and try to be coherent. It feels like you're shouting and slapping me in the face."

"Oh. Sorry. I'll try."

"So... Maelstrom."

"So... We were westbound on a broad reach on a southeast wind, making five or six knots, everything pretty much perfect, and suddenly he was THERE, just off the port aft quarter, overtaking us slowly. His flippers almost touched the ship. Everyone crowded to the weather rail to see. When his head was opposite me, he lifted his head out of the water and said, 'Hello, Granddaughter'."

"He SPOKE to you."

"To all of us, but I was the only one who spoke Dragontongue, or was female. Nearly knocked me off my feet. Have you ever been so close to a lightning strike that the thunder was instant? Your ears ring and your teeth rattle and you feel like you've been hit in the stomach? It was like that."

"What did he say?"

"He told me to climb up where he could see me, so I grabbed the main shrouds and pulled myself up onto the rail. And then he raised his head again, and again that eye just sort of ATE me... his eyes are as long as I am tall... and then he said that I had three dragon marks, all from the same noble house, and he asked me if I was trying to become a dragon."

"And you said...?"

"That I wasn't aware that it was an option, and he... LAUGHED at that.

It was terrifying. And then he said that if I chose to follow that path, I had his consent. His CONSENT."

"And you don't know what to make of that?"

"I don't have a clue in the world. Then he told me to join him in the water, and we would have a chat. So I dropped back to the deck, stripped off my shoes and most of my clothes, and then climbed back on the rail and jumped in. And then Maelstrom submerged and the ship just kept on sailing, and for a moment I wondered if I had just killed myself."

"I can understand that."

"And then Maelstrom came up right underneath me, and told me to settle myself on the front edge of his shell, so I did. And then he caught up with the ship, and got in front of it, and let the ship ride his wake. They told me afterwards that we were doing almost nine knots. This ship has NEVER gone that fast before."

"And you had a chat with the turtle."

"And I told him all about myself. After a while, he said I should prepare to get off, so I made my way back to the aft end of his shell, and called for a line."

"What did the crew do?"

"They threw me a line and pulled me aboard. Also stared at the giant turtle, and shivered in fear, I think."

"That sounds about right. Did you tell Maelstrom about me?"

"I told him that I was looking for something precious that was on the bottom of Hurricane Bay, and he said that when I felt ready, I should come talk to him again, and he would give me some advice."

"The Great Monster Turtle invited you to come talk to him again some time."

"Yes."

"You lead a very strange life, Rose."

"Said the dead unicorn from the bottom of the ocean."

"I also lead a very strange existence."

"So we were made for each other."

"Quite possibly. Are you calm enough to sleep, Rose?"

"Maybe? I don't know."

"I will play something soothing on the fiddle, and even if you can't hear, maybe you can feel it."

"I think... that would be good."

==)»> 4:3: Darkness

"Sleeping tonight, Rose?"

"I spent the day skylarking, so I'm tired. And it's cloudy, so there are no stars to see."

"Skylarking?"

"Wandering around the rigging at high speed. It's something that young sailors do to learn the ship."

"And fledgling sorcerers?"

"Fledgling sorcerers who have terrified the crew by having conversations with the Great Monster Turtle can do anything they want to, even after the captain has returned their passage fees."

"That doesn't explain your motivation."

"It's FUN. And I haven't done it since I was on the 'Sufferance', and being on this stretch of coast makes me nostalgic. Dzee and I used to play tag whenever we could get away with it."

"And Osprey didn't mind?"

"She encouraged it. Topmast monkeys need to know the rigging in their sleep, and be as strong and agile as possible. So a monkey who likes to skylark is good for the ship."

"Ah."

"On the other hand, twenty-two is not sixteen, and I haven't done this sort of thing in five years, and I think I am going to be VERY sore tomorrow."

"My condolences."

"It was worth it."

"You hope."

"I hope. How old are you, Fid?"

"I'm not sure. At least five hundred, probably less than a thousand. The years blend together."

"How many partners?"

"Five, as a ghost. Dozens, before I was killed. They blend together, too."

"All of them?"

"Of course not. The first few are distinct because everything was new, and, since Kellath, they've all been distinct. But in between there were a lot of snacks that I picked up because I was hungry."

"You're making it worse."

"I guess you can't hear the self-recrimination; it's there. I know I'm not good at feeling guilty; I'm not built for it. But eventually I DID learn. It just took a very long while."

"Centuries."

"Yes, centuries. I would change things if I could, but I can't. Why are you dredging through my unpleasant memories?"

"I've been thinking about Maelstrom, and dragons, and the prospect of living for hundreds of years. I would think it would be very easy to become a monster."

"I think so, too."

"But you went through a monster phase, and got over it."

“Is that a compliment?”

“I think it was, yes.”

“A crust of bread is a banquet to a starving man.”

“And a wise magician keeps a fool close at hand.”

“And this fool exists to serve.”

“And I roll my eyes. Good night, Fid.”

==)»> 4:4: Darkness

“Home in Sweetwater, Rose?”

“In Sweetwater, anyway. Not so much home, anymore.”

“Chilly welcome?”

“More like no welcome; no one recognized me. I didn’t catch a ride with a local boatman; I was transported to shore in the ship’s longboat, and escorted to the local inn by sailors who carried my luggage, all one piece of it. And no one realized that the center of attention, with a sword on her hip, and scales on her cheeks, was a girl who had grown up here.”

“Not too surprising, really.”

“I suppose not. Once I was settled, I went to my parent’s house, and my mother didn’t recognize me until I said, ‘Hello, Mother,’ and then she nearly fainted. And my mother does NOT faint.”

"I would not expect the woman who birthed you to be prone to fainting."

"No, not at all. But once she had recovered, she hugged me, and started gathering the family. Two of my brothers are married, now, and my sister has had two more children; that's seven nieces and nephews, all told. My father and my brothers came in from the boats at sundown, and there was food, and I told some stories, and did some trivial magic, and nothing had really changed except that I belonged there even less than I did when I was sixteen. They called me 'Emma' and I never once told them otherwise."

"Would they have listened?"

"Probably not. The person they remember and are fond of was named 'Emerald', and might not have ever existed. And while I'm fond of them, I hadn't been close to any of them in a long, long time."

"Still, it's more family than I ever had. After I changed, I never even saw my mother again; I couldn't."

"Couldn't?"

"Think about it."

"Oh. Right. No, I suppose you couldn't. So you and I are stuck with each other?"

"Gods, I hope so."

==)»> 4:5: Darkness

"So how was Auntie Moss?"

"Strange as always, but really informative. She wants to meet you, by the way."

"Does she now. I thought I was a secret."

"You are. But Auntie Moss hasn't steered me wrong so far, and only a stupid captain hides charts from her own navigator."

"Hmmm. So what did you learn?"

"That she knew that I had sea dragon blood in my family tree, which is why she put it in my tattoo. She says she has enough of the stuff left for another tattoo, by the way, and offered to give it to me."

"The blood, or another tattoo?"

"Both together. She says I have a talent for transformation, and this tattoo will bring it out. And that if I take the tattoo, she has a book with a transformation spell she'll let me copy."

"Nice of her. What's in it for her?"

"Not much, but it makes her happy. I think she enjoys playing dice with the universe."

"That would make you a die."

"Maybe. I've been called worse things."

"Anything else?"

"She told me a bit more about dragon marks. There are five of them; birth, charm, semen, draught, and wound. I already have the first three, and all from sea dragons."

"So... Draught?"

"Drinking dragon's blood. Fresher is better, and given is better than stolen."

"And wound?"

"Blood from the dragon's open wound into mine. That one MUST be fresh, but freely given is still better than taken by force. It's best if all five dragons are of the same type, but are all different individuals."

"So if you want to do this right, you need to find two friendly sea dragons. And the end result of this is?"

"To be that much closer to actually becoming a dragon. It isn't a well-documented path."

"Surprise, surprise. Do you WANT to become a dragon?"

"That's the question, isn't it? The life expectancy is attractive..."

"If you don't mind the fact that 'dragon slayer' is actually considered a profession in some parts."

"There is that. But they don't usually come calling unless the dragon makes a nuisance of herself."

"Or a well-heeled sorcerer decides he wants some dragon bits for spell components. I'm told dragon bones are almost as useful as unicorn horns."

"Ouch. I'm not committed to the idea, or even thinking about it very hard. It's just a path I didn't know existed, and now it's in front of me."

"And you have Maelstrom's consent."

"And that. It was such an odd choice of words."

"You're going to obsess over word choices?"

"You didn't see him, Fid. You didn't hear his voice, or look in his eye, or ride on his back. Damned straight I'm obsessing over word choices."

"You're still feeling it, aren't you?"

"Say what?"

"The thunderbolt feeling in your belly."

"Yeah, I think I am, at least a little bit. They say he's the biggest creature on the planet, and one of the oldest. And he made an effort to talk to ME. That's going to be with me for a while."

"I can tell. So what now?"

"Tomorrow, I'm going to haul my belongings over to Auntie Moss' place, and get a tattoo."

"You're going to stay with her?"

"Her idea. She said there might be side effects."

"And you're definite on the tattoo."

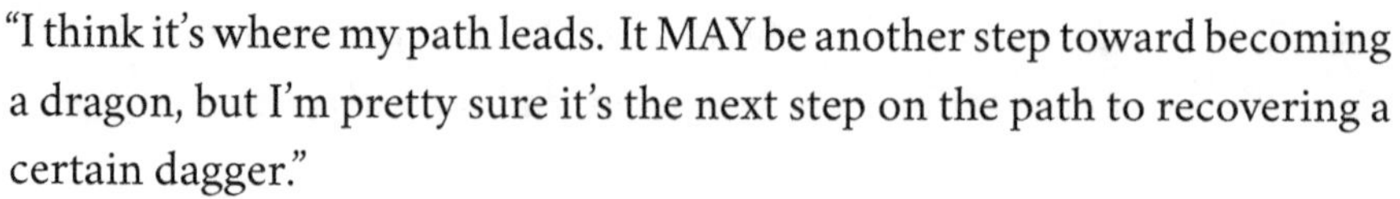

"I think it's where my path leads. It MAY be another step toward becoming a dragon, but I'm pretty sure it's the next step on the path to recovering a certain dagger."

"Then I won't argue with you."

==)»> 4:6: Auntie Moss' cabin

"Are you there, Fid?"

"Always. Mostly."

"Those side effects we talked about? No 'maybe' about them. This is going to be a rough ride."

"I will be here to the best of my ability."

==)»> 4:7: Darkness

"Fid?"

"ROSE?"

"Still not really... I can hear the music, Fid. It helps. Don't stop."

"Never."

==)»> 4:8: Darkness

"Rose? Are you finally dreaming?"

"I must be. I can hear you, so I'm not awake, and I don't have anything like the energy or control to meditate."

"Auntie Moss said you were getting better."

"You've been talking to her?"

"I have, a bit. Mostly I've been trying to reach you, and playing the fiddle."

"I could hear you. I still can, or could until you stopped. It helped."

"Then I'll keep playing."

"I'm exhausted, Fid."

"Rest, then. I'll be here."

==)»> 4:9: A meadow outside of Sweetwater

"Out of bed, Rose?"

"Out of the house, and sitting in the sunlight. Weak as a kitten, but in my right mind. If you can call it 'right' after doing THAT to myself voluntarily."

"Was it worth it?"

"Too soon to tell. I hope so."

"Did you change again?"

"A bit. Not as much. I have more scales, and the old scales are more noticeable, and my smile is scarier."

"Your smile?"

"I have noticeable fangs, top and bottom, and a slight lisp when I speak Kzanti. I'm hoping I can train that away. Dragontongue is a little bit easier, though. Tell me about your conversation with Auntie Moss. I asked her about it, but she just smiled."

"She would. You know that speech that fathers give to young men who court their daughters? The one that goes, 'Mistreat her and I will rip off your genitals and feed them to you while roasting you over a slow fire'?"

"I've heard my father deliver it, and seen one of my brothers come home rattled after receiving it."

"Yeah, well, Auntie Moss gave it to me. I was left with the impression that if she decided I needed to be dealt with, the bottom of Hurricane Bay was not NEARLY far enough."

"That's sweet."

"She honestly scared me. And I'm pretty much indestructible."

"Poor baby."

"You had better be worth this."

"I'm going to pull you up from the bottom of Hurricane Bay."

"Oh. Yeah. Right. I think I'll just play more music now."

"That would be nice."

==)»> 4:10: Darkness

“Tired, Rose?”

“Yeah, I spent the day learning that new spell. I really like it. Eventually I’m supposed to be able to use it to become pretty much anything humanoid, but for now all I can do is the pure human I used to be, a faun, and a crocodilian. That one really shocked Auntie Moss, until I told her about Losty’s heart.”

“The faun didn’t surprise her?”

“She was expecting that one; I had already told her it was a shape I was familiar with.”

“So cavorting with me is educational!”

“That’s not the first word I would have chosen. But between book time and spell work, and not being completely recovered from the fever, I’m beat.”

“I imagine.”

“Tomorrow I think I’m going to hike down to the shore and take the croc for a swim. That should be a lot of fun.”

“Try not to drown; I need you.”

“I won’t drown. I’m a good swimmer, and the croc shape was bred for the water. And how do you expect me to rescue you without swimming?”

“Oh.”

"Don't sulk. Would Master Fiddler do me the honor of playing something soothing?"

"It would be my pleasure."

"That's the other thing that has changed, you know. I can hear your music, now. I had almost forgotten how wonderful it was."

"I regret that I am extremely susceptible to flattery."

"Do you, now? I certainly don't."

==)»> 4:11: Darkness

"You're tired again, Rose. Also happy, I think."

"Yes to both, Fid. I took that walk down to the shore and took a long swim as a crocodilian; I cast the spell five times, all told, and didn't drown once."

"I noticed that. That you weren't dead."

"So I learned two things: Swimming as a croc is pretty much wonderful, and there is no way I'll be able to rescue you as a croc."

"Oh?"

"Crocs swim really well, between the huge feet and the flat tail, and they can hold their breath a LONG time, five or ten times what I could as a human. They can dive easily to depths that I wouldn't have dared to try as a human. But there are still limits, and it's still just holding my breath. I think that I need to find a shape that can actually breathe water before

I can try to rescue you."

"Do you have anything in mind"

"No, but I have an invitation to visit Maelstrom, and if anyone knows, he will."

"That makes sense."

"And I still have to FIND you first, anyway."

"I know. Where, then how, then when."

"Exactly."

"But you're already working on the 'how'."

"It can't hurt. And I have a strong suspicion that part of 'where' is going to be 'hellaciously deep'. So I might as well start working on that when I can."

"Makes sense."

"Speaking of 'where', have you been keeping track of those angles?"

"Not much to keep track of. I can find Drellan easily enough, and now I know Auntie Moss, and I can find her, and there are enough sorcerers who are big enough to see in Ironbridge that I can always find it pretty easily."

"And the angles?"

"Almost an eighth of a circle from Losthaven to Ironbridge, and somewhat less than a quarter circle from Losthaven to Sweetwater."

"That doesn't sound good, but it IS about what I expected. By the time I get all the way around the bay to Skytower, we'll have it nailed down pretty well."

"You're going to Skytower? By circling to the left?"

"Sounds odd, doesn't it? I started out about a hundred miles away, and by the time I actually get there, I'll have traveled more like 3200. But we'll have a really good idea of where you are at the end of that, and then I'll need to spend some time at the Great Library in Skytower."

"The library?"

"Magic is built on three things: Intelligence, Will, and Luck. You build Intelligence by studying, you build Will by casting spells, and you build Luck by having adventures. I need to get smarter. Or at least learn some new things, even if I don't actually get smarter."

"Sounds kind of boring."

"It might be. Sometimes the road just IS. You know that."

"Yes, but I never believe it. I keep hoping I might be wrong."

"And every now and then, I start to suspect that you might be sane, but you always rescue me from the misapprehension."

"As ever, I exist to serve."

"You get all of the good exit lines."

==)»> 4:12: Darkness

"And AGAIN you're tired, Rose."

"Heh. I did an honest day's work. I should be tired."

"You? Honest? Work?"

"Said the non-corporeal entity."

"Ouch. Come and get me and I will non-corporeal you until your toes curl."

"It's a date. But I spent the day fishing with my father. I haven't done that since before I left home."

"It went well?"

"Yeah, it did. He was more than a little afraid of me when I turned up again, but there's something about standing next to a person, hauling on the same net, that breaks down barriers."

"That sounds really good."

"It was. And it may also have solved my next small problem."

"Oh?"

"I mentioned that my next stop was Turtle Bay, and my father said that the town sometimes sends a boat that way on a shopping trip at this time of year, and that he would ask around, and just maybe he would make the trip himself, and provide me with transport."

"And you like that idea?"

"I think I do, yes. I might as well travel with my family as with strangers. And just maybe my father will see who I really am."

"Because that's something that you yourself understand."

"No, because maybe then he will tell me. Brat. You know what I mean; people almost never see each other, and it's worse when parents look at their children, because the parents WANT to see, but they CAN'T."

"You've been hitting the Philter of Profundity again, haven't you?"

"The Philter... Are you sure Osprey didn't just throw you over the side to be rid of you?"

"Yes, Rose. I felt her die."

"Sorry. That was too far. Our moods don't match tonight. Would the Master Fiddler accept my apology, and play me something melancholy?"

"Done, and done."

==)»> 4:13: Darkness

"Another day on the boat, Rose?"

"Sort of. A day on the docks, doing odd jobs and letting people get to know me. It was worth it, though. The Stonecrow clan and the 'Purple Moonlight' will be transporting me to Turtle Bay, starting tomorrow."

"How long is the trip?"

"Four or five days. We'll be stopping to camp on shore every night."

"That's a change."

"'Moonlight' isn't big enough to make the trip in one hop."

"Ah."

"And I have a very strange parting gift from Auntie Moss, in the form of a story. Gods only know where she heard it from, but she swears it's true, and showed me the spot on a map."

"Go on."

"Four women made camp on the shore of a very big lake, stripped naked, and burned all of their belongings. Then one of the women turned into a sword, and then another woman picked up the sword and threw it as far as she could into the lake. And then she turned into a wolf, and ran away. And then the third woman turned into a hawk, and flew away, and then the fourth woman turned into a horse, and walked away."

"That's a very strange story. What's the point?"

"Would Auntie Moss tell me that?"

"Ah."

"But she did say that she's pretty sure that the sword is still on the bottom of that lake."

"Auntie Moss is an evil woman."

"Sometimes, yes."

5: Turtle Bay

There is always life, child. Even in the great depths where there is no memory of light, where it is so cold that the water would freeze instantly if the crushing pressure did not prevent it. There is ALWAYS life.
—Maelstrom the Turtle

==)»> 5:1: The sea floor south of Sweetwater

"What are you up to, Rose?"

"Sitting on the sand in crocodilian form in thirty feet of water with a big rock in my lap, and wondering if I could get far enough into a trance to talk to you."

"It would seem that you can."

"It's good to know. It'll probably be useful. Also easier if I were breathing the water and not holding my breath."

"No doubt. How do your companions feel about their crazy passenger going for a midnight swim?"

"I'm hoping I'll be back in my blankets before they know I'm gone."

"You should probably head back to your blankets, then."

“Yes, Mommy. Look for me when I fall asleep?”

“Of course.”

==)»> 5:2: A beach south of Sweetwater

“You’re not sleeping, Rose.”

“No, but I do have a blanket wrapped around my shoulders. I was a passenger today; I need to convince my brain that I need to sleep. Do you mind coming along for the ride?”

“I am invariably delighted by the treasure of your company under any circumstances.”

“That’s just cruel.”

“Sarcasm makes overly sentimental truth bearable, but it’s easy to overdo.”

“And just like that I stop being offended, and I’m happy and feel flattered. You’re dangerous.”

“I used to be. Then I developed a conscience. But the skills remain.”

“You remind me of ‘The Riddle of the Great Seducer’.”

“Say what?”

“‘The Riddle of the Great Seducer’. It’s an ethical puzzle philosophers use to torment each other.”

“Philosophers are evil.”

"Possibly. The riddle involves a man who is so skilled at the arts of seduction that, once he chooses a target, his conquest is utterly assured; he cannot fail to bring that woman to his bed. The question is, does that then make all of his conquests rapes?"

"Philosophers are REALLY evil."

"Usually."

"It's not that difficult a riddle, though. Think of it in a non-sexual context. If I use deception and misdirection to get you to give me money, that's definitely theft, right? So seduction, regardless of skill, is fundamentally rape."

"That does NOT put your history in a good light, Fid."

"I freely admit that I used to be a monster. Might still be one. Haven't had a lot of opportunities, lately."

"Hmmm. The philosophers came up with an answer to that one, though. Suppose, as a mark, I make the swindler going in, and allow him to achieve a controlled level of success, just for the privilege of watching him work."

"Swindle as performance art?"

"If you like."

"Philosophers are really, REALLY evil."

"Said the monster."

"You knew what I was before you offered to help me."

“Indeed. On that note, good night, Mister Scorpion.”

“Good night, Miss Frog.”

==)»> 5:3: Darkness

“Good evening, Rose.”

“Hey, Scorps.”

“Is that nice? How would you like it if I started calling you, ‘Froggy’?”

“I wouldn’t mind. But you wouldn’t do it.”

“And why not?”

“Because I think that being able to think of me as an attractive woman is really important to you.”

“I think that if I were less shallow I would be offended at your perception of my shallowness.”

“I think that that’s my cue to concede this particular game.”

“Your small edge in talent pales beside my edge in experience. How was your day?”

“Good enough. We sail, we fish, we tell stories. I don’t think they would believe most of mine, if the crew of the ‘Plaything’ hadn’t spread the story of my encounter with Maelstrom. But it’s good, it’s homey.”

“You seem to be happy.”

"I think I am, mostly. But I never forget about you."

"I'm touched."

"I mean it. Rescuing you is the focus of my life right now, and everything I do is done with that in mind."

"I'm grateful, but that sounds kind of ominous."

"It shouldn't. It's just a reaction to the fact that life is fundamentally meaningless, and that you have to find your own purpose. At the moment, rescuing you is mine."

"I shall endeavor to be worth the effort."

"I can hear you leering."

"Oops."

"Idiot. If it was only about sex, there ARE other alternatives besides trying to find a dagger on the bottom of the ocean 500 miles from land."

"But they don't involve me. I'm trying to sell my best points."

"There's a unicorn joke in there somewhere, but I'm not going to make it. The point— and now you've got me doing it— is that you're my friend, and you need my help. And that gives me something to do with my life, as an alternative to trying to rule the world."

"Do you WANT to rule the world?"

"Not really, but the desire seems to be an occupational hazard for sorcerers."

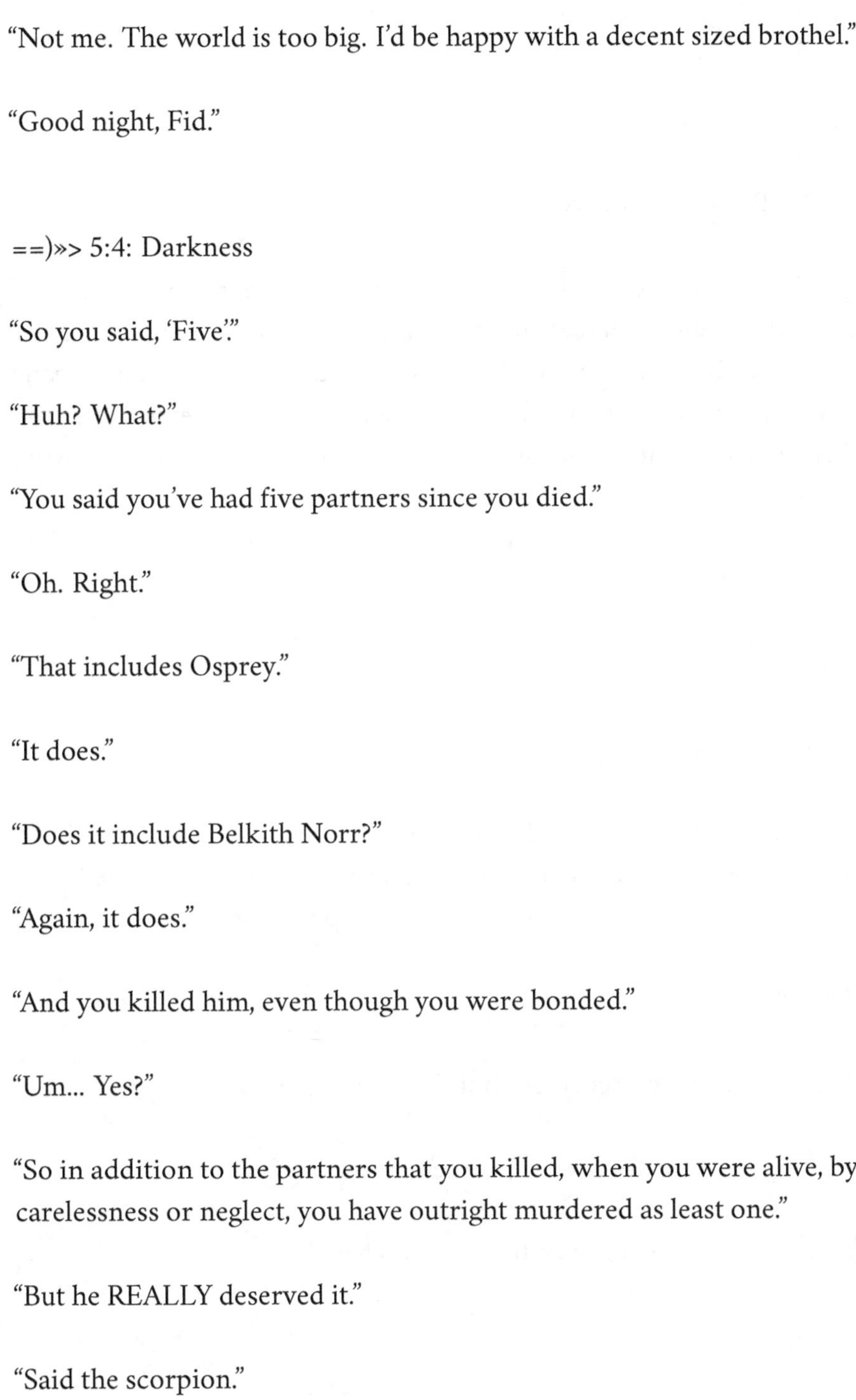

"Not me. The world is too big. I'd be happy with a decent sized brothel."

"Good night, Fid."

==)»> 5:4: Darkness

"So you said, 'Five'."

"Huh? What?"

"You said you've had five partners since you died."

"Oh. Right."

"That includes Osprey."

"It does."

"Does it include Belkith Norr?"

"Again, it does."

"And you killed him, even though you were bonded."

"Um... Yes?"

"So in addition to the partners that you killed, when you were alive, by carelessness or neglect, you have outright murdered as least one."

"But he REALLY deserved it."

"Said the scorpion."

"Is that fair?"

"Don't whine. And you tell me."

"Well... Probably. Is there a point to this?"

"Well... You've told me that the bond, once formed, holds until one of the partners dies, and that you were able to keep Salsi alive, and healthy enough to be useful to you, for over a hundred years, so that means that all of the partners that you've had since your own death must have died violently. And carelessness and neglect are not likely to be an issue since, you assure me, the living partner is the one in control, so it seems REALLY likely that you actually killed one of the partners between Norr and Osprey."

"Oh."

"That's it? 'Oh'?"

"I killed Norr directly, Harrick was killed for associating with me, I had Janeth assassinated, and I neglected Dannel while he self-destructed. And then there was Osprey, who I wanted to keep forever."

"Oh. Wow."

"So, yes, definitely a scorpion. But I'm trying to reform."

"I'm not really thrilled by the prospect of being a frog."

"I want to keep you forever, too. I always have."

"Always?"

“Pretty much “

“How did Osprey feel about that?”

“I’m not nearly stupid enough to have brought it up with her. I probably would have, if you were still around after a decade or so.”

“A decade?”

“Immortality invites the long game.”

“And we’ll call that the exit line. But you owe me stories.”

“Or course.”

==)»> 5:5: A beach north of Turtle Bay

“Not sleeping, Rose?”

“Standing watch.”

“And talking to me at the same time?”

“The world doesn’t go away when I do this; I still have all of my senses, but they’re faded. Though they have been less and less faded as I’ve gotten better at the technique.”

“Ah. Any news today?”

“Not really. We’ll arrive in Turtle Bay tomorrow, so I’ll be ashore for a while. My father and brothers will head home a couple of days after that.”

"And you?"

"I'll try to find a ship that will take me across the mouth of Hurricane Bay, or at least as far as Thirsty."

"Thirsty?"

"Thirsty Harbor is a an island with a really good anchorage, and no fresh water. It doesn't have a lot of permanent population, but there's a fair amount of traffic, because many captains would rather sail back and forth from Turtle Bay to Thirsty, or from Landfall to Thirsty, than to take the long run from Turtle Bay to Landfall. So it's a good destination, as long as you're prepared to pay whiskey prices for water."

"That sounds tragic. And I've never actually HAD alcohol in the real world."

"Now THAT sounds tragic."

"I lost my hands when I was fourteen."

"Oh. Right. I'm sorry. But you still need to tell me about Harrick."

"Damn. Caught. Well then... I killed Norr, and Sulissa and I waited for someone to come along for... I don't know, a year or two. We needed longer and longer periods away from each other as time went on. And then one day Harrick found us, and I walked into his dreams and convinced him to bond with me..."

"I thought you had learned this lesson with Kellath."

"It was different. He was in control, now. Even though he wasn't very strong, but he was bright, and pleasant. And he had legs..."

"And you really wanted to get out of that room."

"Not as much as I want to get out of this... wherever I am. But Harrick bonded with me, and I introduced him to Sulissa, and we gave him advice on getting cash for Sulissa's staff without making her too angry. And then he went home to Ironbridge and got on with being a thief."

"And eventually he got caught."

"He did."

"And the dagger ended up in someone else's control."

"It did. Several different people, but eventually Janeth, who was a Third Circle sorcerer."

"And you've already said that Harrick wasn't very strong."

"You've already heard this one, haven't you?"

"I know what happens when a Third Circle tries to dominate someone with no magical training."

"Yup. So Janeth dominated the hell out of me, and learned how the bond worked, and who I was bonded with, and had Harrick hunted down and killed. And then he forced me to bond with him."

"Just like with Salsi and Norr."

"Well... I didn't LOVE Harrick, but... Yeah."

"I'm so sorry, Fid."

"So I'm turning out to be a sympathetic scorpion?"

"You've always been my friend regardless, Fid. But... Yeah."

"And with that, I think, good night."

==)»> 5:6: A dock in Turtle Bay

"Standing watch again, Rose?"

"Sitting watch, but yes. Of course here the threat is human predators rather than bestial ones."

"Where do crocs fall on that scale?"

"Human. Humans want loot, beasts want food. Crocs would never ambush strangers just for food."

"Ah."

"So... Janeth."

"Janeth was powerful, and smart, but also arrogant. He saw the dagger as a source of healing, and ultimately immortality, but he left it a on shelf most of the time. Which was fine with me. He didn't know about dreamwalking, so I had the run of the population of Ironbridge. I had plenty of opportunities for recreation, but I was also able to shop for someone I really WANTED as a partner, and for someone to kill Janeth for me. As it happens, I found Osprey before I found Dannel."

"You found Osprey in Ironbridge? I though she grew up on board the 'Sufferance'."

"No, she didn't go to sea with her father until she was about twelve years old, when her mother died. I found her when she was seven."

"You started walking in Osprey's dreams when she was SEVEN? That's... creepy."

"I showed up in her dreams as a one-horned faun in CLOTHING. I was decent and respectful. I can do that, if I want to. If I try really, REALLY hard."

"Hmm."

"Honestly. She had had three partners and had had her heart broken twice before SHE approached ME about the possibility of having sex with me."

"A suggestion which you jumped on with all four feet. Still creepy."

"In fact, I was reluctant. Insincere, but reluctant."

"Ever the scorpion."

"I've never denied it. But I truly loved Osprey, just as much as I loved Salsi. And you know that."

"Yeah, I do. So... Dannel."

"He was a fairly clever thug with terrible luck. I provided him with all of the information he needed to rob and murder Janeth, I promised him certain benefits from bonding with the dagger, but also convinced him that, after he stole it, he shouldn't carry it, but keep it somewhere safe."

"Which I assume meant with Osprey."

"You really are a terrible audience."

"Sorry. Go on."

"I knew that Dannel's lifestyle would get him killed soon enough, and, at least at first, he was stronger than Osprey was, so that gave me more energy to work with. He didn't actually die until after Osprey went to sea, and I had nothing to do with his death."

"Other than that you might have helped him avoid it."

"That. Or I might have talked him into some hare-brained scheme that would have gotten him killed earlier. I LIKE hare-brained schemes; they're fun."

"So are you planning to be an influence for caution or for recklessness in my life?"

"I have heard it said that one should always yield to temptation, because you may never get another chance. There is some debate as to whether this is wisdom, or foolishness."

"And you are on the side of?"

"Wisdom, while being wholly aware of the absurdity of finding wisdom in the counsel of foolishness."

"And I knew what you were before I decided to help you."

"Yes, you did."

"Good night, Fid. Gods help me."

==)»> 5:7: A dock in Turtle Bay

"Still on the docks, Rose?"

"Still. I'll be in a real bed tomorrow, and my father and brothers will be back on a beach, so I'm taking a double watch. They're sailing in the morning."

"And you?"

"Asking questions, getting no answers, and looking for passage south. But speaking of getting no answers... Have you added Turtle Bay to your map? What do the angles look like?"

"A nearly perfect quarter circle between Losthaven and Turtle Bay."

"With Ironbridge right in the middle?"

"Yes."

"That's what I expected, but didn't want to hear. You are DEAD in the middle of the bay, more than 400 miles from the nearest land."

"No need to check your charts?"

"I've already done it. I assumed your bearing for Sweetwater was good, got a position. And if that position was valid, then Turtle Bay should have been a quarter circle off of Losthaven, and it is, so we have our position. We'll keep checking, get as close as we can, but we have the basic answer, and it's as bad as it can be."

"But you're not quitting."

"No. Why would I? It's an amazing puzzle, full of mystery and danger, and I get to actually SEE my best friend if I can solve it."

"That's... disturbingly optimistic."

"That's the sunny version. The dark version involves a lot of self-recrimination and hatred of the universe in general and pretty much everything in it in particular and a lot of REALLY foul language and I will keep it to myself, if you don't mind."

"I'd be grateful. Any plans for tomorrow?"

""I'll help getting the 'Moonlight' under way, and then I think I'll see if I can get close enough to the east bay to actually see a turtle."

"East bay? Turtles?"

"Turtle Bay hooks to the south, and is divided into a smaller western bay, which is the port, and a larger eastern bay, which is apparently the breeding ground for all of the dragon turtles in Hurricane Bay. Any human vessel that crosses into the east bay is subject to attack, and the land within a quarter mile of the east bay, and the whole peninsula that divides Turtle Bay from Hurricane Bay, is patrolled by crocs who more or less serve the turtles. There's a fence about 25 miles long that marks the dividing line."

"And you're planning to cross the fence?"

"I'm planning to try to talk my way across the fence. We'll have to see what happens."

"Try not to get eaten."

"If the crocs give me trouble, I'll just give up on the idea. And if I get to the water's edge, I'm not NEARLY stupid enough to go into the water with a dragon turtle without an invitation."

"Said the frog who enjoys the company of scorpions."

"Exactly. Good night, Fid."

==)»> 5:8: Darkness

"You're late tonight, Rose. And not in the bed you expected, I think."

"Nope. Camping out with the crocs."

"So the visit went well?"

"A little too well. They asked me about Losty's fangs, and they liked the answer so well that they gave me a tour of their lands and threw a party for me. I haven't walked that far in YEARS, and THEN I got pretty drunk."

"Back up a bit. What did you tell them about Losty?"

"That he was a warrior with whom I fought a duel, and when he realized he had lost, he asked me to promise to eat his heart, so I did, and his family gave me his fangs in his memory. And suddenly I was a long lost cousin."

"Rose's luck strikes again. See anything interesting on the tour?"

"A couple of clutches of turtle eggs, which are longer than I am tall and probably weigh a ton each. They took me a up a watch tower and pointed out the local geography. They said they weren't using boats at the moment, because there were no adult turtles in the bay, and the young turtles are aggressive and unpredictable."

"And the young turtles are dangerous?"

"The bigger ones are ten feet across the shell, and have heads five feet long. What do you think?"

"That would keep me away. But I'm a notorious coward."

"You're indestructible, and when you were alive, you routinely fought and killed outraged husbands who outweighed you by three to one."

"So was that a bad lie, or exceptionally good induced flattery?"

"I will find a way to make you pay for that."

"Possibly, but you'll never actually use it; I'm too charming. So there was a party?"

"There was a party, and there was nasty green alcoholic stuff— which was different from the stuff they made near Losthaven, but at least as strong and just as nasty— and they told stories, and I made a story out of my duel with Losty, and I told them about meeting Maelstrom, and eventually, when I was really drunk, I stood up and took off my clothes and turned into a croc in front of them."

"How did THAT go over?"

"Pretty well. They started shouting out marriage proposals."

"Marriage proposals?"

"Well, offers to be my companion through my next fertile cycle, which is as close to marriage as crocs get. I regretfully informed them that I could only hold the shape for an hour at a time, and I didn't think that I would actually be fertile through the transformation anyway, but that I was flattered by the offers."

"And then what?"

"And then we all drank a huge toast— the nasty green stuff tastes better when you're a croc, but is still awful— and then the spell wore off, and I passed out cold."

"So for all you know you're hanging from a roasting spit, waiting for them to light the fire."

"No, I'm in the shaman's hut, as is appropriate for a friend of the Great Turtle."

"So tomorrow you'll be back in civilization, and finally sleep in that bed?"

"Civilization, a bed, and a BATH. If the hangover that is hunting me doesn't kill me in the meantime."

"Ah. Good luck with that. Good night, Rose."

==)»> 5:9: Darkness

"Still no civilization, Rose?"

"Nope. Several more marriage proposals, whether or not I'm a mammal, apparently, and an offer to become local royalty, though."

"And the reason for this is...?"

"I'll get to that. In the morning, they gave me a pretty decent hangover cure, and then I sat down with the elders, and asked the questions that had brought me there in the first place. I wanted to know how deep they could dive, and they told me that they tried to stay out of the water unless they could see the bottom. Or course, there are places around here where that's a couple of hundred feet deep, but no more. There are sharks in the darkness, which worry them a bit, but there are also shark-people in the darkness, and they NEVER want to tangle with those in deep water."

"Shark-people."

"Yup. Look a LOT like crocs, with bigger eyes, smaller jaws, and bigger teeth. They can't breathe air or fresh water very well, but if they can get between a croc and the surface, the croc is doomed."

"They sound nasty."

"They are, but Maelstrom hates them, and destroys any settlements they try to build in Hurricane Bay. Out in the Great Ocean, though, they would seem to be common, and Turtle Bay is close enough to the mouth of Hurricane Bay that they turn up around here occasionally."

"I don't see a connection between this and professions of love and offers of dominion."

"Maelstrom showed up."

"Oh."

"Yeah. He surfaced in the middle of the bay, and asked for me in his usual subtle way..."

"He has a usual way?"

"Whatever it is, it is NOT subtle. So I ran to the edge of the water, stripped, crocked out, and swam out to him. And then he took me on a tour of the bay from the water, and we talked some more."

"Why did you change shape?"

"Because Rose the croc swims a LOT better than Rose the human."

"Oh. Right."

"So I asked him about the bottom of Hurricane Bay, and he told me things. It's about two and a half miles deep..."

"Maelstrom gives you mileages?"

"'Not as deep as the width of the mouth of the east bay, but deeper than half the width of the west bay.'"

"That works."

"He also said that it is utterly dark that deep— he has never seen the least trace of light below the half mile point, and very seldom that deep— and very, very cold. He also said that there are creatures that live there, things that eat the dead bodies of creatures that die near the surface, and creatures that eat those things."

"Sounds lovely."

"You're the one who lives there."

"Prison. I am the one who is imprisoned here. And I'm not happy with knowing my neighbors are all scavengers and scavenger predators."

"You're indestructible. I'm the one who will have to deal with them, when the time comes."

"But in the meantime, I'll be the one having nightmares."

"You don't sleep. And if a real nightmare did show up, you'd just have sex with her, anyway."

"I'm trying to be offended, but you're probably right. Is there more?"

"I asked him about the shark-people, whom he calls 'pistrisines', and he said that they could dive that deep, and some of them even lived that deep, but not in HIS bay."

"Good to know."

"I thought so. And then I asked him why he called me 'Granddaughter', and he said that I WAS, that the first sea-dragons had been the result of his relationship with a sun-dragon, back in the long ago."

"That's... I don't know what that is. How do you feel about it?"

"I don't know either. It just IS, I guess. He also told me that he knew about the second tattoo, and approved of it."

"That certainly doesn't hurt."

"No, it doesn't. And then he told me again that I had his consent to become a dragon, and I asked him what that meant, and he laughed again, and that was just as terrifying as it had been the first time. And then he took me back to where he had picked me up, and I crocked out again, and that was that."

"Except that the crocs offered to make you queen."

"That, and threw another party, and got me drunk again."

"You shameless party girl, you."

"And let that be your exit. Good night, Fid."

"Good night, Your Crocodilian Majesty."

6: Thirsty Harbor

Of course there are monsters waiting below the horizon. But are they a threat, or are they a challenge?

—Perrin Ironhand, *Armor and Hob-nailed Boots*

==)»> 6:1: Darkness

"Back at sea, Rose? What happened to the plan for a bath and a bed?"

"The crocs provided me with a bath; they showed me this wonderful little spring-fed lake that was so clear the water was almost invisible, and I played in the water and swam for about two hours. And then when I got back to town, there was a ship ready for me to climb aboard, so I climbed. The hammock is comfortable enough."

"That makes sense."

"Besides, being a passenger gives me time to think. And I always think better when my hair is clean."

"Consider my eyes rolled. What are you thinking about?"

"A few things. Do you want the depressing thoughts, or the insane ones?"

"Let's start with depressing."

"The logistics of rescuing you are... daunting. You're about 500 miles from anywhere, so the rescue is a thousand mile open water voyage, plus time on station to do the dive. So I need to find a ship capable of a thirty day open water voyage with no landfall, and then pay a captain enough to convince him to actually make the voyage."

"That... sounds expensive."

"I could live comfortably for several years on what it will cost. And I'm going to have to pay it in advance."

"Ouch."

"And then I have to find a way to SURVIVE a three mile dive, which probably begins by finding the right shape, but also requires being able to extend the spell by a factor of at least three..."

"Why that?"

"I have about an hour with the spell, now. The descent will take most of that, then the search, then the ascent. So three, at least. I may be able to rush the descent with some kind of ballast, but the ascent will just be me swimming the distance, and the search will take however long it takes."

"Right."

"And then I need a way to tell time while I'm down, because if the spell ends at depth, I die. And I'll also need a compass or something like it, that will function at depth, just to make the search possible."

"Again, why?"

"There are some common locator spells, but they're short range and short duration. I need to be right on top of you— of the dagger— for them to be useful. So that means I'll need to go in and out of trance, and have you lead me in. And even though you can give me compass points, I won't have any external references, so I'll need a device or a spell to find my way."

"And these new toys won't be cheap, either."

"No, they won't. And we aren't home yet. Once I find the dagger and get back to the surface, the ship and I will still have to find each other. And even if the ship does everything it can to stay in one place, it could still drift more than a mile for every hour I'm down, IF there are no local currents. If there are currents or much wind, it will be a lot more than that."

"Yeah, that's depressing. So what's insane?"

"I think I need to eat a shark person steak, or at least drink some shark person blood, to learn the form. And I think that I need to learn the form to do the dive."

"That's more disgusting than crazy."

"I was playing with the idea of going hunting for shark people."

"By YOURSELF?"

"...Maybe."

"THAT is insane. Please don't."

"Try, or think about it?"

"Either."

"I'll give you, 'Try', for now. If I think about it long enough, I may find a way to make it not insane."

"Or you may just CONVINCE yourself that it's not insane."

"Well, considering that my current standard for sanity is trying to find a dagger buried in the mud under two thousand fathoms of ocean five hundred miles from anywhere..."

"That's cruel. I ought to stop talking to you."

"You couldn't."

"And why not?"

"Because you couldn't deal with that much self inflicted loneliness. And because you love me."

"That's presumptive. It may be that I only put up with you because I'm an avatar of unbridled male lust, and you're the only female to whom I currently have access."

"Which still means you won't stop talking to me."

"Ouch. Well played."

"I've been practicing. Am I entitled to a forfeit?"

"If it's within my power."

"Do you know any happy lullabies?"

"A few. As my Lady wishes."

==)»> 6:2: Darkness

"Good evening, Rose. How has your day been?"

"Boring. Frustrating. Hot."

"Ah. Well, SOMEONE had a talk with Auntie Moss last night. She had a suggestion regarding pistrisine blood."

"Oh? And how is Auntie?"

"Cantankerous and enigmatic as usual, but apparently as least a little bit generous."

"Apparently. What did she say?"

"You might be able to get it in trade."

"The blood and flesh of sentients are not commonly traded items."

"That's what I said, but she said that if you find a trader who deals in pistrisine goods, you might be able to back track to an actual pistrisine trader, and then getting some blood would be a matter of negotiation."

"I would say that that sounds like a long trail, except that it stands as part of a trail that is much, much longer. It might just work."

"I am, as ever, at your service."

"That would sound better if you didn't smirk."

“If I didn’t smirk, my reputation wouldn’t allow me to say it at all.”

“Reputation? Fid, Auntie Moss and I are the only people who even know you exist.”

“My self-esteem, then. It I weren’t obnoxious, I would have no personality at all.”

“Idiot. And you have a complex and nuanced personality. Though I admit that the aggregate is pretty much obnoxious.”

“You wound me. I am struck to the heart, and may never recover.”

“You continue to be an idiot. Tell me about Osprey.”

“What would you like to know?”

“Tell me that you didn’t just impose your complex, nuanced, and obnoxious personality on a seven year old girl and overwhelm her.”

“I didn’t.”

“CONVINCE me.”

“Consider my goal. By the time I met her, I was looking for a master that I WANTED to serve. I’m irrevocably a slave, since my death. I met and talked to THOUSANDS of people while the dagger was sitting on Janeth’s shelf, and one of them was a seven year old girl who was smart, and curious, and tough, and brave, and pleasant for all of that, and had the horizon in her eyes.”

“You used that line on me.”

"It's a good line. Particularly when it's true."

"Hmmm. Go on."

"So I thought, 'If life doesn't crush this girl, I think she will grow up to be someone I could be happy serving forever.' And we talked regularly, and after three years, when Dannel killed Janeth, I thought she was the best person I knew to take custody of the dagger. And when her mother died, and she went to sea with her father, she took the dagger along. I didn't mind, because even though being at sea meant that I wouldn't have access to nearly as many people, she was my favorite."

"And she was twelve, then?"

"About."

"And you behaved yourself?"

"Yes. Why wouldn't I? I had access to all the women I wanted whenever we made port, and what I wanted from Osprey was so much more precious than sex."

"But you did get around to sex eventually."

"At her request. I was utterly terrified; I knew that we were risking the most precious thing in my existence."

"But you went ahead anyway."

"Rose... Think about what I am. Do you really think that I'm capable of refusing an offer of sex from my best friend?"

"I very much doubt that you're capable of refusing an offer of sex from someone you hate."

"There you have it, then. And that was still before Dannel died. After he was gone, we made the formal bond, and we had a lot of good years together. More than forty."

"Osprey was SIXTY?!?"

"About. I kind of lost track."

"She didn't look much older than me, even though I knew she had to be older than that."

"She was the oldest person on the ship, but the only one who knew that was Kyle the purser. He had come aboard as a boy, under Osprey's father."

"I'm... I don't know what."

"Hey, I do good work."

"Apparently so. Good night, Fid."

==)»> 6:3: The deck of the "Lonely Gull"

"Not sleeping again, Rose?"

"I slept much of the day to avoid the heat; it's pleasant tonight, and the sky is full of stars."

"Sounds nice."

"I wish... I wish you were here, physically, sitting next to me, sharing this.

And I know that that's not possible, even after— even if— we manage to get to the end of this road, and we can be together in dreamspace whenever we want. And it makes me crazy, because you're the person I want to share it with."

"I'm sorry, Rose. There has NEVER been a time in all of my existence that I could have done that, though. When I had a body, it had four legs..."

"I know. I'm just sulking."

"It occurs to me that we might come closer to what you want than you think. You're the only person I've ever dealt with who could do your trance trick; you're aware of the world around you, and yet in the dreamspace as well. Who knows what we'll have when you're close enough, and I have the energy, to actually pull you into the dreamspace properly. Are you blushing?"

"Gods. Yes. That's a dangerous line of thought."

"We'll have to make sure we have privacy when we experiment, then."

"Stop grinning. Monster."

"As my Lady wishes. Tell me about domination."

"Say what?"

"You said that you knew what happened when a Third Circle tries to dominate an untrained mind. I've been wondering about mechanisms, or at least details."

"Hmmm. All right. Do you know the difference between Will and Charisma?"

“That sounds like a trick question.”

“Clever boy. It turns out that they’re the same thing, but there is so much background noise at mundane levels that you really can’t see that. When you start practicing sorcery, though, the truth becomes apparent.”

“Does it now.”

“Skepticism will get you nowhere. Consider three levels of direction: Suggestion, as in, ‘Someone should fix the hole in the roof’; Request, as in, ‘Would you please fix the hole in the roof?’; and Command, as in, ‘Fix the damned hole in the roof NOW!’. Each applies more force than the previous one, though it matters who is speaking; a stranger gets nowhere, a parent gets further, and the commander of your military unit gets further still.”

“Obvious so far.”

“A really charismatic person will get further that a less charismatic person with the same credentials, and sorcerers ALWAYS have more charisma. A First Circle dealing with a stranger probably out ranks a parent, but doesn’t have quite the pull of a military leader. A Second Circle will get better results with a Request than a military leader will with a Command, and a Third Circle with get better results than that with just a Suggestion.”

“And if a Third Circle actually issues a Command?”

“You mean like, ‘Hogtie your wife and children inside your house and then burn the place to the ground, and then hang yourself after the fire has gone out and you’re sure that they’re dead’?”

“Yeah, like that.”

"You would do what the sorcerer told you to do."

"And there are two more Circles beyond Third?"

"AND that's without actually using magic. There are spells that enhance all of these effects."

"I begin to see why sorcerers get interested in taking over the world."

"Yeah. I got lucky with Drellan; he's one of the good ones. After he explained what happened to me, he told me that he was jealous of my mastery of Dragontongue, and that he would like me to tutor him in it. And then he asked me to tell him what I honestly thought would be a fair price for that service, and I said that I wasn't sure it was fair, but that what I wanted was to learn formal magic, with room and board thrown in, and then he offered me a small stipend on top of that, so I agreed."

"Even though you probably couldn't have refused anyway."

"I'm not sure. I wasn't exactly a mundane at that point, so I probably could have. The point is that he was very careful to give me as little direction as possible. Ethical sorcerers tend to develop some strange speech patterns for just that reason."

"And you WANT to become one of those creatures?"

"I don't see that I have a choice. I'm pretty sure I'll have to break Third Circle to rescue my best friend from the bottom of the ocean."

"Oh. Um... Would my Lady care for some music to watch the stars by?"

"That would be wonderful, Fid. That would be simply wonderful."

==)»> 6:4: A beach west of Thirsty Harbor

"Outdoors again tonight, Rose?"

"Yup. Thirsty Harbor is EXSPENSIVE, and the weather is good, and I have something goofy to do outside city limits tomorrow, anyway."

"Will I regret asking?"

"I want to find out some more about my croc form, and clear shallow water seems like a really good place to do it."

"Such as?"

"I want to know how long I can hold my breath, and how far I can swim on one breath."

"I'm not sure if I should be impressed by your diligence or worried for your sanity."

"Consider the nature of our relationship and the course of our lives for the foreseeable future, and stop impugning my sanity."

"Um... I'm impressed, then. What are you actually going to do?"

"First, I am going to find a decent sized rock, wade out to neck deep water, and then take a deep breath and hold it while I sit on the bottom with the rock in my lap and count scorpions."

"Scorpions?"

"It's a handy three syllable word which reminds me of something meaningful. Maybe."

"And then?"

"And then I am going to take the hundred yards of rope I bought this afternoon, string out a course in ten or fifteen feet of water, rest a bit, and then see how many laps I can swim in one breath."

"I find that I have been forbidden from making appropriate comments."

"Damned straight you have. Play me something sad while I stare at the stars."

"As my Lady wishes."

==)»> 6:5: A beach west of Thirsty Harbor

"And how is my Lady Mad Scientist this evening?"

"Tired, Fid. But content. The answers are a thousand scorpions, and twelve laps, both of which could be pushed if my life depended on it."

"And how many scorpions are there in a day?"

"About a hundred thousand, I think. It's hardly an exact measure."

"There's a joke in there somewhere, about being able to rule the world if I only had a hundred thousand scorpions."

"And YOU make jokes about MY sanity."

"I take refuge in my immunity from retribution."

"We'll see about that. Some day."

“In the worst case, I will take refuge behind my fiddle.”

“That’s a pretty good refuge. Are you prepared to prove it?”

“Always.”

==)»> 6:6: Darkness

“I take it you’ve found a ship, Rose.”

“That I have. The ‘Duchess of Skytower.’ Biggest ship I’ve ever been on, too.”

“Does that matter?”

“She has more waterline and carries more sail; she should be faster over open water, if conditions are good. That will help; it’s a long trip.”

“To Landfall?”

“Yup. Four hundred miles by chart, but given that we’re straight into the prevailing wind, more like twice that in practice. Probably ten days, almost all of it with no land in sight.”

“Wow. Ten whole days out of sight of land. However will you cope?”

“I’m aware of the irony. But you’re indestructible, and if anything happens to the ship, we all die.”

“Pathetic little corporeal ephemerals.”

“Ouch. Where did that come from?”

"Nowhere in particular. I just need to sharpen my tongue occasionally."

"Really."

"No. I don't know. Prison blues."

"Play something sad, and I will listen appreciatively."

"That's not much."

"It's what we have, Fid. And it won't be forever. Now play."

"As my Lady wishes."

==)»> 6:7: The deck of the "Duchess of Skytower"

"Stargazing again tonight, Rose?"

"It's a night for it."

"Osprey loved doing it. On good nights she would sit on the windward rail, and I would play for her. They were good times."

"She could hear your music when she was awake?"

"It was part of being bonded. We could also talk any time we wanted to. I think that anyone who touches the dagger can hear the music, if I want them to. I've never tried that."

"Ah."

"I've been thinking about that riddle that Auntie Moss told you. About the four women."

"It does have four naked women in it, after all."

"Not fair. Though I admit that I can not imagine any story that wouldn't be improved by the addition of some naked women, that doesn't mean that I can't think about the rest of the story."

"Sorry, Fid. That was cheap. Go on."

"It seems to me kind of like a suicide pact."

"How so?"

"They burned all of their possessions, and then parted company..."

"But three of them walked away in good health."

"But the sword didn't. I know a bit about the options available to a piece of cutlery on the bottom of a body of water. It may not be death, but it's damned close. And all four stopped being human, which is a kind of death too, I think. When I was alive, I could talk to anyone who touched my horn, or to my bonded servant, and I could dream walk. But those seem to be unicorn things, not something that any person in animal shape can do."

"Interesting. It makes sense. I certainly don't have a better explanation. I guess there's only one way to find out."

"Which is?"

"Recover the sword."

"I seem to recall that you have a prior engagement with a different piece of submerged cutlery."

"I do, Fid, and you come first. But YOU need me to break Third Circle, and breaking Third Circle means earning more luck, and earning more luck means taking on absurd quests. And this sword seems to be an absurd quest of the first order."

"That makes sense, except... I think I'm kind of jealous."

"Oh, my Darling Idiot. You don't even know if she WANTS to be rescued, and even if we find the sword, the spirit may be gone, and she IS NOT YOU. Got it?"

"Yes, Ma'am."

"Good. Now play me some music to watch stars by."

==)»> 6:8: Darkness

"Whoever he is, I hate him."

"Huh? What? Who?"

"The man who's sleeping next to you. The one you just had sex with. I hate him."

"How do you know...?"

"Because you are really late getting to sleep, and you have a happy, foggy-brained resonance that can't mean much else."

"So you're attacking me for being happy?"

"...Yes. Damn."

"And and then there is the fact that, as far as either of us knows, you are actually incapable of sexual fidelity under any circumstances, assuming you have any contact with intelligent life AT ALL."

"Double damn."

"So why are you attacking me?"

"I'm not jealous of HIM, Rose; I'm jealous of you. You get to have something I can't."

"I know, Fid, and I swear that I'll do my best to make it up to you when the opportunity arises. And it's not like I planned this evening, or even sought it out."

"Oh?"

"We're anchored off Landfall. We made the coast too late in the day to dock— you can't just sail into the harbor in darkness— so we anchored out, and will dock in the morning. And since we were at anchor, the captain invited me to dinner in his cabin, and things went from there."

"I'm sure."

"Fid.... I've never had many opportunities. I was a fairly pretty girl, once, but I have scales on my face, now, and I'm not at all sure about 'fairly pretty' anymore. And I have high and difficult standards..."

"Do you now?"

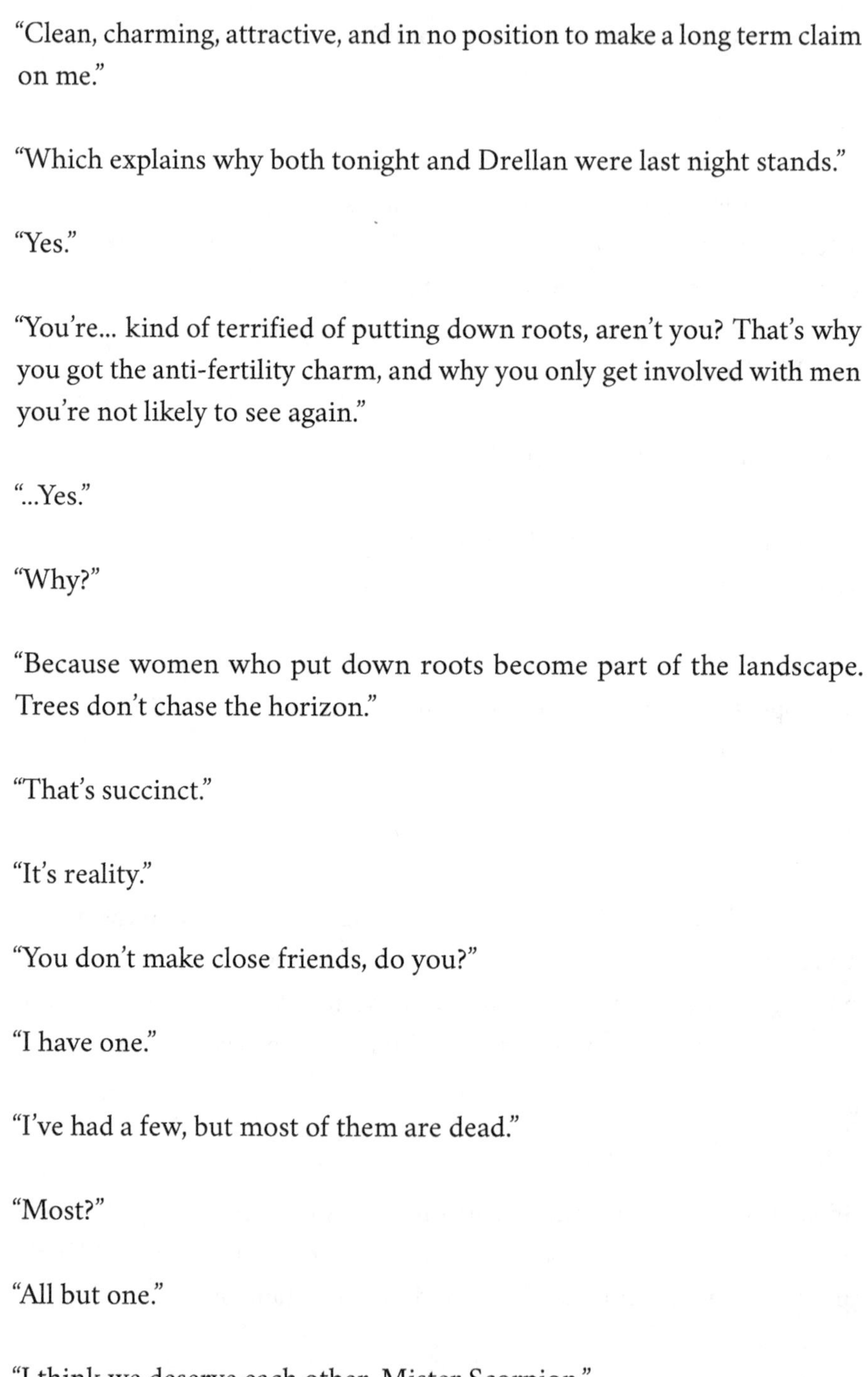

"Clean, charming, attractive, and in no position to make a long term claim on me."

"Which explains why both tonight and Drellan were last night stands."

"Yes."

"You're... kind of terrified of putting down roots, aren't you? That's why you got the anti-fertility charm, and why you only get involved with men you're not likely to see again."

"...Yes."

"Why?"

"Because women who put down roots become part of the landscape. Trees don't chase the horizon."

"That's succinct."

"It's reality."

"You don't make close friends, do you?"

"I have one."

"I've had a few, but most of them are dead."

"Most?"

"All but one."

"I think we deserve each other, Mister Scorpion."

"We probably do, Miss Dragon."

"I'm not a dragon yet, Fid. I may never be."

"You sound like you know what that means."

"You know that I don't."

"I know that you had the heart of a dragon before you got that first tattoo."

"You sound like you know what THAT means. Have you met many dragons?"

"Only Sulissa. But we shared a prison cell."

"Ah. And Sulissa was a paragon of desirable personality traits?"

"Not really. I was trying to give you a compliment."

"I noticed, and I give you full credit. I just wondered if it actually meant anything, because the nature of dragons is something that concerns me."

"Ah. I MEANT that you are fierce and fearless."

"And you get full credit twice, then. Thank you."

"That wasn't really flattery, Rose."

"It feels like it. I'm only rarely fierce, and I know that I'm not fearless."

"You're cautious, but you never let fear stop you. You're an irresistible force."

"An awfully small irresistible force."

"Even so."

"Hmmm. And that sounds like the exit, unless I can talk you into playing me a lullaby."

"You expect me to play you a lullaby while you're sharing another man's bed?"

"I don't expect, I only ask. And he's not HERE, is he, Fid?"

"As my Lady wishes."

7: Glass Fort

If the day to day mechanics of running a war don't break your heart on a regular basis, it's not a war, it's just a gladiator show with really bad seating.

—Perrin Ironhand, *Armor and Hob-nailed Boots*

==)»> 7:1: Darkness

"Good evening, Rose. And how are you tonight?"

"Alone, on dry land, and slightly drunk. How about you?"

"Sharing the first of those, and envious of the other two."

"Business as usual, then. Give or take the alcohol."

"Indeed."

"Do you remember Bekkar? From the 'Sufferance'?"

"I've heard the name. I didn't keep close track of the male crew."

"Ah. Well, I ran into him tonight, bought him a few drinks, learned a few things. He didn't know what the cargo was, but Osprey's last voyage really started in Ironbridge. 'Sufferance' was carrying no significant cargo, just ballast, across the bay from Ironbridge to Silverport, and then came back the same way. Whatever the real cargo was was small enough to be kept in Osprey's cabin, both ways."

"I remember that now. I didn't usually pay much attention to the actual business of running the ship, but I know that there was something unusual and profitable involved, and she was nervous about it."

"So the mystery of WHY turns into a mystery of WHAT. Maybe we'll find some answers in Silverport, but I don't think the odds are good. Not after all of this time."

"Even when there was a lot of money involved?"

"Even so. Nothing valuable was out where anyone saw it. There may have been some bribes involved, but those would have been out of sight, too. Bribes usually are."

"But you're going to Silverport, anyway."

"Might as well. We're half way across the bay from Losthaven and Ironbridge, and following the coast is a LOT easier than finding transport across the bay."

"Oh. I... kind of liked the idea of you sailing over my head, even if it was only that."

"That's... silly. Also sweet. And I can't really argue with you. But there would be no point, at least until I can figure out how to make the dive."

"I know."

"In other news, though... Finding a pistrisine trader is NOT going to be an option; the locals are at war with the shark folk, so there's no trading going on."

"That's no good."

"Well, it's more dangerous, anyway. But war means dead bodies, and since I'm looking for body parts, that means an opportunity to scavenge."

"So you're going to deliberately go into a war zone."

"Yup."

"And you denied being fearless."

"I'm terrified. But it seems the best way to go."

"I would not call what you seem to be feeling right now terror."

"Fine. I'm excited by the idea, too. But I'll try to be careful, and I'm running short on money, and this seems like a good chance to make some."

"Say what?"

"I have a feeling that a Second Circle sorcerer who can use a sword can probably make a decent wage fighting fish people."

"And we have gone right through foolhardy into insane."

"I was a soldier for two years, Fid. There's risk here, but I'll be fine. And I've been telling you that the way to build luck is to push what you have."

"I'm doomed. You're going to be killed, and I'm going spend the rest of my existence in occasional correspondence with Auntie Moss."

"And Drellan. I'd bet you could get a friendship going with Drellan."

"I'm doomed."

"Only if I get myself killed, which would be much worse for me than it would be for you in any case."

"That's REALLY small comfort."

"And I'll do my best to come back and haunt you, and then you can ravish my ghost on a regular basis."

"Really?"

"I'll look into it. It's not my preferred option."

"I don't know, it sounds like a pretty good alternative to me."

"You and Sulissa got sick of each other."

"Yeah, but she was..."

"A dragon?"

"Um... Oops. I meant..."

"I think you should stop talking and make with the music, now."

"I think you're right."

==)»> 7:2: Darkness

"How was your day, Rose?"

"Good. Productive. I found a billet, got a signing bonus, and bought some new clothes."

"Clothes?"

"A loose mid-thigh skirt with a drawstring waist, and a sleeveless vest, both in quilted black silk."

"I'm not impressed, off hand."

"Now I can croc out without getting naked first. It might come in handy."

"I can imagine that. And the billet?"

"I found a recruiter gathering troops to march down to Glass Fort and fight the sharks. He said he wasn't authorized to hire sorcerers, but he offered to take me on at infantry rates until we got down to Glass Fort, where his superiors could make me a real offer. So starting tomorrow, I have room, board, and a small stipend. And that signing bonus I mentioned, that bought the new clothes."

"So you're really going to do this dumb thing."

"It's where the road leads, Fid. I need to learn the pistrisine form, and I need more money, and this will help with both. If I never take risks, I'll never rescue you."

"If you get killed, you'll never rescue me."

"We went over this yesterday, Fid. I have more on the table than you do. And I have, you know, legs? So I get to steer."

"I know, Rose. Just be careful."

"I have always done my best, and will continue to do my best, to be as careful as possible within the parameters of whatever insanely dangerous thing I'm doing at any given moment."

"That is one of the most absurd statements I've ever encountered."

"It's sincere, though, Fid. As much as I want to rescue you, I want to die even less. So try to trust me."

"When you put it that way, I would be an ingrate to refuse."

"Ah. You're on to me."

"Well, I AM the swindler is this relationship. You're the one who stabs things and blows things up."

"Which is why I am getting a job stabbing things and blowing things up."

"Out played again. You're going to destroy my reputation."

"Which, as we have discussed before, you don't really have. Perhaps you should stick to music."

"And THAT, I can do."

==)»> 7:3: A field east of Landfall

"Not sleeping, Rose?"

"Too much noise. I haven't ever tried to sleep in an infantry camp before; there's no rigging or sea to cover the snoring."

"So you're just meditating?"

"From inside my bedroll. With luck, I can slide smoothly from meditation to sleep. And maybe talk to you a bit along the way."

"It may not be a good plan, but it's a plan."

"It was a long day. And I think this job is going to be different than I expected. I may spend most of my time as an instructor."

"Are you that good?"

"No. But I can teach the recruits what it feels like to go up against a big scaly monster with a huge mouth full of sharp teeth."

"I take it that this is a good thing."

"Yes, when you're going to war against big scaly monsters with huge mouths full of sharp teeth."

"And how did this bit of idiocy come about?"

"The recruiter was putting us through our paces, and a young hotshot complained about having to spar with a girl, so I asked the recruiter for permission to do something unorthodox. He gave it, I turned my back on the hotshot, crocked out, turned back, and went for him. I never touched him, but his reputation and his pride may never recover. He can wash his clothes..."

"You're usually not that cruel."

"I was provoked. But it impressed the hell out of the recruiter. He stood his new hires in a line and had me roar into their faces, one at a time. None of them took it very well. It should make better soldiers out of them, though."

"How so?"

"New danger is scarier than known danger. If they can be taught to not flinch when the big jaws and teeth come at them, they'll be that much closer to living though their first fights."

"It's a bit outside my experience."

"It is, isn't it? I ought to teach you to use a sword, someday, when we have access to dreamspace again."

"I can think of so many better uses of our time."

"How did the line go? 'After, or maybe between.'?"

"Hmmm. Between. Once we're together, it's ALWAYS going to be, 'Between.'"

"I can live with that."

==)»> 7:4: Darkness

"No trouble sleeping tonight, Rose?"

"Hardly. Do you know how long it's been since I've walked twelve miles in a day?"

"Quite a while?"

'Too long. Not since I first shipped out, I think. I should do more of it. After my feet recover. If my feet recover. If I don't just saw them off, first."

"Don't do that. You'd look silly with no feet."

"But I'd sleep better."

"I assume you've started marching toward Glass Fort."

"You would be correct."

"How long will it take?"

"About ten days at this pace. They tell me that day three will be the worst, and that it'll be easy by day ten. I guess we'll see."

"You chose this path."

"Don't remind me."

"How can I not? 'I told you so' is practically my name."

"Point made, and I plead for mercy."

"Mercy, I will grant. For now. In the meantime, I've been wondering: Why is it called 'Glass Fort'?"

"I'm pretty sure it's made of glass."

"I'm skeptical."

"Quarried obsidian blocks reinforced with magic in some way. It's old and tough and has never fallen to an enemy."

"That's a thing."

"It's a big thing. Particularly since the sharks make a serious attempt to take it pretty much every generation."

"Really? Every generation?"

"Every fifteen to thirty years since the fort was built. They attack, a whole section of coast is closed for about six months, and then the sharks go away, and things go back to normal. Until the next time. For more than four hundred years."

"What happened four hundred years ago?"

"They built the fort, because the sharks had slaughtered the town that was there before the fort was built."

"Does anyone know why?"

"Nope. Apparently, no one has been able to figure out a way to talk to the sharks. And there never has been any trade, either. Just intermittent war."

"That sounds crazy."

"It is crazy."

"How can they not know? Haven't they at least interrogated prisoners?"

“They’ve tried. They just haven’t gotten any answers.”

“Rose... Prisoners always give up answers, eventually.”

“Unless there’s a language barrier.”

“There are translation spells.”

“Which don’t seem to work.”

“So more crazy.”

“Yes. Fid, as much as I enjoy your company, can I pretend to be dead for a while?”

“Of course. Sleep well, Rose.”

==)»> 7:5: Darkness

“So how was day three, Rose?”

“I hate everyone.”

“Even me?”

“Have you come to bring me new feet?”

“I’m afraid not.”

“Then you, too. Unless you can play me the most soothing music that has ever been played ever.”

"As it happens, I can do just that."

"Then I might not hate you. Maybe."

"Be silent, foolish Dragon, and I will play."

"Hmph."

==)»> 7:6: Darkness

"In pain again tonight, Rose? I thought things were getting better."

"They were. Things were getting so much better that we had weapons drill after we set up camp tonight, and EVERYONE wanted to spar with the crocodile girl."

"Which is why you're sore."

"Which is why I'm sore, but also proud of myself. Even though all I did was beat up kids, they're kids who are trying to be soldiers, and they need to be beaten up a bit."

"So how many did you fight?"

"A dozen, one at a time. After I got first touch on Number Twelve, they let me bow out. I said it wasn't fair if they kept me going until I started to lose from fatigue, and the instructor agreed."

"But you won twelve fights in a row?"

"It wasn't THAT hard. They're all green, and they know I'm not, but they haven't learned what that means, yet. Eventually one of them will ask me how many men I've killed, and I'll tell them something. Still not quite sure what, though."

"Is it that complicated?"

"Fourteen lives. Two duels, one of them against a croc, eleven in battle, and one accidental drunk. What's the answer they want to hear?"

"Just what you said. But list them in numerical order: Drunk, duels, battle."

"Why?"

"It just feels right."

"And you're an expert?"

"How many people have YOU convinced to throw away everything for a life of hardship and adventure?"

"Only myself. I'll probably take your advice."

"See? I'm good for something!"

"Possibly. You're amusing, anyway."

"Amusement is useful."

"That it is. And that's an exit line."

==)»> 7:7: A field east of Glass Fort

"Not sleeping, Rose?"

"No. We made Glass Fort a bit too late to be assimilated, and early enough that we had a bit of free time, even after the nightly 'Beat up the crocodile girl' ritual. Which drew a crowd, tonight. Fortunately, I managed to get out of sight before I turned back to myself, so most of the camp doesn't recognize me."

"Does that matter?"

"Too soon to tell. I hope I end up with a bit of privacy, anyway. I'm enough of a freak as it is."

"And yet you voluntarily subjected yourself to being the crocodile girl in the first place."

"My judgment is less than wonderful when I'm already snarling."

"Not surprising, though I haven't actually ever seen you snarl."

"I don't suppose you have, have you? That may be why I keep you around."

"You don't 'keep' me anywhere, Rose. That's the point of this whole exercise. So that you CAN."

"I haven't forgotten, Fid. Really I haven't. I know that getting you out of there is pretty much the only thing in your world, but it's also the single biggest thing in my world, really it is. But you don't have to FIND the path, and I do."

"I know."

"And your music, and memories of being with you, are pretty much all that kept me sane over the last few days. So I don't forget, and won't. Right?"

"Understood."

"Good. Now earn your keep with the fiddle."

"As my Lady wishes."

==)»> 7:8: A tent east of Glass Fort

"Different surroundings tonight, Rose?"

"Just a bit. I had several interviews, crocked out twice, fought half a dozen wooden sword duels, and signed some papers. Which is what I was planning on, but just a bit scary."

"So what have you signed up for?"

"Ninety days at standard wages for a Second Circle, plus a bonus for unique duties, officer's meals, private quarters and a servant, and any magical training I can cajole out of the other sorcerers. In exchange for which I get to spend four hours a day playing crocodile girl and getting hit with sticks."

"FOUR HOURS A DAY?"

"Four one hour shifts, with an hour in between each. Probably. I think I'm going to get VERY good with a wooden sword."

"Is that useful?"

"I'm going to get one made that handles as much like my rapier as possible, so yes. Deadlier Rose is a happier Rose."

"And you say you aren't a dragon yet."

"I'm not. But I certainly seem to be a crocodile."

"Which is a definite step down the path."

"We shall see."

==)»> 7:9: A tent east of Glass Fort

"Rose? Are you all right? You seem... muzzy."

"Moderately drugged and in pain. It was a long day."

"What happened?"

"Remember the other day, when I went twelve for twelve against recruits? Today I went five for forty-eight against SENIOR veterans. It hurt."

"Your body, but not your pride."

"Hell no. I beat FIVE of them. They expected me to get completely shut down. I expected the same thing. I think I won a fair amount of respect, and made at least one friend."

"Oh?"

"The master healer is a Third Circle who specializes in Necromancy, but he's a hell of a healer. Says that after you have taken a few dozen bodies apart, you learn how to put them back together pretty well. He seems to be right."

"But he's a necromancer?"

"Yep. Calls himself 'Bing the body snatcher'. He's a funny guy, taller than I am, about three times as heavy, and flirts constantly. I like him a lot, and he seems to like me."

"Really."

"Do we have to talk about jealousy again? There is NO threat here, Fid. When I said he flirts constantly, I meant it. And men outnumber women around her by about twenty to one. I'm pretty sure I have the wrong plumbing for Bing's tastes."

"Oh... What kind of name is 'Bing', by the way?"

"Harbinger, cut sideways."

"Of course it is."

"You'd like him. I may even tell him about you. We'll have to see."

"If someone else rescues me because you couldn't keep a secret, it will be YOUR fault."

"I know, Fid. I said we'll see. In the meantime, I also did some pointless interviews in looking for a servant. I didn't expect any of the female soldiers would be interested, and they weren't."

"No one wants a soft billet?"

"You don't survive as a female infantry troop if you don't love your work."

"Ah. Does that mean you are going to find a male servant, or go without?"

"Not yet. I am going to talk to some camp followers tomorrow; I'm more hopeful there. It's usually not too hard to find a whore who's looking for the exit door. I doubt that that's any different when they're army whores."

"You've had a lot of experience with whores?"

"I spent time with them, on and off, when I was on 'Storm Turtle'. I stayed with my shipmates when I went ashore, and if they went whoring, I got dragged along. I had some interesting conversations. Also got some interesting offers, from the clients, and from the girls."

"I imagine."

"Once I got really drunk and admitted that I had had sex with a centaur. They got really excited about that, until I told them that I had been a centaur myself at the time. Then they all just laughed and gave me more brandy."

"I thought you were a whiskey girl."

"I'm a free alcohol girl. Though I admit a preference for whiskey, all other things being equal. And I think I need another dose of something, and then real sleep."

"Until tomorrow, Rose."

==)»> 7:10: A tent east of Glass Fort

"Today was better, Rose?"

"A bit. I hired a servant, spent a fair amount of time being poked and prodded while Bing played comparative anatomy among my various forms, and I did more fighting against somewhat inferior opponents. It's more fun when you don't lose all the time. And it doesn't hurt nearly as much."

"I imagine. So you found a servant?"

"Rescued, more like. Rilla really, REALLY wanted to be soldier; she's fierce. But she's also tiny, and there was NEVER any hope for her in the infantry."

"Oh?"

"All other things being equal, mass rules."

"That wasn't my experience."

"I said, 'All other things being equal'. You were unnaturally fast. And much, much smarter than your opponents."

"And yet you constantly call me an idiot."

"Compared to a sheep, you're a genius. And I only call you an idiot when you play into the role."

"My wit is tragically unappreciated. It would serve you right if I ran off with someone else."

"Let me know when you get an offer. I may warn them of what they're getting into."

"You're heartless. Reptilian, even."

"Oh, THAT was low."

"Can you feel the grin? I think we were talking about your new servant."

"So... Rilla is TINY, very pretty, ANGRY. She signed up because she really liked the idea of hurting people and breaking things. She signed a contract, made the trip down here from Landfall just like I did, and found out the army had no place for her except as a camp follower. She thought about deserting, but she decided she was too proud, so she saves every penny she gets, hoping to buy out her contract, and grinds her teeth a lot. Apparently she hides her anger well, because she gets good tips."

"But she'd rather work for you."

"She'd rather do ANYTHING that gets her out of the brothel, but no one else was offering her a billet."

"Ah."

"I'm going to have a talk with the recruiter. And then I am probably going to have a talk with the recruiter's commander. And then, if all goes well, the recruiter is going to have a talk with Sister Crocodile. I think Rilla would like that."

"They let you duel?"

"It would be a training session. I'd make it hurt."

"If he isn't out of your class."

"I'm willing to make sacrifice moves. I get beat up all the time, and don't care."

"There's that dragon again."

"Grrr."

==)»> 7:11: Darkness

"Good evening, Rose. I would say that you were sleeping the sleep of the just, but I know better."

"Brat. Guess who may have learned a new shape today?"

"Rilla?"

"Hah. Rilla has no magic at all, other than a talent for infuriating former brothel clients."

"She's doing a lot of that?"

"Only when she wants to distract me. She gets much too much fun out of seeing men who were cruel to her back down when she hides behind Sister Crocodile."

"Are you denying that you enjoy it as well?"

"You know me too well. But I don't push people around, I only push back. And grin."

"And Rilla lures men into situations where you can push back."

"Only men who deserve it, but yes."

"Hmmm, indeed. Tell me about this new shape."

"I was picking Bing's brain for information about the sharks, and he showed me his spare parts collection. He's been gathering dead shark folk bits, and using magic to preserve them, so he can figure out how they work."

"Count on a necromancer to show a girl a good time."

"Right. I can tell that there is something in the back of his head that really wants to get a croc on the slab, and he doesn't exactly WANT it to be me, but, well… It's more than a little creepy."

"I can imagine."

"So I told him my theory about why I have a croc shape, and a faun shape, which took a bit of editing on my part, since I didn't want to tell him about you at all. He went to a shelf and pulled down a shark heart that had been preserved by magic, and I carved out a meal-sized chunk, and we boiled the hell out of it, and I ate it. Bing tells me that it will be as much absorbed into my system as it will ever be within three days, so we should know by then."

"And you still deny that you're turning into a dragon."

"I'm experimenting with ritualized cannibalism in the name of magical research. It's not like I'm hunting my neighbors for food."

"Yet."

"Do I have to remind you that I am doing this, quite literally, for you?"

"No."

"Then be a good nuisance and play me some music to digest intelligent beings by."

"As her reptilian majesty wishes."

8: Sharks

All truths are incomplete, including this one.
—Feldspar Greymantle, *Thaumatology*

==)»> 8:1: Darkness

"Good evening, Rose. Have you become Shark Girl yet?"

"Sort of. I knew the form was available the first time I crocked out for training this morning..."

"Say what?"

"When I do my transformation spell... Any spell, all spells, are about imposing your will on the world. All of the mumbo jumbo— all of the gestures and incense and fondling of tokens and recitations of obscene draconic poetry..."

"REALLY?"

"No. Not so far, anyway, but I wouldn't be surprised. Anyway, it's all just force multipliers for your will. Eventually you get to a place— and this is a metaphor, it's really kind of too weird for words— that is like a big room, or a long hallway, with a bunch of doors..."

"And each door is a spell."

"Right. And every door is locked, so you choose the door you want, and then you do more mumbo jumbo that is specific to that spell to create a key, and then you open the door..."

"And the spell goes off."

"Maybe. In the case of my transformation spell, once the door is open, I have a closet with costumes hanging in it. There's an 'Emma' costume, pre-scales me, and a faun costume, and a croc costume, and this morning there was a shark costume that I didn't get to try on until after I had finished my daily beatings. And of course Bing had to be there to watch and take notes. He's never had a chance to observe a WILLING live pistrisine before."

"Is Bing as strange as he sounds?"

"At least. He's got tons of energy and enthusiasm, and he almost always seems to be happy, but his priorities are usually weird and often just plain creepy."

"So why 'sort of'?"

"Because I pretty much hated being in the shape, and Bing wanted me to hold it as long as possible."

"Hated the shape?"

"Breathing HURT. And I couldn't talk, just gesture."

"Breathing hurt? What was wrong?"

"Sharks aren't built to breathe air. They can, at least for a while; Bing says he's seen them stay functional for hours out of water, but it isn't good for them. I get the impression that he's performed a lot of experiments on captive sharks, and they've often been fatal."

"As you said, just plain creepy."

"Yup. Sharks don't breathe in and out; they pull water, or air, in through their mouths and push it out through vents under their ribs, so the flow is continuous."

"That's weird."

"It's necessary. Bing went into a long explanation of the science behind it all, which I couldn't really follow. Dragon blood taught me to read, and Drellan taught me Thaumatology, but I'm still an ignorant fisher girl when it comes to Physics and Alchemy and Biology. I'm not very happy about that, or about being reminded of it."

"And you couldn't talk?"

"I didn't know how. Even with a translation spell in effect. I've never thought about it much, but the translation spell I know only works on incoming information, and doesn't help at all going the other direction. And pistrisines use different apparatus to communicate than humans do; we talk with air going OUT through our throats; sharks don't have that option."

"Which explains why they've never gotten any information out of their prisoners."

"Actually, Bing has gotten a LOT of information out of pistrisine prisoners, but none of it was linguistic, and most of it was by way of dissection."

"Bing sounds creepier all the time."

"He's a necromancer to the bone. He just doesn't look like one, at first glance."

"So how DO sharks talk?"

"There are some structures in the exhaust vents that produce pops and clicks and whistles. Bing thinks they would work better under water, since that's what they're designed for. He's got some sort of idea to try that out tomorrow."

"Other than just going for a swim?"

"The ocean is behind enemy lines."

"Ah."

"Is my life impossibly weird, Fid?"

"You're asking the ghost of a unicorn who's bound to an object on the bottom of the ocean."

"There is that."

"But yes, you're the single most peculiar person I have ever considered a friend. And while that's not a long list, you're VERY different from any of the others. What brings this up?"

"I think the other sorcerers are growling at me behind my back. When I got here, everyone wanted to learn my transformation spell, but I've done everything I can think of to teach it, and NO ONE has gotten it."

"I take it none of them has three dragon marks, or a transformation tattoo from Auntie Moss."

"Exactly. They've realized that the reason they can't fly is that I have wings and they don't."

"Is this a problem?"

"Difference isolates. I get along with Rilla because she owes me, and lives with me, and has actually gotten a chance to know me. And I get along with Bing because he's manic about learning new things. I think that if a dragon threatened to eat him, he would beg to be swallowed whole so he could observe the process."

"Bing is crazy, isn't he?"

"Oh, yeah. But... Oh, hell, Fid, I'm complaining about being lonely to someone who is a hundred times lonelier than I am."

"I take solace in your intention to make it up to me in great detail."

"And he proves that he can still make me blush. But you're right, I very much do."

"So we share weirdness and loneliness and discontent, but are content in each other. And on that note, good night."

==)»> 8:2: A tent east of Glass Fort

"You're late tonight, Rose."

"And exhausted. But I wanted to let you to know nothing had happened to me, so I'm doing a trance rather than trying to sleep right away."

"What happened?"

"Bing got me into the fortress. There are some flooded cells there where they can keep prisoners alive, if they want to. They have one prisoner, the only one at the moment, who has been there for something like a hundred years. Apparently sharks live a LONG time."

"So it would seem. What was the point?"

"I got to be a shark in sea water, which was a lot more comfortable. The water in the cells isn't even too stale; there's some kind of wave pump system that keeps the water circulating."

"That's... surprisingly humane, given what you've told me."

"I think it's more a matter of bored mages working on pet projects. And it turns out that Bing hasn't done anything crazy to live prisoners, just read the notes of his predecessors. The rule seems to be that captured sharks are dead meat anyway, so they're available for anyone who has a use."

"These are really nice people you work for."

"I'm not thrilled, but remember what happens to humans captured by the sharks."

"That sounds fatal."

"Everyone HOPES it's fatal; no one has ever escaped to say otherwise."

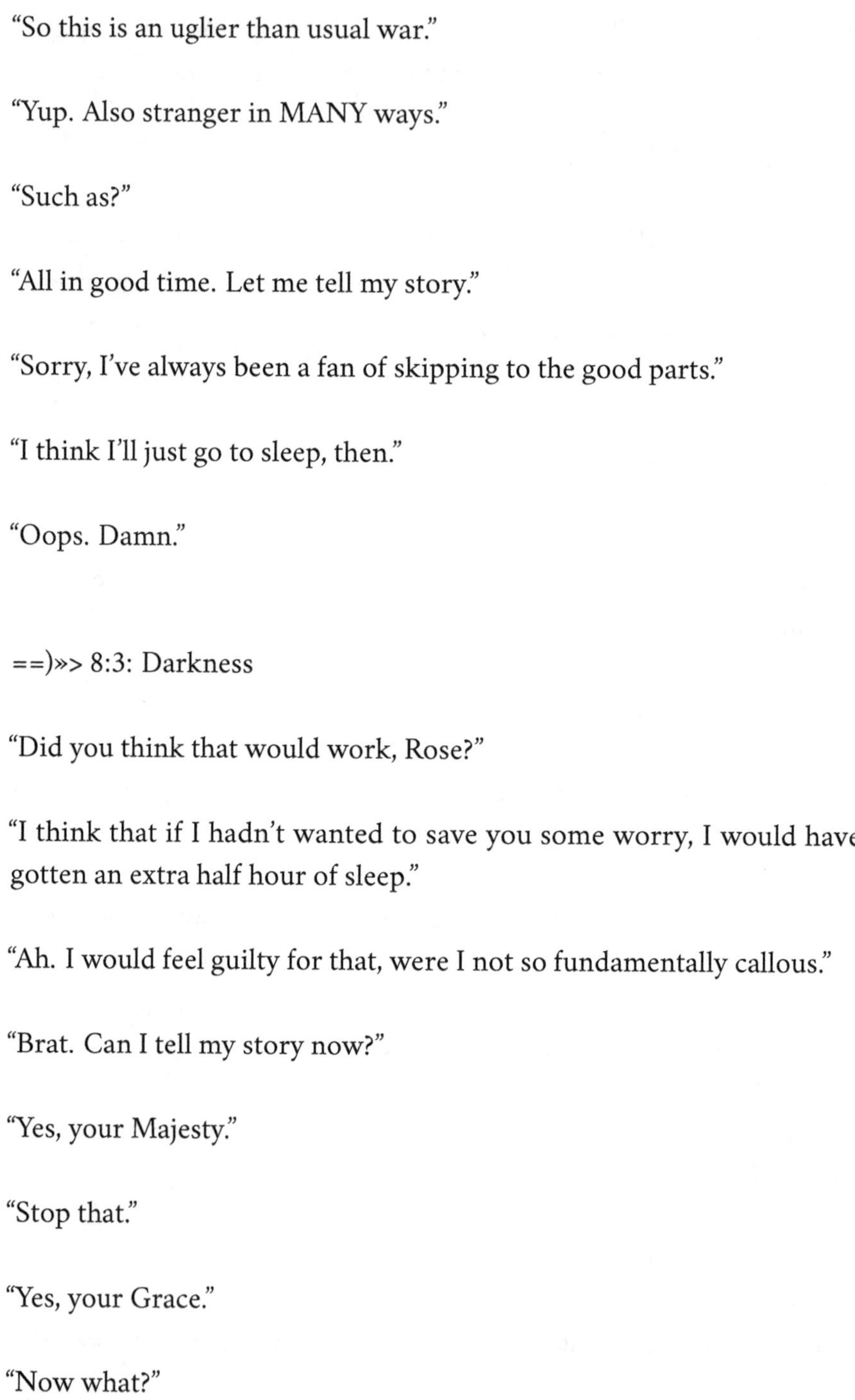

"So this is an uglier than usual war."

"Yup. Also stranger in MANY ways."

"Such as?"

"All in good time. Let me tell my story."

"Sorry, I've always been a fan of skipping to the good parts."

"I think I'll just go to sleep, then."

"Oops. Damn."

==)»> 8:3: Darkness

"Did you think that would work, Rose?"

"I think that if I hadn't wanted to save you some worry, I would have gotten an extra half hour of sleep."

"Ah. I would feel guilty for that, were I not so fundamentally callous."

"Brat. Can I tell my story now?"

"Yes, your Majesty."

"Stop that."

"Yes, your Grace."

"Now what?"

"If I can't call you a Queen, I can still call you a Duchess. You let the kobolds do it."

"The KOBOLDS!?!... Fine. Brat. Can we continue?"

"Yes, your Grace."

"You do realize that I'm supposed to WANT to rescue you, don't you? Anyway... Once I was in the cell, the other prisoner started talking to me, and I cast my translation spell, so I could understand him. I tried to talk to him, but didn't know how to form the words. I managed to learn a few words, but not nearly enough. But I did learn that, because sound travels so easily in water, the hundred year prisoner has been in contact with the rest of the sharks all along."

"That's BIG information."

"I thought it was. When I got out of the water, there was a squad of troops waiting for me. Bing was still there, though, and he told me that he and I had been summoned to meet with the head sorcerer of the army, pretty much the head of everything, a Fourth Circle named Norastras who specializes in divination."

"Is this going to be bad?"

"No, just even more strange. Norastras is OLD, and slight. Stand him next to Bing and you'd pick him as the necromancer. Of course, you'd probably guess Bing was a wine seller... Anyway, we talked minor pleasantries, and then Norastras asked me about my ability to communicate with the sharks."

"And you led with the truth. I'm so ashamed. My tutelage has been wasted on an imbecile."

"Hush. Yes, I told him the truth. I also told him that the sharks had open communication with their prisoner. He wasn't surprised. It turns out that it's REALLY hard to surprise a high-level diviner..."

"As opposed to, say, a low-level sorceress who gets hit in the head with sticks a lot."

"You are SO lucky I'm not cruel enough to shut you out. But remember that I might have a limit."

"Yes, your Grace."

"Anyway... He asked if I was interested in trying to learn more of the pistrisine language, and I said that I was, and he said he would arrange for me to have access to the flooded cells as I wished. And then he said that he was going to tell me a secret, since I was likely to learn it from the prisoner eventually, and THIS way, he could swear me to secrecy first."

"An oath you are now going to break?"

"An oath to never tell a living person."

"And it turns out that she is NOT utterly inept as a swindler, after all. I am vindicated."

"You're a nuisance, but yes, I cut you a loophole. Now shut up and let me use it."

"Yes, your Grace."

"That was old the second time."

"I'm nodding. Really I am. Also leering lasciviously, if you really want to know."

"At WHAT?"

"Umm... A carefully cultivated memory?"

"Idiot. Anyway... I now know why this goofy war is being fought the way it is. The sharks don't want territory they can't use, and humans are much too much work as a food source. It's about breeding rights. For a shark to be allowed to breed, he has to either wound, or be wounded by, a surface dweller."

"Two questions: He?"

"Yup. The society is female dominated, and they really only need about one male for every hundred females, so they can afford a LOT of casualties in the selection process."

"Riiight. And second, wounds struck are on the honor system?"

"Apparently the sharks have some NASTY truth spells, of the 'Die a horrible lingering death if you lie' variety."

"Of course they do. How does Norastras know all of this?"

"Divination. Generations of it, apparently. But that's also why the army knows months in advance when the next invasion is going to happen, and where each new skirmish is going to occur."

"I didn't think diviners could actually see the future."

"They can't. But they can sense that plans are being made, and that troops are being massed."

"So the topsiders are always waiting for them, and the sharks can never pull off a surprise."

"Yes. And the topsiders— our side— well, MY side anyway, I don't know about you— have instructions to let the sharks back off if they want to after first contact. Command doesn't WANT prisoners; they know that the sharks will leave as soon as they reach some quota of blooded warriors, and dead sharks don't count toward the quota. But it's difficult to get soldiers to stand their ground when the enemy present their backs..."

"I've been told. So what are you going to do?"

"I'm going to add going for regular swims in the dungeon to my routine. And for right now, I'm going to play dead for a while."

"As my Lady wishes."

==)»> 8:4: Darkness

"Good evening, your Grace."

"You're never going to let that go, are you?"

"Probably not."

"I shouldn't complain; at least you're talking to me."

"Problems, Rose?"

"A riddle: Which is worse: Being alone, or being surrounded by people who won't talk to you?"

"As bad as that, Rose?"

"Not quite. Rilla seems to like me, and Bing finds me interesting, Cagey finds me amusing..."

"Cagey?"

"The old shark in the dungeon; the other sharks call him 'The Old One in the Cage', so I think of him as Cagey. Actually I think of him as a three note whistle-click that means 'Cage Person', but, well, translations across disparate vocal systems get dodgy."

"It sounds like it."

"But beyond them, the troops seem to have gotten it into their heads that Sister Crocodile is the real me, and that the girl with scales on her cheeks is some kind of spy for the sharks, and the other sorcerers all resent me for knowing a spell that they can't seem to learn, and I seem to be followed by disapproval all the time. I wonder if I wouldn't be better off just ALONE."

"I would be happy to trade places with you so that we could each develop an informed opinion."

"I know, Fid. But I also find myself wishing I could just be with you on the edge of the waterfall more or less forever, and forget about everything else completely."

"I think I could adapt to that. But I know that you couldn't."

"Probably not."

"Would her Grace's mood be improved by some music?"

"Almost certainly. And Fid... Thank you."

"I exist to serve."

==)»> 8:5: Darkness

"Good evening, Rose."

"Hey, Fid."

"You seem... Happier. Less down-trodden, anyway."

"Yup. The war is ending, and we get to leave this place behind."

"What happened?"

"The sharks have had enough for now, just like always. One, maybe two skirmishes, and they'll head out to sea for another generation."

"And they've ANNOUNCED this?"

"Hell no. I heard it from the sharks, first, then had a talk with Norastras, who confirmed that it matched his divinations. And of course he asked me to keep it to myself. But in less than a month I should be back on the water and headed for Silverport, and I can forget all about this little puddle of misery."

"I know it's been hard. For both of us, really. When you're unhappy it wears me down. I kind of wish you'd have sex occasionally. I get jealous, but the emotional feedback feels good."

"Does it now? I'll have to keep that in mind."

"Just don't get carried away."

"Never that many opportunities, Fid. And I'm sure my sessions with Cagey haven't helped. He's even lonlier than you are."

"I thought he had unlimited conversation with the outside."

"Only during wars. Most of the time, there are no sharks that close, unless one of them makes a point of paying Cagey a visit. And that's dangerous; the locals kill sharks on sight, even if there's no war."

"So he goes for YEARS without any conversation at all?"

"Yup."

"Poor bastard. How does he stand it?"

"He's become something of a mystic. Good language teacher, though. Says my accent is atrocious, which is no surprise."

"No, it's not. Will you miss him?"

"I wouldn't go that far. He's interesting, I've enjoyed the language lessons, but there's no question he would rip my heart out and eat it if he got the chance."

"That does constrain friendship just a bit."

"Just a bit. Though it says something about this experience that, even with that, he's been one of the high points."

"It'll be over soon."

"That it will. Chase the luck for me, Fid? I could use some happiness."

"As your Grace wishes."

"Brat."

==)»> 8:6: Darkness

"Good evening, Rose. Is that... GUILT? What did you do?"

"I bought out Rilla's contract."

"Say what?"

"Rilla signed up for twenty-five years, or until properly discharged. As far as the army goes, she's still a camp-follower, and they don't want to let her go. And Rilla is particular about having given her word, and doesn't want to desert."

"So you bought her out. How bad is it?"

"I'm dead broke. And in debt to Bing, actually."

"That's... expensive altruism, Rose. What now?"

"I go back to Landfall with Bing, and serve as his assistant for a while. Rilla will come with as my servant, but I'm pretty sure I can talk her into working directly for Bing, and talk Bing into hiring her."

"So how long will it take to pay off Bing and rebuild your stake?"

"...A year?"

"...Ouch. Just... Ouch."

"I'm sorry, Fid. I couldn't leave her there. She's my friend. And you... You're immortal, and you and I will have time. I'll find a way to make this up to you."

"No, I will DEVISE a way for you to make it up to me."

"That sounds terrifying."

"It should. But you'll enjoy it anyway."

"And you can STILL make me blush."

"I live for it."

"How angry are you?"

"Not angry. Disappointed, and impatient, but I'm always impatient. I will cope."

"Thank you."

"I exist to serve. Your Grace."

==)»> 8:7: A field north of Glass Fort

"Why is my Duchess awake this evening?"

"I'm letting things around me calm down a bit before I actually try to sleep, and thought I'd check in with you."

"This lowly personage is grateful for your attention."

"I acknowledge that I'm doing penance, but you're heartless."

"Literally, certainly. Figuratively my heart exists, though it may well be frozen stone. The result of isolation and neglect."

"You're going to run out of penance tokens REALLY quickly at this rate. Idiocy aside, guess what I did for the first time ever today?"

"Set fire to your eyebrows?"

"What? No! I rode a horse."

"As opposed, presumably, to being ridden by a horse. And there is that blush again. Damn, I'm good."

"Good is not the first word that comes to mind."

"Ah. Well. How sore are you?"

"Pretty damned sore, thank you. But this is a LOT easier on the feet than the trip out was."

"You should ask the horse's opinion."

"I tried. He tried to bite me."

"I would say that that's an answer. Though I'll admit that I've tried to bite you on occasion as well. Usually successfully."

"Different circumstances, Fid. And never with horse's teeth."

"I'll give you that."

"I am SO glad to be away from Glass Fort."

"I can tell. You're... energized."

"Happy?"

"Not quite yet, I think. But certainly happier."

"I'm still sorry that I put us on this detour, Fid."

"You followed the path as you saw it. Fate turned against you. Life, or in my case existence, goes on."

"Fid? That doesn't sound like you. That was sweet, and gentle, and... Is something wrong?"

"I'm just trying to push through YOUR melancholy, Rose. I'm in a very quiet place, and what you whisper there becomes thunder, here. Even when I don't know what I'm hearing. Though I'm learning."

"This isn't what you used to say."

"Things change. I think that we're cheating the rules of the bond by length of relationship."

"Is that good?"

"I think so. I hope so. If the true bond is going to form over distance, though, I wish it would hurry."

'I do too, Fid. I do too. Am I allowed music in my penance?"

"Of course. I may be hard, but I'm not cruel."

"Good night, Fid."

==)»> 8:8: Darkness

"Good evening, your Grace."

"And to you, your Nuisanceship."

"You're happy tonight, Rose."

"I think I am, yes. We told campfire stories. I told one about having been haunted by a unicorn's ghost, once upon a long ago."

"How did that go over?"

"Quite well. They may have even believed me. Though Bing was disappointed that I had never tried to engage the unicorn in my own shape."

"Bing continues to find new ways to be creepy."

"I just laughed. Rilla turned a bit green."

"And what did you tell them became of this ghost?"

"I told them the truth: That he sailed away with the owner of his binding object."

"An incomplete truth, then."

"All truths are incomplete, Fid. Some are more obviously incomplete than others."

"I'll give you that."

"How did you do it, Fid? Survive through four years with no contact at all?"

"I almost didn't. I was very close to sliding off into the void when I found you."

"You seemed manic. I knew you were very unhappy. I didn't know it was that bad."

"A fact of my existence is that I can end it by deciding to. Being aware of that makes me careful of my thoughts. But I was only close; I wasn't there yet. And now... I don't LIKE waiting; I've always been impatient. But there is a dragon waiting for me with open arms at the end of the road, and I WILL survive the journey, however long or convoluted it may be."

"Damn, that's sweet, Fid. Sometimes you make it really hard to remember how charming you can be. But I swear that as long as I draw breath, I will be on that road. Give or take a detour."

"If you hadn't taken this detour, you wouldn't have been my Rose."

"There is that. Until the day, Fid."

"Yes. Until the day."

==)»> 8:9: An open field east of Landfall

"Stargazing, Rose?"

"You can tell?"

"I can tell a few things, and I can guess. Is it safe?"

"I have a sword at my side, and a crocodile in my pocket, among other things. I'm safe enough."

"You never know. There could be a minotaur in the woods."

"Really."

"You never know. They're sneaky."

"Are they?"

"You don't know about minotaurs, do you?"

"Apparently not."

"Minotaurs are to humans what unicorns are to deer and cows and horses. Or maybe more accurately, what unicorns are to centaurs."

"Humans aren't herd animals..."

"Minotaurs are sneaky. A minotaur on the edge of town can impregnate every fertile woman in the town in a matter of days. And if someone figures out what's going on, then the killing starts. The bellow of a minotaur will freeze a human, or a hundred humans, in their tracks. And then the minotaur will cut down all of the men like wheat."

“This is a campfire story, Fid.”

“If you like. I’ve met a few. In dreamspace. Unicorns and minotaurs stay away from each other.”

“Have you. All right, then, Storyteller, how does one deal with a minotaur?”

“You kill him from a distance. A very great distance, preferably from ambush, before he can start bellowing. Plugged ears help a little, if you’re far enough away.”

“What does a minotaur do with the infertile women, then?”

“He ignores them, as long as they stay out of his way.”

“So I’m safe.”

“If he can sense the magic of your tattoo. If you don’t mind getting to know him a LOT better than you had planned on. If your charm actually holds up against fertility magic that is that strong.”

“You’re ruining my stargazing, Fid.”

“I’d be happier if you were doing it from the deck of a ship, is all.”

“So would I, Fid. So would I.”

9: Landfall

It is not enough to see flight as a means of transport; lesser creatures have been doing that for millennia. We have taken to the sky; let us master it. We have found our wings; let us dance!

—Xart Windchaser, *Flight*

==)»> 9:1: Darkness

“Good evening, Rose. You seem... good, tonight.”

“I’m sleeping in a rich man’s bed.”

“Excuse me?”

“I am sleeping in a bed that belongs to a rich man. He isn’t sharing it with me, nor is it even the bed in which he is accustomed to sleep. It’s just a REALLY nice bed in the room Bing gave me for the duration of my stay with him. It’s kind of like sexual afterglow made into furniture.”

“So your first statement was not only incomplete, but misleading.”

“Not deliberately so; it’s a natural limitation of the genitive case.”

“Fancy talk for an under educated fisher girl.”

"Heh. My education was erratic, but it took place. Did I ever tell you how Drellan taught me to read Kzanti?"

"It would seem not."

"I grew up speaking Kzanti, but was illiterate; after the first transformation, I could speak, read, and write Dragontongue. And I knew a translation spell that I could use for a couple of hours a day, at that point. So Drellan gave me a Kzanti story book, and told me to copy it into Dragontongue. When I ran out of magic each day, I was supposed to compare my copy, which I could still read, with the original, which was in a language I knew but couldn't read, and try to figure out as much of Kzanti text as I could. By the time I had finished copying the book— it wasn't very long— I had a basic handle on Kzanti text. And then he gave me a Kzanti book on Thaumatology, and told me to go through the same process, with the added step of trying to understand the content of the book along the way. And he gave me a book on Kzanti grammar, and a Kzanti dictionary, just to confuse things. His words."

"Sounds... dry. Didn't you feel cage bound?"

"Are you joking? Learning things, chasing information that you WANT, is just another way of chasing the horizon. I couldn't do it forever, because every answer asks two more questions, and at least some of those questions are the 'What would happen if I...?' kind, and you don't find THOSE answers in books. But when you're out in the world, eventually the sun goes down, and you have to stop chasing and sleep. When you're chasing things in a library, you can keep going until your head collapses onto the page."

"Which is something you've done repeatedly, I gather."

"Oh, yeah. Drellan used to growl at me about it, because then I would crash for a day and a half. But it was pretty wonderful, all told."

"You're a very strange creature, Rose Stonecrow."

"Said the dead unicorn from the bottom of the ocean."

"And on that note... Enjoy your rich man's bed, Rose."

"Count on it."

==)»> 9:2: Darkness

"And how is the scholar tonight, Rose?"

"Ambivalent. I love the material, hate the instructor."

"Problems with Bing?"

"No, Bing's great. His senior apprentice, Gorsheg, is supposed to be tutoring me and he's making me crazy. He's already been over all of the stuff I'm working on, but he's only a late First Circle, and I'm mid-Second somewhere, so I out-rank him, and he resents it. Plus the usual junk about my ability to do transformations. Mostly, I only go to him when I can't find a book I need."

"Not the best way to work."

"Not even close. On the other hand, I REALLY love the work. Math is like a giant toy box full of puzzles, and every time you solve one, you get another one to play with. And the rest is almost as much fun."

"That's a lot of excitement. For having your clothes on, and all."

"I really ought to hate you."

"For making you blush when no one else is looking? It's the highlight of my existence at the moment."

"Consider my eyes rolled."

"Do you doubt me?"

"I... am baffled and occasionally awe-stricken by the improbability of our friendship, that's all."

"I prefer to focus on my gratitude."

"You're being sweet again. It's confusing."

"It's SUPPOSED to be confusing. If I made sense, I might find that I was insignificant."

"I think that's true of all of us, Fid."

"Well, then."

"In other news, I might learn how to become a kobold."

"And why would you want to?"

"Why not? I don't have any reason to believe that there's a limit to the number of shapes I can learn, and the process seems to really excite Bing."

"Beyond just giving him an excuse to hunt down parts of intelligent beings that are still in edible condition."

"I admit that he seems to enjoy the hunt."

"Just be careful, Rose. Don't end up in his collection."

"He's my friend, Fid. It'll be fine."

==)»> 9:3: Darkness

"Good evening, Rose. How was your day?"

"Boring and kind of frustrating. I spent the whole day being naked at an artist."

"That sounds stranger than usual. What happened?"

"Bing wanted to document my tattoos, so he hired an artist to paint them. And because I'm a good little student, I obeyed the master's request, and spent the day in the artist's studio, lying on a board, while he made copies of the handiwork of Auntie Moss."

"That explains the boring. Why frustrating?"

"Because it was hot in the studio, and given where my tattoos are, it was easier to just pose naked. And I might as well have been in croc form for all the interest the artist showed. It made me feel undesirable. I didn't like it."

"Are you sure you had the right plumbing?"

"Yes. When I first got there, he showed me some of his work, which included several female nudes, two of which he pointed out as former lovers."

“So you think it’s just you.”

“I don’t know what else to think.”

“I’m sorry, Rose. He has awful taste.”

“Hardly. You didn’t see the former lovers.”

“Ah. I will hate him on your behalf, then.”

“No, he doesn’t deserve that. He’s nice enough, really. Clean, charming, cute, AND talented. I was hoping something would happen, and was disappointed.”

“You see? I was going to hate him anyway.”

“You could just hate everyone on spec; it would save time.”

“Everyone but you, my dragon.”

“Awww.”

==)»> 9:4: Darkness

“So who do I get to add to my list of hated jealousy objects tonight, Rose?”

“Trosteg. The artist I told you about yesterday.”

“I knew I should have started hating him yesterday. What changed? Did you drag him back to your rich man’s bed?”

“No, we made do with the floor of the studio. And I thought you said that it was good for you when I had sex."

"I said it was a mixed blessing, and I'm choosing to concentrate on the negatives."

"You're not being fair, Fid."

"I'm dead and in prison. I don't have to be fair."

"You do if you want me to talk to you."

"Ah, but I still have a pocket full of Penance tokens."

"Conceded. But you're still a brat."

"Acknowledged, and with no intent to change. So what happened?"

"I took off my scales."

"That... sounds disgusting. And painful."

"One of my forms is my pre-transformation human self. I just have to cast the spell."

"And how did this come about?"

"Trosteg made a comment that the pattern of the scales obscured some of the original design, and I told him that the original tattoos had been there before the scales. He said he wished he could have seen the designs then, so I did the spell and showed him. And then I helped him pick his jaw up off the floor, and then nature took its course."

"Ah. Nature. Her again. Hasn't been around here much, lately."

"And I learned that I can't maintain the transformation spell and have an orgasm at the same time. Which is interesting, if not particularly useful. That upset him a bit, but I calmed him down, and I did the spell again, and he went back to work. We're still on schedule to be done tomorrow."

"You're going back?"

"The original estimate was for three days, yes."

"I'm going to go sulk, now."

"Fid?"

==)»> 9:5: Darkness

"Didn't you go back, Rose?"

"I went back. We finished the illustrations on schedule."

"But..."

"I told him I wasn't interested in a second helping, and put just a touch of magic behind it."

"Domination?"

"A little bit. There is a large ethical jump between calling a person to your bed, and holding a person at arm's length."

"At least as much difference as between eating your victims alive, and having them butchered, broiled, and sauced first."

"Jealousy makes you mean."

"I don't deny it. But... Why?"

"Because yesterday he was the first opportunity I had had in months, and today he wasn't you."

"That's good to hear. Even if I don't believe it."

"Still mean."

"Honest. Which doesn't mean you aren't as well. I just don't think I'll ever be able to believe that particular sentiment in the pit of my non-existent stomach."

"Do you want me to swear fidelity to you?"

"No, because you'll regret it before this is over, and you'll resent me for it. Just wallow in your excessively comfortable bed, and think about what a charming and generous person I am."

"That, I can do. Good night, Fid. Until the day."

"Until the day."

==)»> 9:6: Darkness

"You seem smug tonight, your Grace."

"Maybe a little."

"And?"

"Rilla has been gradually making herself indispensable around here, and today Bing finally officially put her in charge of the household."

"Which is something you were counting on."

"It was. But it also means that many of Gorsheg's responsibilities, and his power in the household, have now been ceded to Rilla."

"This sounds politically ugly."

"A bit. There was a small power struggle, but a battle of wills between a spoiled apprentice sorcerer and a former army whore can have only one conclusion. Particularly with me AND Bing on Rilla's side."

"I might feel sorry for the fellow, if I didn't know he deserved it."

"Exactly."

==)»> 9:7: Rose's room

"Rose? What's wrong?"

"I think I'm going through another transformation. It feels like it. Keep an eye on me. I may need help."

"Of course, Rose. What happened?"

"Kobold blood."

"KOBOLD?"

"I have no idea what's wrong, Fid, I just know it's happening. Please stay as close as you can."

"Always, Rose. Always."

==)»> 9:8: Rose's room

"Keep playing, Fid. It helps so much."

"Always."

==)»> 9:9: Darkness

"Getting to the end, Rose?"

"Gods, I hope so. I don't imagine you've talked to Auntie Moss?"

"You know I did."

"And?"

"Kobolds are distant dragon cousins. So are crocs, but kobolds are much closer. And there are stories— many stories— of dragons taking kobold form and just... slumming, I guess. So the donor for your blood might have been a dragon once or twice removed, close enough to count as a dragon mark."

"A kobold mark. WONDERFUL."

"You're recovering faster than last time. You have a sense of humor. For you."

"Brat."

"Kobold."

"NOT funny, Fid."

"I concede the point. Keep healing, Rose. I'll continue to play."

==)»> 9:10: Rose's room

"Rose? What's wrong?"

"I'm not human, Fid. I look into the mirror and I'm not ME any more. The damned kobold blood took away my face, and my hair. I'm a monster."

"Rose... You are, and you always will be, MY Rose. You know how little appearances matter to me."

"But... I'm a freak."

"Rose... You are Emerald Corrosion Flower Stonecrow, and you have ALWAYS been a freak. What do you think it means to chase the horizon? You've ridden the back of the Great Monster Turtle. You've feasted with crocodilians; you've spoken to shark-folk. These are not things normal people do, but they're part of your day to day existence. You have NEVER been ordinary, and I have always known that. And if it's now a bit more obvious to the casual observer than it was, what does it matter? You're still YOU."

"I'm a monster."

"By what definition? Are you dangerous, and beyond the control of the society you live in? That's been true since your first transformation. Are you a threat to your society due to malice or callousness? That you are not, and NEVER will be. What IS a monster?"

"But..."

"Here's what you are going to do. First, you're going to get a good night's sleep. Then, tomorrow, you're going to put on your Emma face, and get dressed as if your sister Ruby were dressing you for a party, and then you're going to go see your artist friend. You are going to tell him what happened, and demonstrate, if it's necessary, and then you're going to put your Emma face back on, kick his legs out from under him, and make him forget his name. And tomorrow night, you're going to come back here and tell me how much better you feel, and what a wonderful friend I am."

"...Really? You want me to put on girly clothes and have sex?"

"Yes."

"And that will make me feel better?"

"Absolutely."

"And you'll surrender all of those Penance tokens if you're wrong?"

"Only if you make it a double or nothing wager."

"Wow. You're really that confident."

"Yes. And it's hardly a bitter prescription."

"You might have just revolutionized the whole medical profession."

“Hardly. Doctors who prescribe sex too often tend to be called pimps.”

“Ah... Thanks, Fid. You’re a good friend.”

“I’m a monster. But I do my best.”

==)»> 9:11: Darkness

“Good evening, Rose. And how was Trosteg?”

“Generally pretty good, I think. When I left him, he was semi-conscious and muttering about never being able to walk again.”

“And how are you?”

“Much better, thank you. It would seem that my physician knows his business.”

“I’m glad. And now I have all of these extra Penance tokens to torment you with.”

“Brat.”

“Token.”

“Yes, Master. My apologies, Master.”

“I could get used to this.”

“I could decide you’re not worth it.”

“Liar.”

"We'll see. In other news... The kobold form was waiting for me the first time I shifted into Emma this morning. I haven't tried it yet. I told Bing about it this afternoon, though, so that's the first thing on the agenda for tomorrow."

"Do you care?"

"Not much, but Bing does. I care about the fact that there seems to be another new form waiting out there that I can't quite reach. I'm hoping it'll become available after I use the kobold."

"Are you sure it's a real thing?"

"No, not really. I don't KNOW anything about the workings of the spell, other than what I've observed."

"And it helps to eat intelligent beings."

"Or drink their blood. I'm trying not to think about that stuff too much."

"Just tell yourself that it's normal draconic behavior."

"And on that note..."

"Until tomorrow, Rose."

==)»> 9:12: Rose's room

"Your Grace is unreadable this evening."

"I'm not surprised. What do you see?"

"I think you are feeling high levels of both unhappiness and excitement, which seem an improbable combination."

"You're getting too good at that, Fid. You're right on both counts."

"An explanation?"

"How about an explanatory story? This morning Bing gathered his apprentices, and I put on the kobold—which feels a lot like a minitature croc, by the way— and Bing poked and prodded and measured, and when I went back to me... I didn't return to the same place I had set sail from."

"That sounds bad."

"It would have been worse if it had happened simultaneously with losing my face. Since I'm more or less at peace with that, more or less..."

"You are still my Rose, regardless..."

"...This was more of an extreme irritation. But my native form has a tail, now, and I've become a toe walker."

"Come again?"

"Humans walk on their heels, mostly. Crocs and kobs and sharks and fauns have elongated feet, and walk on their toes."

"So your base form used to have plantigrade feet, and now it has digitigrade feet."

"Where do you get this stuff?"

"The original unicorn information dump was full of REALLY obscure information."

"In addition to being ethically void."

"That, too. And I can understand your irritation. I have some small knowledge of having my anatomy involuntarily rearranged."

"You're being sweet, again, Fid. And stabbing me a bit at the same time."

"Ah. You noticed. But you were telling me a story?"

"When Bing saw I was in a form he hadn't seen before, there was more poking and prodding and measuring, during which Bing and I speculated on what might have caused the change, but we really don't understand my transformation spell well enough to make a decent guess."

"Understandable. I'll ask Auntie Moss. Sometime. Auntie Moss doesn't like me, much."

"Bing suggested that I try to reset by shifting to one of my older forms, specifically the human. I started to do the spell, realized that the previously out-of reach form was now available, and went for that instead."

"And?"

"And I turned into a kobold with wings."

"Which is why you're excited."

"Just a little."

"What next?"

“Bing is putting together an overnight trip to someplace outside the city that has lots of open space, so that I can experiment with flight, and he gave me a very strange book about flying.”

“Strange how?”

“In the first chapter, the author talks about how hideously dangerous flying is. And then he talks about the fact that the standard sorcerer’s flight spell, which is over my head, and that Bing has never bothered to learn, is crippled by safety features, because its forerunner was fatal three times out of four.”

“Fatal?”

“It would seem that it’s really easy to get dead when you’re traveling at ninety miles an hour.”

“NINETY?”

“Oh, yeah.”

“It sounds like you’ve found another horizon.”

“Oh, yeah.”

“Don’t forget about me, Rose.”

“Never.”

“But...”

“Ninety miles an hour. Damn.”

"Try to get some sleep, my dragon, and I'll play you a lullaby."

"Good night, Fid."

==)»> 9:13: Darkness

"Tired, Rose?"

"Brain blasted. Also footsore. Today was my first significant walk on new feet."

"Why brain blasted?"

"Because I've spent a lot of time with that 'Flight' book, and it's beating me up. It would have been incomprehensible before I came to stay with Bing, though."

"What's so difficult about it?"

"Consider it a description of an orgy involving Physics, Engineering, Thaumatology, and Common Sense."

"Now my brain hurts. Common sense?"

"Things like, 'Get a comfortable pair of optically high quality goggles, and wear them if you have any suspicion that you will exceed 20 miles per hour.'"

"That's common sense?"

"Get a bug in your eye at 30 miles per hour, and tell me."

"Ah."

"Bing tells me that sorcerers in general think that old Xart, the author, was crazy, but Bing thinks that's because no one wants to take the time to test his theories."

"Until you, anyway."

"Not sayin'. Yet. We'll see. I intend to investigate his comments on winged flight as thoroughly as I can, though. I'll worry about the magic driven stuff when it becomes relevant."

"After you rescue me."

"Maybe..."

"Heartless."

"I'm a dragon, remember?"

"You're playing my own insults against me. That's not fair."

"It's too true to be an insult any more, Fid. I'm trying to get used to it."

"Yes, your Grace."

"Good night, my Monster."

"Good night, Rose."

==)»> 9:14: Darkness

“In pain, Rose?”

“Memories of pain. It's all been healed, now; Bing talked a friend who specializes in healing into coming along today, because he suspected what would happen. So two broken ankles, a broken shin, and three various broken wing bones later, I'm fine. But all of that pain jangles the nerves.”

“That must have been a really awful landing.”

“Nothing that bad. I botched a couple of dozen landings, but only broke myself five times before I got it sorted out.”

“You broke bones, got patched up, and went right back up.”

“Umm... Yes?”

“You're crazier than I thought you were. And that's saying something.”

“I FLEW, Fid. With my own wings. By the end I nailed five landings in a row, and on my last flight I did a ROLL. You should have seen Bing's face. He was TERRIFIED. And then I did a climbing turn, came in hot, did a perfect flare, and landed flat-footed. It was AMAZING. It was... Better than sex is going too far, but a DAMNED good substitute.”

“Don't forget me, Rose.”

“Don't be stupid.”

“I'm not.”

“Fid, YOU are still the center of my life. Some day, we're going to be back in dreamspace, and you're going to cobble together a form with wings, and I'm going to teach you how to fly. Because as good as this is, and it is unquestionably WONDERFUL, sharing it with you will be even better."

"I've never given a moment's thought to being able to fly."

"And I'd never given a moment's thought to being a centaur— among other things— until I met you. And that worked out pretty well."

"You can teach me to fly, Rose."

"I can hear the grin. You're winding me up?"

"Every chance I get. Even when you terrify me."

"I terrify you?"

"Constantly. But you wouldn't be you if you didn't."

"I am intrigued by the idea of terrifying an indestructible immortal monster."

"Rose... You know the old story about the sorcerer who couldn't be hurt because he had taken his heart out of his chest and hidden it where no one could find it?"

"I know the story. Not sure I see the point."

"Have you heard the story about the monster who was immortal and indestructible, and who chose to leave his heart outside his chest, out in the world where anyone could find it and damage it?"

"No..."

"You're living it."

"Damn, Fid. There's no follow up to that."

"There isn't supposed to be. At least until tomorrow night."

"And I'll always be here."

"I know."

10: Revenant

A boat is a tool, and should be a friend. But a ship is your mother.
—Sailor's proverb

==)»> 10:1: Rose's room

"Restless tonight, your Grace?"

"Itchy feet. I promised Bing a year, and it's almost up, and I'm not sure how to proceed."

"Are you thinking about staying on?"

"No. I wouldn't do that to you, anyway, but I just know I've been here too long. And as soon as I start to think about leaving, this place starts to look like a prison."

"I thought you were happy, for the most part."

"I have been. It's a nice prison. And I can walk away any time I want, I guess, but I'm not a walker, and I'm really afraid that the sea might be closed to me."

"I'm not seeing that."

"Emma can go anywhere she wants, but only for an hour at a time. My true form is just too weird, and I don't see how I can book passage on a ship and stay out of sight for a whole voyage."

"Ah."

"If I have to walk, I have to walk. But it's a damned long way."

"I have no ideas."

"I didn't expect you to. You could play me a lullaby, though."

"I can, and I will."

"Good night, Fid."

==)»> 10:2: Darkness

"You're tired tonight, Rose."

"I've been doing honest work."

"That sounds unpleasant."

"No, it's kind of exciting, actually. I bought a boat."

"I did not see this coming."

"I didn't either, but it works. Sailing will get me to Silverport, and on to Skytower, much faster than walking, and I won't have to worry much about cargo load, and it'll be safer than being on land. I hadn't considered it because I thought it was out of my price range."

"What changed?"

"I bought a wreck."

"Hear my eyes rolling."

"I can fix it easily with magic, it'll just take a little time."

"Hmmm. You should at least get a good story out of it."

"Which you want to hear."

"I wait with bated breath. Which, since I don't breathe, is pretty much the only option."

"Brat. Anyway... There was a storm last night, and I woke up early this morning, because I was still restless, and I wore Emma down to the docks, just to talk to the water. And I found this old man standing next to an empty slip, turning the air blue. It turned out that the slip wasn't empty, but that his boat had sunk during the storm. I listened to him go on for a while; he was a really accomplished vulgarian. Eventually he wound down, and I asked him about the boat, which set him off again, and then I asked him if he would consider selling it, as it was. He was shocked, but he said he would, and I made an offer, and he accepted it. So now I own a sunken boat."

"Your ability to plumb new depths of crazy never ceases to amaze me."

"It was floating yesterday, which means it's all there, no matter how poor its condition. That means I can use magic to repair it, plank by plank, until it's as good as new. It won't actually take that much magic, or more than a few days. The biggest job was getting it out of the harbor, and I've already DONE that."

"You got a sunken boat out of the harbor in one day?"

"I bought some empty barrels and used them to float it off the bottom, and then Sister Shark towed it out of town. Towing a twenty-five foot boat through water when you can stand on the bottom is kind of like pulling an empty horse cart over level ground."

"I'm impressed. I still think you're crazy, but I'm impressed."

"So now I have a swamped boat on the beach about three miles north of town. Tomorrow I'll pull it farther up the beach and start fixing it."

"And assuming this all goes as planned, when will you start heading east again?"

"Two weeks. Three at the outside."

"Which is a LOT better than the 'never' I was beginning to worry about."

"Have I EVER given you any reason to believe that I was going to put down roots here, or anywhere?"

"I am ever at your mercy, Rose, and have no control whatsoever."

"Idiot. You KNOW I'll come for you. You DO."

"When the sun is in the sky, I have no doubt that it will rise again tomorrow. But the nights are long and cold, and I forget."

"Is that you, or did you steal it from somewhere?"

"Would I admit it if it were stolen?"

"Probably not. Good night, my scorpion. Your heart is safe for at least one more day."

==)»> 10:3: Darkness

"You're late tonight, Rose. And exhausted, I think."

"And sleeping in the boat, because I'm too tired to walk into town. But she's DONE, Fid. Tomorrow I give her a new name, raise her sails for the first time since I've owned her, and sail her into the harbor. The day after that, probably, I'll take Bing and Rilla out for a tour of the harbor, and the day after that I'll start loading her up for the trip."

"A new name?"

"I think she deserves one. She wore out her old one."

"And the name is?"

"'Revenant.'"

"That's... quite a name."

"It fits. And my best friend is a ghost, so I'm disinclined to be afraid of the undead. At least the lesser ones."

"Speaking as your ghostly friend, I would be grateful if you were just a bit more superstitious."

"She takes her revenge against the sea that killed her by rising and conquering her enemy all over again. It's a good name, and she's a good boat. It'll be fine."

"You're far too trusting, Rose."

"What? Are you afraid I'm going to get tangled up with some undead thing, and dedicate my life to rescuing it?"

"Ouch."

"It'll be fine, Fid. And a spooky name will frighten the riffraff. Maybe."

"We can hope. Would her Grace like a lullaby?"

"Her Grace would like that very much indeed."

==)»> 10:4: Rose's room

"Not sleeping, Rose?"

"Meditating on my way to sleep, I hope. This way I can talk to you, a bit, and maybe fall asleep as well. It would be a shame to waste my last night in this wonderful bed."

"And we'll finally be moving forward again."

"We've been moving forward right along, Fid. It just hasn't always been obvious. But tomorrow the road will be clearer than it has been in a long time."

"Fifteen months."

"I know, Fid, and I've said I'm sorry. But now I have my fourth Dragon Mark, and I have Wings, and a head full of new knowledge, and some new books, and some new spells... It's been worth it, and I promise I'll make the wait up to you somehow."

"You keep saying that."

"And you keep doing that invisible leer whenever I do."

"Heh."

"And making me blush."

"Heh."

"Be useful and play me a lullaby."

"As her Grace wishes."

==)»> 10:5: Aboard "Revenant"

"You've... MOVED, Rose. Enough that I can see it."

"Fair winds and calm seas, with a lightly laden boat that seems to enjoy running."

"And you're still not sleeping?"

"Not just yet. I'm taking a little time to take in my surroundings, and to talk to my best friend."

"You would have talked to me in any case."

"I know. But this way I have the stars overhead, and the sound of the water, and I can feel the boat around me in a way that I wouldn't if I were asleep."

"You're getting poetic on me, Rose."

"Maybe a little. I'm acutely aware that I'm somewhere I've never been before. I actually own the bed I'm sleeping in— the metaphorical bed, anyway— and there isn't another person around for miles. It's an odd feeling."

"How do you ever cope with the isolation?"

"Brat. I'm trying to identify with an ungrateful friend."

"Yes, your Grace. And I can feel your excitement. And you've MOVED. You're actually closer to me than you have been for a year and a half."

"New horizons, Fid. New scenery, new challenges. Same old you."

"I regret my immutability."

"Don't. The march of the stars is wonderful, but the North Star holds them all together."

"Aww."

"Do I give you grief when YOU get poetic?"

"No, but you haven't built your personality around obnoxiousness."

"Play me something melancholy and MAYBE I won't try to forget you exist. Maybe."

"Token!"

"Sorry, those all expired the moment we set sail. You can't harass me for delaying after the delay is over."

"What? Wait! I hadn't used them up yet!"

"Just play, Fid. And remember that I'm going to be getting closer to you every single day for a while."

"As your Grace wishes."

==)»> 10:6: A coastal hilltop

"Something's different tonight, Rose. I don't know what."

"I've grounded the boat and made camp on high ground. There's a big storm coming, and I want nothing to do with it."

"You left the boat on the beach?"

"No, I sailed up a small river until the boat grounded, and then stripped the boat and pulled it up the nearest hill, rolled it over against a couple of big trees, and made camp underneath it."

"That sounds like a lot of work."

"I've been going on it since noon, but when the Great Monster Turtle tells you to do something, it's a really good idea to do it."

"And you didn't lead with that. I'm rubbing off on you. I'm not sure I like it."

"And it's only been a year and half. Imagine how charming I'll be after fifteen years of your influence."

"Or a hundred and fifty. I look forward to it in any case. But you're still avoiding the story of the day."

"Maelstrom showed up. You should really warn me when he's in the vicinity."

"All of Hurricane Bay is in the vicinity; he can be anywhere in it in less than four days, maybe less than three."

"Still. Even though I am pretty sure he likes me and doesn't want to hurt me, having a turtle's head that's bigger than your boat surface next to you with no warning is... difficult."

"And he said?"

"He congratulated me on my fourth mark, and asked to get a good look at me, so I hove to and stood up on the windward rail, with one hand braced against the mast. And he surfaced again, staring straight at me. Then he turned slowly to the left, and looked at me with his right eye, then he turned to the right, and looked at me with his left eye, and then he looked straight at me again."

"Sounds like a lot of fun."

"I've never been so terrified. Just the weight of that stare..."

"I can imagine. Maybe. I can feel the echoes."

"And then he told me that I wore the mark well, and that I was beautiful, and that I was very lucky that I had managed to find a source that was from the same noble house as the first three."

"Say what? The kobold?"

"Maelstrom was amused by my confusion about that. Kobolds have dragons in their family tree, and apparently most dragon types have contributed to the soup at one point or another. My blood donor must have favored the sea dragons."

"Lucky Rose."

"And then he said that when I was ready for the fifth mark, which I wasn't yet, he would be honored if I were to take it from him."

"The Great Monster Turtle wants you to cut him so that he can bleed into your open wound."

"Yes."

"That's... I have no words. I don't even have any THOUGHTS."

"I know. I was so rattled that I really didn't notice that he had disappeared."

"That's rattled."

"Almost as rattled as I was when he surfaced under the boat, and told to take my place on the front of his shell."

"Gods."

"Can you imagine telling the Great Monster Turtle to wait while you furl the sails?"

"You didn't."

"Hell yes I did. Maelstrom can swim fast enough to roll the 'Revenant' if she gets cross winded, and that boat is my life at the moment."

"Only you, Rose."

"So eventually I ended up on the shell just above his neck, and I told him about everything I've done since Turtle Bay, and he asked me if I was ready to tell him what my secret quest was."

"Um... Wow?"

"What could I do? I told him who you were, and how I met you, and what your situation was, and he said that he was aware of a tiny spark on the bottom in the depths of the bay."

"A tiny spark."

"A VISIBLE tiny spark. He told me that he would do his best to make sure that no one else got to you before I did, and that you should pay him a visit sometime."

"I've thought about it, a little, but besides being terrifying, he never seems to sleep."

"He said that if you knocked on his door, he would answer."

"And you want me to do this?"

"It'll be fine, Fid. He knows that hurting you would hurt me, and he likes me."

"Unless he decides that I'm a bad influence, and that you'd be better off without me."

“Try not to seem like a bad influence.”

“I’m a UNICORN!”

“You’re my best friend. It’ll be fine. I’ve looked into his eyes in the real world. You can handle a little mind speech.”

“Maybe.”

“At any rate, by this time it was noon, and he pointed out the mouth of a small river on shore, and told me that there was a big storm coming, and that I should get as far away from the ocean, and the water, as I could for a few days. So here I am.”

“I wondered where you were getting your weather reports.”

“Like I said, when the Great Monster Turtle gives you weather advice, you take it.”

“I imagine.”

“I’m going to sleep now, Fid. Say, ‘Hello,’ to Maelstrom for me.”

“NOW?”

“Sooner started, sooner over. It’ll be fine. And I’ll be sound asleep, and you can come back and tell me all about it.”

“You’re heartless.”

“No, I’m a dragon.”

==)»> 10:7: Darkness

"That was terrifying."

"But you survived."

"Maybe. I'll let you know when the surreality wears off. It may be a while."

"You'll be fine. Tell the story."

"PUSHY dragon. You take after your grandfather."

"That's a compliment I never expected to hear. Tell the story."

"So I reached out to him, knocked on his door, sort of, as requested, and he just WALKED into my dreamspace."

"Um... wow. I didn't see that coming."

"I didn't know it could happen. I've always kind of thought the dreamspace was inside of me, that I had complete control over it, but, well, not when the Great Monster Turtle is involved."

"I tried to warn you."

"Not really."

"All right, I told you how I reacted."

"Rose, he could have shredded me like a butterfly's wing. I have NEVER been so terrified."

"But what happened? What did he say?"

"He just appeared, in the shape of... One of those big fresh water snapping turtles, I guess, but bipedal, with plantigrade feet, and he said that I ought to choose a form and come talk to him, so I put on Brother Faun, and CLOTHES, and..."

"You wore CLOTHES? You really must have been terrified."

"I keep telling you. And I walked up to him, and bowed, and he shook my hand and said he was pleased to meet me, and asked me to give him a tour. So I showed him the waterfall grove, and the clocks, and my statues; he was really taken by the one of you as a mermaid."

"I look forward to seeing that one myself."

"He asked me why I had so many statues of you as a human, and none with scales, and I said I had never seen you since you had had scales..."

"So many? I thought there were only three of me."

"I've made a few more since then."

"How many?"

"A couple of dozen? Thirty? I've kind of lost track."

"THIRTY?"

"I get lonely. It helps."

"Someday you are going to do something this sweet that isn't completely crazy, and I'll have no idea how to react."

"I'll see what I can engineer. Anyway... He asked me about my music, and I played 'Chasing the Luck' because it's one of your favorites, and then we played a game of Territories."

"You played Territories. With the Great Monster Turtle."

"It was humiliating. He said he would coach me, and that I would get better with time."

"Which is to say that you now have a standing invitation. To play Territories. With the Great Monster Turtle."

"Yes?"

"You may have just permanently out-weirded me, Fid. I'm impressed."

"I'm still terrified."

"You'll get over it."

"Gods, I hope so."

"You know that there are some people who actually chase terror, Fid?"

"Crazy people."

"They say that they do it because it makes them feel alive."

"I have no response for that."

"You aren't supposed to. Good night, my scorpion."

"Good night, my heart."

==)»> 10:8: A coastal hilltop

"Bored, Rose?"

"You have no idea. I've been trying to work on studying, and on practicing magic, but the rain is driving me crazy, and there's no place to go."

"So you're meditating because?"

"Because there is some chance that you'll decide to check in on me, and help relieve the boredom."

"Poor Rose. Without drawing parallels to my current situation..."

"You have all of dreamspace to play with. And a turtle to play Territories with."

"...I have been rained in a time or two over the centuries. When I had a servant, we would set up a tarp and retreat to dreamspace. When I was alone, I would try to find shelter, and think evil thoughts of the entire universe."

"This would be a REALLY good day to spend in dreamspace, if we had the option."

"Any day with you, Rose."

"How do you DO that? There's no lechery in your words, or in your tone, and I STILL blush. Or something. My body doesn't really blush anymore."

"You could always put on Emma for the occasion."

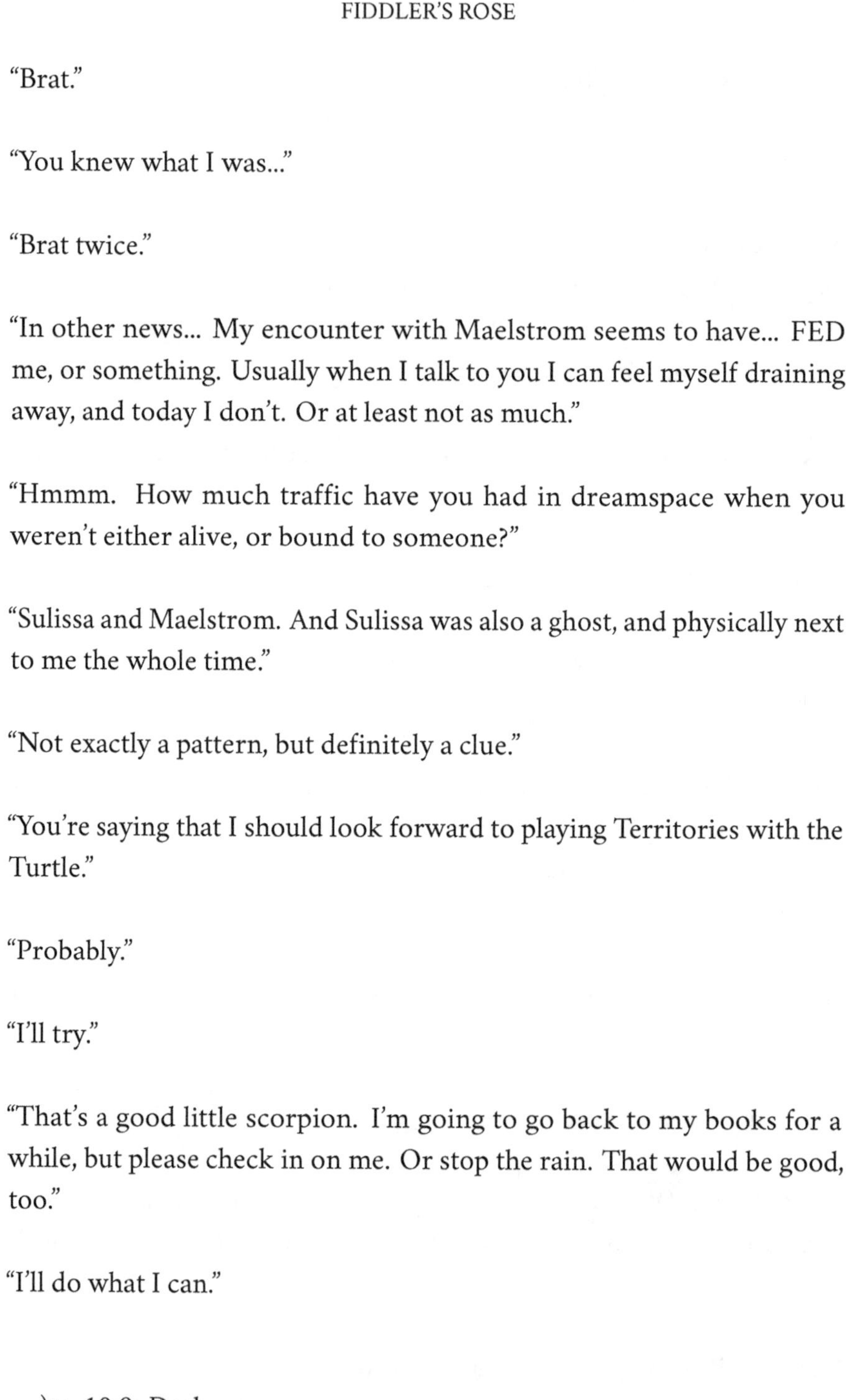

"Brat."

"You knew what I was..."

"Brat twice."

"In other news... My encounter with Maelstrom seems to have... FED me, or something. Usually when I talk to you I can feel myself draining away, and today I don't. Or at least not as much."

"Hmmm. How much traffic have you had in dreamspace when you weren't either alive, or bound to someone?"

"Sulissa and Maelstrom. And Sulissa was also a ghost, and physically next to me the whole time."

"Not exactly a pattern, but definitely a clue."

"You're saying that I should look forward to playing Territories with the Turtle."

"Probably."

"I'll try."

"That's a good little scorpion. I'm going to go back to my books for a while, but please check in on me. Or stop the rain. That would be good, too."

"I'll do what I can."

==)»> 10:9: Darkness

"You're tired tonight, Rose."

"Back on the water, and half a day away from my last camp. It's good to be moving again, but this morning was a LOT of work."

"But you're MOVING."

"I was. Anchored now. Also have a belly full of fresh fish, so that helps. The stuff I've been living off of for the last few days doesn't have much variety, or taste. And now my supplies of the stuff are almost gone; I should probably stop at a village soon and stock up."

"You've been deliberately avoiding people, haven't you?"

"Mostly. It hasn't been hard, particularly if I scout ahead from the air occasionally. From a thousand feet up, the horizon is forty miles away."

"You can take off and land from the boat, or do you go to shore?"

"I heave to, throw a boarding ladder over the side, shift to Sister Wings, and take off. When I come back, I land in the water, shift back to Sister Dragon, climb back into the boat, and sail away. I've tried to land in the boat, but there's ZERO margin for error; it's like trying to land on a tightrope, with a broken ankle or worse waiting if you miss. The odds are too bad."

"Sister Dragon."

"Yes?"

"They all have names. Emma, plus Sister This and Sister That. There's no Rose."

"Ah. You noticed."

"You don't know who you are, anymore."

"Of course I do. I just don't know what I look like. But that doesn't really matter."

"Then who are you?"

"I'm the Corrosion Flower. Also, the Heart of the Unicorn."

"Ah. That."

"Yes, that, silly Fiddler. Forever and always, unless you've changed your mind."

"Never."

"Well, then. I refuse to worry about what face looks back at me from the mirror. Though I wish I could hold onto Emma for more than an hour at a time; it would make my life simpler."

"You can't recast it before it expires?"

"No. Not any more than I can renew Sister Shark. Holding a form takes too much out of me to cast the spell again. A lot of longer term spells interfere with each other like that."

"Ah. That's what stands between you and doing the rescue dive right away."

"Clever scorpion. Though if you had been really clever, you might have asked me about this as soon as I learned the shark form.."

"You said you needed to be Third Circle; I didn't know why. I thought the answer was probably outside my Thaumatology."

"You TRUSTED me? That's... kind of unbelievable. I'm touched."

"Of course I trust you, Rose. You're my heart."

"Damn, Fid. The day just CAN NOT come too soon."

"Just keep sailing."

"As soon as the sun comes back up."

"Until the day, Rose."

"Until the day."

11: Silverport

If you have to promote an officer without seeing him in combat, play a strategy game with him, to see if he can think. And then play a bluffing game with him, to see if he has any nerve.

—Perrin Ironhand, *Armor and Hob-nailed Boots*

==)»> 11:1: Darkness

"Good evening, Rose."

"Good evening, Fid... Have you been talking to Maelstrom again? You seem stronger."

"I have, and I think that I am. Or at least I have more energy. My ego has taken a horrible beating."

"Have you been playing Territories again?"

"Yes. Every time I lose, he spots me ten more stones for the next game. He says that I'm bound to win eventually, and that then he'll start taking stones back one at a time. And of course he looks forward to the day when we'll play with no handicap."

"And how long will that take?"

"I suspect that it will be millennia."

"Ouch."

"We'll see. Do you play?"

"I know the rules."

"Once you've rescued me, we'll have to play occasionally."

"Between other activities."

"Of course. There is no possibility of 'Instead.'"

"You're nothing if not consistent, Master Fiddler."

"As the scorpion pointed out, it's my nature."

"Indeed. Good night, Fid."

==)»> 11:2: Aboard "Revenant"

"Restless tonight, Rose?"

"Planning and calculating. There's a town about ten miles down the coast, and I'm probably going to try to buy some supplies there."

"And the problem is?"

"I don't know what kind of reception I'll get in my true form, and I'd rather not risk it, so I'm planning to put on Emma about half a mile out. Which would be fine, but there's no way I'll get into town and back out again in the single hour the spell lasts, so I'm going try to be ready to refresh the spell."

"Which means?"

"I'm going to go barefoot, and wear a hooded robe on top of my loose vest and skirt. That way I can pull up the hood, drop back to dragon, and then shift back to Emma. With luck, no one will notice."

"I don't like the risk."

"I don't either, but I can play some domination games if I have to. And if I don't figure out some way to get back into human civilization, I'm going to be stuck in this boat until the end of time."

"Or the boat sinks."

"You're a BIG help."

"I exist to serve."

"Play something soothing, and maybe I'll be able to sleep."

"As her Grace wishes."

==)»> 11:3: Aboard "Revenant"

"Are you nervous, Rose?"

"A bit. Standing by to repel boarders."

"That doesn't sound good. What's going on?"

"The trip into town went well enough. I had to recast the transformation twice, but as far as I know, no one noticed, so that was good."

"And the problem?"

"I'm being followed. I'd forgotten how much social armor having a reputation gave me. This afternoon I was just a tall, skinny red-haired girl who was all by herself on a boat. Apparently that attracted some predators."

"What do they want?"

"Rape and or robbery, I imagine, with murder as collateral. I'm going to try to talk them out of it, but I'm not hopeful."

"But you're only nervous, not frightened."

"I'm pretty sure I won't be able to talk them out of their stupidity, and will have to kill them instead. I'm not happy about that."

"But you're still not frightened."

"Something can go wrong; I could end up badly hurt, or dead. But the smart money is heavily on me, and I have no way of convincing them of that without proving it."

"And that means killing them."

"I think so, yes. At least some of them. With luck they'll learn their lesson and run away."

"What if they come back with friends?"

"Then I'm in trouble."

"Be a dragon, Rose. Don't let compassion kill you."

"You're a terrible influence. We'll just have to see. It won't be long, now. See you on the other side."

"Rose?"

==)»> 11:4: Aboard "Revenant"

"Rose? What happened?"

"You had to tell me to be a dragon."

"I ask again, what happened?"

"They're... I... Hell. From the beginning."

"That never hurts."

"They had a lantern on their masthead, so it was easy to see them coming. Sister Dragon sees a lot better in the dark that humans do; I could have killed them all with mage-bolts, if I had wanted to."

"I would have voted for that."

"Shut up, Fid. Not funny."

"Sorry."

"When they were about fifty yards away, I hailed them. I didn't say anything aggressive, just commented that it was late, and that they should anchor."

"Reasonable. Sort of."

"They said that they had lost their anchor, and that they wanted to raft up with me, and I said that they would be better off on shore. They kept coming, and then they got a good look at me; I was standing in the cockpit with one hand on the mast."

"Not good?"

"No. They started shouting about monsters, and one of them apparently already had a bow in his hand, because he stood up and shot at me. I ducked and raised an arm over my face, and got an arrow through my forearm for it. I was going to.. I don't know, roar, maybe, and sneezed out a lightning bolt at the archer..."

"You can breathe lightning?"

"I can SNEEZE lightning, apparently; I was as shocked as they were, and we all just stopped for a moment."

"Except for the archer?"

"Except for the archer, who was out of the equation. There were four of them left, and they started shouting about killing the monster, so I went over the side. I surfaced behind their boat, bit off the arrowhead and pulled the shaft out of my arm. Then someone saw my head, and somebody stood up with the bow to take another shot, and I realized that I had more lightning available, and I used it."

"Down two?"

"Yup. And then I went back under water and came up on the far side of 'Revenant', and I could hear the three surviving idiots shouting and panicking and trying to get away as fast as they could. So I climbed back into the boat, and I thought to myself that it was well over."

"But it wasn't."

"No. I HEARD Sister Dragon say, 'No! They attacked our HOME!' And then I shifted to Sister Wings and flew after them, and killed them all with mage-bolts from the air. Then I landed in the water, shifted back to Dragon, sailed their boat back here, and rafted it to the 'Revenant'. "

"And THEN it was over."

"And then I sat down on the floor of the cockpit and meditated so that you could find me, because Sister Dragon doesn't know how to cry."

"I'm sorry, Rose."

"I've always had a temper. I've always had a bit of the berserker in me; it helped me stay alive, back on the 'Storm Turtle.' But this... By the time the last one died, he was curled up in the cockpit, weeping and begging for mercy, and I just kept hitting him until he was dead."

"Again, I'm sorry, Rose."

"What's happening to me, Fid? If this is part of being a dragon, I don't want it."

"I think... I am confident... This is part of being a dragon, yes, and you will have to deal with it. But the Corrosion Flower is stronger than the dragon, and the main reason that this happened is that you were blind-sided by it, and the next time you won't be, and the next time you'll be able to control it if you want to."

"You sound awfully sure of that."

"I know that I need you to be that strong, Rose, and therefore I believe that you are."

"That's backwards. Or maybe sideways."

"It's practical. One chooses the best tools available, and then believes in them to behave as they should, because doubt will destroy you if you give it a foothold."

"And now I'm a tool?"

"You are the finest and most beautiful weapon that has ever been forged in the history of the world."

"That's... damn you, Fiddler Centaurson."

"Perhaps. Now put on Emma's face, and cry yourself to sleep, and I will play you every lullaby that I know."

"I'm proud to be your heart, Fid."

"I know. Sleep."

==)»> 11:5: Darkness

"Good evening, Rose. Things are back to normal?"

"They are now. I spent the morning cleaning up from last night."

"The entire morning?"

"I hauled the idiots' boat up above the tide line, stacked the idiots under it, and then dug out enough around the boat so that an animal that wants to eat the bodies will have to dig first. Of course I stole everything that was worth stealing along the way. And an ear from each of them."

"And then you ate the ears."

"Yup. Well, Sister Croc did. I don't know if they were really evil, or just drunk and stupid, and I have no idea what religion they practiced, or what idea of the afterlife they believed in, but they are NOT going to Crocodilian Hell."

"You went to a lot of work for men you have good reason to hate..."

"I went to a lot of trouble for men that I killed for no good reason. It wasn't battle rage; you can't cast spells from inside a battle rage, even simple ones like Mage-bolt. Certainly not the transformation. What I felt last night was cold and... I'd say, 'alien', but it WASN'T. It was definitely all me, just part of me that I haven't ever seen before, and may not have always been there."

"Sister Dragon."

"Except I know that Sister Dragon isn't a separate person, she's still ME. I just... Did your personality shift when you became a unicorn?"

"Of course. But I was only fourteen; I didn't really know who I was in the first place."

"Not helpful."

"Sorry, just true."

"I know. I've been through three of these transformations, now. I didn't really notice a change in the way I thought after the first two. I didn't notice a change after the third one, until last night."

"You'll get through this, Rose. WE will get through this."

"I don't want to be a monster, Fid."

"We've been over this before, Rose..."

"And you said that a monster had to pose a threat to society due to malice or callousness. What would you call what I did last night, Fid?"

"What I would have told you to do."

"You're callous as hell, Fid."

"Ouch."

"Not helpful."

"You lost control. They threatened you, hurt you, and made you angry, and they paid. And you've given them more courtesy than I think they deserve. Call it penance, get back on the path, and try to do better next time. You can't take it back, so go forward."

"Already moving forward, Fid. But also dealing with the echoes."

"But the echoes are things of the darkness, and you have me and my music to help chase them."

"I suppose I do, Fid. And I think that's your cue to start playing."

"As her Grace wishes."

==)»> 11:6: Darkness

"Nervous tonight, Rose?"

"A bit. Silverport is on the horizon; I'll be there by mid-morning. And then will come all the rigamarole of trying to not be noticed. And the possibility of drawing more idiot would-be predators. I REALLY want to just sail past, but I came all this way to ask questions in Silverport."

"Life was simpler when you made that decision."

"You mean I had human feet and a human face and long red hair that I really liked..."

"All of which you will have tomorrow morning when you sail into Silverport."

"For an hour."

"It'll be fine, Rose. It'll be easier in a larger town. And you KNOW you can deal with the predators."

"I can PROBABLY deal with the predators, but it leaves scars."

"Scars are sexy."

"Not the ones on my soul."

"Ah. Those."

"Yeah, those. The ones that stay with you no matter what shape you wear."

"Just like tattoos from Auntie Moss."

"But unwanted and a lot less decorative. You have a strange sense of humor, Fid."

"Solitary confinement will do that to you."

"You can always play Territories with Maelstrom."

"Oh, yes, an hour or two of abject terror with a side order of crushing intellectual inferiority."

"He still terrifies you? Haven't you convinced him to like you yet?"

"He likes me fine, I think. I just can't get past the idea that he could shred me with a thought."

"He can kill me just as easily when I'm near him; I don't let it bother me."

"But you're mortal; ANYTHING can kill you. I've gotten used to being indestructible."

"You're whining. And it sounds cowardly."

"OF COURSE it sounds cowardly. I'm a COWARD. Why do you think I keep you around?

"Say what?"

"I get to bask in your fearlessness."

"That's... sweet. Kind of disturbing, and probably not strictly true, but sweet anyway."

"It is absolutely true."

"Or at least after you have discounted that I'm willing to dedicate myself to getting you out of the mud, and that I actually like you much of the time."

"There is no such thing as complete truth and I reserve the right to mold the fragments as it suits me."

"Fine. But I'm hardly fearless."

"Perhaps. But you're unquestionably courageous. You have fits of caution, but you always get over them, and charge ahead when the time comes. The safe path would have had you married and with three children in Sweetwater. If you say, 'Ninety miles an hour' to a normal person, they turn pale and look away. Your eyes light up and you say, 'When?'"

"Guilty. Chase the luck for me, Master Scorpion?"

"As my Heart wishes."

==)»> 11:7: Darkness

"You're drunk, Rose."

"A little."

"And not sleeping in either the 'Revenant' or in a bed. A hammock?"

"I'm in my hammock on the 'Storm Turtle'."

"And thus begins tonight's story."

"If you wish. I knew there was a big ship at anchor as I approached Silverport; as I got closer, I realized it was the 'Turtle', and decided not to hail it, but I had to get a good look at her; she was my home for two years. I was wearing Emma, and someone recognized me, and they asked me aboard, and I went, and we swapped stories..."

"And you held onto Emma?"

"For a while. The spell was going to expire soon, anyway, and I had already told them that I was a sorceress, and I had hinted that I had gone through a lot of changes. I begged them to not panic when I gave them an example, and then I let Emma drop."

"How did that go over?"

"As well as I could have hoped. I made sure I had my back to the rail the when I did it, so that I could go over and escape if things got ugly, but about half of the people there knew me from before, and were willing to give me some leeway."

"Lucky Rose."

"A bit. And of course then I had to show them Sister Crocodile, and that led to a short stint with the Master at Arms, who acknowledged that I was keeping myself fit, and may have learned a few things. And then I went into town as Sister Dragon with an escort from the 'Turtle' to keep things on an even keel, and then I came back here and there was brandy and more stories and now I'm in my hammock."

"And where does the story go from here?"

"The 'Turtle' has some shallow water work ahead of it, and they've been trying to acquire some small boats for that, and in exchange for use of 'Revenant' and support on that raid, I get transport to Skytower and escort into towns along the way as needed."

"And if they lose 'Revenant'?"

"Then I'll be very unhappy, but also have her fair market value in hand."

"And if they get you killed?"

"Then I'll be dead and you'll be lonely. The most dangerous thing in my future remains a certain utterly non-negotiable salvage dive, so please try not to be a mother hen about the other risks along the way."

"Yes, your Grace."

"Humph. Play me a lullaby, and try not to worry. I'll be fine."

"As my Lady wishes."

==)»> 11:8: The deck of the "Storm Turtle"

"Star gazing, Rose?"

"Not really, too much moon. Just a bit restless."

"And the why?"

"Nothing has really come out of the Silverport visit, for one thing. I found a few people who remembered Osprey and 'Sufferance'; there aren't too many female captains. And I was able to confirm that 'Sufferance' offloaded NOTHING, and took on only water and basic supplies. But I had already heard that, so this is just confirmation."

"A small waste of time doesn't explain your mood."

"No, I suppose not. It's the way people look at me, particularly on board the 'Turtle'. I EXPECT odd looks when I'm ashore as Sister Dragon, but I used to LIVE on the 'Turtle', and now I feel alien here. Before, I was a good topmast monkey, and a decent fighter, and a fairly pretty girl. And everyone knew all three of those things, and I got variations on two parts of respect and one part of lust from pretty much everyone. And now... It's more like one part respect and one part fear. I understand that, but it doesn't make me happy."

"I'm sorry, Rose."

"I miss being human, Fid."

"I know, Rose."

"I'm not... anything, Fid. I'm not human, I'm not a dragon, I'm this weird thing that doesn't fit anywhere."

"You're my heart. And someday I will make you forget all about this, and you won't have to CARE what species you are."

"You're sweet, Fid. But sex doesn't solve everything."

"It solves a lot of things, and helps you forget all of the others."

"You're an idiot."

"You're smiling."

"Yeah, I am. Play something happy for me, Fid, and then I'll try to get some sleep."

"As her Grace wishes."

==)»> 11:9: Darkness

"What are you up to, Rose?"

"What? Nothing. Really. Just sleeping. I'm TIRED."

"I can tell that you're tired. But you're also grinning, even though you're sound asleep."

"Maybe."

"Tell."

"I was awake at dawn, and we wouldn't have the tide until mid-morning, so I asked the Captain if I could do something kind of strange. He said yes, and I climbed onto the rail at the main shrouds, shifted to Wings, and dove off. And then I practiced landing on the ship."

"I thought you said the risk was too high for that."

"On 'Revenant', yes. But on the 'Turtle' the ratlines on the main shrouds might as well be a crash net. I come in low and slow, climb hard just before I hit the ship, and then skim up the shrouds and grab on just as my wings stall. It's easier than landing flat footed."

"Did anyone know that Sister Wings existed before you pulled this stunt?"

"Of course not. That would have spoiled the fun."

"You're insane."

"Maybe a little. When the spell wore off, I rested for a while, then once we were properly underway, I did it some more. The timing is trickier when the ship is moving, but I'm told that the effect is spectacular. Apparently it looks like I am sliding up the shrouds sideways."

"So you went flying, and learned a new trick, and you're happy. But something else has changed, too."

"The fear is gone, Fid. Or mostly gone. Now it's envy. And you know what? Envy is a LOT easier to live with. It's FRIENDLIER."

"Friendlier?"

"They're curious, they want to know as much about flying as they can. I've gone from being a freak to being a celebrity. Celebrity is more fun. AND I get to fly a lot."

"There would seem to be method to your madness."

"I don't know about method, but there does seem to be joy. Joy and madness are a pretty potent cocktail."

"And that's an exit line if I've ever heard one. Good night, my Heart."

"Good night, Fid."

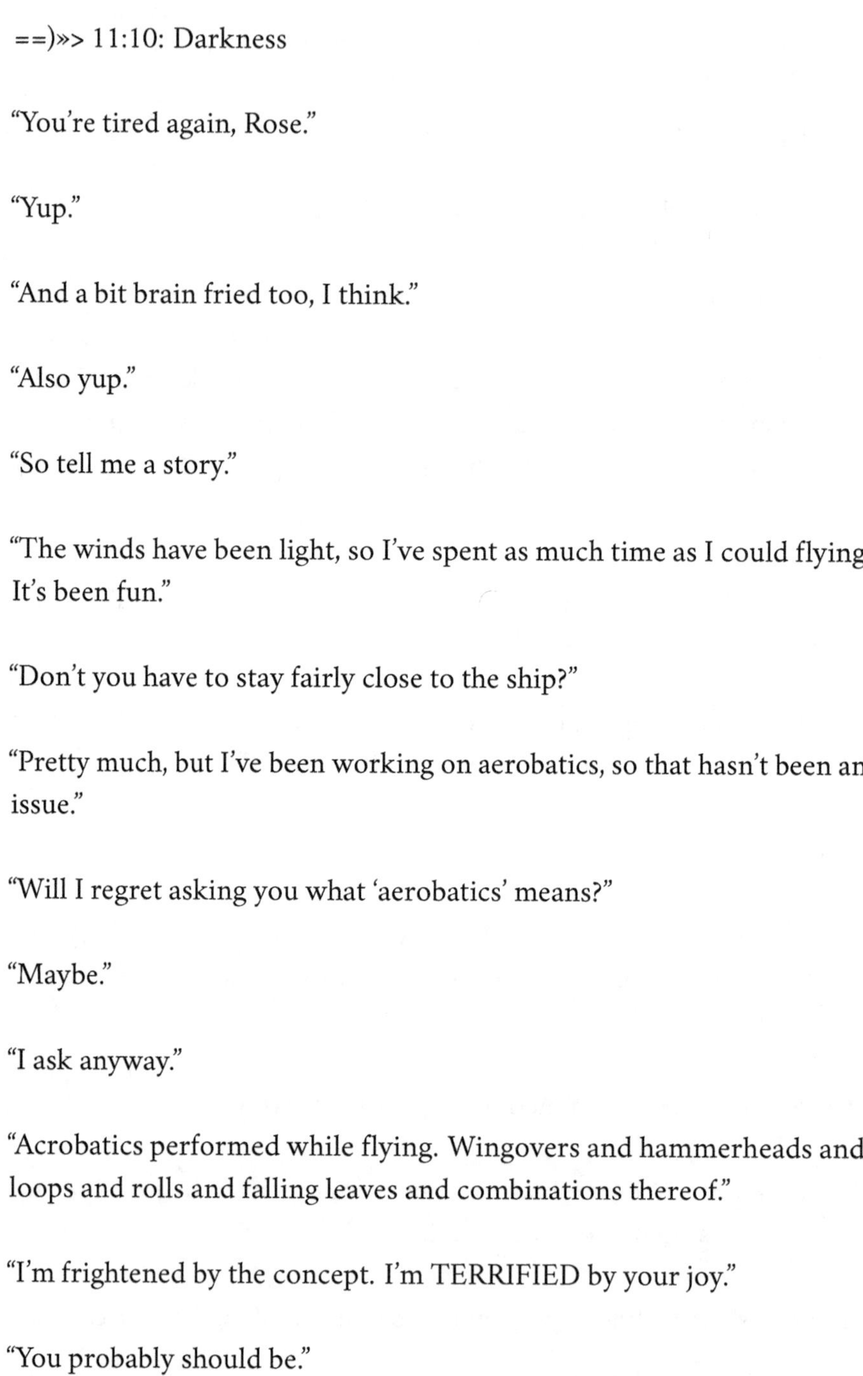

==)»> 11:10: Darkness

"You're tired again, Rose."

"Yup."

"And a bit brain fried too, I think."

"Also yup."

"So tell me a story."

"The winds have been light, so I've spent as much time as I could flying. It's been fun."

"Don't you have to stay fairly close to the ship?"

"Pretty much, but I've been working on aerobatics, so that hasn't been an issue."

"Will I regret asking you what 'aerobatics' means?"

"Maybe."

"I ask anyway."

"Acrobatics performed while flying. Wingovers and hammerheads and loops and rolls and falling leaves and combinations thereof."

"I'm frightened by the concept. I'm TERRIFIED by your joy."

"You probably should be."

"So your body is tired. What taxed your mind?"

"A little book called, 'Flight'."

"Ah."

"It's an amazing book, Fid. It's where I got descriptions of the tricks I was doing today, among other things. It's full of math and science and Thaumatology, but it's also got some amazing stories. Though most of them end badly."

"Oh?"

"They're mostly cautionary tales, of the, 'Here is something that will make you dead' variety."

"For instance?"

"It seems that there was a sorcerer, a landsman, who was a passenger on a ship at sea. The ship was making about 6 knots on a broad reach in a 15 knot wind. The sorcerer decided to fly up to the masthead to get a better look at things..."

"I see this coming..."

"The standard flight spell lasts less than a quarter hour, and has a top speed of less than 3 knots. So by the time the sorcerer realized he was in trouble, he was over the ocean and heading away from the ship at about 10 knots. He corrected as best he could, and the ship turned to follow him, but that only reduced the speed gap to about 6 knots."

"And the reason he didn't just hit the water and stop getting blown away?"

"He couldn't swim."

"I thought I saw this coming."

"Ten minutes at 6 knots is a mile, more or less. And then ten minutes for the ship to get there. They never found his body."

"He couldn't recast the spell?"

"He should have been able to, but he was probably panic stricken. And really, that would have only prolonged the inevitable."

"And you wonder why I worry."

"I'm practicing so that I know what to do in odd situations. For instance, I know that I can recast my shape shift spell in flight, if I have about a thousand feet to spare."

"Please tell me that you didn't work that out experimentally."

"No, I got it from Xart. But I did try it out..."

"Gods, Rose. You're going to make me old before my time."

"You're immortal."

"Even so."

"And I'm going to do my best to keep you company as long as you'll have me."

"Give or take the occasional thousand foot free fall."

“It was FUN!”

“I have left my heart in the keeping of a suicidal maniac. I’m doomed.”

“You have given your heart to the only living being who has the slightest inkling what an incredible treasure it is.”

“Damn, Rose. Point and game to you.”

“I think this calls for a forfeit.”

“Which would be?”

“A lullaby, silly Fiddler. What else?”

“As my Lady wishes.”

12: Storm Turtle

A plan can be brilliant and well executed and still lose.
—Perrin Ironhand, *Armor and Hob-nailed Boots*

==)»> 12:1: Darkness

"Back in the 'Revenant', Rose?"

"Yup. Doing a recon mission for the 'Turtle'. I asked the Captain if he would like me to do a few flyovers and check the accuracy of his maps of our target, and he said yes. So now the 'Turtle' is anchored a day out, and he sent me forward with 'Revenant' and two crew. They're going to mind the boat and fish, and I'm going to do the flyovers."

"As much as I hate the idea of you going alone into enemy territory, that makes sense."

"I just wish magical recon were as easy. They aren't supposed to have any major mages, but... Damn, I'm an idiot."

"That's an unfairly tempting straight line, Rose."

"I've been listening to the officers making plans and just fell into their thought patterns, and forgot that I DO have a way to do basic magical recon: YOU."

"Should I feel heroic?"

"Maybe. Could you take a look around and see what other sorcerers are in the area?"

"Give me a moment... Two to the south, about your size, right on top of each other; those are the sorcerers on the 'Turtle', aren't they?"

"I would assume so. The 'Turtle' has two Second Circles on her crew."

"And five to the north, also all on top of each other. Three about your size, one about Drellan's size, and one bigger."

"Nine bleeding hells."

"So that IS as bad as I thought it was?"

"Offhand, it's insurmountable. Three Seconds on each side cancel, which leaves a Third, plus a Fourth or Fifth, unanswered on their side."

"So now what?"

"So tomorrow I fly my recon as planned, and the next day we go back to the 'Turtle', and try to talk them out of committing suicide."

"You're going to do the recon anyway?"

"I'm going to do the recon so that I can argue from a standpoint of courage. If I say, 'I just did a flyover of a hostile sorcerer who is two or three circles over my head, just so I could come back here and tell you to let this go,' it MIGHT carry some weight."

"But you're not sure?"

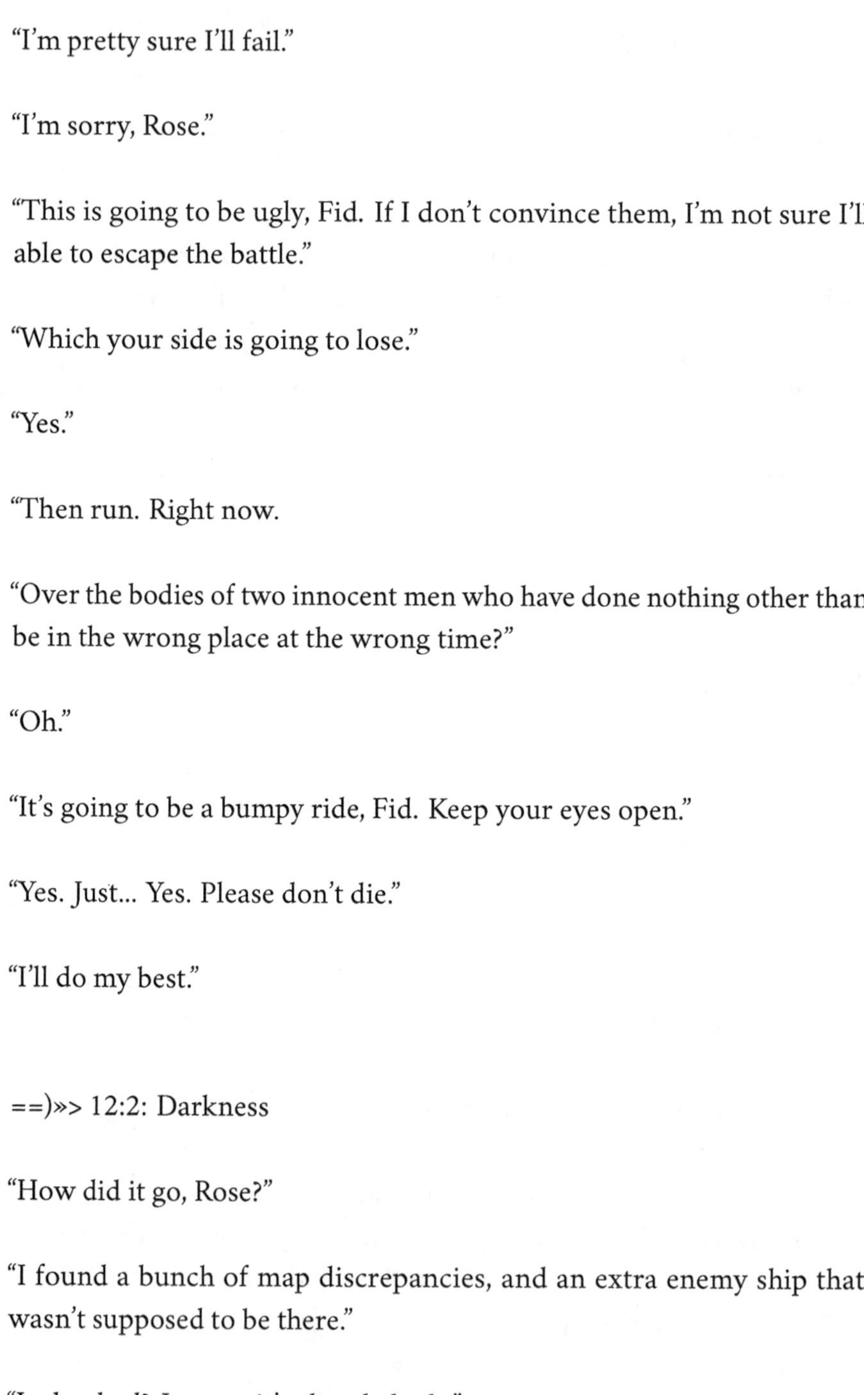

"I'm pretty sure I'll fail."

"I'm sorry, Rose."

"This is going to be ugly, Fid. If I don't convince them, I'm not sure I'll able to escape the battle."

"Which your side is going to lose."

"Yes."

"Then run. Right now.

"Over the bodies of two innocent men who have done nothing other than be in the wrong place at the wrong time?"

"Oh."

"It's going to be a bumpy ride, Fid. Keep your eyes open."

"Yes. Just... Yes. Please don't die."

"I'll do my best."

==)»> 12:2: Darkness

"How did it go, Rose?"

"I found a bunch of map discrepancies, and an extra enemy ship that wasn't supposed to be there."

"Is that bad? I mean, it's already bad..."

"We're being set up for a bloodbath, Fid. They have the edge in magic, and in manpower, and they have prepared defensive positions."

"Still not willing to run?"

"I have friends on the 'Turtle', Fid. I have to try to keep them away. And I still have two men from the 'Turtle' with me."

"They'd make good pets. Really."

"It will be fine, Fid."

"You don't know that."

"I'm not in immediate danger and will take as few risks as possible in attempting to bring this awful situation to an acceptable conclusion."

"Humph."

"Stop whining and live up to your name. Something restful."

"I have a selection of dirges."

"I don't HAVE to rescue you, Fid."

"You have to have a reasonable chance of survival to threaten me."

"Just play."

"As her Grace wishes."

==)»> 12:3: Darkness

"So? Has the stupid raid been cancelled?"

"Not yet, Fid. At the moment, we're just advancing to the boat release point, as scheduled. But we're not committed to anything yet, either."

"But you can snag 'Revenant' and sail away any time you want, right?"

"Could. Won't. I gave my word to go along if they decide to fight."

"WHAT!?!"

"Soldier's logic, Fid. The word of a coward can't be trusted, so I have to prove I'm not a coward to give my report any weight."

"But... but..."

"It's the way things are, Fid. If I could walk away from this I wouldn't be me."

"I'm going to sulk, now. I'll talk to you tomorrow night, if you're still alive. Maybe."

"Fid?"

==)»> 12:4: Aboard the "Storm Turtle"

"Are you safe?"

"Yes, Fid, I'm safe."

"Safe for now, so that you can give me a 'Tomorrow I die,' speech, or really safe?"

"Really safe. The raid has been canceled, and we're on our way back to Silverport."

"Why Silverport?"

"We need to dispose of the cockle boats, other than 'Revenant'. That's where we got them, and that's where they go back to. Once they're sold, it will be on to Skytower and the idiot who commissioned the raid."

"So you're just a passenger until Skytower."

"Unless some idiots decide to attack the 'Turtle' in the open ocean. That hasn't happened in all the years the 'Turtle' has been sailing."

"I guess I'll forgive you if you ask, then."

"Not going to ask, Fid."

"But..."

"You're the biggest thing in my life, but not the only thing. And you don't own me, and if you aren't willing go along with that, you can tell me to stop chasing you."

"I... Fine. But I reserve the right to sulk when you take stupid risks."

"Sulk all you want. Just come back to me when you're done. And remember that sulking hurts you more that it hurts me."

"You're being logical. That's not fair."

"I'm sorry, Fid. I'll try to find some time to practice being irrational."

"Grrr."

"What did you tell me the other day, Fid? That you needed me to be strong enough to deal with the dragon influence, so therefore you chose to believe that I WAS that strong, because it was the only acceptable outcome? This is a variation on the theme. Choose to believe."

"I'll do my best."

"Besides, if I manage to get myself killed, I'm sure that Auntie Moss will find some other lunatic girl to come after you, eventually."

"Not helping AT ALL."

"Fid... What kind of person would be willing to dedicate her life to rescuing a friend from a prison that was five hundred miles from nowhere, under 2000 fathoms of ocean?"

"Ummm... One who was loyal... and fearless... and not entirely sane."

"And how many people, in your centuries of existence, would even bother to apply for that job?"

"Um... One?"

"Are we good now?"

"Yes, your Grace."

"Good. Now think some lustful thoughts, and put them into music."

“As my Lady wishes.”

==)»> 12:5: Darkness

“Back on ‘Revenant’, Rose?”

“Yes. It would seem that I wore out my welcome on the ‘Storm Turtle’.”

“How so? I thought they liked you.”

“They did. But a lot of them also blamed me for getting the raid canceled, and the attitude of the ship was unfriendly. So I suggested that the Captain might want to pay me off and send me on my way before we got any further from Skytower, and he agreed. So ‘Revenant’ and I are alone with you for another three weeks or so.”

“I’m always alone with you, Rose.”

“You know what I mean.”

“I do. I’m sorry that this happened. You liked being on the ‘Turtle’.”

“I did, And this makes the trip that much harder, and longer. But the Captain made sure I had plenty of supplies, and actually paid me a bonus for my work, which was extremely generous of him.”

“You might have saved his life.”

“Which is why he paid me. But his wallet doesn’t know that, and the ship’s purser scowled so much as he was paying me that I think he hurt himself.”

"It would serve him right."

"It doesn't matter. It's done, now. How's Maelstrom?"

"Worried about you."

"I should have seen that coming. Do NOT push him that way, Fid. No good can come of it."

"He's odd. Sometimes he is RIGHT there in front of you, just another person playing a game, and a moment later he does something that reminds you how old and huge and powerful he is. I MAY get used to it, but I sure haven't yet."

"You may be working on being the best friend he has, Fid."

"ME?!?"

"Who else does he talk to? Who else CAN he talk to?"

"Oh. Right. I've been too busy being terrified to think about that."

"That's the problem, Fid. You let the fear loose, and it messes up your thinking."

"As opposed to ignoring both fear and thought?"

"I don't do things thoughtlessly, Fid. Insanely, sometimes, but never thoughtlessly."

"Yes, your Grace."

"If you're going to be that way, it's time for the fiddle. Something... I don't know, surprise me."

"As her Grace wishes."

==)»> 12:6: Aboard "Revenant"

"Rose, why are you meditating in the middle of the afternoon?"

"Why are you checking in on me in the middle of the afternoon?"

"I was bored."

"So was I."

"But aren't you supposed to be, you know, sailing?"

"'Revenant' is sailing. I'm just supervising in a haphazard fashion."

"'Revenant' can sail herself?"

"Sure. You can't single-hand for any length of time if the boat can't sail herself."

"But... How?"

"The sheets all lead back to jam cleats that I can reach from the helm; the boat is balanced for a bit of weather helm, with a line through a block to a ballast stone. If the wind gets ahead of the boat, the jib gains drive, and the mizzen loses drive, and the boat turns to restore balance; if the wind gets behind the boat, the mizzen gains drive and the jib loses it, and the boat turns to restore balance; in a gust, the ballast stone lifts and the boat turns into the wind, and when the gust is over, the stone pulls the tiller back, and the boat rebalances herself. Simple."

"WAY too much sailor talk for me."

"I could yammer at you about Xart's aerodynamic scaling factors, if you'd rather."

"Will that be more humiliating than playing Territories with the turtle?"

"Maybe. One way to find out."

"Pass. I'd threaten to yammer at you about musical theory, but you'd probably enjoy it."

"I probably would. When did you have a chance to study musical theory?"

"Salsi could read and write, and one winter we holed up in a place where there was a bit of a library, and she found a book on musical theory. She read it to me, and I copied it down in dreamspace. I've reread it several times, at this point."

"I did NOT see that coming."

"I have hidden depths."

"You would have to, given that you cultivate an air of superficiality."

"I'm too honest for that. I tend to think of myself as fundamentally superficial, with some interesting history."

"You sell yourself short."

"Do I? The theory is all very nice, but the fact remains that the most important thing in music, to me, is making girls want to dance."

"I doubt that, on two counts. First, you can do a LOT more with your music than inspire dance."

"Maybe. Second?"

"You can make the girls want to do ANYTHING with magic."

"Which makes getting the job done WITHOUT magic twice as sweet."

"Again, I did not see that coming. That's twice in one conversation."

"Rose... Do you have any idea how precious you are to me? And not just because I have no one else on tap to rescue me. You talk to me because you WANT to, day after day, without the slightest hint of magical persuasion. You joke about walking away, but you COULD, and you DON'T. That's... amazing."

"Three. And I think I need to break trance so that I can shift to Emma and cry."

"Don't. That wasn't the point. I just... I think I need to stop talking and play something."

"I think that that would be a VERY good idea."

"As my Lady wishes."

==)»> 12:7: A beach north of Silverport

"Stargazing, Rose?"

"A bit. Getting ready to run past that pirate lair we didn't raid tomorrow night."

"At night?"

"I stopped here in the middle of the afternoon; I'll sleep in tomorrow, and sail all night long, so that I'll go past their lookouts in darkness. Or a least that's the plan."

"So tonight you're staying up late so that you'll sleep later in the morning?"

"If it works. We'll have to see."

"What will you do if they see you anyway, and come after you?"

"Hope that they send a small boat with no sorcerer, and then kill them from the air."

"And if they send a larger boat, or a sorcerer?"

"Then I'm in trouble, and they're stupid, because a boat this size isn't worth that much trouble."

"Always calculated risks."

"Whenever possible. At least, as opposed to blind risks. But a deliberate blind risk is insane, even by my standards."

"That's good to know. That you have standards."

"Ouch. And not fair."

"But you smiled."

"Yes, I did."

"Then I have justified my existence for another little while."

"Maybe. It may be an insurmountable task."

"Does the Lady appreciate my company?"

"Yes. At least most of the time."

"Then my case is made. Contingent, of course, on the ability of the Lady to justify her own existence."

"That's just cruel. But again, I smile. And sitting under the stars on a clear night is as good a time as any to contemplate the value of one's own existence. Though it would be nice to have a warm body to snuggle up to."

"Alas, I can do no more than provide background music."

"You probably should, then."

"As her Grace commands."

==)»> 12:8: Aboard "Revenant"

"Is something wrong, Rose?"

"It's raining, and there's a storm coming in. I may not be able to maintain contact for long. But the good news is that I won't have to worry about pirates in this weather."

"Storm gods instead of pirates? I dislike the choice."

"I'm not thrilled with it, but that's how the dice have fallen. I'm wet, and cold, and before long I'm going to be at least a little worried about losing the boat."

"I REALLY dislike the choice."

"I'll be fine, Fid. I've already stowed the jib and the mizzen, and the main is double reefed. And in the worst case, I can just put on Sister Shark and head for the bottom. It's really hard to drown when you can breathe water."

"There is that. Be careful, Rose. Be lucky."

"I'll do my best. Keep an eye out for me; see you on the other side."

"Always."

==)»> 12:9: Aboard "Revenant"

"Is this the other side, Rose?"

"Not quite, but getting there. The rain has stopped, and the wind has dropped quite a bit; it will take a while for the waves to calm down. Still double reefed, but done bailing, and able to let the boat steer while I check in with you."

"But you're fine? No injuries or problems?"

"I'm fine. Had a real lesson in the logic behind an old sailor's saying, though. 'If it's not secured, it's overboard; if it's not sealed, it's wet.' And, as it was often pointed out, there were no guarantees on either of those."

"How bad was it?"

"As advertised. Cold and wet and scary. But we managed. 'Revenant's' a good girl."

"You sound like she's alive."

"Said the ghost in the dagger. But yes, she is. Any boat worth sailing in is alive, and if you don't understand that, you should probably stay on shore."

"That was always my choice, actually."

"Yes, but if you had never gone to sea, you would never have met me, and we wouldn't be having this grand adventure."

"Said the person who is not imprisoned in a mud bank at the bottom of the ocean."

"Not a valid path, Fid. Would Osprey have been the woman you loved if SHE had never gone to sea?"

"No."

"Well, then."

"So what now?"

"I'm going to keep on until sunset, or at least until my eyes start to cross. Then I may take a day off; I'm already tired, but I want to put some more miles behind me."

"Would her Grace care for some music, in the meantime?"

"A bit. Before too long I'm going to hoist the jib and the mizzen, shake out the reefs, and let 'Revenant' RUN."

"Well, then. I shall endeavor to be quick, but I can promise that I'll be FAST."

"Joy and madness, Fid."

"And undead ladies racing the wind."

==)»> 12:10: A beach south of Skytower

"Where ARE you sleeping, Rose?"

"I have 'Revenant' pulled well up from the beach, inverted, and partially buried, and I'm sleeping underneath her. It's a cozy little cave."

"And the why?"

"Because I'm going to abandon her for a few days while Sister Wings and I check out Skytower."

"Why not just sail in?"

"Because the harbor is too big and too complex for me to try to find my way as Emma without having some idea of where to go and who to talk to. I don't even have a map, at the moment; Wings can get that for me, and maybe a bit more. I'm hoping I can find a place to land and shift to Emma, though that will be tricky, what with the nudity."

“Say what now?”

“I thought that would get your attention. I’ve never bothered to wear clothes as Sister Wings, because anything that wasn’t skin tight would get in the way, and, well, kobold. But it might not be safe to deal with people as a naked kobold, but if I switch to Emma...”

“Naked Emma has other problems.”

“Right. So I’ll bring clothes for Emma, and hope I can find a place to land and dress without being seen, or at least without being seen too well.”

“You really enjoy making me nervous, don’t you?”

“Maybe. But I don’t have to try very often; I seem to do quite well on that score just by living my life.”

“Agreed.”

“And I was more or less human when I started on this trip, and I’ve had to figure things out as I go along. My main goal in Skytower is to learn how to hold a shape for longer than an hour, and once I’ve done THAT, everything will be simpler.”

“I’m a big fan of simpler. It’s usually safer.”

“Getting eaten by a dragon is REALLY simple.”

“I said, ‘usually’. Are you likely to be be eaten by a dragon?”

“Not that I know of, but it’s unknown territory.”

“Not making me happy, Rose.”

"Just giving you a bit of perspective. Skytower is a civilized place. I'm not a threat, so I should be able to take a look around without raising anyone's hackles."

"But..."

"Do you have a better idea?"

"No."

"Then be calm, and play me a lullaby. I have a long day ahead of me tomorrow."

"As her Grace wishes."

==)»> 12:11: The top of the Skytower

"Where ARE you, Rose?"

"On top of the Skytower. I knew I was going to fly up here sometime, and this seemed like as good a time as any. I know no one will mind if I camp up here."

"No?"

"I'm more than a quarter mile above the city, and there are no stairs. Though there is a floor drain; I hadn't expected that."

"You flew up a quarter mile?"

"Not the first time, but it was easy this time; I found an iron works with a big thermal on top of it, and just rode my way up."

“And you’re camping up there?”

“I hadn’t planned on it, but it seems likely. Though I may decide it’s just too cold and windy.”

“I have said this before, but you really are not sane.”

“I’m me. And I am seeing something that VERY few people have ever seen. I didn’t know what to expect, in fact.”

“So tell.”

“Do you want the full tour?”

“Sure.”

“Skytower. 1500 foot tall thing made from a single piece some kind of almost white stone. The cross section has sixteen sides. It’s about a hundred yards in diameter at the base, and about ten yards in diameter at the top. It has no doors or windows, and there are rumors that it has an interior structure, but no one really knows anything. The top is flat, and has human-scaled crenelations. And since that makes the top a big bowl, there is a floor drain that is just big enough for my hand to fit into. No one knows who built it or why.”

“That’s... more than a little creepy, Rose.”

“There’s general agreement on that point. Though the locals have gotten used to it, and ignore it for the most part.”

“And you’re planning to spend the night there.”

“Yes, Mother.”

"Consider my eyes rolled."

"If anything odd happens, I'll go over the side; there's enough air between here and the ground to summon Wings and land safely."

"Fine. Have you actually learned anything useful?"

"I've found a place to land 'Revenant' where she'll be safe from molestation at least for a few days, by which time I'll have made longer term arrangements. There are LOTS of inns. Also lots of four and five story buildings with roofs that Sister Wings can hide on, and alleys and... Well, just lots of places to hide generally. And for the most part, people don't look up if you don't give them a reason to."

"And you don't."

"I try not to. Mistakes happen. One of the most interesting discoveries is an enclave of dragon-folk. I'm going to have to check them out further; I didn't even know there WERE such people."

"Dragon-folk?"

"I've only seen them from a distance. They look a lot like Sister Dragon, but with no tails and plantigrade feet. I'm hoping to make friends."

"And take a bite out of one of them?"

"No! Well, metaphorically, maybe. Never hurts to have an extra set of skin to jump into."

"Does it bother you how easily you have slipped into ritual cannibalism?"

"Fid, there are so many things about my current existence that bother me that I've lost count. I have a big box labeled, 'Worry about these later' that will no doubt drive me crazy some day."

"As opposed to your current mental state."

"As opposed to my current highly functional but peculiar and lonely condition, yes. Though I think I have a long term solution to the loneliness worked out."

"Oh?"

"You, silly Fiddler."

"Oh. Right. Me."

"At any rate, I'm going bid you good night, and spend a little time enjoying the view of the city and the sea by starlight, and then I'll try to get some sleep."

"As her Grace wishes."

13: Skytower

Never cheat a kobold you aren't planning to kill.
—*The Book of the Blind King's Wisdom*

==)»> 13:1: Darkness

"Back on 'Revenant', Rose?"

"Yep. Back on the water, and an hour or two out of Skytower harbor. I'll make port in the morning, and then on to the next adventure."

"How is this different from Silverport?"

"I need to find a job and long term housing, so that I can find a teacher and do the magical study I need. Skytower is the best place to study magic on Hurricane Bay, and the only place I'm likely to find a teacher in advanced Thaumatology."

"So more delays."

"I'm coming for you as fast as I can. In a chariot drawn by snails."

"I'm certainly getting that impression."

"I would say that I'm in a hurry to get on with my life, but... I don't really know what my life will be once I've rescued you. I suspect that my horizon will be a lot bigger than it used to be by that time."

"But in the meantime..."

"In the meantime, you have been down there for nearly six years, and I have been chasing you for nearly two, and the delays are making us both crazy. I know it too well... In other news... How is my grandfather?"

"Maelstrom? He just is, mostly. Shows up every couple of days, humiliates me in a charming and patient fashion, and then goes away."

"Have you ever had a conversation with him?"

"Other than telling him about your exploits? Not really."

"He must have some amazing stories."

"He might. On the other hand, he spends most of his time in a half-dream state, wandering through the ocean and eating fish by the ton."

"And you're not curious?"

"OF COURSE I'm curious. But also terrified, remember?"

"Tell him I asked. That might get him talking."

"It just might at that. Where is this newfound wisdom coming from?"

"Damned if I know. Might be the company I keep."

"Since that's been mostly me, lately, I suspect that that is not correct."

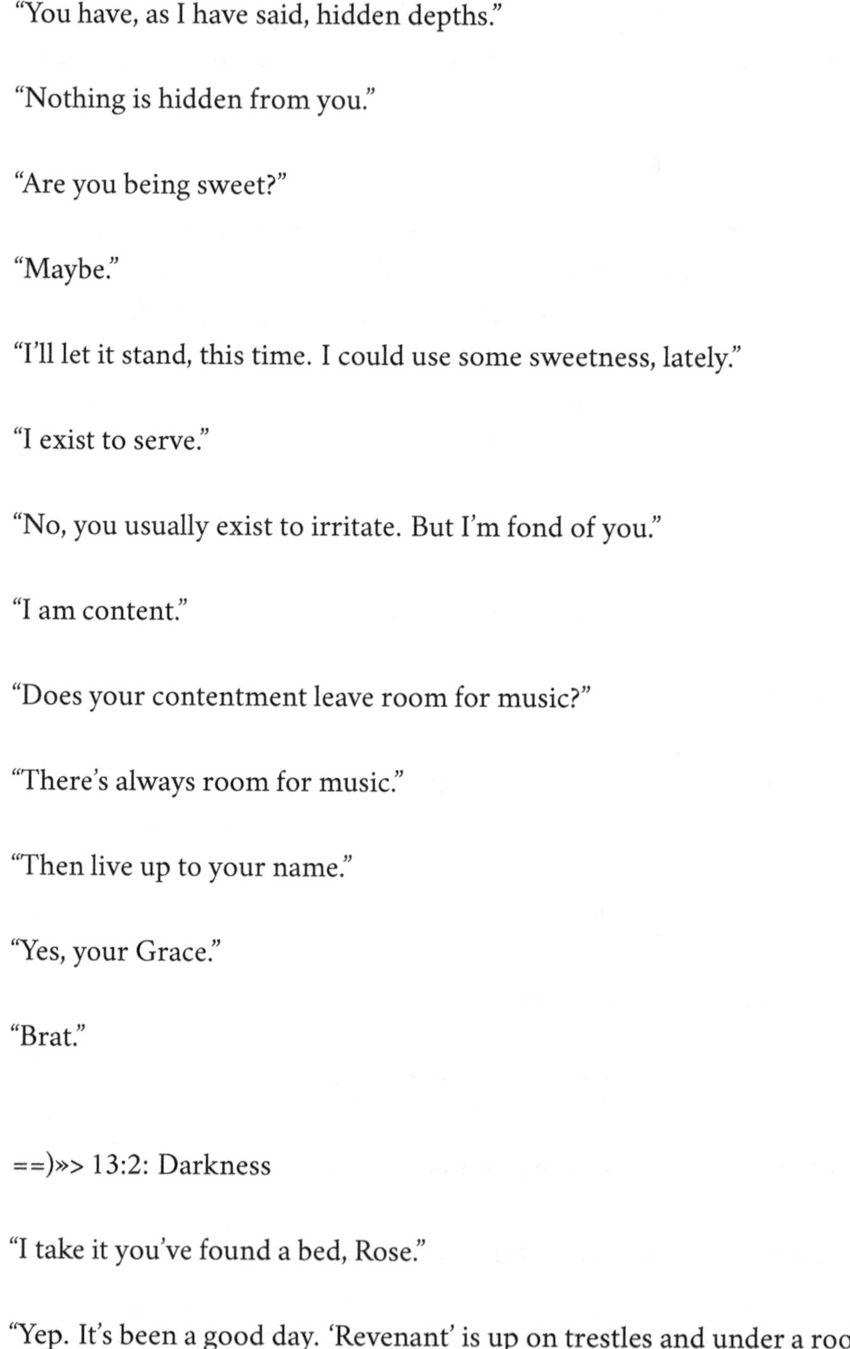

"You have, as I have said, hidden depths."

"Nothing is hidden from you."

"Are you being sweet?"

"Maybe."

"I'll let it stand, this time. I could use some sweetness, lately."

"I exist to serve."

"No, you usually exist to irritate. But I'm fond of you."

"I am content."

"Does your contentment leave room for music?"

"There's always room for music."

"Then live up to your name."

"Yes, your Grace."

"Brat."

==)»> 13:2: Darkness

"I take it you've found a bed, Rose."

"Yep. It's been a good day. 'Revenant' is up on trestles and under a roof, and I have a clean room with a comfortable bed, a good lock, and easy access to the roof for Wings. Tomorrow I start looking for a teacher and a job, preferably as a two-in-one."

"Is that likely?"

"High level sorcerers often have jobs that they would love to fob off on mid-level sorcerers who will work for a bit of training. I just need to find one that I get along with. I've had two good teachers, so far, so I'm hopeful."

"Unless your luck has run out."

"There is that. But it's a big city, so there are plenty of chances to roll the dice again."

"What about the dragon-folk?"

"I'll investigate them as I have time. I suspect that if I wander the edges of their enclave as Sister Dragon, no human will notice me, but the dragon-folk will. Which might get me a conversation, or might get me attacked as an abomination. I'd prefer to know which in advance."

"Do I detect caution? Are you sure you're really my Rose?"

"Reasonable caution, Fid. As always, and you know it. I think I need to find the local kobold slum, and start asking questions there."

"Kobolds don't get an enclave, just a slum?"

"The kobold enclave is guaranteed to be a slum; they're KOBOLDS."

"Oh."

"And the nice thing about kobolds is that, even if they regard Sister Dragon as an abomination, they can be counted on to run away rather than attack, so they're safe to approach."

"Wow. You really are being cautions."

"I'm in a big city where my best living friends are an innkeeper and a few wharf rats, all of whom I met yesterday. Carelessness is suicidal. It's just... I'm lonely, Fid. And I know I have no right to complain to YOU about loneliness, but, well, there's no one else, and that's part of the problem. I want to be held, I want to have sex, I want... I don't know, some warmth, maybe."

"I know, Rose. I can feel it. And I could and would deal with all of that myself, except..."

"Yeah, I know. Five hundred miles and two thousand fathoms. I'll be all right, Fid, and I know you're there, and I know how much you care, and... I worry about becoming reckless."

"That's reasonable. Knowledge is armor."

"Yeah, it is, isn't it? If Master Fiddler would do me the honor of playing... I don't know. Something that will make me feel better."

"I will do my best."

==)»> 13:3: Darkness

"Good evening, Rose. How went the search today?"

"I found the kobolds."

"There is something fundamentally not exciting about kobolds."

"I admit that. At least the ones with no wings. But in this case it turns out that they pretty much define the slum at the edge of the dragon-folk enclave, so I should be able to make some inroads there."

"Remind me again why you're so fascinated by the dragon-folk."

"Because they might just be willing to accept Sister Dragon as she is, and then I just might find a place to live where I more or less fit in, and don't have to hide my true form all the time."

"You could always bully the kobolds into sheltering you."

"One, not fond of bullying my way into anywhere, and two, the queen of the kobolds is still a kobold. I just spent three months on a small boat. I would like my standard of living to improve, not degrade."

"Ah."

"On the other hand, the queen of the kobolds has next to no living expenses, and that might not be a bad deal. We'll just have to see. Is there any news on your end?"

"I visited Auntie Moss."

"Brave boy. Why?"

"I asked her if she knew anything about the history of the Skytower."

"And she said?"

"That she knew nothing sure enough to repeat, and then she asked about

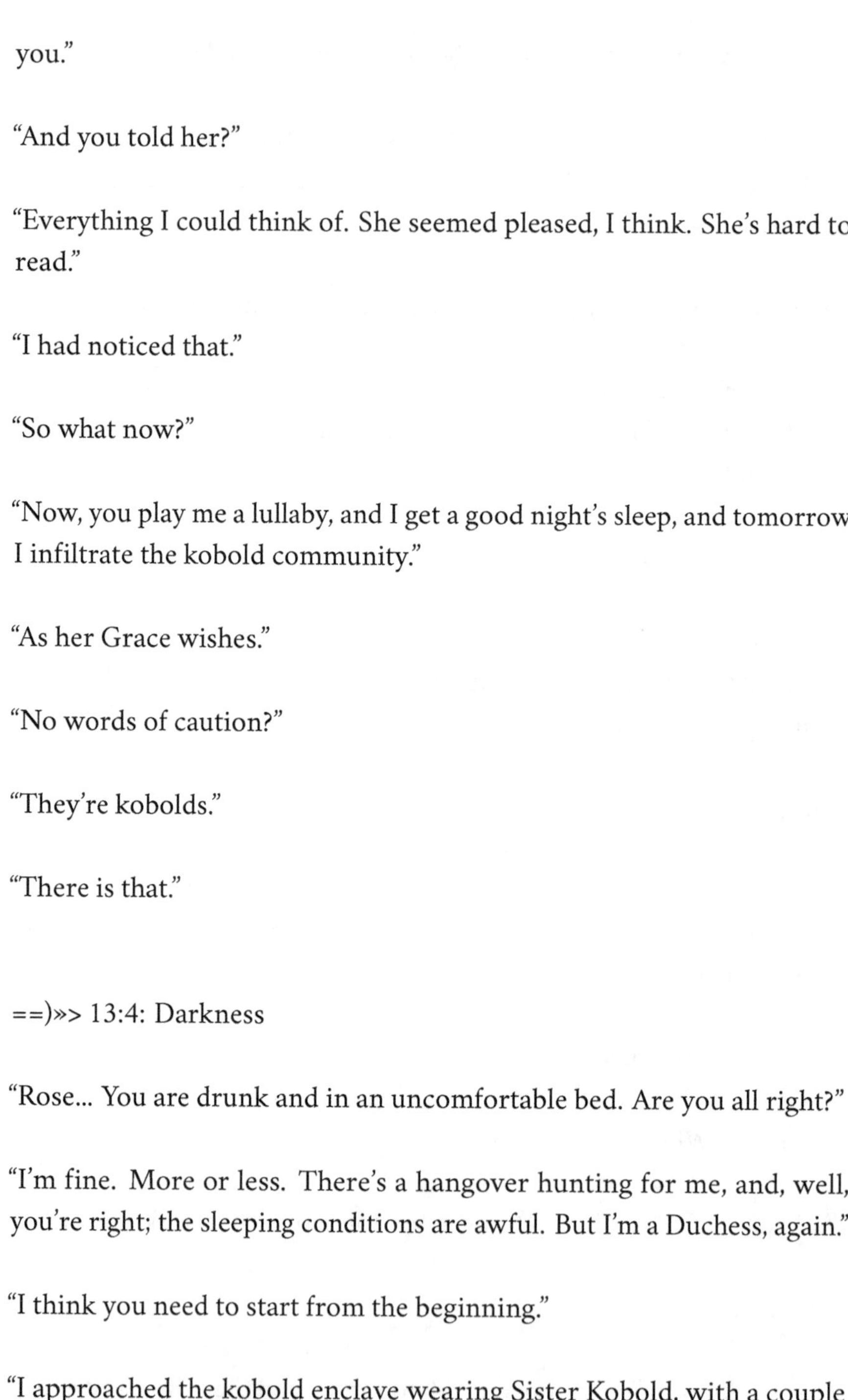

you."

"And you told her?"

"Everything I could think of. She seemed pleased, I think. She's hard to read."

"I had noticed that."

"So what now?"

"Now, you play me a lullaby, and I get a good night's sleep, and tomorrow I infiltrate the kobold community."

"As her Grace wishes."

"No words of caution?"

"They're kobolds."

"There is that."

==)»> 13:4: Darkness

"Rose... You are drunk and in an uncomfortable bed. Are you all right?"

"I'm fine. More or less. There's a hangover hunting for me, and, well, you're right; the sleeping conditions are awful. But I'm a Duchess, again."

"I think you need to start from the beginning."

"I approached the kobold enclave wearing Sister Kobold, with a couple of bottles of cheap brandy in a shoulder bag. When challenged, I said I had come down from Losthaven, which eventually led me to a couple of kobs who had REALLY come down from Losthaven."

"This could be colorful..."

"It got really colorful when one of them noticed the croc teeth around my neck, and asked me about them. I said I had won them in a duel, and then she— the kob from Losthaven— started talking about a human called Duchess Red who had actually beaten a crocodilian in a duel, and had a set of croc teeth from it. And then someone decided that I must be wearing THOSE teeth, and that I must have stolen them from Duchess Red, and that she was a friend to kobolds, and that I should be punished."

"REALLY colorful."

"So I shifted to Sister Dragon and bellowed that I WAS Duchess Red, and that I could prove it, and shifted to Emma, and waited for the insanity to subside."

"And no one stabbed you?"

"Not that I noticed."

"And then?"

"And then I reached into my bag and pulled out a bottle of brandy and suggested that we should all be friends."

"And they went for that?"

"Given a choice between fighting someone who outweighed them each by more than three to one, and had appropriate teeth and claws, and

DEMONSTRATED magic, against a shot of brandy? They're kobolds. What do you think?"

"So it turned into a party."

"It turned into a party. Tomorrow, I should be able to have an intelligent conversation with their elders, such as they are. If the hangover I'm sure to have doesn't kill me."

"Next time buy better brandy."

"My brandy was good enough. It was the stuff that the kobs brought out after my brandy was gone that may kill me."

"You drank kob liquor."

"AFTER the brandy. My judgment may not have been great."

"I think my fiddles need tuning."

"You wouldn't dare."

"No?"

"You are the sweetest and most wonderful person in the history of the world, and the very best friend I have ever had, and I will give you anything you ask for if you will only PLEASE not tune the Ogre at me."

"Marker."

"What?"

"I'll remind you when the time comes. In the meantime, I will play the most soothing melody I know. Softly."

"You really are a pretty wonderful person. Some of the time."

"Perhaps. Sleep."

==)»> 13:5: Darkness

"Good evening, Rose. I take it you survived the morning?"

"It was a near thing, but yes. And I think the end result was worthwhile."

"Rare, for hangovers."

"Definitely. But after I woke up, I had a talk with the kob elders about the dragon-folk. Well, about a lot of things, but that was the one I cared about most. I got some opinions, and some names. Then I came back here and wrote a letter, and then Emma delivered the letter to the dragon-folk, and then I came back here, took a second dose of the hair of the dog, and then went to bed."

"A short, but good day, then."

"Exactly. How was your day?"

"Exciting! I have learned how to remove myself from the consciousness of the entire world."

"Really? How?"

"Fall overboard in 2000 fathoms of water."

"Cheap."

"All I had."

"You are not forgotten. And you know it."

"I fear that it is all too easy to forget."

"Fid... Do you have any idea how much time and effort it is going to take me to pay you back for what your music has done for me?"

"I could try to do a calculation. I certainly look forward to collecting the debt."

"And I look forward to paying it. In the meantime, would you be willing to extend me a bit more credit?"

"As my Lady wishes."

==)»> 13:6: Darkness

"You seem happy tonight, Rose."

"I am. It was a good day."

"I wait eagerly."

"There was an answer to my letter waiting for me this morning. It seems that I had no need to worry about my reception among the dragon-folk. They seem to practice some kind of dragon-worship, and anyone who is closer to being a dragon than they are is accorded reverence."

"Accorded?"

"Provisional reverence. If you turn out to be parasitic or evil, you still end up out on your ear, or perhaps at the bottom of the harbor."

"Ah."

"So I went down to their enclave as Emma, and then shifted to Sister Dragon, and they welcomed me with open arms. They seemed to like me, and they liked my stories about Maelstrom. I asked about renting a room, and got several offers of adoption, and a few proposals of marriage, including, I think, one for a simultaneous marriage from a pair of brothers."

"And you said?"

"Provisional 'No' to all of the adoptions, and a much firmer 'No' to the proposals."

"But not, apparently, an unconditional 'No' to those, either."

"I don't know the customs well enough. An honest answer would be, 'No, but I wouldn't rule out occasional horizontal entertainment,' but I don't know if that's a possibility in their culture, and would prefer to find out, first."

"But you're tempted."

"Not really. My libido is still human. But loneliness and friendship can break down a lot of barriers, and I'm a long way from home."

"You have a home?"

"Of course I do, silly Fiddler. It's about 500 miles southwest of here, and about 2000 fathoms straight down."

"I hear that it's an unpleasant neighborhood."

"I'm planning to relocate as soon as I can get back there and pick up a few personal items that no one else wants."

"Then why bother?"

"Sentiment makes the worthless precious. Game suspended. Stop fishing for compliments and live up to your name."

"As her Grace wishes."

==)»> 13:7: Darkness

"You've relocated."

"I have. I've rented a room from the eager bothers, as it happens."

"And you're sure you haven't actually married them by mistake?"

"Fairly sure. I've made it clear that I'm not settling in Skytower permanently, in any case. And they're really too much in awe of me to try to collect on any spousal duties. It's kind of sweet."

"That kind of thinking leads to world domination."

"Or at least failed attempts at it. But it'll be fine. The brothers are doomed to low status until one of them dies, but they're intelligent and hard working, so they're fairly affluent, have a big house, and can afford to rent a room cheaply."

"Until one of them dies?"

"They hatched from the same egg, which is rare, and not well regarded. They're legally the same person."

"Which is why they proposed a joint marriage?"

"Exactly. The traditional resolution is for one to kill the other in a duel, but they don't want to take that route, so they're trapped in a barely adult status."

"And your presence changes that?"

"Not really, but it gives them some reflected glory, or something. And they're charming, and we may end up being good friends."

"I'm jealous already."

"Don't be that way."

"I'm... Teasing, sort of. When you're lonely, I can feel it, and my situation is worse. But when you have friends, I wish I were there, and a part of me worries about losing you."

"NEVER GOING TO HAPPEN. For one thing, you have too many of my markers, and I pay my debts."

"That... is possibly the most wonderful thing anyone has ever said to me."

"Silly Fiddler. In the meantime, I offer another marker for a lullaby."

"Done."

==)»> 13:8: Darkness

"You're excited tonight, Rose."

"A bit."

"And the reason?"

"I spent most of the day with the dragon-folk's community sorcerer. He's a Third Circle named Dlef."

"So back to apprentice status?"

"No, he treats me as an equal, and can't seem to wait to start trading spells."

"That sounds good. But I doubt that's all."

"He gave me a spell to learn, and as soon as I had it down, we went on a walk through the city."

"What did I miss?"

"The spell was a personal illusion. It takes less than half of the energy of my shape shift, and can be cast on top of itself, or on top of the shape shift. I'm free, Fid. As long as I don't run out of energy, I can wear Emma's face all day long without attracting any attention."

"As long as no one steps on your tail."

“Spoilsport.”

“I exist to serve.”

“Do you know how long it’s been since I’ve had a chance to go for a walk through a city with someone who lived there and just see the sights?”

“I’m guessing that would be, ‘Never’”.

“You would be right. It was a lot of fun.”

“Can Dlef teach you what you’re here to learn?”

“Well...”

“That would be no.”

“That would be no. But it all adds up, and he’s willling, and I’d be a fool to not accept his generosity.”

“What’s in it for him?”

“Companionship, prestige, and some small measure of religious ecstasy that I hope will wear off soon.”

“Are you still moving forward?”

“Always, silly Fiddler. This just gives me something to do while I’m looking for the teacher I NEED.”

“If you say so.”

“Don’t be that way, Fid. I’m allowed to be happy, sometimes. I’ve been hurting ever since I lost my face, back in Landfall, and now I'm surrounded by people who don't think I'm a freak, or a monster. THEY think I'm beautiful. I still don't, but they do, and it's WONDERFUL. And you should be happy for me, even if you can't feel it."

"Again, if you say so."

"Good gods. That's why you've been so needy lately. I've been telling myself that I've been running on nothing but determination for months, but I've been leaning on you the whole time, and you don't have any reserves, either."

"No, it's... Maybe."

"So maybe we should both relax, and see if letting my emotional wounds heal a bit might heal yours, too."

"Are you telling me to be patient?"

"Yes."

"I'm really bad at patient."

"I know."

"Really, REALLY bad."

"Yes. But we have each other, and we can and WILL get through this."

"If you say so."

"I do. And I'm smarter than you. So play something that makes YOU happy, and I'll fade away for the night."

"Yes, your Grace."

==)»> 13:9: Darkness

"Good evening, Rose. How is life in Dragonland?"

"Pleasant. Strange. Kind of cozy."

"How strange?"

"Well.... No. We'll get back to that. First, I have a lead on finding the teacher I need. It seems that THE broker for magic items in Skytower is a fellow named Cinnabar. Which means he knows his way around the magical community, and if I can get him to talk to me, he can almost certainly connect me with my teacher."

"That's really good news."

"IF I can get him talking to me. But it's really only a matter of time, and probably not that much. If he wasn't social, he couldn't do his job."

"And so, back to 'strange'."

"I live with two males, and deal with a third daily, and they all flirt constantly. It's flattering, and it's really good to be wanted, but... They honestly think I'm beautiful, and I still think, in the pit of my stomach, that I'm a monster. And my libido is still human."

"So you're suffering from an embarrassment of riches."

"Sort of. There are other issues. Dlef is really sweet, but three times my age, and kind of inept, socially. So he would be a really long shot if we were all human."

"And the twins?"

"Turo and Ollie are utterly a package deal. They're best friends, and just GOOD people, but there is this subtle, continuous competition between them. It's probably inevitable when society expects them to kill one another. So I have become one more thing for them to fight over, and I will NOT declare a winner."

"So there's no real possibility there."

"Not unless I can figure out a way to have sex with each of them without either of them knowing who was first."

"That sounds impossible."

"Pretty much...Gods. I hate my brain, sometimes."

"You just figured it out, didn't you?"

"Yes. Damn it."

"So tell."

"Put them both to sleep magically, bathe, sex with one, more magical sleep, bathe again, sex with the other, more magical sleep, morning."

"That sounds like it would work."

"I know."

"Having sex with people just to validate your planning skills is..."

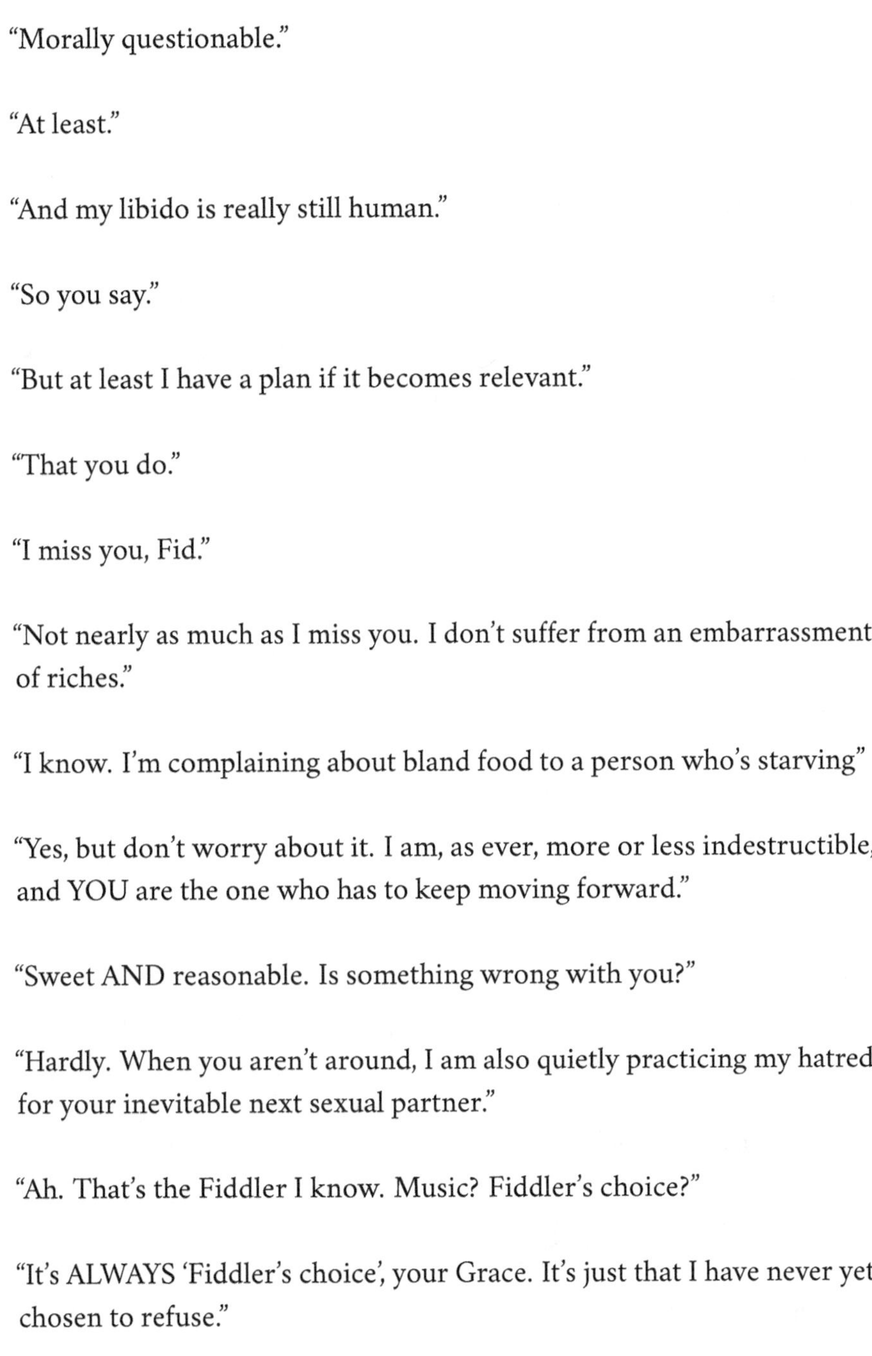

“Morally questionable.”

“At least.”

“And my libido is really still human.”

“So you say.”

“But at least I have a plan if it becomes relevant.”

“That you do.”

“I miss you, Fid.”

“Not nearly as much as I miss you. I don’t suffer from an embarrassment of riches.”

“I know. I’m complaining about bland food to a person who’s starving”

“Yes, but don’t worry about it. I am, as ever, more or less indestructible, and YOU are the one who has to keep moving forward.”

“Sweet AND reasonable. Is something wrong with you?”

“Hardly. When you aren’t around, I am also quietly practicing my hatred for your inevitable next sexual partner.”

“Ah. That’s the Fiddler I know. Music? Fiddler’s choice?”

“It’s ALWAYS ‘Fiddler’s choice’, your Grace. It’s just that I have never yet chosen to refuse.”

==)»> 13:10: Darkness

"Is something wrong, Rose?"

"No. Yes. Maybe... I'm confused."

"Thank you for admitting that. Why don't you tell me a story?"

"I met Cinnabar."

"Good, I think."

"He's my red-haired cousin from Losthaven, five years ago."

"HIM?"

"Yes."

"The dragon semen donor?"

"Yes."

"That's...interesting."

"He didn't remember me."

"Not surprising, really."

"But I had sex with him anyway."

"I did not expect that."

"I never lost Emma's face."

“Ah. That explains...”

“And THEN he recognized the tattoo.”

“Ah.”

“And then I told him what I’ve been up to for the last five years, without ever saying WHY...”

“That was a wise omission...”

“And then I introduced him to Sister Dragon.”

“Did you, by any chance, eat him?”

“What? No!”

“Ah, well. One looks for happy endings where one can.”

“He says he can coach me on the Thaumatology I want, and get me access to the Great Library. AND he wants to take me on as an assistant in his magic brokerage business.”

“That seems sudden.”

“I told him I’d think about it.”

“That was a good choice.”

“I don’t know what happened, Fid.”

“That seemed like a succinct narrative.”

"I mean, I don't know what the game is, or where I am in it. I know that Nab..."

"Nab?"

"Cinnabar."

"Oh."

"I know that he's... ethically sloppy. He is, and was, a Third Circle sorcerer, and when we first met he rolled me into bed on a whim, and then disappeared. I doubt he used any magic; a Third Circle doesn't NEED magic to make someone with no training do something they might have done anyway. But he definitely didn't make any effort to protect me."

"Sounds like a unicorn, so far."

"And I'm ALMOST certain that he used no magic on me this evening, just charm and lots of practice, and the fact that I NEED his help."

"Again, ethically sloppy."

"Right. And I'm even more nearly certain that if he DID use magic on me, I would've been aware of it when the spell wore off."

"But still not absolutely sure."

"Still not absolutely sure."

"So you're wandering through a swamp blind-folded."

"Yes."

"And you need his help, specifically."

"Yes."

"And there's no way I can convince you to back away and find another path."

"You might, if you had another path to offer."

"So you're going to proceed with small steps, and all possible caution."

"That or stand still."

"And there's no chance of that."

"No, not really."

"Then we go forward."

"We do. Pay attention, Fid. If I seem to be behaving oddly, call me on it."

"Is that likely?"

"I don't know. He's stronger than I am, and I'm not absolutely sure of my defenses or his intentions, and we need to be vigilant."

"I shall be so."

"Good. In the meantime... Play something that will make us both happy."

"I will do my best."

14: Cinnabar

If you would be truly free, leave all of your fear and half of your conscience behind.

—Feldspar Greymantle, *Thaumatology*

==)»> 14:1: Darkness

"Good evening, Rose. How are you this evening?"

"You tell me."

"I can't. I don't understand what I'm feeling from you."

"That makes two of us."

"Story?"

"I spent the day with Nab. He showed me his collection of magic; it was amazing. Everything from nearly useless junk to things worth a king's ransom."

"Did it give you itchy fingers?"

"A bit, but I've never been a thief. And I didn't see any of the things I really WANTED, either."

"Ah."

"We did talk money, a little bit. He's going to pay me something he thinks is a trifle, and is a fortune by my standards."

"Ship chartering money?"

"Not for me. But I had the value of a ship in my hands a couple of times, if Nab is to be believed."

"Do you?"

"I have no idea. I do seem to be unable to say, 'No', to him, though."

"That doesn't sound good."

"It's not as bad as that. There's a big gap between 'I want' and 'I won't', and everything he's asked for has fallen into it. But something feels wrong."

"You had sex with him again, didn't you?"

"Yes."

"Closer to 'Won't' than 'Want'?"

"Yes."

"No wonder things seem wrong. Run away, Rose. You're over your head."

"I'll be all right."

"That's a lie."

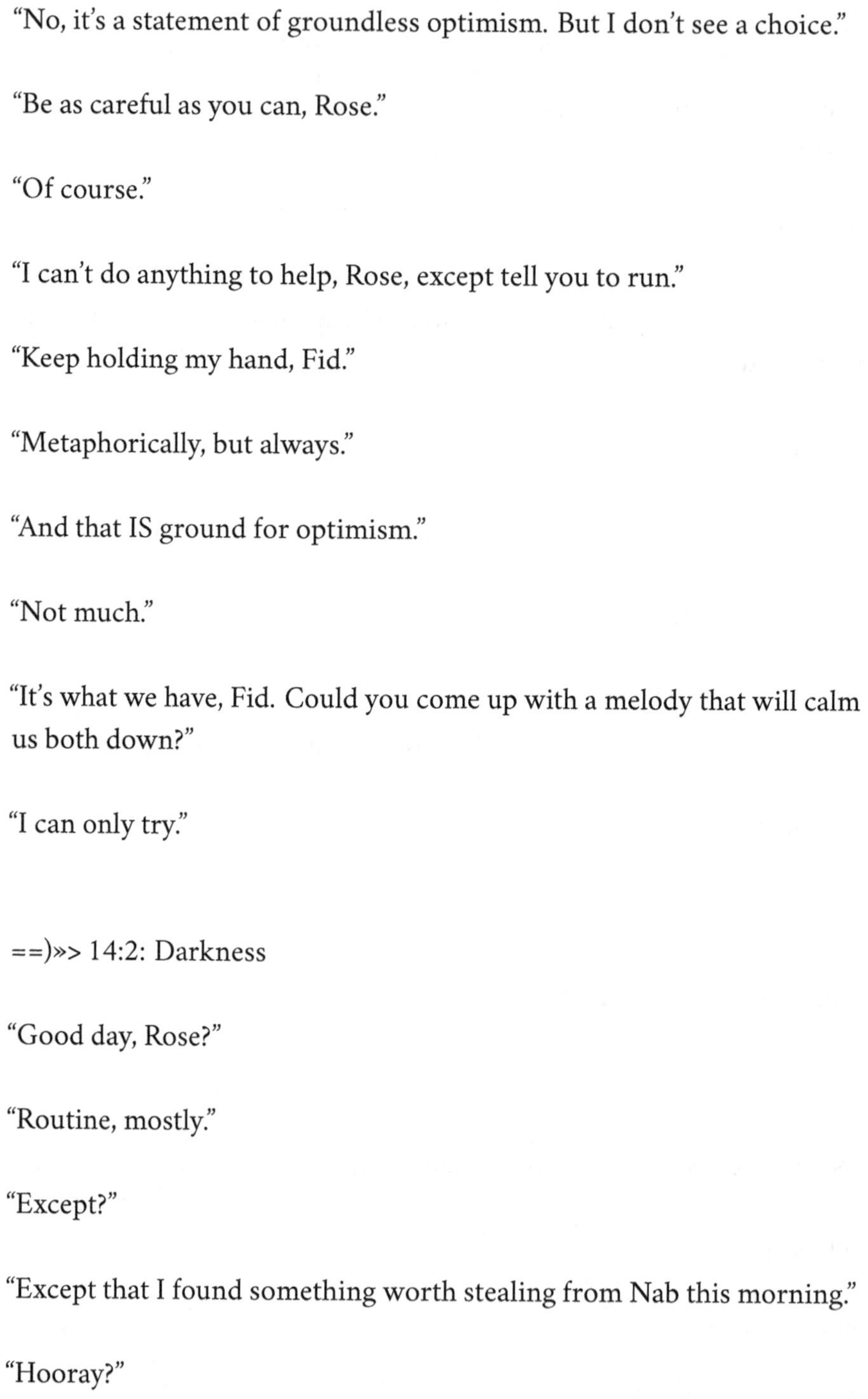

"No, it's a statement of groundless optimism. But I don't see a choice."

"Be as careful as you can, Rose."

"Of course."

"I can't do anything to help, Rose, except tell you to run."

"Keep holding my hand, Fid."

"Metaphorically, but always."

"And that IS ground for optimism."

"Not much."

"It's what we have, Fid. Could you come up with a melody that will calm us both down?"

"I can only try."

==)»> 14:2: Darkness

"Good day, Rose?"

"Routine, mostly."

"Except?"

"Except that I found something worth stealing from Nab this morning."

"Hooray?"

"I'm not going to try to steal it. I had Nab set it aside for me."

"And what was the premium on that?"

"Nothing, really. I asked, he said yes. When I have the money, I pay for it, it's mine. Easy."

"And how far does this set back the 'Saving for Ship Charter' plan?"

"Not sure. Maybe six months."

"Ouch. Is it worth it?"

"Maybe? I think so. I MIGHT be able to do the dive without it, but I'm not sure."

"Six months for maybe. I'm not happy with that trade. What are we talking about anyway?"

"A Frost-walker amulet."

"Which does?"

"Keeps the owner warm under really absurd conditions."

"And this is useful because?"

"Long term, it means I can wear an illusion over silk pajamas and never worry about the weather ever again."

"Charming. And for this, I spend an extra six months in prison."

"In the short term, your neighborhood is full of FREEZING water. Sister

Shark is not bad with cold, but I don't think she can deal with that much of it. And if she can't, then the dive fails, and I have to find another one of these things, or something like it, and start saving money for another charter."

"So six extra months for a sure thing, against an unknown chance of failure."

"Right."

"Damn."

"Right."

"Get the thing."

"Right."

"I'd be happier if waiting didn't involve you being Nab's private whore."

"It's not that bad."

"Isn't it?"

"It's the road, Fid. I don't love it, I don't hate it, it just is. And at the end of the road, we'll be together, and Nab will fall off the edge of the world."

"I'd rather push him off the Skytower."

"That would be colorful, but also too much trouble."

"Spoilsport."

“Possibly. Play me a lullaby, and try not to be too impatient.”

“As her Grace wishes.”

==)»> 14:3: Darkness

“Good evening, Rose. What’s puzzling you tonight?”

“I had a long talk with Dlef tonight about customs among the dragon-folk.”

“And?”

“We talked about Turo and Ollie, mostly.”

“Good for them.”

“It seems that their status is basically, ‘Adult but unmarried’, which is the lowest adult status. They’re stuck there unless they can get married, and because of all of the complications with their being twins, no one wants to marry them.”

“We’ve been over this.”

“The new wrinkle is that I determined that I really could get them the next step up the ladder if I married them.”

“You’re insane.”

‘You’ve said that before.”

“You keep finding new ways to illustrate it.”

"Given your history, would you really mind that much being bound to a runaway bride?"

"Put that way... Not really."

"Didn't think so."

"So you're really going to do this?"

"Still don't know. I'm not willing to take a vow that I'm planning to break, so Dlef would have to come up with something that would convince the elders that the marriage was legitimate, and still leave me room to run. He's not sure he can do it, but he's going to work on it."

"How do the twins feel about this?"

"Haven't asked them, and won't, until I'm sure it can be done. No point getting their hopes up."

"But you're willing if Dlef can work it out, and they want it?"

"How could I not be? They're my friends, this costs me little or nothing, and it will help them a great deal. It's not like I'm ever going to get married the way my mother would like me to."

"No?"

"Of course not. I'm not sure what species I am, I have neither interest in nor ability to have children, and I'm involved in a non-negotiable relationship with a dead unicorn."

"Non-negotiable?"

"Assuming he's not a complete idiot."

"Damn."

"Silly Fiddler. In the meantime, would Master Fiddler be willing to play something happy and soothing?"

"He would, and he will."

==)»> 14:4: Darkness

"Where are you, who are you with, and why are you drunk?"

"There was some kind of big party in Kob-town, and I decided to crash it."

"You're in bed with a kobold."

"Maybe."

"Gods, Rose, what's wrong with you?"

"Other than being drunk and in bed with a kobold?"

"Isn't that enough?"

"I'm chasing a little bit of transitory happiness, and it was working, at least until you started to give me grief about it."

"Hmph. How does your human libido feel about this?"

"Confused, but satisfied."

"And how is your partner going to feel about waking up next to someone who outweighs his original partner by three to one?"

"We've had that experience. He had sex with Sister Kobold, but fell asleep next to Sister Dragon. And things being what they are, it will likely be Dragon he tells his friends about."

"Hmph, again."

"You're just angry because you can't bring yourself to feel jealous of a kobold."

"I can still hate him."

"Don't. Please. He made me happy and tomorrow I probably won't be able to pick him out of a crowd."

"Hmph the third time. And I'm going to go sulk."

"Fid?"

==)»> 14:5: Darkness

"Good evening, Rose. What's the good news?"

"The good news you won't like is that I have learned the name of last night's playmate. He came by sometime today and left a bottle of brandy with a signed thank-you note."

"That's... bizarre."

"Yes, but also sweet."

"Also expensive."

"Well, it's that awful green kobold swill, so not exactly worth a king's ransom..."

"Sanity prevails."

"But it's top shelf awful green kobold swill. So he was really trying. As I said, it was a sweet gesture."

"You implied that there was good news I WOULD approve of?"

"I found a plan for a magical clock that I like in the Library today."

"Hooray?"

"I need a clock for the dive, and this one is nearly perfect. It's an amulet, it's precise, and it's within my ability to manufacture. "

"And the time cost for manufacture?"

"Maybe six weeks."

"Only."

"I've had similar things I didn't like as well run through my hands working with Nab, and this won't take any longer to make than it would to earn the money to buy one of them."

"As her Grace says."

"Don't be that way. We need it, we're going to have it, that's good."

"It feels like you're putting down roots."

"No, I'm... I may be stuck in the mud, but that's not the same thing. I AM coming for you. The day WILL come."

"As her Grace says."

"Damned straight I do."

==)»> 14:6: Darkness

"What's wrong, Rose?"

"Another kobold party."

"That explains the drunkenness, but not the unhappiness."

"My playmate from the other week is dead."

"Say what?"

"According to his friends, he was so inspired by the fact that he had had sex with the Mighty Sorceress Duchess Red that he decided he was ready to make his mark on the world, and came up with some hare-brained get rich quick scheme, and was dead in less than a week."

"Ouch. I'm sorry, Rose."

"You know what I like about you, Fid?"

"I suspect that any guess I make will be wrong."

"You were already dead when I met you, so getting involved with me won't get you killed."

"That's... You know better than that, Rose. This is a single occurrence, not a pattern."

"Doesn't matter."

"This is the swill talking. You aren't cursed. This is... What's the life expectancy of a male kobold?"

"Twenty-five years. Maybe thirty."

"And a female?"

"Maybe one-twenty?"

"And the difference?"

"Males get themselves killed in stupid ways, and females stay home and hatch eggs."

"And the lesson here is?"

"Male kobolds make lousy pets."

"More or less. I'm sorry your playmate is dead. But... He wasn't really even a friend, was he? You only know his name because he signed the thank-you note."

"Yes."

"Then mourn him as seems appropriate, but don't blame yourself. And stay away from the green swill; it rots your brain."

"Yes, Mommy. You said you had a collection of dirges?"

"I do."

"Play me one or six."

"As my Lady wishes.

==)»> 14:7: Darkness

"You seem much better tonight, Rose."

"Time, sobriety, and kindness all help."

"Kindness?"

"Dlef said I looked down, this evening, and gave me a present."

"Which was?"

"About four ounces of his blood."

"Apparently your madness is contagious."

"It was a sweet gesture!"

"I don't deny it. But it was also... around the bend from normality."

"Granted."

"And are you going to drink it?"

"Already have."

"I should have known."

"Can you think of any drawbacks?"

"Other than triggering another metamorphosis into something less manageable than your current form? None at all."

"Oh. Right."

"This was reckless by YOUR standards, Rose."

"It will be fine."

"You have no way of knowing that. How did Dlef know to give the stuff to you?"

"We've talked about my shapeshifting, and where the forms came from. I haven't mentioned the faun, though."

"Why not?"

"Because it breaks the pattern, and only makes sense if I tell the whole story about the unicorn ghost in dreamspace, and I'm not willing to do that."

"You still have SOME sense, then."

"Brat."

"Perhaps. In any case... I have nothing polite to say, but if you permit me, I will play for you, and hope for the best."

"That would be wonderful."

==)»> 14:8: Darkness

"Good evening, Rose."

"And to you, Master Fiddler."

"Let's play a guessing game, shall we? I'll guess, and you'll tell me if I'm right or wrong."

"If you insist."

"You're drunk, and in a bed not yours, and not alone."

"Yes."

"You are feeling some mild discomfort that is probably the result of drinking green kobold swill."

"Yes.

"The bed is too comfortable to belong to a kobold."

"Yes."

"The green swill was the bottle your deceased playmate gave you."

"Nahm. He was called Nahm. And yes."

“You’re in bed with Dlef.”

“Yes.”

“So we have ‘What’, but I remained baffled as to ‘How’.”

“Well...”

“From the beginning.”

“There were no side effects from drinking Dlef’s blood.”

“Good.”

“And the dragon-kin shape developed, just the way I thought it would. As far as I can tell, it looks exactly the way I did during those two days between losing my face and growing a tail.”

“Is that good?”

“It’s interesting, that it’s the same shape. And I’m glad I have it.”

“Well enough. Continuing?”

“I thought I should show Dlef the new shape, since he had been the blood donor, and I was still feeling kind of melancholy, and I thought drinking a toast or two in Nahm’s honor, from the bottle he gave me, would be appropriate, and I was pretty sure that Dlef would go along.”

“Which he did.”

“Which he did.”

"And a couple of toasts turned into half a bottle each."

"Yes."

"And that led to sleeping in Dlef's bed while Fiddler adds another name to his hate list."

"No! Well, yes, we had sex, but I explicitly forbid you to hate Dlef. He's been my friend, and he will remain my friend, and you aren't allowed to hate him."

"Stop me."

"Please, as a favor to me, do not hate my friend Dlef just because he's lonely and I have self-control issues."

"Yes, your Grace."

"Are you being cruel, or just teasing me?"

"I'm not capable of being cruel to you on a more than momentary basis, Rose, and you know that. But I am worried about you."

"I'm worried about me, too."

"Then run."

"Not yet. I'm not done here yet."

"We've had this discussion before, and I can't win, so I'm going to go sulk. Until tomorrow. Or next week. Or whenever."

"Fid?"

==)»> 14:9: Darkness

“Once again, you’re unreadable, Rose.”

“I’m getting married, Fid.”

“The twins?”

“Yes.”

“So this isn’t exactly a surprise.”

“No.”

“So what’s the problem?”

“It’s all a little too surreal for me to digest, I guess. This isn’t a path I expected my life to go down.”

“I can understand that.”

“I’ve been living in their house for over a year, and we all agree that I’m going to go away eventually, and may never see them again, but... I can’t escape the idea that it MEANS something, but I don’t know what.”

“Tell me a story while you think about it.”

“Dlef came by this evening with the vows he had worked out, and I looked them over, and then we presented them to Turo and Ollie...”

“And they jumped on the idea.”

“No, they seemed to have an objection they couldn’t explain, and I finally figured out that it was about consummation."

"Ah."

"So I told them my idea for confusing the order, and they liked that, and signed on. They even added an extra wrinkle; they're going to toss a coin, and switch bedrooms, or not, depending on that. That way, I won't know which was first, either."

"This is too surreal for anyone, I think."

"But it's going to happen anyway."

"So it would seem."

"Fid... Don't play wedding marches. Really, please, don't. FIDDLER CENTAURSON IF YOU DON'T STOP PLAYING WEDDING MUSIC THIS INSTANT I WILL NEVER SPEAK TO YOU AGAIN."

"Really?"

"No. Damn you."

"I promise I'll only go through the list once. And you might wake up before I'm done."

"I'm doomed."

==)»> 14:10: Darkness

"You're happy tonight, Rose."

"I found the other device recipe that I needed in the Library today."

"I assume that that's good?"

"It's GREAT. I wanted a compass, and this is an actual navigator. It doesn't just tell you your heading, it tells you where you are in the world, and even your altitude."

"And how much time will this take to build?"

"Three months?"

"But you really need it."

"I really need the compass. The rest is just bonus."

"But three months."

"Yes. I'm sorry."

"Of course you are. How are your studies going?"

"Well enough. I have a decent understanding, and a ton of notes, but I don't have the necessary ability yet."

"And to get that?"

"I need to hit the road and chase Luck, mostly."

"But first you need to save up ship charter money."

"And get married."

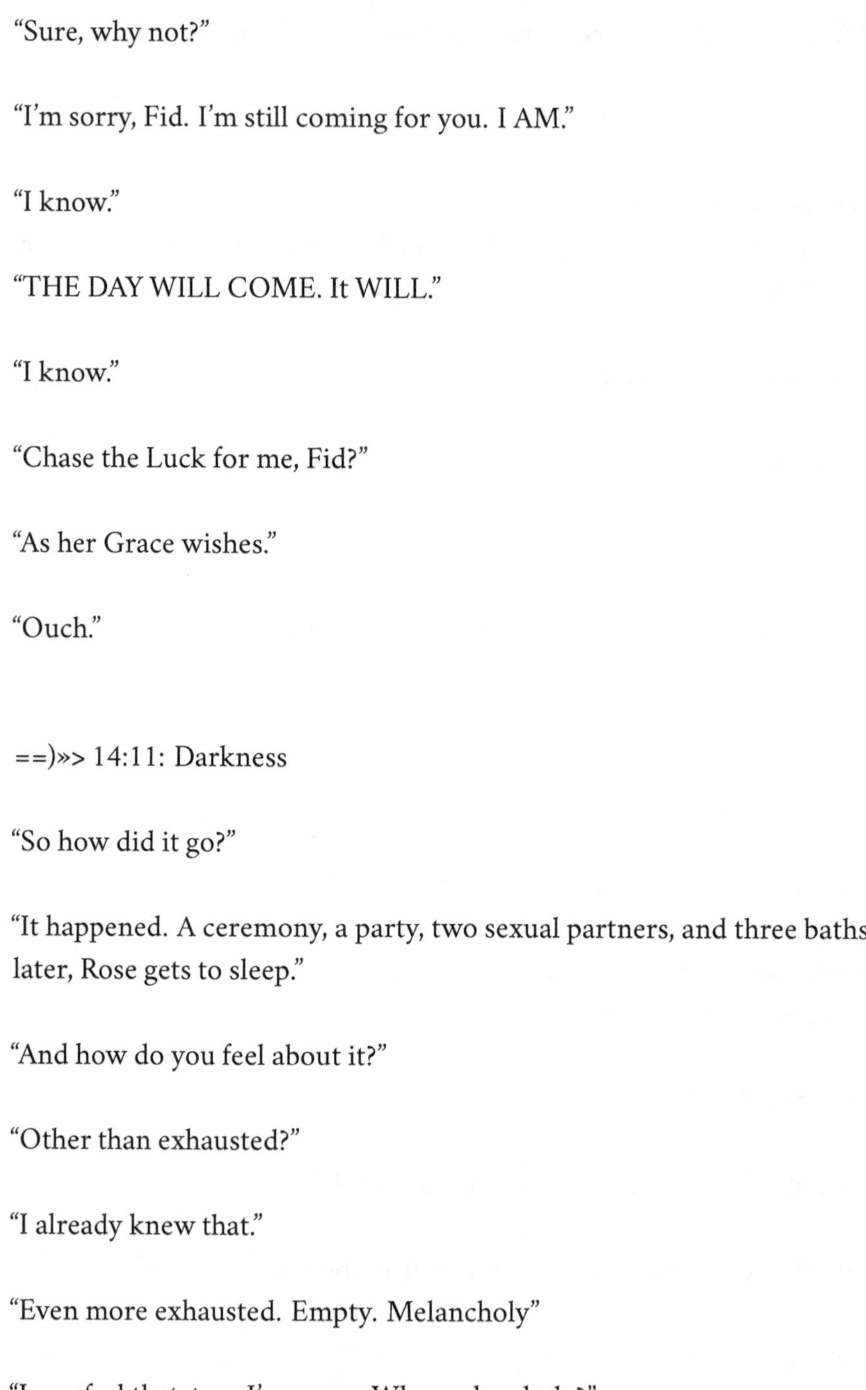

"Sure, why not?"

"I'm sorry, Fid. I'm still coming for you. I AM."

"I know."

"THE DAY WILL COME. It WILL."

"I know."

"Chase the Luck for me, Fid?"

"As her Grace wishes."

"Ouch."

==)»> 14:11: Darkness

"So how did it go?"

"It happened. A ceremony, a party, two sexual partners, and three baths later, Rose gets to sleep."

"And how do you feel about it?"

"Other than exhausted?"

"I already knew that."

"Even more exhausted. Empty. Melancholy"

"I can feel that, too. I'm sorry. Why melancholy?"

"I can only guess. I have some great friends here, Fid..."

"Three good friends, two of whom are now also your husbands, and an abusive employer whom you will not walk away from."

"As you say. There's so much I like here. I could almost put down roots, but I know I won't."

"Forgive me if I'm glad for that."

"You keep me honest. You remind me that I CAN'T."

"Which means?"

"Deep down, I know that I'll never put down roots, that it would kill me if I did. And being so close to being able to take root here just... hurts."

"Ah. I'm sorry for you pain, Rose. But glad you're who you are."

"In other news... The twins paid off the Frost-walker as a present to me..."

"I approve of this..."

"And Dlef gave me... something odd and kind of wonderful."

"Which was?"

"A glass ring pendant."

"And?"

"It's made from the neck of the bottle that Nahm gave me, polished to have no edges, and made almost indestructible with magic."

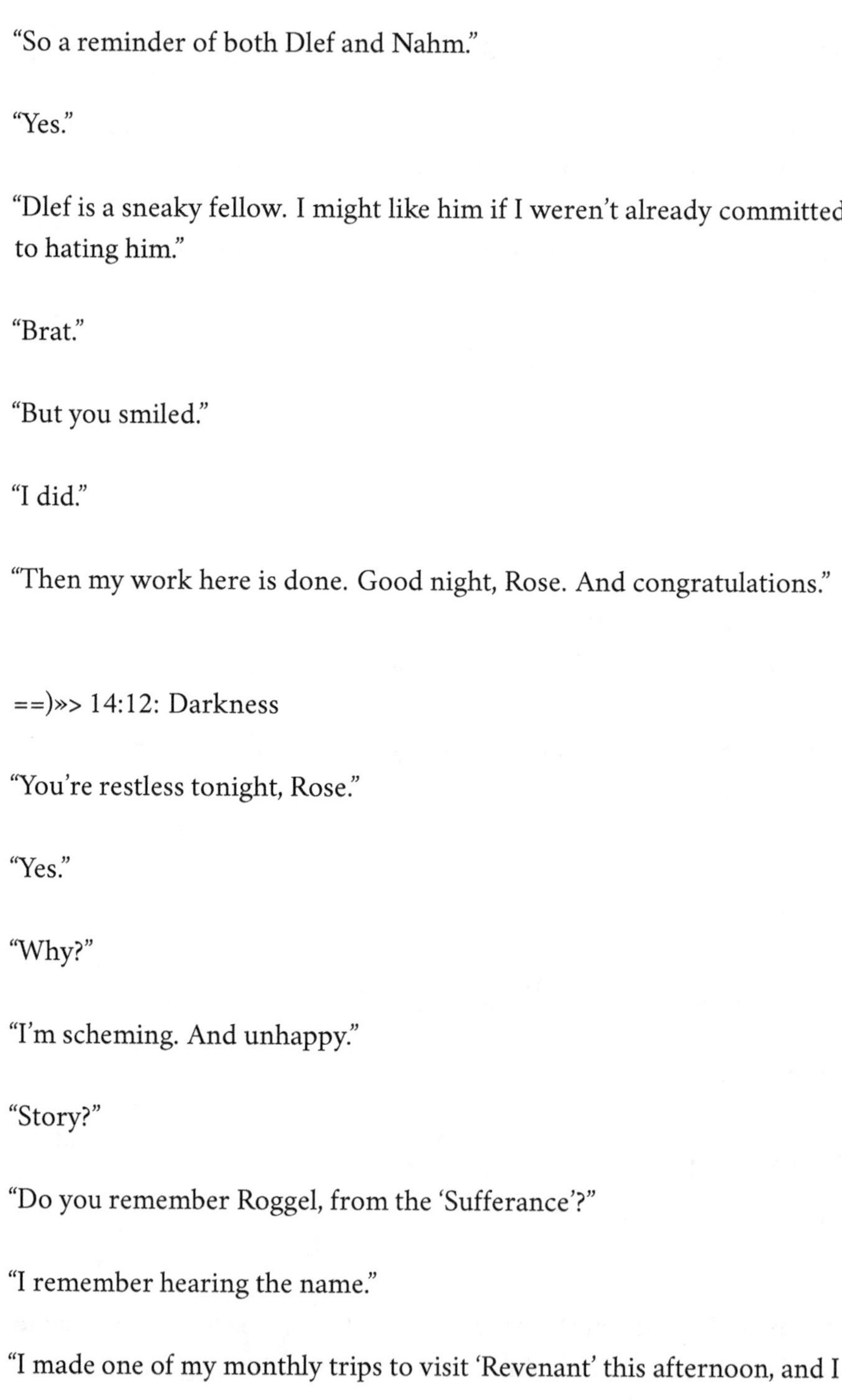

"So a reminder of both Dlef and Nahm."

"Yes."

"Dlef is a sneaky fellow. I might like him if I weren't already committed to hating him."

"Brat."

"But you smiled."

"I did."

"Then my work here is done. Good night, Rose. And congratulations."

==)»> 14:12: Darkness

"You're restless tonight, Rose."

"Yes."

"Why?"

"I'm scheming. And unhappy."

"Story?"

"Do you remember Roggel, from the 'Sufferance'?"

"I remember hearing the name."

"I made one of my monthly trips to visit 'Revenant' this afternoon, and I ran into him. He's still sailing, just happened to be in port, and recognized me. Or more properly Emma."

"She stands out."

"She does. So we talked a bit, and he told me that he was pretty sure he had seen Dzee in a brothel across the river last night. He hadn't spoken to her, and wasn't absolutely sure it was her, but he thought so."

"That's... I like Dzee. She was fun. Sweet."

"And always much too trusting. After Roggel went on his way, I went over to check the place out. I put on Roggel's face, found Dzee, and bought some time with her."

"Definitely our Dzee, then."

"Yes, and she's in a bad way. Not sick or hurt, but desperately unhappy, and trapped there."

"She's a slave?"

"Not technically, but in practice. If they catch her going out the door, they'll beat her; it she manages to get away, they'll report her to the watch as a thief, and put a bounty on her head. Which results in the girl being beaten, and often hobbled."

"Dzee has seen this?"

"More than once."

"What happened to her?"

"She and Lyssa stayed together after 'Sufferance' paid off, found work, kept sailing. And then Lyssa was killed in a bar fight about three years ago."

"A shame. I always liked Lyssa."

"I did too. But that left Dzee alone, and small, pretty, kind, and alone is not a tenable situation dockside. So she ended up in a brothel in short order."

"Ah."

"And now I have to get her out."

"I am tempted to ask, 'Why you?', but I already know the answer."

"You do."

"Do you have a plan?"

"Most of one."

"Will I hate it?"

"Probably not, actually. And it involves leaving Skytower for Losthaven, which should make you happy."

"What will Nab say?"

"Whatever he wants. I'm not going to tell him."

"How about the twins?"

"That will be hard, but they knew it was coming. Same with Dlef."

"When?"

"I think I can get her back here tomorrow, and then out to sea as soon as the weather breaks. There's a storm coming in."

"Which matters because?"

"'Revenant' doesn't like big waves."

"Ah."

"Would you play me a lullaby, Fid? I have a long day ahead of me."

"As my Lady wishes."

==)»> 14:13: Darkness

"Home safe, Rose?"

"Finally. Sister Wings isn't fond of high winds."

"How's Dzee?"

"Sound asleep, alone, in a clean bed, and with a chair wedged against the door."

"A chair?"

"The boys have been very gracious, but she isn't used to dragon-folk. Had never even spoken to one before."

"Ah. So, from the beginning?"

"Right. From the beginning. I taught Dlef how to look like Osprey in the morning..."

"Because?"

"You know that patience you're so bad at?"

"Yes..."

"Find some. At sundown, Dlef and I crossed the river and went to the brothel. Dlef was wearing Osprey's face, and I was wearing Gorsheg's...

"The obnoxious apprentice from Landfall?"

"Right. I went in and bought some time with Dzee while Dlef loitered in the lobby, waiting for 'Gorsheg' to do his business. Once we were alone, I gave Dzee my clothes, and gave HER Gorsheg's face, and then she went out to the lobby, found 'Osprey'..."

"Who was someone you were sure Dzee would recognize..."

"And the two of them headed back to Dragon-town. I put Lyssa's face over Sister Dragon, on the assumption that no one would ask a scantily clad woman too many questions on a busy night in a brothel, and found a top floor window, then shifted to Sister Wings and dove out."

"And then you came home."

"And then I got caught by the wind and blown out of town before I could find a safe place to land, and had to walk home."

"Which is why you're so late."

"Which is why I'm so late. Also exhausted. I checked in on Dzee before I went to bed, though, which is how I know about the chair in front of the door."

"Ah. And now what?"

"And now we keep Dzee out of sight for a few days, until the weather breaks, and then 'Revenant' will take us to Losthaven. In the meantime, we'll get some clothes for Dzee, and I'll say my goodbyes to Dlef and my husbands."

"Ah. Would the conquering hero care for some appropriate music?"

"The conquering hero would love to hear a lullaby."

"As my Lady wishes."

15: Dzee

The only cure for restless feet is death.
—*The Book of the Blind King's Wisdom*

==)»> 15:1: Rose's room

"Not sleeping, Rose?"

"Not yet. I just wanted to check in with you before it got any later."

"It's appreciated. How did the day go?"

"Well enough. Dzee spent a lot of time sleeping, and most of the rest of it trying to adapt to being around dragon-folk, including me. I spent the day gathering supplies, getting clothes for Dzee, and saying my goodbyes to Dlef, Turo, and Ollie."

"On your back?"

"What goes on between me and my husbands is none of your business."

"So not Dlef."

"Brat."

“But you are up past your usual bedtime, and not planning to sleep anytime soon.”

“Not saying.”

“Don’t have to. What’s up tomorrow?”

“Dzee and I walk a handcart full of stuff down to the docks, get ‘Revenant’ in the water, and sail away with the evening tide. I’m planning to make the trip in one hop, since I ‘ll be able to leave Dzee on the helm while I sleep.”

“Won’t they be looking for Dzee?”

“Let them. Dzee will be wearing Bing’s face, and no one associates Emma’s face with Dzee.”

“And then you’ll be at sea.”

“And then we’ll be at sea.”

“And Dzee will start worrying about being eaten by the dragon on the other side of the boat.”

“No.”

“Optmist.”

“Brat.”

“I exist to serve. Enjoy your evening, Rose. And good luck on the morrow.”

==)»> 15:2: Aboard "Revenant"

"All went well, Rose?"

"Without a hitch."

"And the boat is sailing herself?"

"No, it's a bit too rough for that, but Dzee is on the tiller and grinning like a fool. She's a sailor at heart, and hasn't been on the water in far too long."

"Sounds good."

"It is. I feel like... I don't know. I miss Dlef and the twins already, but it is just SO good to be moving again."

"I can tell. It's a good feeling."

"Does your repertoire include anything that fits this situation better than 'Chasing the Luck'?"

"Not offhand. I'll think about it while I play, though."

"Thank you, Master Fiddler. I wish I could share the music with Dzee, but it would be hard for her to be happier."

"Then let us chase."

==)»> 15:3: Aboard "Revenant"

"Eventful day, Rose?"

"You know it was, don't you? You're the one who told him I'd be at sea again."

"Maybe..."

"Dzee almost died of fright. Things had been so busy, I had never told her that the Great Storm Turtle was calling me, "Granddaughter." He surfaced under the boat..."

"And she just loved it."

"No, she started screaming and couldn't stop. I had to shift to Emma and hold her to get her calmed down."

"Sorry."

"No, you aren't. But someday you're going to get Dzee in dreamspace again, and you're going to apologize to her. And you're NOT going to use magic to get her to forgive you."

"I have other options...

"And you're NOT going to use sex to get forgiveness, either. Or you'll have to answer to me."

'Yes, your Grace."

"Damned straight. Anyway, eventually I got her out of the boat and up to the front edge of his shell for a conversation. Of course she doesn't speak Dragontongue, so I had to translate, and she only shook her head or nodded when he asked her questions. But she loved it. If she ever remembers how to talk again, I don't think she'll shut up about it for days."

"So will YOU forgive me?"

"Eventually. I have no real choice in the long run. But I can make you pay for a long time."

"Yes, your Grace."

"And I have to admit that having Maelstrom carry us for a few hours made the trip shorter."

"You mean I'm actually useful?"

"Occasionally."

"I'll do my best to avoid it in the future."

"Most likely. I'm told that you're becoming proficient at Territories."

"I've had a good teacher, and my handicap has stabilized. I'm not sure that means I'm becoming proficient."

"Maelstrom's actual comment was that you've finally proved that you are smarter than the stones on the board. I extrapolated."

"That was kind of you."

"He also told me that you were worried about me, and that made him worried about me."

"I WAS worried about you. I still am."

"But did you have to tell the Turtle?"

"He asked me direct questions. Have you ever tried to lie to him, or evade his questions?"

"Objection withdrawn. And you were actually looking him in the eye, weren't you?"

"BOTH eyes."

"Damn."

"Exactly."

"Things should be better, now, though. Now that I'm away from Cinnabar. I... didn't think he had gotten inside my head, but he must have. This is the first time I've gone three days without seeing him..."

"Without having sex with him..."

"Without putting on Emma, at his request, and having sex with him, in over a year. Yes. Gods, Fid, what was wrong with me?"

"I did my best..."

"I know you did, Fid. I should have listened. I'm not sure I could have, though. But now...I don't know, my mind feels clearer."

"That is... amazing news. But I'm still worried."

"So am I. I'll keep you posted. In the meantime... I think I need to relieve Dzee at the tiller, and let her get some sleep. If she can."

"Does she know you're talking to me?"

"It hasn't come up yet. Should I tell her?"

"Your call. At least as long as I'm on the bottom of the ocean."

"Now THAT worries me. Good night, Fid."

"Good night, Rose."

==)»> 15:4: A rented room

"Not sleeping again, Rose?"

"Practicing my 'Rose Mark Two' face for wandering around Losthaven."

"Mark Two?"

"The face they know around here. Mark One is the one you know, before any transformations, pure human. Mark Two is the one Drellan knows, after I got the third dragon mark. She has fine scales that you wouldn't notice from more than five feet away. Mark Three is what I looked like after the second tattoo from Auntie Moss, Mark Two but with more obvious scales. Mark Four is the one I only had for a couple of days in Landfall, with a dragon head and full scales, but plantigrade feet and no tail. And Mark Five is my current form, with digitigrade feet and a tail."

"And where are you doing this practice?"

"In an inn in Losthaven; I'm sharing a room with Dzee. Tomorrow I'll pay Drellan a visit, and see what I can work out."

"What do you have in mind? You're hardly his apprentice anymore."

"No, I'm going to try to set up Dzee as his housekeeper. She's had enough adventure, I think, and Drellan is lonely but doesn't have a clue what to do about it."

"He can't be THAT lonely, then."

"He isn't; he's pretty self contained. But I lived with him for three years, and I have a pretty good idea of how his mind works. People baffle him."

"Ah."

"And I've already explained the situation to Dzee. I told her what I have in mind, and she's willing to try to get to know Drellan. After a while, if she's interested, I'll suggest to Drellan that Dzee might be more than a housekeeper."

"And you need to be involved because?"

"Because Drellan will never make the first move, otherwise, and if Dzee makes the first move, he'll be suspicious, and it might ruin everything."

"YOU made the first move on him."

"Yes, but I had known him for three years, and was going away, so there was no chance I was trying to take advantage of him."

"Ah. And where does all of this scheming leave you?"

"Not quite in the cold. I'm going to leave Dzee with custody of 'Revenant', which she'll like, and I should be able to talk Drellan into storing the rest of my stuff; there isn't that much. And then I'm going to cross Dragon Lake, spend some time getting re-acquainted with the local crocs and kobs, and see if I can arrange an audience with the Empress herself."

"Because, having survived acquaintanceship with the Great Monster Turtle, you have no fear of lesser dragonkind."

"No, because I need a lot of money, and she's reputed to HAVE a lot of money, and I MAY be able to provide her with some lucrative service or other."

"Like what?"

"I have no idea."

"You're going to walk into the lair of a major dragon and ask for a job, on spec."

"Pretty much."

"Damn. Gonna have to move the Crazy Bar again."

"Say what?"

"The Crazy Bar. The, 'Rose can't possibly try something more insane than this', bar."

"You might want to just give that up."

"I would. But I'm waiting for the day that I propose something so insane that it causes you to collapse in a fit of hysterical laughter, and I'll be able to say, 'But it's not nearly as insane as these six (or seven, or eight) things that you've already done,' and you'll have no choice but to go along with what I want."

"No choice?"

"It's not a perfect concept."

"You're kind of cute when you're stupid."

"I know. I cultivate it. But you still intend to visit the Empress."

"I do. But as always, I'll do the insane thing as carefully as possible, and it'll be fine."

"Do you really think she'll offer you a job?"

"Not at first, no. But it'll put the idea in her head, and THAT may lead to something."

"That almost makes sense. Almost."

"You don't use brute force on things that are bigger than you, Fid. You nudge them, and hope they'll shift to the path you want."

"Like the rudder on a ship. Force multiplies."

"Exactly."

"Don't get eaten."

"I'll do my best. In the meantime, I need to do a few more experiments before I sleep."

"Ever in my thoughts, Rose."

"Until the day."

==)»> 15:5: Darkness

"And where are you sleeping tonight, Rose?"

"Still in the inn. Tomorrow we'll clean out my old room at Drellan's house, and then I'll be back on the road, more or less."

"So things went well with Drellan?"

"They did, though I ambushed him, a bit. I went to his house alone in the morning, with food and beer, and we caught up on the last three years. And THEN I mentioned Dzee, and then I went back to town. And I came back, WITH Dzee, and more food, and more alcohol, in time for supper."

"And they seemed to hit it off?"

"I think so. Drellan is attracted to Dzee, and Dzee is a bit in awe of Drellan, and I couldn't have expected things to go any better."

"And the day after that you go looking for the Empress?"

"More or less. I need to re-establish myself with the local kobs and crocs, thought that may be easier than I expected."

"Oh?"

"Stories have been carried from Skytower to Losthaven. The locals had started to forget me, and then they started hearing rumors from the east, and now I'm here in person."

"With a dragon snout and a tail."

"Yep. The impact I had last time around hasn't completely gone away, either. There is now a small kobold enclave on this side of the river, near the south end of the lake. The kobs don't sell in the square on market days, but they buy, occasionally, and the kobs have a market of their own where some of the humans shop. And there is still some traffic in kobolds for unskilled labor. "

"Not bad for something you did as a hobby three years ago."

"It wasn't exactly a hobby, it was... I don't know, trying to be decent, I guess. I need more of that. I feel kind of... soiled, after Skytopwer."

"Cinnabar?"

"Yes, but more than that. I think back over my relationships with Dlef and the twins, and..."

"You regret getting married?"

"No, that was a good thing. But I regret Nahm, and pretty much everything I did there has this... greasy feeling. But Dlef and Turo and Ollie were all my friends, and I'm actually kind of proud to be married to the twins, as silly as that sounds. Am I contradicting myself?"

"A bit."

"I'm confused, and I don't like it."

"And I'm dead. Also on the bottom of the ocean. Not too fond of either of those, either."

"But you aren't going to stay on the bottom of the ocean."

"And you aren't going to stay confused."

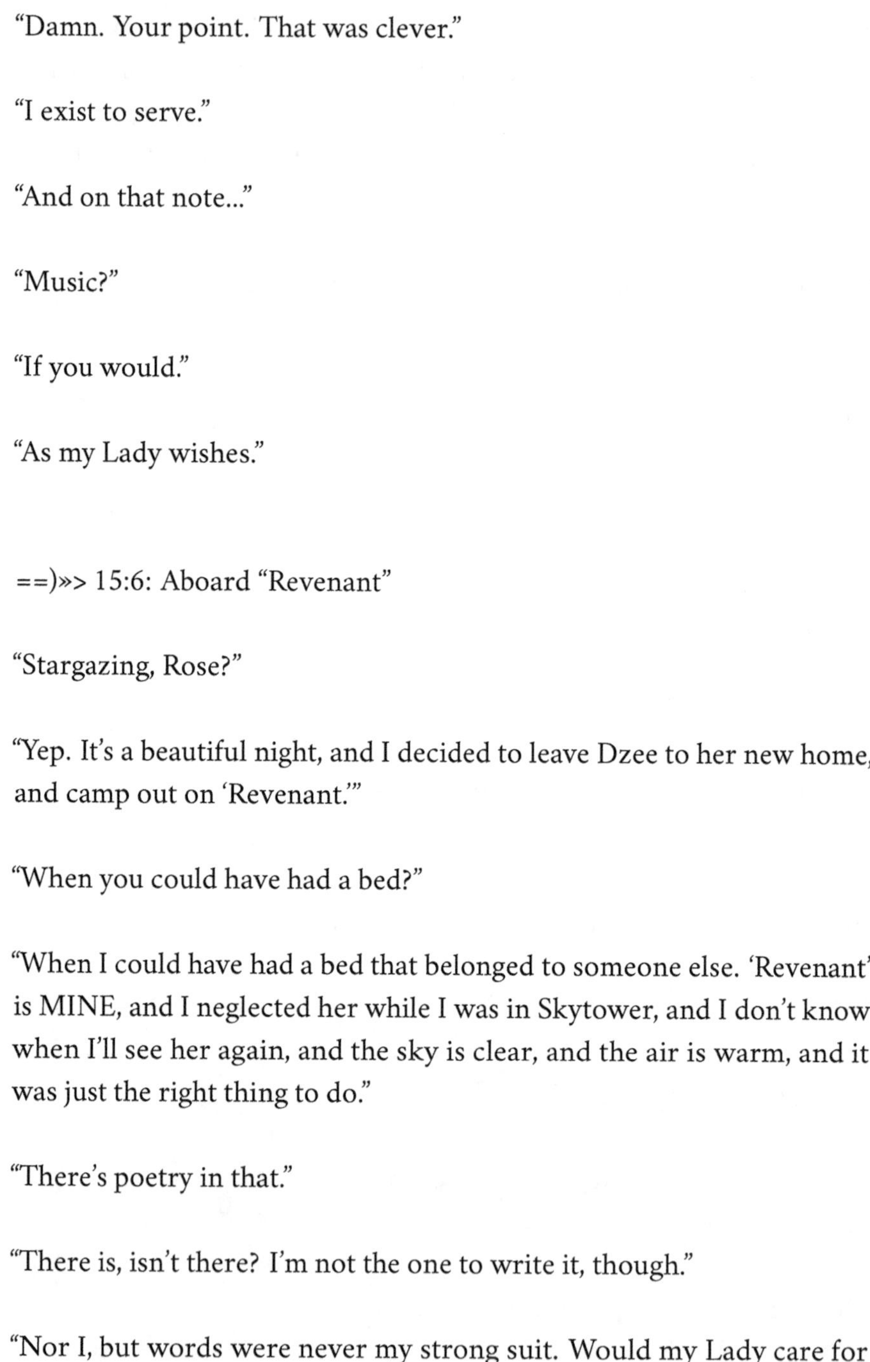

“Damn. Your point. That was clever.”

“I exist to serve.”

“And on that note...”

“Music?”

“If you would.”

“As my Lady wishes.”

==)»> 15:6: Aboard “Revenant”

“Stargazing, Rose?”

“Yep. It’s a beautiful night, and I decided to leave Dzee to her new home, and camp out on ‘Revenant.’”

“When you could have had a bed?”

“When I could have had a bed that belonged to someone else. ‘Revenant’ is MINE, and I neglected her while I was in Skytower, and I don’t know when I’ll see her again, and the sky is clear, and the air is warm, and it was just the right thing to do.”

“There’s poetry in that.”

“There is, isn’t there? I’m not the one to write it, though.”

“Nor I, but words were never my strong suit. Would my Lady care for some music?”

“That would be... perfect, Fid. And thank you.”

“I serve with pleasure.”

==)»> 15:7: Darkness

“Good evening, Rose. Sleeping among the kobolds tonight?”

“I am, though the accommodations are a bit better than their equivalent in Skytower.”

‘And why would that be?”

“These kobs are a bit more affluent, or at least a bit less desperately poor. And there, I was a strange person who showed up out of nowhere, and here I've been heralded by a legend, and may have exceeded the expectation.”

“Oh?”

“I look enough like a kobold to be considered exotically beautiful, and I'm a giant, more or less. I never really tried to just BE with the kobs in Skytower as Sister Dragon. I always tried to slip in as Sister Kobold. They always recognized me fairly quickly, but the experience is different. Today, it's closer to worship.”

“That just sounds SO healthy.”

“Which is why the Duchess maintains a Fool to keep her honest.”

“Once again, I serve a purpose. I'm going to have to demand double wages.”

"Done."

"And you call ME a spoilsport."

"I also call you an idiot. Among other things, a few of which are complimentary. In spite of myself."

"Yes, I've noticed that my charm was irresistible."

"And on that note... Good night, my Scorpion."

"Good night, my Heart."

==)»> 15:8: Darkness

"Back on 'Revenant' tonight, Rose?"

"Yes. The sky isn't as clear, but it's QUIET. Or at least quiet compared to a kobold warren."

"Ah. How was your day?"

"Busy enough. Satisfying enough. I brought Dzee down to kob-town and introduced her around, and found a kob willing, and able, to teach Dzee Dragontongue."

"And the why of that?"

"Dealing with kobs is a useful skill if you live in Losthaven, and it's a lot easier if you speak their language."

"I thought you said a lot of them spoke Kzanti?"

“Most of them speak SOME Kzanti, but when you speak their language, it tends to make them friendlier. And speaking Dragontongue— learning Dragontongue— will give her something in common with Drellan. He’s made a little progress in the last three years, but he would be happy for more practice.”

“Ah. So tomorrow you take off into the swamp?”

“That’s the plan. I think I’m going to travel REALLY light, just a couple of daggers and some money. That way I can do most of my travelling as Sister Wings, and I won’t have to worry too much about being ambushed, either; not too many pursuers can take to the air.”

“What I’m hearing is that you’re going to go gallivanting among the sex-crazed kobolds stark naked.”

“Wow. Have you been taking lessons in obtuseness?”

“”No, it’s all natural talent.”

“I’m impressed.”

“The comment still stands.”

“No, the comment falls on its face and snores drunkenly. The kobolds are not sex-crazed...”

“Could you, or could you not, have any male kobold you wanted any time you wanted?”

“Probably could, but that’s not the...”

“Of course it is.”

"Male kobolds are available to me, not that I want them, AT ALL, because I'm perceived as a source of status. They curry favor any way then can, and would provide sex as part of the package if I were interested. Which I'm not."

"But you're still going to be naked."

"But I can conjure any illusory clothes I want any time I want."

"Still naked."

"Everyone is naked under their clothes, Fid."

"Most clothing has, you know, mass?"

"Fid... Why am I going to wander around the swamp in the first place?"

"To acquire more luck, so that you can become more magically powerful."

"And?"

"To try to swindle the Jade Empress out of enough money that you can hire a ship to come rescue me."

"Right. And what does this mean you should do with your stupid comments about my wardrobe or lack thereof?"

"Keep them to myself. Though I reserve the right to imagine you naked while I think extremely lustful thoughts."

"I would be deeply disappointed if you didn't. Good night, Fid."

"Good night, Rose."

==)»> 15:9: Darkness

"And where are you tonight, Rose?"

"In a kobold town about 60 miles northwest of Losthaven."

"And how are you getting along?"

"Well enough. I have a bit of a reputation here, but not really enough to be useful."

"Useful?"

"Yeah. Saying, 'Hello, I'm a kobold friendly sorceress who's looking for an audience with the Empress, can you tell me how to find her?' just doesn't carry much weight if they haven't heard enough about me to know if I can be trusted at all."

"Ah."

"So the job becomes that much slower; I have to actually make friends in every town, not just be taken as friendly. I wish I knew some healing spells; healers are always welcome."

"I'd be happy to help you with that, except..."

"Five hundred miles and two thousand fathoms. I know."

"So what are you planning now?"

"Hang around for a few days and make friends, I guess... Wait a moment. Why 'What are you planning?' Why not, 'What are you going to do?'"

"Damn. Busted. All right, I have an alternative to suggest."

"Really."

"I played a game of Territories with Maelstrom last night— I won, by the way, so I may outgrow my handicap in less than a thousand years, after all— and he asked me when you were going to chase the sword."

"The sword?"

"Four naked women. One of them turns into a sword and gets thrown in a lake. The other three turn into animals and wander away."

"Oh. THAT sword."

"Maelstrom seems to think it's important, and also that wheedling a small fortune out of a dragon may take a very long time, and that now is probably the best time to chase the sword."

"Does he now. And how does he even KNOW about the sword?"

"I babble when I play Territories. It's supposed to distract him."

"Sure it is. One piece of crazy at a time. Maelstrom thinks I should chase the sword."

"Also Auntie Moss."

"You asked her about it?"

"After Maelstrom put it in my head, sure."

"And what did she say?"

“That there would never be a better time, and that you might get bogged down with the Empress for a long time.”

“Did she.”

“Bing and Dlef and Drellan, too, for that matter.”

“You discussed this with ALL of them?”

“It seemed important.”

“How about Cinnabar?”

“I want nothing to do with him that doesn’t include him being dead.”

“Ah. Nice to know that there’s some limit to your meanderings.”

“I take Maelstrom’s word seriously. And since you think I’m an idiot, I though I would collect some opinions from people you trust.”

“Hmm. The last time we talked you didn’t seem too enthused about that particular quest.”

“That was before it was an option to dealing with a less than friendly dragon.”

“The Empress isn’t hostile.”

“She’s a dragon.”

“So’s Maelstom. Sort of.”

“And he sought YOU out. You didn’t walk into his home.”

"I'm trying to wrangle an invitation."

"Still."

"I'll think about it. Come look for me an hour before dawn?"

"As her Grace wishes."

==)»> 15:10: Darkness

"Sleeping finally, Rose?"

"I guess so. No thanks to you and your committee of advisers."

"I exist to serve."

"Someday, I'll find a way to make you pay for that line."

"I look forward to it. In the meantime..."

"In the meantime you've made your point. I'll head west to Ironbridge, and then north up the Iron River. Though I'm going to stop at the major kobold villages along the way. And I'm pretty sure they're having a banquet for me here tonight, so I'll have to stay for that."

"But you're going to chase the sword?"

"Yes, I'm going to chase the sword. It's probably what Auntie Moss wanted me to do three years ago, when she told me the story."

"Maybe. Who can tell with Auntie Moss? And if you had turned north then, instead of completing the circuit of Hurricane Bay, you wouldn't have had Sister Shark, or Sister Kobold, or Sister Wings."

"And if we're playing might-have-beens, I would still have been human."

"I don't think Maelstrom would have liked that as well."

"Probably not. And I'm getting used to this, slowly. And if I can extend Sister Shark—and I need to— I can extend Emma. So it'll work out. Eventually."

"It's never quite the same, is it? I had hands in dreamspace almost as soon as I lost my hands in the real world, but it's just never quite the same..."

"It is what it is. And I suspect I'll be awake in the very near future. Until tonight, Fid. And until the day."

"Until the day, your Grace. Until the day."

16: Silver Faun

Your grandmother was young, once, and I know first hand that she was wilder than you are now.
—Auntie Moss

==)»> 16:1: Darkness

"Good evening, Rose. Same bed as last night.?"

"Yep."

"And slightly drunk. More green kobold swill?"

"Yep."

"Does it get any better with practice?"

"Maybe. It gets less awful. I can't imagine it'll ever be GOOD."

"So how was the day?"

"The usual. I play the politician and try to get the kobs to like me, and try to avoid making promises I don't want to keep. I need to get used to it; there's going to be a lot of it in my future before I get to the Empress."

"Of course, you may win a huge fortune in the course of your sword quest."

"I might also sprout wings and turn half-way into a dragon."

"But you've already... That... It's a joke until you realize it's a joke, and then it's not, and then it... My head hurts."

"And you're not the one who's slightly drunk. How long have you been talking to Bing?"

"What? Where did THAT come from?"

"Now that I'm committed to the sword quest, I've had a little time to consider the interesting bit of news that you blurted out while trying to convince me. How long?"

"I wouldn't say 'blurted', it was a calculated release of significant information..."

"How long?"

"Since shortly after you started spending time with Cinnabar. I needed advice. Or at least I wanted it."

"And Drellan?"

"About the same time. And the same reason."

"And Dlef?"

"The first night after you docked in Losthaven. I used the fact that you were safe off the ocean as an introduction."

"And what did you tell any of them about yourself?"

"That I was a spirit bound to an object you owned."

"That's almost true."

"It's completely true. It's just not the complete truth."

"I suppose. And I really can't be angry with you, can I? Your existence is as much your secret as mine, maybe more. And I can't fault the choices."

"Are you giving me credit for wisdom?"

"Maybe. Wow. That actually kind of hurt to say."

"Shame on you."

"Shame on you for fishing for compliments."

"How long have you known me?"

"About nine years."

"So you know that ship has long since sailed."

"And I knew what you were... Ah, my scorpion, what would I do without you?"

"Sleep soundly?"

"Not if I keep drinking green swill."

"I disavow all responsibility."

"Just play me a lullaby and I'll absolve you of all of your lustful thoughts."

"It would have to be a very long lullaby."

"Sooner started..."

"As her Grace wishes."

==)»> 16:2: Darkness

"Three times is a pattern, Rose."

"Say what?'

"Travel a day and stay sober, then rest a day and sleep drunk."

"Ah. You're on to me. But this is the last night of that."

"I'll believe it when it happens."

"You're my conscience now? That's first class absurdity."

"But if you had listened to me in Skytower..."

"Point taken. But tomorrow I'll be in Ironbridge, and I may not sleep sober, and the day after that I'll probably travel, and almost certainly WILL sleep sober. And in any case, the next time I get drunk, it will be on decent whiskey. That much I can assure you."

"You're swearing off green swill?"

"I'll be out of kobold country, and no one will be offering it. Thankfully."

"I thought you were a fan of free alcohol."

"Not when it's green swill. It takes social obligation to make me choke that down."

"Which is how you ended up in bed with Dlef."

"Will you stop? Do you want to start comparing relative culpability for Nahm and Kellarth?"

"No."

"Then stop riding me for my mistakes. We try to learn and move on, both of us, right?"

"Right. Of course, Dlef doesn't think it was a mistake, particularly."

"Dlef wasn't ENTIRELY a mistake. But I WAS stupid, and I was lucky it didn't end badly, and can we PLEASE talk about something else?"

"Yes, your Grace."

"Damned straight."

"Lullaby, your Grace?"

"If Master Scorpion would be so kind."

"As my Lady wishes."

==)»> 16:3: Darkness

"Good evening, Rose. You're... unreadable this evening. Or rather, you're feeling something I have no reference for."

"Really? I wonder why. Would Master Scorpion care for a story?"

"I suspect I should be afraid, and that I have no real choice."

"You would be right on both counts."

"I choke down my apprehension and request that you get on with it."

"So I got to Ironbridge this afternoon, and decided that I'd splurge on a real bed, because I may not have another chance for a while. And I decided to put on Nab's face, because I don't care if I get him into trouble, and it's a lot safer to be a man traveling alone on foot than a woman, and Sister Dragon's voice sounds more like a man, anyway."

"Understood..."

"So I found a decent looking inn, and got a room, and decided to have some food and a drink or two before I shut myself in for the evening."

"Reasonable."

"And while I was at the bar, minding my own business, the bar maid got in a fight with a fellow, and shouted at him, 'You think you're the Silver Faun, but you're really just a tired old plow horse.' And everyone who heard it laughed, and the man stormed out."

"Uh-oh."

"You think you see this coming, but it gets worse. I got the barmaid's attention, and asked her about the Silver Faun comment, and she told me that there was an old story about a Silver Faun that came to women in their dreams and had amazing sex with them."

"Is there now?"

"So I asked for more details, and she said it was just a story, but that her grandmother swore that she had had sex with the Silver Faun herself."

"Her grandmother."

"So I asked if her grandmother was still alive, and she is, and I told her a bit more about who I really was, and showed her Emma's face, and then I bribed her into bringing me to meet the old woman..."

"Which made the innkeeper REALLY happy..."

"He was after I bribed him, too."

"Spendthrift."

"Are you joking? There was no way I was going to let this go. So the barmaid took me to meet her grandmother, and I asked about the Silver Faun. She was reluctant to talk about him..."

"And then she told you that she had made it all up and that you were an idiot."

"...until I tapped my index finger to the middle of my forehead and said, 'I've met him.' And then she gave me a huge smile and told me that she had had sex with the Silver Faun several times when she was young, and that it was the best she had ever had, and she's been through three husbands and a couple of men on the side since."

"Really."

"She said that she didn't know a single woman her age who hadn't had sex with the Silver Faun at least once, and most had done it several times."

"That's... quite a story."

"How long was the dagger sitting on Janeth's shelf?"

"Maybe fifteen years?"

"And how thoroughly did you have your way with the women of Ironbridge during that time?"

"I guess it must have been really, REALLY thoroughly."

"It would seem so."

"I have no idea what to say."

"Are you at least slightly embarrassed?"

"More than slightly."

"That's more than I hoped for, actually. I'm amused as hell."

"You're not mad?"

"How could I be? I know what you are, and it's downright hilarious to know that I can walk up to any seventy year old woman in Ironbridge, whisper 'Silver Faun' in her ear, and see her get a dopey grin, for just a second. You're a legend. It's just... charming."

"I guess I am pretty wonderful."

"Don't get smug. You are what you are, and I know it, and this kind of thing is just part of being with you. Eventually, I'm going to get you up into the real world, and you'll have the run of every dreaming woman within whatever your hunting range is, and the Silver Faun is going to ride again. It's just part of the deal, and trying to hold you back would break your heart, so I won't."

"That's..."

"NOT DONE. If I ever hear ONE WORD to indicate that you coerced or frightened even ONE of your playmates, I will find a way to put you in a cage, and I will find a way to punish you. Do you understand?"

"Yes, your Grace."

"DO YOU UNDERSTAND?"

"Yes, Rose. I do."

"Well, then. And that leaves me deeply amused, and even more deeply frustrated. Does Master Fiddler have any music to prescribe for this rather peculiar condition?"

"I'll see what I can come up with."

==)»> 16:4: Darkness

"You're tired tonight, Rose."

"It was a long day; I spent most of four hours in the air."

"I have no reference."

"I haven't done more than about two and a half before, with longer intervals in between. This was one up, one down, one up. I overdid it. But I wanted to get outside the cluster of civilization that stretches upriver from Ironbridge."

"Because?"

"Because I blew my budget on bribes chasing the Silver Faun story, and I didn't have enough money to stay in an inn every night anyway, and I REALLY want to be far enough from the nearest dwelling that they don't stumble on me while I'm sleeping, because being awakened by people with spears who are screaming 'Monster!' at you is no fun at all."

"I can't argue with that."

"Damned Silver Faun."

"I did NOT put you up to that."

"No, but you set up the story, sort of. And you KNOW I couldn't begin to walk away from it."

"You mean you're a creature of impulse?"

"Sometimes. Don't rub it in."

"Spoilsport."

"I guess. But it was SUCH a good story."

"I exist to serve."

"I ought to bring you back there, come the day, and let you look up your old lovers."

"You won't get any revenge there, Rose."

"I don't know. The idea of you explaining your absence to a septuagenarian sounds like fun."

"You really are tired. Why wouldn't the septuagenarian want to be young again in dreamspace?"

"You're right. I am tired. That isn't funny any more. Kind of sweet, though, now that I think about it. Giving Granny a chance to fornicate until her brain melts."

"Or her heart gives out."

"Tell me you haven't."

"Of course I have. Never exactly on purpose, though."

"I don't know if that's horrible or sweet."

"Decide it was probably sweet and stop thinking about it. Please."

"That's... surprisingly good advice. Coming from you."

"Maybe. Maybe your judgment is just impaired by exhaustion."

"Maybe so. In that case, play me a lullaby and wish me good night."

"As my Lady wishes."

==)»> 16:5: Darkness

“Will I regret asking how you came by the whiskey?”

“It’s not whiskey.”

“Not green swill?”

“Gods no. Pretty much the opposite. It’s Dryad Brandy. It’s GOOD.”

“That sounds dangerous.”

“It is. You know the stories about people who wander into dryad’s groves and never come out again?”

“Yes...”

“Half a pint of this stuff a day, and permission to stay, and the dryad wouldn’t need any other magic.”

“And how much have you had?”

“Twice that. Maybe three times. I’m LOOPED.”

“ROSE!”

“It will be fine. I have defenses, after a fashion, and she doesn’t intend to keep me. She says I belong to Auntie Moss.”

“Ah. So how did this come to pass?”

“I was getting near to the end of my second hour in the air, and I was hurting because I overdid it yesterday, and I saw this oddly ordered grove of trees and decided to investigate, and maybe rest there. And Auntie Rowan saw me land, and saw my tattoos, and saw me shift from Wings to Dragon, and she invited me in."

'This would be easier if you would stop giggling."

"What would be the fun in that?"

"My inability to share your inebriation occasionally amounts to torture."

"Poor Fid. He can service more women in one night than most men get near in a lifetime, but he has to do it all sober."

"I will remind you that I have not been near ANY women in seven years."

"Oops."

"And may be losing interest in the only one who seems likely to come near in the foreseeable future."

"Aw, poor, poor Fid."

"STOP GIGGLING!"

"Aw, you're funny when you're angry."

"Until tomorrow, Rose. Or the next night. Maybe."

"Awww..."

==)»> 16:6: Darkness

"Are you sober tonight, Rose?"

"Mostly. Auntie gave me a half pint of her brandy, told me a sip or two at bed time would help with the fatigue and soreness."

"And you drank the whole bottle?"

"No, I took one moderate sip. And that was plenty, This stuff has a LOT of kick, even when you're ready for it."

"And how far have you come today?"

"Three hours worth. That puts me about nine hours out of Ironbridge, total, about halfway to the confluence with the Green River."

"How long is the whole trip?"

"Fourteen or fifteen hundred miles, about fifty hours by air. I've got a ways to go, yet."

"And you're sure you know where you're going?"

"I had enough of an idea to start with, and I have a better one since talking to Auntie Rowan."

"And her brandy."

"And her brandy. Which isn't entirely brandy, and may make you really happy, but doesn't make you stupid."

"You say."

"Auntie Rowan says. And since she told me that when I questioned the wisdom of trying to explain things to me while I was loopy, I'm inclined to believe her."

"Really."

"Don't be grumpy. You should try to talk to her. She isn't as grumpy as Auntie Moss."

"I'll consider it. She'll be a devil to find, though; she's in the shadow of Ironbridge. I had enough trouble finding YOU, and I know exactly what you look like."

"She probably looks a lot like Auntie Moss, if that helps."

"It might."

"Well, then. In the meantime, will Master Fiddler accept my apology for drunkenly tormenting him last night, and play me a lullaby?"

"He might."

"And on what would that depend?"

"I don't know. I'll take your marker."

"A small one?"

"Good enough. You're forgiven."

==)»> 16:7: Darkness

"Tired again, Rose?"

"I did four hours today. I think I'm getting used to it, and I have faith in the restorative power of the Dryad Brandy."

"That sounds dodgy. How much do you have?"

"Maybe ten doses left. Maybe less."

"Will that get you there and back?"

"It won't even get me THERE. But it will get me past adapting to heavy flying every day."

"You hope."

"It's what I have."

"Hmmm. The other day you were telling me about the shape of the journey, and never finished."

"Five more hours by air to the Green River confluence, three more to the Damnation confluence, and then one more to the Garfish confluence. Then something like twelve hours up the Garfish, past a due west stretch, and a northwest stretch, and when it turns due north, I go west for an hour or two until I get to a BIG lake. Then follow the shore line around to the left for another ten hours until I come to a bay about thirty miles long with a peninsula that runs about halfway up the middle of it. The sword is in the lake at the tip of the peninsula."

"And you got all of that from Auntie Moss, back when?"

"Enough of it. She gave me landmarks; I've been looking for confirmations and distances ever since. The bay is pretty distinctive."

"And you can keep track of all of that?"

"At 250 feet up, which isn't TOO bad a climb, I have a 20 mile horizon. And I have my Navigator."

"Which tells you what, exactly?"

"Distance and bearing to the Skytower, bearing to the North Pole, and distance to the center of the world. If I concentrate on the increments, it will scale down to inches or tiny fractions of a degree, if I want it to."

"Why the Skytower?"

"It's the way the spell was designed. It gives a unique value for every point on the planet, though, so if I kept a notebook of readings, I could make a really accurate map."

"But you don't keep the notebook."

"I keep track of important places."

"Better you than me."

"You're such a coward when it comes to numbers."

"I'm a coward generally."

"You're not, you know. You're just a worrier."

"I may resent that. I reserve the right to declare my own cowardice."

"And yet you continue to play Territories with Maelstrom. Cowards run away from their fear; they don't invite it to play table games."

"I... am going to retreat into my music while I think about that."

"As you will. Until the day, my Scorpion."

"Until the day."

==)»> 16:8: Darkness

"I thought you were going to ration that stuff."

"I was. I did. I just found a new source."

"Should I be afraid?"

"Nah. I saw what looked like a dryad's grove, stopped to look, got invited in."

"This is the beginning of a 'never seen again' story."

"It's fine. Auntie Willow was REALLY impressed that I had more than half a bottle of Auntie Rowan's brandy left after three days, so of course she invited me to try out HER brand new batch..."

"Never seen again..."

"Just stop. Dyads like me because I'm interesting and polite, but they don't want to keep me."

"So far."

"Why would they?"

"I would."

"You pretty much have. For all the good it's done you."

"It's a long term investment. Which I would prefer to not see dissolve into a puddle of Auntie Willow's brandy."

"Auntie Willow seems to think that I'm only partially soluble to bottled happiness."

"Does she."

"She does. She says that there are two things in my life that pull on me at least as strong Dryad Brandy ever could, and that the combination makes me safe."

"Two things?"

"The horizon in my eyes, and the ghost of a unicorn."

"Ah. Please tell Auntie Willow that I'm flattered, and would grace her with a deep bow if the circumstances permitted."

"I will. Bow from a unicorn, or a faun?"

"Again, as circumstances dictate, but you're needlessly pushing the hypothetical."

"Maybe, but it sounds funny when you use big words."

"You are well and truly looped. I think I will leave you with a lullaby."

"Good night, my Scorpion."

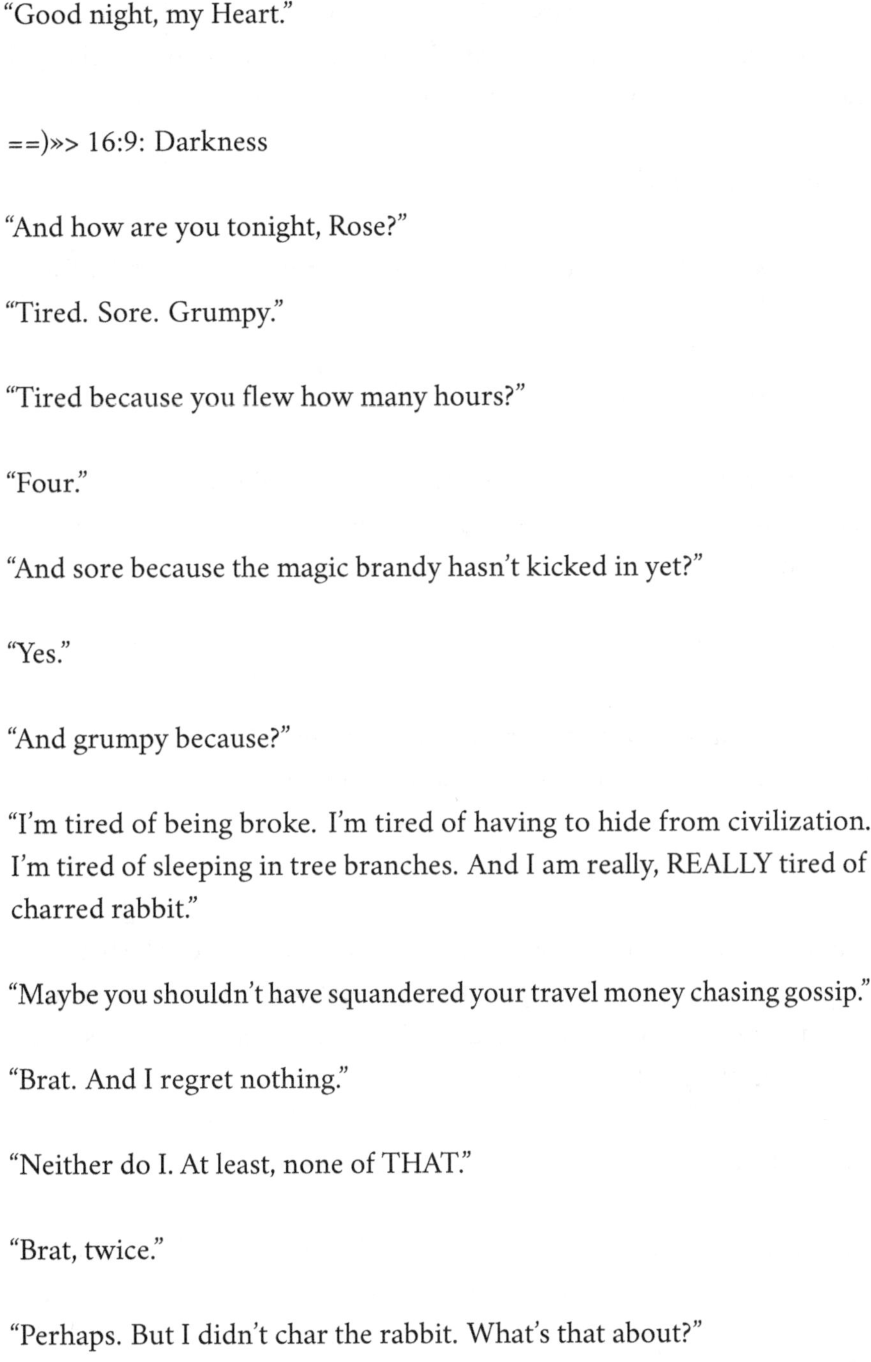

"Good night, my Heart."

==)»> 16:9: Darkness

"And how are you tonight, Rose?"

"Tired. Sore. Grumpy."

"Tired because you flew how many hours?"

"Four."

"And sore because the magic brandy hasn't kicked in yet?"

"Yes."

"And grumpy because?"

"I'm tired of being broke. I'm tired of having to hide from civilization. I'm tired of sleeping in tree branches. And I am really, REALLY tired of charred rabbit."

"Maybe you shouldn't have squandered your travel money chasing gossip."

"Brat. And I regret nothing."

"Neither do I. At least, none of THAT."

"Brat, twice."

"Perhaps. But I didn't char the rabbit. What's that about?"

"It's my staple food. Rabbits are easy to catch with a mage bolt from the air, but a mage bolt is intended to drop an adult human, so I get charred rabbit meat in the middle of a circle of burning grass, most of the time."

"Sounds delightful."

"Emma would hate it. Sister Dragon doesn't mind, fortunately. But it gets old."

"Didn't you have better fare yesterday?"

"Dryads are vegetarians, and prepare food that's really tasty to humans. I didn't have the energy to shift to Emma, and Sister Dragon was less than thrilled."

"Ah."

"But the company was good, and there was plenty of Happy Juice, so it worked out. At least until tonight, when I'm back to my usual."

"Where are you, anyway?"

"About thirty miles north of the Green River confluence. The banks of the Iron are fairly heavily populated between the Green and Damnation confluences, so I'm trying to stay as far away from the river as I can without getting lost."

"Lost is bad."

"Lost is very bad, though I'll find my way eventually. In this part of the world, every river eventually flows into Hurricane Bay."

"Eventually."

"Yeah, I really don't want to have to rely on that. If I get that lost, it'll take at least ten days to sort things out."

"Lost is very bad."

"I want this to be over at least as much... ALMOST as much as you do, Fid. Trust me on that."

"I know. What's next?"

"Tomorrow I head northeast, cross the Iron, and try to get to the Damnation confluence. The day after that, I find the Garfish, and start following that."

"So tomorrow will be the last time you worry about dodging civilization for a while?"

"Until the return trip, as far as I know. I really don't know what to expect on the shore of the big lake."

"Soon enough."

"Soon enough. And for now, would Master Fiddler be willing to play me a lullaby?"

"He would, and he will. Sleep well, Rose."

==)»> 16:10: Darkness

"You've found another dryad."

"I have."

"And I take it you've escaped the clutches of civilization, and are safely on your way up the Garfish River?"

"That, too."

"So how much longer to the sword?"

"At least a day longer than I planned on."

"What does that mean?"

"It means that I'm going to take tomorrow off. I'm NOT going to fly, I'm going to trade lies with Auntie Apple, and I'm going to sleep in something that resembles a bed two nights in a row, and I'm going to go for a swim, and I'm going to eat real food as Emma or maybe Sister Faun, and I'm not going to worry about much of anything for a day."

"Wish I was there."

"So do I, Fid, so do I."

"But that doesn't answer the question."

"Three or four days to the lake, and then three or four more to the sword."

"Once you start moving again."

"Once I start moving again."

"Until tomorrow, then. Enjoy your rest, Rose."

"Until the day, Fid."

"Until the day."

17: The Lake

The pickpocket feels righteous when chained to a murderer.
—*The Book of the Blind King's Wisdom*

==)»> 17:1: Darkness

"Good evening, Rose. How was your day of rest?"

"Great."

"And have we segued into a 'never seen again' story?"

"Not quite. Though Apple REALLY wants me to fall in love with her and stay here forever."

"Is that likely?"

"Not staying forever. I'm leaving tomorrow morning as scheduled."

"Good to know."

"Though I did promise Apple that I'd pay her a longer visit on my way back to Losthaven, and that someday I'd bring you to visit her."

"I can hardly object if I'm included."

"No, you can't."

"Did you happen to learn anything interesting along the way?"

"Several things. None that I'm inclined to talk about."

"Spoilsport."

"That's my line. And yes, if you insist."

"You're no fun at all."

"It depends on who you ask, I think. And the circumstances. And the day will come when I make you eat those words."

"I'm counting on it."

"In the meantime... Good night, my Scorpion."

"Goodnight, my heart."

==)»> 17:2: Darkness

"Good evening, Rose. I see you escaped your dryad on schedule."

"Mostly. I got a late start."

"Did you."

"But I spent four hours in the air, anyway. I think I'm at the point where the river turns and runs due west for a while."

"So you won't be getting too much farther away for a day or two."

"I suppose not. Is that an issue?"

"It seems to be. You were really hard to find, tonight. It's been getting harder every night for a while, and then it was much easier when you were with Auntie Apple..."

"Cousin Apple. 'Auntie' just seems weird for her."

"Of course it does. But you were bright and easy to locate when you were with... COUSIN... Apple, and tonight you're much dimmer than you were three nights ago.."

"I don't like the sound of that. I'm somewhat more than a thousand miles from you, now, and will be something like fifteen hundred miles out when I get to the sword."

"You're already out of range of the fiddle."

"Say what?"

"I've been playing, and you haven't heard, just now."

"Damn, Fid. That hurts."

"Get the sword and hurry back."

"I will. You know I will. But... It's easier from inside a dryad's grove?"

"Apparently."

"We'll experiment with that, the next time I find one. I'm worried we'll

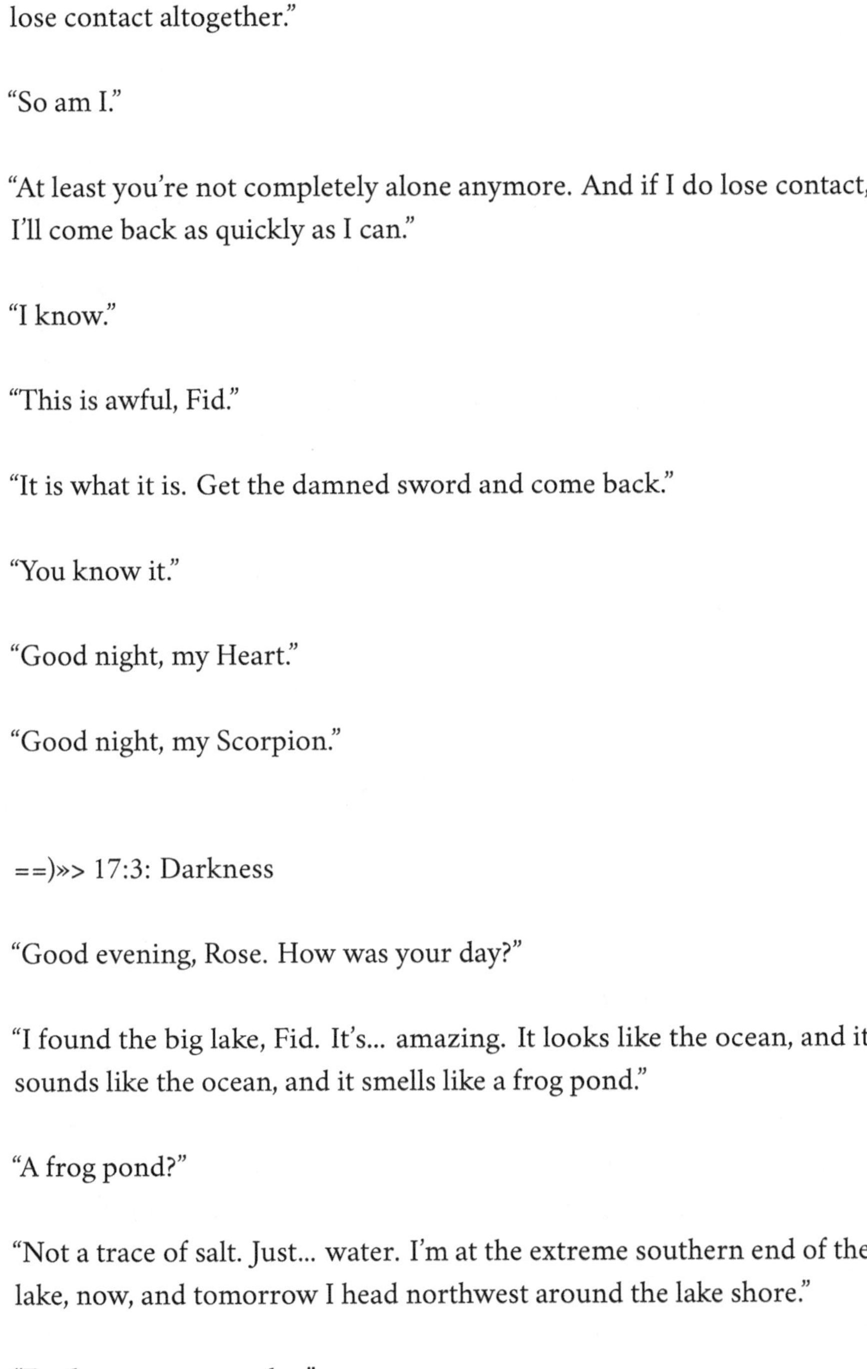

lose contact altogether."

"So am I."

"At least you're not completely alone anymore. And if I do lose contact, I'll come back as quickly as I can."

"I know."

"This is awful, Fid."

"It is what it is. Get the damned sword and come back."

"You know it."

"Good night, my Heart."

"Good night, my Scorpion."

==)»> 17:3: Darkness

"Good evening, Rose. How was your day?"

"I found the big lake, Fid. It's... amazing. It looks like the ocean, and it sounds like the ocean, and it smells like a frog pond."

"A frog pond?"

"Not a trace of salt. Just... water. I'm at the extreme southern end of the lake, now, and tomorrow I head northwest around the lake shore."

"Farther away every day."

"I know, Fid. But I'll be back soon."

"I'm counting on it."

"Look for me in the morning, will you? If we're going to lose contact, I want to have you as fresh in my mind as I can."

"Of course. When?"

"A bit before sunrise. I should start flying as soon as I have enough light."

"As her Grace wishes."

"Really? I'm getting weepy at the prospect of going a day without talking to you, and you're playing the 'Your Grace' game?"

"We deal with our pain as is our nature."

"I guess I can't argue with that. Until the day, Fid."

"Until the day, Rose. Until the day."

==)»> 17:4: Lakeshore

"Good morning, Rose. Did you sleep well?"

"Good morning, Fid. And I did, thank you. This is so strange. I feel like I'm saying goodbye to you, and yet for all we know, you will be right there tonight, just the way you always are."

"I might be. But I might not."

“But I’ll always come for you.”

“I know that, Rose.”

“Look for me every evening at the usual time.”

“I will, Rose.”

“And every morning, too.”

“I’ll see you, Rose, if you can be seen at all.”

“Sooner started, I guess...”

“I suppose.”

“Don’t run off with any mermaids.”

“Run off? Never. I reserve the right to the occasional dalliance, however.”

“Of course you do. Until the day, my Scorpion.”

“Until the day, my Heart.”

==)»> 17:5: A meadow

“What manner of creature are you?” the minotaur asked.

“I’m not at all sure I should answer that,” Rose replied. “What are you doing in my dream?”

“What are you doing on my land?”

"Hmmm." Rose said. "Would you agree to trading an answer for an answer?"

The minotaur thought for a moment. "We will try it. It might be amusing. I repeat, what manner of creature are you?"

"I was born human. I'm told that I'm turning into a dragon. I seem to be somewhere in the middle. My turn: Why do you say this is your land?"

"Because I have claimed it, and I defend it against all who enter it. Which leads back to: What are you doing on it?"

"Passing through. What are you doing in my dream?"

"Interviewing a trespasser. Where are you bound?"

Rose smiled. "Somewhere north of my current location. What are your boundaries?"

The minotaur growled. "All land within a hard day's walk of my fortress is mine. Does your destination have a name?"

"No. Where is your fortress?"

The minotaur thought for a moment. "Between the fingers of the reaching arm. Is your destination a place, or something other?"

Rose smiled again. The minotaur had some cleverness; that made the game both more fun, and more dangerous. "I seek something other than a place. Why are you so hostile?"

"You are an invader, or a thief. Why should I think you are not?"

Rose thought about that for a moment. "I don't have a good answer for that one. Could you tell me what makes you think I am invader or a thief, and then I can try to answer the charges?"

"There is only one legitimate way to approach my fortress, and everyone knows it, and you are not on it."

"Not everyone, apparently, because I didn't. What's the legitimate way?"

"How can you not know?"

"Because I haven't spoken to anyone since I left the far south edge of the big lake, some time ago."

"You have traveled more than two hundred miles without speaking to anyone? That is not possible."

"I didn't travel on foot."

"I allow no boats in my territory."

"I'm only passing through, and should be out of your lands to the north tomorrow."

"See that you are."

"I'll do my best. But out of curiousity: What's the legitimate way to approach your fortress?"

"There is a road that runs due south out of my gates. You would find it if you traveled due west from where you are now."

"I'll keep that in mind." Rose felt something push against her magical defenses. "What was that?"

"You are a sorceress."

"Perhaps. What did you try to do?"

The minotaur shrugged. "I wanted to see your human form, but you stopped me. I do not tolerate such things."

"I don't think it's up to you."

"This is MY place. I am a god here. If you will not do what I want, I will break your bones until you wish for death."

"You can't do any damage that will carry over to the real world."

"Damage? No, I can not. But pain carries over quite nicely. You will not be the first one I have broken."

"You MIGHT be able to do that. I'm not sure. But there is one thing I can do, that most people can't, that you can't do anything about."

"And what would that be?"

"I can leave."

==)»> 17:6: Cherry Dryad's grove

"Rose?"

"I'm here, Fid."

“It’s been a very long three days.”

“Two and a half. But long, in any case.”

“Where are you?”

“In a dryad’s grove on a small island in the bay with the sword, about a mile off the east side of the peninsula.”

“So you have the sword?”

“Maybe tomorrow.”

“And then you’ll head south again?”

“Oh, Fid... No, not right away. But I can talk to you from here, and I’ll head south as soon as I can. I’ve stumbled into something.”

“Is this about chasing the luck?”

“Maybe. Not particularly. There’s a minotaur that has made the peninsula into his private kingdom, and I may need to bring him down.”

“I’m not fond of minotaurs, but that seems a bit much.”

“Aunt Cherry— the local dryad— says he’s evil, and needs to be put down. She’s doing the enigmatic dryad thing, and isn’t willing to tell me the story directly; I have to find out the reasons on my own.”

“Why not just leave?”

“Because I’ve met the minotaur, and I’m willing to believe that he might need to be put down.”

"You've MET him?"

"In dreamspace. He's... unpleasant. Also pushy. If you can find me, but can't contact me, it's because I'm sleeping with shields up."

"Which is why I found you meditating tonight."

"Yeah."

"What makes you think he needs to die?"

"Besides being a bully with a lot of magic power? There are the tree girls, for starters."

"Tree girls?"

"Over the years, several of the minotaur's concubines have managed to swim to Cherry's island. Others have drowned on the way. None of them are able to swim the three miles to the far shore, and they're stuck here."

"And Cherry turns them into trees?"

"Cherry has a stasis spell that turns them into humanoid trees, because that's the only way to protect them from being pulled into dreamspace by the minotaur and tortured every night."

"That sounds fairly evil."

"I thought so. Cherry is trying to work out a way for some of the tree girls to tell me their stories without getting tortured by the minotaur again. She says that I need to hear what they have to say."

"Is there some rule that says dryads can't give straight answers?"

“Maybe... Fid, can you try to play something? To see if I can hear?”

“Of course... How was that?”

“Faint but beautiful.”

“Would her Grace like to hear a lullaby?”

“You can’t imagine how much.”

==)»> 17:7: An arena

“You are still in my territory,” said the minotaur.

“I liked the setting better yesterday,” Rose answered.

“Yesterday you were a stranger; today you are an enemy.”

“Why? You told me to leave your territory, and I did. I just didn’t get any farther away.”

The minotaur growled. “You’re with the witch.”

“I am a guest of Cherry the dryad, yes. But her island is not your territory, and you know it.”

The minotaur growled with more vehemence. “You have not left my claimed range.”

“Ah, well. You have me there. But you really don’t have a right to ask that, do you?”

A two handed battle ax appeared in the minotaur's hand. "You are an enemy and I will destroy you."

"You aren't very good at this, are you? You already know that you have no power over me, here, because I can leave before you react. So threatening me with an ax that only exists in dreamspace is just a bit pointless."

"I. Will. Destroy. You."

"Maybe. Maybe not. But if you want me to waste any more time talking to you, you need to be polite."

The ax disappeared. The arena shifted back to the previous day's meadow. "Is this polite enough? I have given you something; let me see your human face."

Rose overlaid herself with an illusion of the shape she called 'Emma'. "Is this better?"

"It is an illusion; you will not let me change your shape."

"I won't let you do ANYTHING to me; I'm not stupid. And calling something an illusion when we're both inside a magical construct at the interface of your dreaming consciousness and mine is just a bit... odd."

"You are wearing clothing."

"And you aren't.. It seemed a reasonable choice."

The minotaur growled again. "What do you WANT?"

"Something that isn't yours, which isn't in your possession, and is outside

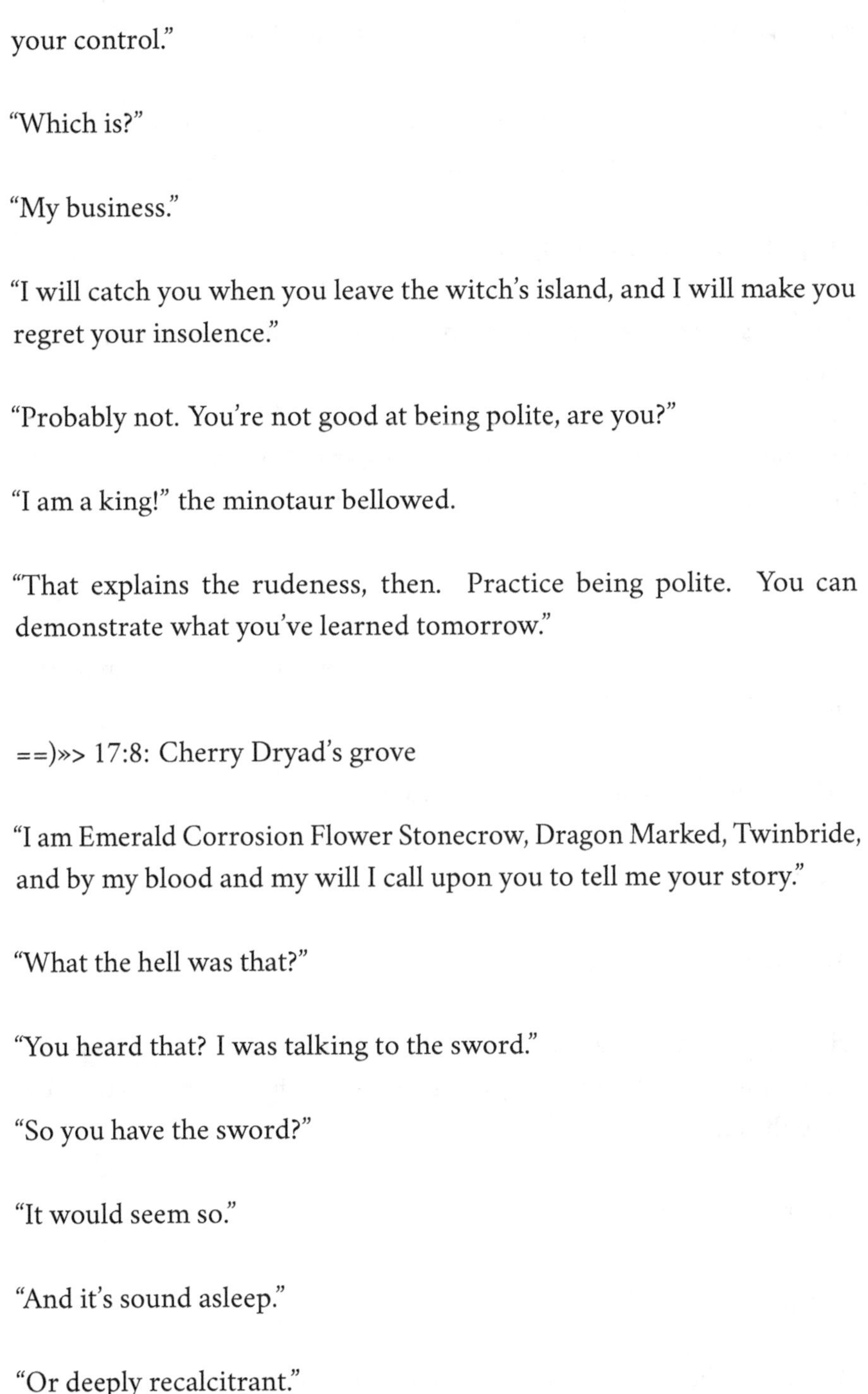

your control."

"Which is?"

"My business."

"I will catch you when you leave the witch's island, and I will make you regret your insolence."

"Probably not. You're not good at being polite, are you?"

"I am a king!" the minotaur bellowed.

"That explains the rudeness, then. Practice being polite. You can demonstrate what you've learned tomorrow."

==)»> 17:8: Cherry Dryad's grove

"I am Emerald Corrosion Flower Stonecrow, Dragon Marked, Twinbride, and by my blood and my will I call upon you to tell me your story."

"What the hell was that?"

"You heard that? I was talking to the sword."

"So you have the sword?"

"It would seem so."

"And it's sound asleep."

"Or deeply recalcitrant."

"So story. Was it hard to find? What does it look like?"

"It's a broadsword, made of what seems to be dark gray bone. It's all one material, hilt, guard and all, looking kind of like a casting."

"Shaped by magic. Probably dragon bone."

"That was my guess. It's not sharp at all, more like a wooden practice sword."

"Dragon bone swords only cut when the spirit of the sword wants them to. Kind of like unicorn daggers on that score."

"Do tell."

"It's really handy when the spirit of the blade wants to set the handler up for a really nasty cut."

"THAT sounds like the voice of experience."

"Maybe. Not saying."

"Belkith Nor."

"Fine, yes, but that was only part of it. It's pretty much impossible to sucker someone into striking a fatal blow against himself, no matter how sharp the blade is."

"Granted."

"So why am I hearing you do this?"

"Because the best way I could think of to summon the spirit of the sword was also the method I use to make my conscious mind available to a certain pushy unicorn."

"Ah."

"A state which I'm hoping still appears as 'conscious' to a certain obnoxious minotaur."

"We can hope. So... More story."

"The end of the peninsula is pretty square, and about a mile wide; there's an occupied watch tower at each of the corners."

"A watchtower?"

"The minotaur has a wall across the southern end of the peninsula, water to water, with a watchtower at either end, and a gatehouse in the middle. He has about a dozen other watchtowers around the edges of the peninsula, including the two at the end. There seems to always be an archer on top of each of them."

"And they haven't seen you?"

"They've done their best to ventilate me, but they aren't used to shooting at things overhead. By the time their arrows get to me, they're moving at half speed. I stay high and don't get too close."

"I'd tell you to be careful, but you'd just laugh."

"I AM being careful. Necessary risks, remember?"

"Trying to forget, actually. But back to finding the sword..."

"I have a spell that will show me every sword within a thousand feet, but I can't maintain it and an alternate shape at the same time. So I had to choose between being Sister Shark, and flashing the locator spell several times, or being Sister Dragon, and holding the locator spell while I swam along the shore. Dragon doesn't swim as well as Croc or Shark, and can't breathe water like Shark or hold her breath nearly as long as Croc, but, well, she does all right. "

"So you shifted back to Dragon and held the locator spell."

"Right. I hit the water a little bit southwest of the western tower, which is a bit farther into the bay, shifted to Dragon, activated the spell, and started swimming. I found the sword right away, but it was in a pretty deep hole. I tried to get to it as Dragon a couple of times, then gave up and shifted to Shark, swam to the bottom, and flashed the locator spell. Twice."

"And got the sword."

"It was NOT easy. It turns out Sister Shark likes breathing fresh water less than she likes breathing air. It feels like breathing smoke, and gives me these weird underwater quasi-coughs that HURT. So to cast the locator spell I had to exhale completely, calm myself as much as possible, and then cast the spell and find the sword. All while holding onto Sister Shark REALLY tightly, because a forced transformation to Dragon that deep might have killed me."

"Why do you tell me things like that?"

"Because you want to know."

"Not really. I mean, I want the information, but I'd be happier with the near death parts scrubbed out."

"No you wouldn't."

"Yes... No, you're right. But warn me first."

"I'll try. Would Master Fiddler be willing to play me a Fiddler's Choice while I wait for this sword to show some sign of life?"

"He would, and he will."

==)»> 17:9: An arena

"You are STILL in my territory!" the minotaur bellowed.

"Are we back to this again?" Rose answered. "Stupid unpleasant background, stupid unpleasant minotaur, and no hope of improvement. You get ONE chance to make things better before I raise my shields and get a good night's sleep."

The minotaur growled, but the area melted into a meadow. "What is it that you WANT?"

"Still none of your business. Though I would be happier if you put some clothes on."

"Show me your human form again, and I will."

"Done. Why do you care?"

"You are beautiful."

"No I'm not. Though I imagine that you find this form more interesting than the dragon girl."

"I do. Why do you care if I wear clothes?"

"Because, in order to tolerate your presence, I have to distract myself from knowing that you are, at base, a rape machine. It's easier to believe the lie when you're not naked."

"My concubines love me!"

"Do they? Even the ones who drown trying to get to Cherry's island, when they don't know how to swim?"

"The witch ensorcels them and draws them to their doom."

"Sorry, that won't play with me. I know too many dryads."

"My concubines are happy here!"

"And that's why your kingdom has thirty miles of border, and 29 of those miles are water, and yet there is not a single boat in your kingdom, and your girls are never taught to swim."

"The water is dangerous. They are protected on the shore."

"And behind the wall? The one that blocks that last mile of border that isn't water?"

"The world must be kept out."

"And the girls must be kept in."

"They. Love. Me."

"Prove it."

“Stop hiding behind the witch, and camp on the peninsula that separates my bay from the lake. I will send a squad of my daughters to hunt you down and bring you to me.”

“Did you say ‘daughters’?”

“What of it? Yes, my concubines are also my daughters, and my granddaughters, and my great-granddaughters. I am the only male ancestor most of them have had for more than a dozen generations. It is the way of my kingdom.”

“Well, THAT is a three-headed chicken.”

“What?”

“A truly strange and remarkable thing.”

“What is?”

“The way of your kingdom.”

“Your opinion does not matter.”

“It might not. It might matter very much. We’ll have to see. In the meantime... SOME of your concubines occasionally try to escape, right? They risk death by swimming to the island. Don’t they ever just go over the wall and head south?”

“No.”

“Never?”

“Never.”

"But some of them are willing to risk death by swimming to Cherry's island."

"Those who have displeased me are exiled to the small eastern peninsula. My displeasure sometimes leads them to risk the water."

"Really. And how do you express your displeasure?"

"As long as they do their assigned work, I ignore them completely."

"And THAT drives them to risk death?"

"I told you, they love me. All of them."

"And being ignored by you drives them to risk death in escaping."

"Yes."

"You know, I was told that you were really easy to hate."

"By the witch?"

"Perhaps. Whoever it was, they were right."

"I will break you."

"Perhaps. Perhaps not. But neither tonight."

==)»> 17:10: Cherry Dryad's grove

"I am Emerald Corrosion Flower Stonecrow, Dragon Marked, Twinbride, and by my blood and my will I call upon you to tell me your story... Look,

I know that you're in there, to some extent, because there's still magic in the blade, and if you were gone, the blade would be dead. I have reason to believe that you were on the bottom of the lake as a kind of suicide attempt, which had no real hope of succeeding. I want to know your story; I want to know why you and your three friends did what you did. So I'm going to continue doing the 'blood and will' thing twice a day, every day, until either you talk to me, or I get fed up with having baby cuts on my forearms, and believe me, THAT is going to take a long time. But I promise you that if you tell me your story, and if I can't change your mind about killing yourself, I will put you back into the lake, only this time it will be so far from shore that no one will ever find you again. So I have things to do this morning, and I'm just going to leave you to think about that, and we'll try again this evening... Oh, and after you cut through all of the formal titles, my friends call me Rose, and I would really like to be your friend. So think about it."

18: Minotaur

The smarter an animal is, the easier it is to domesticate.
—*The Book of the Blind King's Wisdom*

==)»> 18:1: Cherry Dryad's grove

"Hello, Sword. This is Rose, blood and will, you know the song. I'm sitting in a grove of trees that belongs to a very nice dryad named Cherry, and I'm in a contemplative trance that makes me more open to communication with non-corporeal beings. I'm holding you, the sword, with hands that have been smeared with my own blood, because that seems to be the way this is done, and I would REALLY like to talk to you. Before very long my friend Fiddler, who is a ghost bound to an object that is very far away, and I are going to talk for a while. You're welcome to listen, but I would love to have you join in, because I REALLY want to hear your story. And as I said this morning, I'm willing to put you back on the bottom of the lake if that is what you want. But you need to tell me that."

"Good evening, Rose. Still sword watching?"

"Yes. I wish I knew if there was enough left of her to understand me."

"If you could arrange for my dagger to make contact with the sword, I could probably find out in short order."

"Oh?"

"I can pull ghosts into dreamspace, if they're close enough."

"Interesting. We may try that route, someday, if nothing else works in the meantime."

"Other than that, how was your day?"

"Busy. Tiring. I did FIVE flights, since I knew I had a safe place to sleep, and I explored the peninsula pretty thoroughly from a hundred yards up.."

"How did THAT go?"

"Learned a lot. Saw the minotaur in person, almost got killed..."

"ROSE!"

"Remember how you told me that when a minotaur bellowed, humans froze?"

"Yes?"

"I didn't."

"Didn't freeze, or didn't remember?"

"Either. Both. It was a near thing, though. One of his watchtowers is as close to Cherry's island as you can get, and he must have gotten word that I was in the air. He was in that tower with several of his women when I flew by after my third flight, and he bellowed at me. I fought it off. It came close to freezing me, and came REALLY close to making me lose Sister Wings, but I stayed in control. Which was good, because if I had lost my wings I was too low to get them back again before the splat."

"If I had a heart, it would seize."

"You don't even have a metaphorical heart."

"I do too, and it's in the custody of a suicidal maniac."

"I am NOT suicidal, and only occasionally maniacal. Anyway... The bellow messed up his archers, too, so I didn't get punctured while I was remembering how to fly."

"Remembering how to... This just gets better and better."

"But the good news is that I have heard the bellow, now. I have an idea of what it does to me, and I can prepare myself for it."

"That's good, I guess."

"I was heading back to the island to rest, anyway, and I got some water, and something to munch on, and I spent most of the next hour sitting on the shore of the island where King Horns could see me, making obscene gestures."

"I'm not sure if that's charming or stupid. Probably both."

"He bellowed at me several more times, which was apparently really hard on his archers, but I sort of got used to it. I still cringe whenever he does it, but I think that in a fight, the act of inhaling deeply and actually doing the bellow would be more of a handicap than my cringe."

"You're thinking of trying to fight him?"

“It’s a possibility. But only if I think the odds are heavily in my favor.”

“You couldn’t just seduce him as Emma and stab him in his sleep?”

“I think that if he ever came near physical Emma, as opposed to illusion Emma, he would own her. His magic is tuned to mammals, which is why it doesn’t work too well on me.”

“And I seem to recall that Emma was a mammal.”

“Yes. But I still haven’t decided to try to put him down, yet. I don’t LIKE him, but that doesn’t carry a death sentence. Cherry says that I’ll change my mind.”

“So, other than terrifying minotaur encounters, what did you actually learn?”

“The peninsula is a farming community. They have horses and cows and pigs and sheep and goats and chickens. They have grain fields and pastures and orchards. They have lots of timber, and they seem to be harvesting THAT carefully.”

“The minotaur is a FARMER?”

“It would seem so. I saw several hundred people working the fields, all of them women. There’s a smithy and a windmill and something I think was a sawmill. The one thing I didn’t see was any houses. The buildings are in clusters every mile or so, up and down the peninsula, and every one of them has a big building that seems to be a barracks or a dormitory.”

“The minotaur is a farmer.”

“The minotaur is the center of a stable, sensible community that has been rolling along smoothly for more than a hundred years. Do you know how rare that is?"

"Pretty rare. Not unheard of."

"I don't like him AT ALL, but on the face of things, he's a good king. I know Cherry says he needs to die, but so far I don't see it."

"Do you trust Cherry?"

"She's a dryad that I've known for three days. She has her own agenda. But I have no reason to believe she would lie to me."

"So you keep asking questions."

"Which is actually the task Cherry set in front of me."

"It is, isn't it? What next?"

"Tomorrow, I go south and talk to a sorcerer Cherry writes letters to."

"Say what?"

"He has a hawk familiar, and they write letters to each other. He has minotaur stories that Cherry thinks I should hear."

"How far is it?"

"About thirty miles, just outside the minotaur's claimed territory. There's a town at the end of the minotaur's road called 'Threshold' that's the official access point to the minotaur's lands. The sorcerer lives there."

"Should be interesting."

“Should be. And not as tiring as today was. But for now... Might I have a lullaby, good Fiddler?”

“As her Grace wishes.”

==)»> 18:2: A meadow

“What do you WANT?” the minotaur growled.

“I want something to happen that has nothing to do with you, and that I have to wait for,” Rose answered.

“Why were you spying on my lands?”

“I wasn’t SPYING, I was sight-seeing. It seems we’re going to be neighbors for a little while, and I thought I would look around. Spying implies hostile intent, and I have none.”

“So you say. But you did not stop even when your life was in danger.”

“My life was never in danger. I have no intention of getting close enough that I can’t dodge an arrow. You should tell your ladies not to waste their time. You should also be proud of your community; it’s beautiful.”

“It’s... You like it?”

“It’s well laid out, and well maintained, and your workers seem to be happy. At least I didn’t see a trace of any overseers with whips, so I got that impression.”

“I... you... Thank you. I try very hard to take care of my people.”

"Are they all your daughters?"

"The ones in the fields are. Those who are not are less domesticated, and more fragile, and are kept... contained."

"Where do the others come from?"

"Sometimes women run from intolerable homes. Sometimes I am allowed to buy female criminals."

"But you do trade with the outside world?"

"Yes."

"What do you trade?"

"They bring me iron and gold, and sometimes food. Sometimes they bring me interesting weapons to study and duplicate and improve upon. I give them blades and some leather goods."

"You manufacture weapons?"

"My goal is to be acknowledged as the finest smith in the world. I have yet to see a blade that I have not be able to reproduce and improve upon."

"That's quite a claim."

"It is the truth."

"I have no reason to doubt you, but I've never seen your work."

The minotaur did something with his mouth that might have been a smile. "Come to the front gate; I will give you a tour, and perhaps a demonstration."

Rose smiled back. "I'll think about it."

"You would be welcome to stay for the rest of your life."

"I'm sure I would. I probably won't think about it very hard."

"As you wish. They are beautiful blades."

"I'm sure. And on that note, I'm off to sleep."

==)»> 18:3: Cherry Dryad's grove

"Hello, Sword. Once again, I am Rose and I call upon you, by my blood and by my will, to at least consider talking to me. And once again I have things to do today, and I don't really have very long to spend doing this right now, but I'm still going to keep doing it twice a day until..."

"Winter. My name is Winter."

"Hot damn. You're... HERE."

"I am here. And I have listened to you, and to your friend the ghost, and I have heard his music. I will consider telling you my story. But you have been polite, and I thought you should know that I was truly listening, and that you should have my name."

"That's... Thank you. I'm very grateful. I've traveled over a thousand miles to find you, and am glad that you are... I'm very pleased to meet you, Winter, and I repeat, I'll return you to your retreat, if you'll let me try to understand."

"We shall see. For now, I know that you have somewhere to be, and I have been quiet for a very long time, and I have never been full of conversation. I will continue to listen."

"And you're welcome to. Until tonight, Lady Winter."

"Until tonight, Rose Dragon-marked."

==)»> Four: Cherry Dryad's grove

"Winter, I don't know if you can hear me, but I thought I would hold the sword and get into a trance for a little bit WITHOUT cutting myself first, just to see if you can still hear me, because while I don't MIND cutting myself to open the link, I would really rather not if it isn't necessary..."

"I can hear you, Rose. There is more than enough of your blood on the blade."

"Thank you for answering so quickly. Fiddler should be here soon, and I have a lot to tell him, and you're welcome to listen, if you would like. And I know he would love to hear from you, if you can hear him without the blood, and I would like to know if you can... Why do I always babble like an idiot when I talk to you?"

"I do not know that, Rose. Perhaps you are not sure I am listening. If you are holding the sword, I am."

"That's good to know. I've wondered... Do you think of the sword as your body, or is it only an anchor?"

"I am the sword, and the sword is me."

"Also good to know. Do you mind if I keep asking questions, or would you rather I were quiet?"

"I will speak in my own time, Rose. I am used to the silence. But I enjoy hearing your conversations with Fiddler."

"As you wish."

"Why do I think I just missed something?" Fiddler asked.

"You didn't JUST miss it," Rose answered. "Winter, the Lady of the Sword, introduced herself this morning. I believe she's still listening, and will introduce herself to you if you behave yourself."

"That's an excessively high premium."

"As it may be."

"How was Threshold?"

"Educational. I flew past it and entered the town on foot from the south, so that no one would think I was coming from minotaur country, and Cherry's friend Badger met me on the south edge of town, and brought me back to his house for a LONG conversation. And I delivered two bottles of Cherry's Dryad Brandy that she had promised him."

"So the conversation consisted mostly of giggling fits."

"No, I told him that the stuff would knock him off his feet, and that he should approach it VERY cautiously, and for the most part we made do with water."

"My Rose has an iron will."

"When she needs to. He'd managed to borrow a sword that the minotaur had made, just to show me, and it was... amazing. He might actually have a shot at being the best smith ever."

"That's quite a claim."

"It was quite a sword. I've never seen a piece of jewelry that was better finished, and it was beautifully balanced, and felt like it was alive in my hand. It's edge was barely a rumor. I had no way to test how well it would hold an edge, but other than that..."

"You might want to be careful giving another blade too much praise when you're talking to a different one, and you have a third blade in your lap."

"Jealous, Fid?"

"Perhaps. And I feel an obligation of kinship to defend the Lady Winter."

"I think that she can speak for herself, and that she knows I mean her no slight. After all, she's not the work of a forge, any more than your dagger is."

"Hmm. Nicely recovered."

"I've been practicing."

"Don't I know it. Continuing..."

"Badger is fascinated by the minotaur, and collects stories about him. So... First of all the minotaur seems to have told the truth about escape attempts; Badger hasn't heard a single story of a woman who left the minotaur. Not one."

"And there are hundreds of women there, who have been raised there, cradle to grave."

"Yes."

"And NONE of them has ever gone over the wall?"

"None."

"That's... If you tell a hundred humans, 'Step through this door, or you'll die,' three of them will refuse."

"Yes."

"You REALLY need to talk to some of the tree girls."

"Yep. Other than that, though... It seems that the minotaur actually marked his border several decades ago. A group of women brought out stone markers and set them at about 100 yard intervals over more than 100 miles."

"That's a lot of stones."

"It took them several months. But it's been marked, and a couple of dozen of heavily armed women walk the line every spring and every fall. People are allowed to cross the line to cut timber, and even plow and harvest crops. Any buildings built on the wrong side of the line are destroyed by the minotaur's patrols, and anyone who actually SLEEPS on the wrong side of the line is dealt with by the minotaur personally."

"In dreamspace."

"In dreamspace. Women are treated to the best dreamspace sex he can give them, and then invited to come to the gates and join the community, and men..."

"...are raped and tortured until they regain consciousness."

"It's worse than that. First, they are turned into women and treated to the best dreamspace sex he can give them, and THEN they are raped as men as violently as a minotaur who is something like twelve feet tall can manage— the real minotaur is something like eight feet tall, by the way, which is scary enough— and THEN he tortures them until they start to gibber. Many men never recover. Badger says he doesn't know of anyone who's ever been willing to spend a second night on the wrong side of the line."

"I'm horrified, and ashamed to be a practitioner of...SOME of the same arts, and really, REALLY curious as to why his victims don't wake up before they break that thoroughly."

"I was wondering about that, too. Also about the pleasant sexual prelude. That seems strange."

"It does. Though with most men, even if the initial experience is pleasant, the... echoes are toxic. That's pretty much what I did to Kellarth, and it killed him."

"But Kellarth didn't object when it was actually happening, did he? It was only when he was awake, and dealing with his memories, that it destroyed him."

"Yes. At least I think so."

"How did you find me, three years ago?"

"What?"

"The very first thought you sent me, three years ago, was my name. How did you find me? How did you know it was me?"

"You were a new light; I had been aware of Drellan, though I didn't know his name, and you popped up next to him, and I recognized you."

"HOW did you recognize me?"

"Well, I KNEW you. From before, on the 'Sufferance'."

"And because you knew me, you were able to find me even in the middle of all the other sorcerers in Skytower and Ironbridge."

"Yes..."

"Is it easier to influence people if you know them better?"

"Maybe. I've never really thought about it. When I was alive, I always had plenty of strength to do whatever I wanted to do, and after that, I was able to draw enough strength from my partner to do whatever I wanted to do."

"But you never really TRIED to torture anyone."

"Except Belkith Nor."

"And he had a personal power of near zero when you attacked him."

"Yes. What are you thinking about?"

"Have you ever seen a spider kill a fly?"

"Can't say I have."

"The fly gets caught in the web, and then the spider bites it once, which stuns the fly, and then the spider binds the fly really thoroughly, and THEN the spider eats."

"Catch, then bind, then torture. So the pleasant part of the ritual is the binding."

"Right. Even though being a woman tends to unhinge most men, anyway."

"Evil doesn't really do your friend the minotaur justice, does it?"

"I'm thinking not."

"So you're really going to try to kill him, aren't you?"

"Not yet."

"Have you suddenly become sane?"

"No... Fid, it's a three stage question. First, does he deserve to die? Second, should I be the one to kill him? Third, CAN I kill him? We're still dealing with Question One at the moment."

"I thought you had settled that."

"No. I mean, he's evil, and I hate him, but... He's built a stable community, and his subjects seem to be happy, mostly. He may not have had any right to the territory he claims when he claimed it, but he's held it for many generations, and it's his, now. He defends it brutally, but his actions are only defensive. I don't see anything in that list that warrants a death sentence."

“So where does that leave you?”

“It leaves me waiting to talk to a tree girl or two.”

“And if they add nothing of significance to the soup?”

“I thank Cherry for her hospitality, tell her I’m not the solution to the minotaur, and head for home.”

“But you don’t think that’s going to happen.”

“No, I don’t.”

“Because?”

“Because Cherry has already talked to the tree girls, and knows things that I don’t, and is convinced that I’m going to kill the minotaur for her.”

“That’s a disturbingly strong argument.”

“It is, isn’t it? I think that that is enough, for now, though. I am going to break this trance, have a shot of Dryad Brandy, endure another session with King Horns, and eventually get some real sleep. Though I really look forward to being able to sleep without shielding myself from the minotaur, one of these days.”

“Would her Grace care for a lullaby first?”

“Her Grace would LOVE a lullaby, Master Scorpion.”

==)»> 18:5: A meadow

"You are still here," said the minotaur.

"I'm still waiting. I would prefer to be elsewhere."

"Perhaps I should build some boats, and come after you."

"That wouldn't be wise. Your ladies don't swim, and water is my element."

"But you fly."

"Water is one of my elements, then. Many things can go wrong across a mile of open water."

"I would not know. That is why I stay away from it."

"Indeed. Tell me, how do your ladies earn your displeasure?"

"What?"

"You said that some of you ladies earned your displeasure, and you exiled them to the eastern peninsula."

"It is none of your business."

"True, but I'm curious, and you insist on questioning me, so I thought I'd ask."

"The community has certain expectations of each of its members. Those who are unable to meet them are, as you say, exiled."

"What obligations?"

“Things that have nothing to do with you.”

“Fair enough. How did you come to be here, then? What made you decide to make this community?”

“I grew tired of being hunted, and put thought into finding a better way. I started to approach farmers and herdsmen and smiths in dreamspace, and I asked them questions, and they taught me things.”

“But you didn’t leave the women alone, and you still got chased and hunted.”

“And I usually ended up killing most of my teachers, which made me sad. But they attacked me, and I had no choice.”

“And then you built a community?”

“First I built a farm of my own, and it was good, but I had to follow my nature. Women came to me, and men followed the women, and then I had to run, again.”

“And THEN you built a community.”

“I tried to take over a small town with a wall, but the word spread to other towns before I was ready, and they destroyed my work, and nearly killed me. And I realized that I needed a place where I could defend ALL of my land, and then I found this place, which gave me sixteen square miles of land behind a wall only one mile long.”

“That’s efficient.”

“I lured women to me, and I built, and we all worked, and the community grew, and now it has been stable for more than a century, and I have been able to concentrate on becoming a bladesmith."

"And you've stopped luring in outside women?"

"I take no women from Threshold. I visit women from other communities, in dreams, but I seldom find one worthy of being called as part of my family. Sometimes they come to me on their own, and I welcome them."

"And they adapt to the life?"

"They do not live long; the life is hard for one not bred to it."

"But their daughters adapt?"

"Their grand-daughters, at least."

"What is it that makes your lives so difficult?"

"Theirs, not mine. I do not bear a child every year."

"Every... Thank you for your civility. You've given me much to think about."

19: Winter

There is always at least one thing you fear more than death. It's wise to learn what that thing is.

—Perrin Ironhand, *Armor and Hob-nailed Boots*

==)»> 19:1: Cherry Dryad's grove

"Good morning, Winter. I don't have much to say, but I said I would check in with you every morning and evening, so here I am. As always, I'd love to hear your story, but I'm in no hurry. Though if I start heading back to my home in the south, it will be a lot harder to return you to your place in the lake."

"Good morning, Rose. May I ask you some questions?"

"You can ask. I'll give honest answers, but not necessarily meaningful ones."

"You are very fond of word games."

"I am. And talking to Fiddler encourages me."

"Why does he call you, 'Your Grace?' Are you a noble?"

"It's a joke. I've spent a lot of time with kobolds, and because I speak their language better than they do, and because I'm not one of them, they often call me, 'Duchess.' Fiddler pushes that a bit to address me as, 'Your Grace.'"

"And why do you call him, 'Scorpion?' He is not really some kind of monster, is he?"

"He's not a scorpion, anyway. It's another joke, but a darker one. It's a way of reminding him that, as much as I care about him, I have no illusions as to what he is."

"I don't understand."

"Do you know the story of the scorpion and the frog?"

"No."

"Ah. It goes like this: Once there was a scorpion that wanted to cross a river, and he asked a frog to carry him across on its back. The frog refused, saying that it was just an excuse to get the frog within reach of the scorpion's stinger. The scorpion insisted that the frog was being foolish, because if he stung the frog, they would BOTH die in the river. The frog thought about it, and agreed. Halfway across the river, the scorpion stung the frog anyway. The frog shouted out, 'Why?' and the scorpion replied, 'It is my nature. You knew what I was before you agreed to help me.'"

"That is an awful story."

"It is, isn't it?"

"But you say it to him with affection."

"That's because he's MY scorpion."

"I still do not understand."

"Fiddler is a unicorn. He's dead, and his spirit is bound to a dagger that was made from his horn. He's limited by being dead, and he's trying very hard to be as good a person as he can, but he is still, at base, a monster, and he still deals with the compulsions of his nature. So the name recognizes that I know all of that, and still have affection for him, but also reminds him that he needs to be on his best behavior all the time."

"That is a very complex word game."

"It is that."

"Does the dagger belong to you?"

"No. I hope it will, some day. But at the moment it belongs to no one except Fiddler."

"And he is not content with that?"

"Fiddler would very much rather the dagger belonged to me."

"But you are not sure?"

"Fiddler will gain powers when he is bound to me that I want him to have, and the binding will give ME powers that I wouldn't mind having, but the idea of OWNING him makes me nervous."

"Why?"

"Because he's a PERSON, and there's a wrongness to that."

"Even when he desires it, and will be made stronger thereby?"

"Even when there are, for him, no drawbacks at all."

"That is a paradox."

"It is, isn't it? When I was young, my sister and her friends used to go out of their way to hear love stories, and they dragged me with them. And I realized that it really is a fine and noble thing to lay your heart on the table in front of another person and say, 'I belong to you, body and soul.' But I also realized something that my sister and her friends missed: If you are standing on the other side of the table, and you pick that heart up and say, 'Yes', THAT is an act of pure evil."

"That is very much a paradox."

"Maybe. But it's also true."

"I don't understand."

"There are problems with being owned; you lose freedom of action. But you also gain freedom from responsibility, and that's no small thing. There are advantages to owning, too, but doing so extracts a price against your soul."

"Will you refuse to pay that price, if you have the opportunity to bind Fiddler?"

"No. I'll pay it, however reluctantly."

"Why?"

"Because it's best for him, and it's what he wants, and that's more important to me than what I want. No, that's not right. My desire to see him happy exceeds my desire to be happy. And in this case, well, I'll be pretty happy most of the time, anyway."

"Thank you for answering, Rose. We will talk more in the evening."

"Good day, Winter."

==)»> 19:2: Cherry Dryad's grove

"Good evening, Winter."

"Good evening, Rose."

"Good evening, ladies!"

"You're quick to the mark tonight, Fid. Almost as if you were waiting in ambush," Rose said.

"Maybe I was," Fiddler responded. "Since you and the Lady Winter have been starting the party without me, I thought I'd keep my eyes open and make sure I didn't miss anything."

"But you missed the morning session, " Rose said. "We talked about you."

"Should I be worried?" Fiddler asked.

"You should always be worried," Rose answered.

"Rose, I think you're making the sword giggle, " Fiddler said.

"I regret nothing," Rose replied.

"Lady Winter," Fiddler said, "I would like to apologize on behalf of my friend, who I believe was raised by fish, and has no manners at all."

"No apology is needed, Master Fiddler," Winter said. "And I believe that you are telling the story wrong."

"I have never... seldom... Oh, never mind, I'm almost certainly guilty, anyway," Fiddler said. "And thank you for speaking to me, Lady Winter, I'm pleased to make your acquaintance."

"And I, yours, Master Fiddler," Winter answered.

"And now that THAT is out of the way... I got a new magic tattoo, today," Rose said.

"Is it likely to be as hard on you as the last one was?" Fiddler asked.

"I doubt it. It probably won't even follow me from shape to shape, but we'll see," Rose said.

"And the why of it?" Fiddler asked.

"Aunt Cherry designed it. The ink contains some of my blood, and some blood, or sap, or what have you from a tree girl who's willing to talk to me. My tattoo is between my shoulder blades, and Amaranth is getting a similar one that's located so that when I sit at the base of her tree and lean against it, the tattoos will touch and form a link," Rose said.

"Amaranth?" Fiddler asked.

"The tree girl," Rose answered.

"That actually sounds kind of practical," Fiddler said. "Given that it's magic."

"The only drawback is that Cherry decided she could do a better job of the tattoo on Emma than on Dragon, so I'll have to talk to Amaranth as Emma, with the attached time constraints. Nothing is perfect," Rose said.

"Except me," Fiddler said. "Well, I used to be. When I was alive."

"Idiot," Rose said.

"You made the sword giggle again," Fiddler said.

"Someone did," Rose said.

"So tomorrow?" Fiddler asked.

"We'll try, tomorrow," Rose answered. "Auntie thinks the marks may have to heal a bit before they work."

"Then perhaps I should tell my story tonight," Winter said. "In the calm before the storm."

"Hell, yes!" Fiddler said.

"Please," Rose said.

"You seem to know something of my sisters, and of the day we parted company," Winter said. "For we were sisters, created in the same act, by the same sire. We were collectively a magical item called 'The Panoply,' even though there were four of us and we were never physically attached to each other."

"Panoply?" Fiddler asked. "Isn't that a soldier's arms and armor?"

"We were intended to be a collection of things that a wandering noble warrior needed," Winter answered. "A sword, a horse, a hound, and a hawk. And servants; we could all take human shape, as needed, at least when we were together and functional."

"So you're really more retinue than equipment," Rose said. "Interesting."

"I have heard that the sword is made of dragon bone, but I would not know; I have no memory of being anything but Winter of the Panoply. I came into being with language, and a great knowledge of swordplay, and little else. Spring, the horse, remembered more. That was part of her function."

"The horse was the source of memory?" Rose asked.

"She had the most, for one thing," Winter answered. "There were five things in the original spell: A dragon bone sword, a large red hawk, an enormous yellow wolf, a well-trained horse, and a human woman. Spring said that she had been a young widow of talent and good pedigree, but with no prospects. She entered the ritual voluntarily, in return for some payment to her family; I think that is also part of why she remembered so much of her life before. I think she even remembers the name she was born with, though I am not sure."

"She sold herself into the spell," Rose said.

"Yes," Winter answered. "She came out of the ritual with three forms: A horse, a human woman, and a centaur. She provided the humanity for the other three of us. She inherited some of the horse's knowledge of being a horse, but her humanity was utterly dominant."

"I think I'd enjoy meeting her," Fiddler said.

"Remember the rules, Scorps," Rose growled.

"Spoilsport," Fiddler answered.

"Absolutely. Winter, my apologies for my idiot friend," Rose said.

"You are both very strange," Winter said.

"Stranger than that," Rose answered. "Please, continue."

"Summer, the wolf, also had three forms: A wolf, a human woman, and a wolf-human hybrid monster that walked on two legs and terrified everyone who encountered it. She had been born a wolf, but had no memory of anything that had taken place before the ritual."

"And the hawk must have been Autumn," Rose guessed.

"She was. She only had two forms, hawk and human. Her human form was the smallest of us. Spring and I were fairly normal, though she was a bit taller than I, and Summer was bigger than most men in her human form, and bigger still as a hybrid."

"And you were either a sword or a woman," Rose said.

"Yes, I only had the two forms, but because I was an object, and immortal, I gave immortality to my sisters. I could shift the shape of the sword as it was being drawn from the scabbard, and I could shift from sword to woman wearing any clothing in my wardrobe, or none at all."

"And yet, on that last night, you all burned your clothing," Rose said.

"My sisters burned their clothing. I burned my scabbard," Winter replied.

"So that magic is lost to you?" Rose asked.

"There was no magic in the scabbard. I just needed to have a scabbard of some kind. A rag would have done," Winter answered.

"But that still leaves the question of why you chose to be exiled to the bottom of the lake," Rose said.

"We were tired of serving unworthy masters, and we were told, from the beginning that we MUST have a master, or we would lose the ability to shift shape, and become horse, hound, hawk, and sword," Winter said. "I became dormant on the lake bottom, until you awakened me. We believed that the others would lose their human memories, and become simply animals. Immortal animals, as it happens, but still animals."

"Do you think the others are still alive?" Fiddler asked.

"I am certain of it," Winter replied. "I can feel their presence, off in the distance. I think that if I were to choose a master it would summon them to me, even after all these years. That was a task that was given to me, from the beginning, if we ever found ourselves masterless."

"THAT is interesting," Rose said. "Are you likely to do that?"

"I have considered choosing YOU, Rose Dragon-marked," Winter said. "It is not something I consider lightly, and I do not know your wishes on the matter."

"I've never felt a need for horse, hound, or hawk, but a dragon bone sword is hard to resist," Rose said. "Do you think that your sisters would like to return to being part of the Panoply?"

"They would love to be sisters again, in the service of a good and just master," Winter said. "We tried so many times to find one, and failed over and over again, which is why we gave up. It is not enough to BE a good master, Rose Dragon-marked. You must make certain that you never bequeath us to one who would make us miserable."

"That does complicate things," Rose said. "But at the rate I'm going, I may end up being a full-fledged dragon, and that makes the matter of bequests a lot less urgent."

"Perhaps," Winter said.

"And I honestly don't know my own mind on the matter, yet," Rose said. "In the meantime, I think that I'd like to hear more of the history of the Panoply, if you're willing to tell it."

"I am, and I will," Winter said. "Our first master, the one for whom the Panoply was made as a gift, was a GOOD man. He would have been horrified to know that Spring had sacrificed her humanity to be part of the magic. He tried very hard to always be on the right side of things, and was always faithful to his wife, and never used any of us for sex."

"That's just WRONG," Fiddler said.

"Manners, Fid," Rose growled.

"Sorry, Winter," Fiddler said. "I've been in exile a very long time. Please continue."

Winter paused before she continued. "Our second master was the first one's son, and he was still a good man, but less than his father in at least one way: He did use the four of us for sex, and told us to not let his wife know."

"Secrets are bad," Fiddler said.

"Usually," Rose said. "Not always. And it's WINTER's story, Fid."

""Yes, your Grace," Fiddler said.

There was another pause, and then Winter said, "Our third master, the son of the second, never married. He felt no need; he had four slaves at his disposal. He even loaned us to his friends sometimes; we REALLY hated that. And then one day he staked us in a game of chance, and LOST."

"I want to think things got better, but I doubt it," Rose said.

"They did not. Over the years, we occasionally had a master who was ALMOST as good to us as the second had been, and sometimes we had masters who were worse than the third. Most were somewhere in between. But the bad ones were REALLY bad. There was one— who had gotten possession through a game of chance that was almost certainly rigged— who realized that our injuries did not carry from one form to another, and that when we shifted back, we were fully healed..."

"Don't tell me..." Rose said.

"He took to beating us all regularly, and took particular pleasure in breaking Autumn's bones," Winter said. "One day he told Summer, in human form, to take me, in sword form, to gather firewood. We went, and when we came back, she dropped the wood, and we cut off his head."

"Because compulsions based on 'never' and 'always' don't hold," Fiddler said.

"I did not know that," Winter said. "But it certainly seems to have been true. That was the first time we had to find a new master. We got a taste of what would happen if we did not choose, and we did not like it. Spring was always our leader, but as the days went by she become more submissive and indecisive; Summer become more short tempered and violent, and Autumn lived in her hawk form, and spent most of her time soaring. She followed us, and always slept near our camp, but that was all we saw of her."

"So you found a new master," Rose said.

"We did," Winter said. "I remained myself, and none of us lost the ability to shapeshift, but it was very hard. We never let it get that bad again, until the last time, and that was on purpose."

"That must have been a very hard decision," Rose said.

"It was. We talked about it whenever we were between masters, and sometimes when we had masters, too, when we had privacy. We all hated the idea of losing each other. Autumn didn't mind losing her humanity so much, otherwise; Summer did, she really liked being human. And Spring was terrified of the idea, because her humanity was so much of who she was. Summer and Autumn were intelligent animals who could assume human form, but Spring was a human who could turn into a horse. It was a big difference."

"And you?" Rose asked.

"I am a sword who can think, and I have remained as such," Winter said. "But I miss my sisters a great deal."

"But you have the right to choose a new master in their absence?" Rose asked.

"It had always been my choice, before, though we always discussed it to some extent," Winter said. "I was the one who made the offer, and we felt the bond form when the offer was accepted."

"But only when you were already masterless," Rose said.

"Yes. Our master could pass us to someone else at will, though it was the transfer of the sword, of me, that triggered the transfer," Winter said.

"Interesting," Rose said. "If it's not too much of an intrusion... What can a dragon bone sword DO?"

"You could've asked me that one, Rose," Fiddler said.

"Then feel free to answer for me, Master Fiddler," Winter said.

"Dragon bone is harder, stronger, and tougher than steel, and only weighs about a third as much. And as a sword, it probably has a volitional edge," Fiddler said.

"Volitional edge?" Rose asked.

"My edge is as sharp as I wish it to be," Winter answered. "As dull as the edge of a stick, or as sharp as an edge can be."

"As sharp," Fiddler offered, "As the sting of a perfect insult, or the dreams of a thousand bladesmiths."

"I... will remember those, Master Fiddler," Winter said. "I am a sword first and always, but I am human enough to recognize poetry when it is directed at me."

"You have an admirer, Fid," Rose said.

"I have many admirers, but most of them are more than 60 years old," Fiddler said.

"And a hundred years from now, they'll all be dead, and I'll still be harassing you about them," Rose said.

"And I'll be happy about it," Fiddler said.

"You are both very strange," said Winter.

"Thank you," said Rose.

"What she said," said Fiddler.

"Sorry, Winter," Rose said. "That was rude of us. Fiddler and I have been having these conversations every day for three years, and we're not used to having an audience."

"I understand," Winter said. "I think."

"And thank you very much for trusting us with your story," Rose said. "I have to admit that I understand why you chose to be exiled in the lake. Do you still want to go back to it?"

"I never WANTED to become dormant, Rose," Winter said. "But it seemed to be the best choice."

"And now?" Rose asked.

"And now there seem to be options, and I would like to investigate them," Winter replied.

"Good enough," Rose said. "And on that note, I suppose I should try to get some sleep, and soldier through my nightly interview with the minotaur."

"Well, then I will wish you both a good night," Winter said.

"Good night and thank you again, Winter," Rose said. "And good night to you as well, Fid."

"Good night, Winter," Fiddler said. "And thank you, once again, for finally speaking to me. And Rose... Good night, my Heart. Until the day."

"Until the day, Fid," Rose said.

==)»> 19:3: A meadow

"It would seem that you are still waiting," the minotaur said.

"You could just ignore me," Rose answered. "You seem to ignore my hostess."

"The witch blocks me. She is an irritant, and I would drive her out if I could. Much like you."

"Thank you. You are charming and your hospitality is without peer."

"WHAT DO YOU WANT?"

"Well, I'm having a fair amount of fun just irritating you, but I have a question or two I'd love to have you answer as well."

"Ask. I promise nothing."

"You said that your concubines each produce a child every year. I know a bit about minotaurs, so I know most of the children are daughters. But you must have a son every year or two. What do you do with them?"

"I seem to have a son born every two or three years. There is no real pattern to it. I raise them to survive. I teach them to fight, and to hunt, and how to stay out of sight if necessary."

"Generous of you. What do you do with them when they change, and become minotaurs?"

"I give them a choice. They can either have a sword, and a pack full of supplies that they will need in the wild, and go off to fend for themselves, or they can have the same sword, and a good suit of armor, and they can challenge me for my kingdom."

"Which do they choose?"

"Most leave. A few challenge."

"And die?"

"Of course."

"Do they ever come back?"

"They know that their exile is forever."

"But they never come back to challenge?"

"Two have. They have died as well."

"Did you accept their challenges, or just cut them down with arrows?"

"I fight them. I would not use arrows on one of my own kind."

"Interesting."

"Are you satisfied?"

"On that score. For now."

"My turn, then. Do you have any idea when you will leave?"

"The time is getting close. I'm waiting for one more thing, and I'll have it soon, I think."

"Make it at soon as possible."

"It's out of my hands, but I'll do what I can. And on that note... Once again, thanks for the information, and good night to you."

20: Amaranth

There is always something more horrible. Always.
—Feldspar Greymantle, *Thaumatology*

==)»> 20:1: Cherry Dryad's grove

"Good morning, Winter. Another busy day in front of me, leaning against a tree that used to be a person, but I wanted to check in with you, because I said I would, and I wanted to thank you again for trusting us with your story. And I wanted to tell you that, if you choose to trust me with responsibility for yourself and your sisters, I will accept."

"I was certain that you would, Rose."

"Certain? Why?"

"Because you see the need, and are the only person available, and that is who you are."

"I didn't think it was that obvious. Fiddler says that it's a good thing that I hate responsibility, because I have no ability at all to escape it once I have it."

"Fiddler is wiser than he pretends to be."

"I'll pretend you didn't say that, but you're right."

"Your conversations with Fiddler make me miss my sisters even more, though our conversations never sounded like that."

"We are, as you have said, very strange. But I'm SO grateful for his friendship."

"That is very plain."

"And on that note... Good day, Winter. Until this evening, I imagine."

""Enjoy your day, Rose."

==)»> 20:2: Cherry Dryad's grove

"Good morning, Amaranth. I don't know if you're listening, and if you are, if you're able to respond, so I'm going to yammer at you for a bit, and hope that you're willing and able to respond. My name is... My friends call me Rose, and I would like to be your friend, I think. If you really need the whole name, which is getting loaded down with titles, I guess it's Emerald Corrosion Flower Stonecrow, Dragon-marked, Twinbride. But that's kind of an overload, so Rose will do just fine."

"I hear you, Rose."

"So we have a link. That's good. Thank you for speaking to me."

"I think you have gone to some trouble for the privilege; it would seem rude to refuse."

"Did Cherry tell you why I wanted to talk to you?"

“The enchantress said that you had questions about my Master.”

“He’s still your Master even though you had to become a tree to escape him?”

“He will always be my Master.”

“Would you be willing to just tell me your story? From your first memories, until the time you came here and were transformed?”

“I will. You are thinking about killing him, are you not?”

“I... Yes, I am. I haven’t decided. I was going to lie to you, but I can’t. You would know. And I can feel that you still love him, and are loyal to him. That’s... This is an INTERESTING bond we have. Kind of frightening.”

“I will tell you my story. I still love my Master, but I understand that he may need to die. At least, I understand partially. There is much sadness.”

“That’s... Thank you. Please begin.”

“I am Amaranth Five Second, the seventh child of my mother, Amaranth Four. My older sister Amaranth Five First died of a mishap when she was young, and I was the next of my mother’s children to be born, so I was allowed to become the next Amaranth.”

“Allowed?”

“Each daughter of the Master is allowed to have only one living child, but if the child dies young, a second is allowed to grow up.”

“What happens... We’ll get to that. Do ‘Firsts’ die often?”

"Is one in twenty often? I think that it happens that way. I only know of one Third, among all of the Sisters."

"I see. Please continue."

"I was raised with the other children; we were all raised together in the Master's fortress. I have a few memories of living in the nursery when I was very young, but I spent most of my childhood living in the Children's Barracks. We were taught to take care of ourselves, how to work the fields, how to prepare food, how to make clothing, how to use the sword and spear and bow. We knew that we were blessed to be the daughters of the Master, and to be destined to become his brides."

"You were happy?"

"Yes. How could we not be?"

"You never wondered about the world outside the peninsula?"

"No. Some of the older Sisters went out to patrol the boundaries, but the outside world was frightening, and the community was safe. Everything we needed was there."

"And when did you leave the Children's Barracks?"

"On the fifteenth anniversary of my birth. The Master had started to visit my dreams as soon as I began to bleed. He told me that he loved me, and how lucky I would be to become his bride, and bear his children, and he taught me about sex, so that when the time came for me to have sex with him in the real world, I would enjoy it and not be afraid."

"And that— sex in the real world— happened on your fifteenth birthday."

"Yes."

"And how soon did you become pregnant?"

"Right away. He visited me for three nights, and then he said that I was with child, and I went off to my duties as an adult."

"So you were pregnant first, before you ever went out to an adult barracks?"

"Yes."

"And almost all of the adults around you were pregnant, too?"

"Yes."

"And you still got all of the farming done, and managed to patrol the wall, and staff the towers..."

"Yes. Most of us were at least three-quarters minotaur, so we were all strong and healthy, and everyone knew when they had become pregnant, and when their child was due, so everyone knew how much and what kind of work everyone was capable of. Everything gets done on schedule, and a new child is born every day."

"Every day. And how many of those ended up in the Children's Barracks?"

"About one a month."

"Right. Did you have any brothers?"

"Yes, there were always a few boys around. They trained with us, and if one of them challenged the Master, all of the girls who were at least nine years old, and all of the adults who were not on watch duty, would come to see the fight."

"Which the Master always won."

"Of course. He is the Master."

"Of course. Please continue. What was life like once you were an adult?"

"I wasn't an adult, yet, at that point. You are really not considered an adult until your child is born, and is old enough to move out of the nursery and into the Children's Barracks. Most of the time before your first child is born is spent learning things that can't be taught well in a classroom. And then your child is born, and for three years your life is centered around the nursery, and your daughter."

"But you still have another child every year."

"Of course."

"And once your child is in the Children's Barracks?"

"Then you are really an adult, and become part of the regular duty rotation."

"For the rest of your life?"

"No, when you daughter has HER daughter, your status changes. You are allowed to specialize in a specific task, if you wish."

"But you keep having another child every year."

"If you can. I only bore two more children after my grand-daughter was born. That was why I was exiled."

"That was why... We'll get to that. Was your own mother still alive then? Were you in contact with her?"

"Yes, she was alive to see her great-grand-daughter born, though she had already stopped producing babies by then. She had thirty-four in all; she was fifty-five when Amaranth Seven was born, which was old, because I was a Second."

"She had stopped producing babies, but wasn't exiled?"

"No, women who produce at least twenty-five children are immune to exile."

"But not you."

"No, I only produced seventeen."

"What happened then?"

"The Master came to my bed every night for ninety days before he exiled me, and I was re-assigned to the east Tower, and the Master stopped visiting my dreams."

"And how long were you there before you decided to swim to the island?"

"Almost a year."

"And what made you decide to go?"

"I just became more unhappy every day, and I finally decided that I had to try. I wanted to be DEAD, I wanted the loneliness to end, and I thought that maybe the Enchantress could help me, but maybe I would die in the attempt, and I would not mind dying."

"There are easier ways to kill yourself."

"I would not kill myself. That is cowardly, and a betrayal of the Sisterhood, and of the Master. But I wanted to be dead, and did not mind taking bad risks."

"But you lived anyway."

"If I had not done my best, that would have been a suicide. So I DID do my best, and I lived."

"And then what happened?"

"The Enchantress was good to me, and gave me food, and gave me something that she said would help me to sleep dreamlessly for my first night."

"But only one night?"

"She said that I was allowed one day to settle in, and that the potion would kill me if taken repeatedly."

"And what happened on the second night?"

"The Master came to me in my dreams, and he hurt me."

"How did he hurt you?"

"How many ways are there? He kicked me and punched me and stomped on me and stabbed me and set fire to me and broke my bones and cut bits off of me..."

"He's the god of his own dreamspace."

"And every time I thought that there simply wasn't enough left of me to hurt any more, he healed me and started in again."

"Did he ever say why?"

"I had betrayed him a second time. First by being infertile, and second by leaving my duties."

"Did you try to fight back?"

"No. He was my Master. His judgments are always just."

"Of course they are. How long did you put up with that before you decided to become a tree girl?"

"Only one night. The Enchantress came to me in the morning, and told me that it was possible to escape from the Master's wrath, and I said I would do it."

"I'm very sorry to make you relive that, Amaranth. One more question, or series of questions, and I will leave you alone."

"You are my sister, Rose. I do not understand all of your feelings, but I experience them."

"And I yours, Amaranth. I think that Aunt Cherry may have an evil streak for that. But my question... You bore... seventeen children, all told?"

"Yes."

"And you raised one daughter, Amaranth Six?"

"Yes."

"What became of the other sixteen?"

"They were given to the Master."

"And what did he do with them?"

"He ate them, of course. One every day, sometimes two. How else would he live?"

"That's..."

"What's wrong, Rose? Why does that upset you? Is it not the way of things?"

"We come from very different worlds, Amaranth. It's... Let's just get through this. Did he eat them raw, as soon as they were born?"

"No, they were usually about ten days old. Babies do not come on a schedule, so he allowed a buffer, to make sure that he always had at least one every day. And he did not eat them raw, he had them prepared in every way you can imagine. Working in the kitchen was a favorite task of the women who had stopped bearing children, and had retired in honor."

"I think that's all the questions I have for now, Amaranth. Thank you very much for your help."

"You are my sister, Rose. Please visit me again. I am lonely."

==)»> 20:3: Cherry Dryad's grove

"Good evening, Winter. I have had a very, very bad day, and I really need to talk about it, but I'm NOT going to tell this story more than once. Though if you have anything to say, I would love to hear it."

"My world is very dark and simple, Rose. I have no news, but I can tell that you are... upset. Unhappy. RATTLED."

"Rattled is a good word. Also shaken. Also pretty much shredded. I have never, in my entire life, wanted to be held as much as I do at this moment, and my best friend is something like 1500 miles away and is a DAGGER, and the only friend I have in reach is a SWORD and I kind of hate my life and the vast majority of people and things in it and... And I'm going to sit here with a sword in my lap and just generally ache for awhile until Fiddler comes looking for me, and I would be really grateful if you would just be there and be my friend in the meantime."

"You have my friendship, Rose. I deeply regret that I am currently limited to a form which is incapable of a hug."

"Thank you, Winter. That helps."

"I do have a volitional edge, Rose."

"Say what?"

"If you choose to hug the sword, I can guarantee that it will not, under any circumstances, cut you."

"Aw, damn, Winter, now I need to cry."

"I think that is probably for the best, Rose."

==)»> 20:4: Cherry Dryad's grove

"Good evening, Rose. What did I miss this time?"

"Winter bought a piece of my soul that I didn't know was for sale. Other than that, it's been awful."

"Amaranth?"

"Yes. Cherry was absolutely right. He needs to die."

"That's a leap."

"The women... His daughter-concubines, the Sisters, are completely besotted with him. They love him, they worship him, they think he can do no wrong. They have completely bought in to his weird little pocket society."

"And that carries a death sentence?"

"A couple of days ago, Horns mentioned that every one of his concubines is expected to bear a child each and every year, about 400 children a year on the average. About a dozen of those are allowed to grow into the next crop of concubines..."

"Which leaves about one a day..."

"I didn't ask, because I didn't want to make him stop talking. When the same numbers came up with Amaranth today, I didn't ask again, at least until I had a good picture of what else was going on."

"And the punchline is?"

"Dinner. He eats them, one every day, plus a second if there happens to be a surplus."

"And doesn't THAT just put dream-rape and torture and enslavement into perspective."

"Just a bit."

"So now what?"

"I have no idea. I need to see him dead, but I really don't want to die in the process."

"Talk to Badger."

"Come again?"

"I can't imagine anyone not being horrified by this news. I'm horrified, and I'm a genuine monster. So if you talk to Badger about this, he might have some helpful ideas, and if he doesn't, he can make sure someone else gets the job done if you fail."

""You're being disturbingly intelligent."

"Sorry, but your life is on the line. I promise I'll go back to being an idiot when things calm down."

"That's still disturbing. Also reasonable."

"In the meantime... What's wrong with you?"

"I'm... Part of me is in love with the minotaur."

"The one you just said you needed to see dead."

"Yeah."

"I'm lost."

"Me too, mostly. It's the damned tattoo."

"The one that lets you talk to Amaranth?"

"Yeah, that one. It's a bit more potent than that, though. For one thing, it DOES follow me in any shape I assume, so I have three, now. The key point at the moment, though, is that it doesn't just let us TALK; we get inside each other, feel each other's feelings. She started calling me 'Sister', and I can't argue with that. Amaranth was taught to love and revere the minotaur from the moment she was born, and I can FEEL that, and it feels like it's MINE, not something alien. So even though the infantophagy horrifies and sickens me, even though I have actual physical memories of being tormented in dreamspace for several hours, I have a... reflex... to love the bastard. And add to that my own revulsion at the infantophagy coupled with Amaranth's memories of having given birth to SIXTEEN babies that that bastard ATE, and PART OF ME STILL LOVES HIM."

"Gods."

"Pretty much. I'm going to sleep with my shields up tonight, though. If I meet him in dreamspace, I don't know what will happen, but it will probably get out of control."

"Sounds wise. So Badger tomorrow?"

"Probably. Unless I ... unless one of us gets a better idea."

"Understood. Lullaby?"

"Six of them. Please."

"As my Heart wishes."

==)»> 20:5: Cherry Dryad's grove

"Winter?"

"Yes, Rose?"

"Do you know what a rag doll is?"

"A children's toy?"

"Yes. I never got very attached to them; I didn't play with dolls, much. But my sister had one that she slept with every night, pretty much up until she got married."

"I... see, Rose."

"Tonight, my friend, you're my rag doll. If you don't mind."

"I am flattered, Rose. I wish I could do more."

"Me, too, though I'm very grateful for what I have."

"Thank you, Rose. And while we are talking... Are you really willing to take responsibility for my sisters and me? To become the master of the Panoply? Because I would be honored if you would take the role."

"I... That's... Yes. And I am flattered."

"And now, Rose, you will be able to face the minotaur armed with a properly bonded dragon bone sword."

"Thank you again, my friend. And you know... You're not a half bad rag doll, either."

==)»> 20:6: Cherry Dryad's grove

"Good evening, Rose. How was your day?"

"Long. Tiring. But good for all of that."

"And the story?"

"To start, last night Winter offered me the Panoply, and I accepted."

"So someday I may have a room mate, or four."

"I hadn't thought of it that way, but Yes, I suppose so. Beyond that... I was a lot saner this morning; the emotional spillover from Amaranth seems to have faded significantly."

"That sounds good."

"You have no idea. And once I got myself sorted out, I flew down to Threshold and had a talk with Badger."

"You actually took my advice. Mission accomplished?"

"With dividends. Badger wants to help me kill Horns, AND he's writing a letter explaining the situation, and he is going to have his hawk deliver copies to all of his several pen pals, so that word will spread, and people will take action if he and I fail at our assassination."

"That sounds like you have an actual plan."

"We do, but we're still refining it."

"And?"

"It starts with me disguising myself as a minotaur, and marching out of the woods on the Threshold road up to the edge of arrow range from the wall, announcing myself as one of Horns' sons, and challenging Horns to a duel for the kingdom. And then I walk back to the woods and disappear for two days."

"Just how far are these woods from the wall?"

"Horns has everything within a mile of the wall clear cut, and grazes sheep there to make sure it stays short."

"Are you sure Horns doesn't have any cavalry?"

"If I hear hoofbeats behind me, I'll shift to Sister Wings and get out FAST. It'll break the gambit, but beats being dead."

"Why two days?"

"Because I doubt that Horns will be waiting at the wall, ready to fight a duel to the death, and if I'm going to issue a challenge and leave, that would give me time to walk back to Threshold and get a good night's sleep before the duel. If I were actually doing the walk, it would require a 60 mile day, but that's possible."

"Barely."

"Barely for a human. Not really too difficult for an eight foot tall minotaur who is used to walking all day long. And I wouldn't actually be doing it, anyway."

"And you think that Horns will accept the challenge?"

"I think it's likely. He's vain, and all of the guards at the gate will hear the initial challenge, so the Sisterhood will know about it. You may be able to convince people to accept infantophagy, but you'll NEVER get them to stop gossiping."

"I can see that. So what happens after two days?"

"The fake son marches out of the woods and fights a duel with his father. And the invisible sorcerer who is following the fake son roasts Horns with a lightning bolt or two."

"While he's invisible?"

"Supposedly. But even if he loses that spell as soon as he casts the first lightning bolt, he'll be far enough away that he'll be able to get off one or two more before Horns can get at him. And I can sneeze at least one bolt of my own at him, and if Horns goes for Badger, he'll have to turn his back on me, and if he does THAT, Winter and I will hamstring him, and then Badger will be able to roast him at leisure."

"And Badger will be up for this idiocy after a 30 mile walk?"

"Badger will be relatively fresh because his pet air elemental will carry him out from Threshold to the edge of the woods."

“What about...”

“We’ll have our ears plugged in case Horns bellows.”

“That’s good, but... This is NOT a low risk plan, Rose.”

“Faint heart never won fair maiden.”

“There’s a fair maiden involved?”

“Several hundred of them. Depending on your definition of maiden. And it’s more of a metaphorical victory anyway; I’m not collecting them.”

“You should. It’s fun.”

“I have rather more than I can handle already, thank you.”

“You do, don’t you? Now I’m jealous.”

“And you’re back in idiot mode. I’ve actually missed it.”

“I try to keep in practice. And terror brings it out in me.”

“It’s not a bad plan, Fid.”

“You’re still putting your life on the line for a bunch of strangers who haven’t actually asked for your help, and probably don’t want it.”

“He EATS a baby every day, Fid.”

“Fine. Just... be careful. Do you have any idea what to do with the Sisterhood once Horns is dead?”

"Just guilt."

"Guilt?"

"I'm going to destroy their society, Fid, and if I try to help them fix it, which I have no real ability to do, I'll get tangled up for YEARS. Do you want that?"

"Hell no."

"So guilt. Badger has some ideas, and will offer help. And honestly... Several hundred very large, hard-working women who have significant farming skills AND have been trained to fight with sword, shield, spear, and bow should be able to figure out how to survive."

"Should. If they find a leader, they might turn into a rampaging army."

"Might. I won't be here. I still have a dagger to bring up from the bottom of the ocean."

"Oh, yeah. That. I wondered when you were going to remember that...

"Can't forget that, Fid. Ever. Or at least not until the dagger is in my hand."

"Good to know. Would her Grace care for a lullaby?"

"Her Grace would like that very much, Fid."

"As my Heart wishes."

21: The Best Bad Plan

The Executioner doesn't wear a hood to hide his identity; he wears a hood to signify that he is acting as the hand of the people.
—Perrin Ironhand, *Armor and Hob-nailed Boots*

==)»> 21:1: Cherry Dryad's grove

"You should make me a scabbard, Rose."

"Winter? You've been quiet lately."

"I have had little to say. But I listen, and I watch."

"You can hear? You can SEE?"

"I have a master, now, Rose. My abilities are coming back to me."

"Really? Would you lay that out for me?"

"Of course, Rose. I am yours, remember?"

"Oh. I'm still not at ease with that. But, please."

"When you found me, I was truly dormant. If you had not been a sorceress, if you had not addressed me with blood and magic, I am not sure I would have heard you."

"Nice to know that the ladder marks on my arm served a purpose."

"Once I had heard you, though, all you needed to do was touch the sword with bare skin."

"Or scales."

"Or scales, it would seem. I could hear and speak to anyone who touched the sword. But now that I have a master, now that the Panoply is being called back together, I can hear the world around me, and see it to some extent."

"Hearing makes sense. What do you see?"

"I sense objects, and beings. Things that move are easiest, and complex things, or stationary things that touch each other, are hard to differentiate. It is like being underwater in dim light; there is no color, or texture, only shape."

"So you can hear me talk to Cherry."

"Yes."

"And you can hear me talk to Fiddler from a trance if I'm holding you."

"Yes."

"Interesting. We'll have to experiment a bit, if things ever calm down."

"As you wish."

"So what were you telling me about a scabbard?"

"I believe that I have regained my ability to shape the blade, and a scabbard. So if you make me a scabbard, even a shoddy one, and concentrate on your ideal sword, and then draw me forth, I can become that sword. And transform the scabbard into something that fits in the process."

"What does the scabbard need to be?"

"A piece of cloth or leather large enough to enclose the blade. Clean is better, and in good condition is better."

"Intriguing. I'll see what Cherry has around here. I've been depending on illusory clothing, mostly, and Cherry might as well. But I can certainly get something from Badger, and I'll be seeing him at least once more before the assassination."

"You mean the duel."

"The execution. But you're right, Horns needs to think of it as a duel. And it might still go horribly wrong."

"You are my master, Rose, and you will go into the battle with me at your side. No one has ever lost a battle as my master."

"That's... really comforting, Winter. Thank you. Though the past never guarantees the future."

"It is the right path, Rose."

"I hope so. Are you sure you wouldn't rather that I just packed up and headed south?"

"If you did that, Rose, I would regret choosing you as our master. But we both know that you won't."

"One of us does. But thank you for your confidence."

"I am a sword, Rose. I miss my sisters, and I know that there is more to the world than a strong hand and a noble cause, but really, there does not need to be."

"Not going to try to answer that, Winter. Thank you."

==)»> 21:2: Cherry Dryad's grove

"Hello, Rose. How was Threshold?"

"As expected, Winter. I had a couple of new wrinkles for the plan, Badger had a few new wrinkles, and tomorrow I'm going to issue the challenge."

"It is right, Rose."

"Gods, I hope so."

"Did you do any shopping?"

"That's amazingly subtle. Yes, I've come back with a spool of silk ribbon that should do the job."

"Ribbon?"

"I'm a sailor first and always, Winter. Ribbon is the child of fabric and rope, and I KNOW rope. Watch and learn."

"As you wish."

"And... What do you think?"

"I should not have doubted you."

"I was born a wharf rat. It's in my blood. Now what?"

""Just convince yourself that the sword already has the shape you wish it to have, and draw it forth."

"Damn, that's sweet. Using other people's magic is fun."

"I am glad you approve."

"Care to do some sword drills?"

"As you wish."

==)»> 21:3: Cherry Dryad's grove

"Hello, Amaranth."

"Hello, Rose."

"I have something for you to think about."

"Yes?"

"What do you want to do if the minotaur— your master— is dead? Do you want to go back to sleep, and just be a tree? Do you want to regain your humanity, and try to rejoin the sisterhood? Do you want to regain your humanity, and try to make your way in the rest of the world?"

"I do not know, Rose."

"You don't have to decide right now, but you need to think about it, because the minotaur might be dead three days from now, and you'll need to have an answer."

"I understand, Rose. I will give it much thought."

"Good. And Amaranth... If you choose humanity, and wish to travel with me, that would be fine."

"Thank you, Rose. I will remember that."

==)»> 21:4: Cherry Dryad's grove

"Good evening, Rose."

"Good evening, Fid."

"You seem... oddly happy. Exhilarated."

"You give a girl a sweet custom sword to play with, and she begins to have aspirations to feats of heroism."

"I can parse that as far as involving the Lady Winter."

"Winter has been demonstrating her ability to shift her shape, and I have then been doing a few sword drills with the best sword I have ever held. She gives me delusions of being a first rate duelist."

"You might BE a first rate duelist as long as you have Winter in your hand."

"That would be nice. I could use it."

"So you're going ahead with the challenge?"

"We haven't had a better idea."

"Running away still works."

"Were you really this much of a coward when you were alive?"

"Of course not. But I wasn't utterly dependent on the well-being of someone who was emotionally irreplaceable, either."

"Aww."

"Damn it, Rose, I'm serious."

"So am I, Fid. Winter has called this one. Can you honestly tell me that you think I could walk away from this fight, and still be myself?"

"No."

"So we go with the best bad option on the table, and that means a staged duel with an assassination."

"Fine. But why are you on point? You can throw lightning from the sidelines."

"Badger has never studied the sword AT ALL, and he can throw lighting twice as hard and three times as fast."

"Fine. So just what is the best bad plan?"

"I show up at the edge of the woods on the Threshold road tomorrow at dawn, walk three quarters of the way across the cleared space, shout out my challenge. Then I stand the spear that I have with me for the purpose in the ground, walk back to the edge of the woods, and come back here. Horns sends someone out to recover the spear, reads the details described in the letter tied to the spear, and two days later we meet on the road in the middle of the cleared space."

"And you kill him."

"Or he kills us, but yes."

"The letter on the spear is a nice touch. It lets you deal with all sorts of details that would be boring to shout."

"Badger suggested the letter, I came up with the spear."

"So what are you going to do with the time between the challenge and the fight?"

"I'm going to practice with my new sword, and I'm going to start building a boat."

"A boat?"

"Any of the tree girls who decide to return to humanity will need a way off the island."

"You have time to build a boat? To say nothing of tools..."

"Between my magic to weld the wooden seams, and Cherry's ability to grow any plank I want on demand, we don't really need tools, or much time. All we really need is someone who understands how to make a boat."

"Which you do."

"Which I do. You know, I have this intense desire to practice sword drills beside your waterfall while you provide accompaniment."

"That's a good desire, but I have a few others that would come first."

"Those, too."

"In the meantime, would her Grace care for a lullaby?"

"Her Grace would be deeply grateful, Master Scorpion."

==)»> 21:5: Cherry Dryad's grove

"Hello, Amaranth."

"Hello, Rose."

"I hope you don't mind some company. I'm taking a break from boat building, and, well, I wanted to just experience this strange bond we have a bit more while I still can."

"While you still can?"

"I fight the minotaur in two days, and after that, if I'm still alive, I'm going to go back south and get on with my life. I may never come back here, so that will probably be the end of this bond of ours. And if you leave the tree, even if you come with me, that will probably be the end of it, too. The link is built to allow communications between a human and a tree spirit, and likely won't work between two humans."

"I had not thought of that, Rose. I will miss this bond. It... makes me happy. I have not felt much of anything since I have been a tree. But I enjoy being your sister, even though you confuse and frighten me."

"Are we really that different?"

"You know it, Rose. You can feel it. How far have you traveled in your life? How far are you from home?"

"I think I'm about fifteen hundred miles from the place I was born, though I'm not sure that's my home. And I imagine I've traveled ten thousand miles, so far. Though that's a really loose number."

"And I have lived my entire life in the same fifteen square mile kingdom. I have never been past the gates. The world you live in is HUGE, and it terrifies me."

"It's not so bad, Amaranth... Is that the only name you have? 'Amaranth' seems a bit long for daily use."

"They called me 'Amma', most of the time."

"That's easier. I was going to say that I would have gone insane in your world, but I don't know that; I wasn't raised there. I do know that none of the girls I grew up with had anything like my hunger to chase the horizon. My sister and her friends wanted to fall in love and have babies, and I wanted to be elsewhere, to see everything. I didn't hate my life, but it wasn't enough."

“And that is why you killed your baby.”

“Why I... Wow. It wasn’t a baby, it was just a possibility of one, but yes. Becoming a mother would have made me hopelessly unhappy, and I know that I would have inflicted that on my child. So I made the choice to not have it, and then I took steps to never be in that situation again. I was in a situation with no good solution, so I took the best bad solution. Why are we talking about this?”

“Because I know you are horrified by my master’s diet, and I want to know if his action is different from yours in kind, or only in scale.”

“That’s... You have a lot of depth that I didn’t notice at first, Amma. It’s definitely a matter of kind.”

“Why?”

“I did an irresponsible thing, and when faced with the consequences, I took responsibility, and made sure that no child was born. Because an unwanted child ruins two lives. So I made a small mistake, and I took responsibility for it.”

“But you killed it.”

“I killed a ball of slime that would have become a baby if allowed. It was NOT a person. Look into me, Amma. You can see pretty much all that I am. I’ve killed nineteen people. You should be able to see how I feel about each and every one of them. And how I feel about that ball of slime. It was NOT a person.”

“Yes, Rose.”

“And you know that we can’t lie to each other over this link.”

"Yes, Rose."

"Well, then. The contrast to that is that King Horns— your master— deliberately engendered fifty thousand pregnancies, which produced fifty thousand babies, which he ATE. I made a mistake, and took responsibility. He acted deliberately at every single step of the process, FIFTY THOUSAND TIMES. It's enormously different in scale, but it's also different in kind."

"I understand, Rose. Do not be angry at me."

"I'm not, Amma. There is a small, stupid part of me that wishes I had been a normal girl, one who didn't react to the idea of motherhood with horror. But I'm not that person, not even a little bit, and I know that I could never be. Being tired makes you wish for foolish things."

"I do not think I have ever been that tired, Rose. Or at least, never when I was not also happy."

"You're lucky in that. You know that if I live, if I kill King Horns, you and your sisters will be orphans."

"Thank you for caring, Rose."

"But that's all I'm going to do. Care, and then turn and walk away. It's another best bad choice; there's really nothing meaningful I can to do help, and I have my own problems."

"They will survive, Rose. Or they won't."

"They?"

"I will not be with them. I may be here, or I may be following you, if you will have me."

"You're my sister, Amma. How could I turn you away?"

"You confuse me, Rose."

"I confuse everyone, including myself. I need to go back to boat building. Thank you for the conversation, Amma."

"Thank you for being my sister, Rose."

==)»> 21:6: Cherry Dryad's grove

"May I ask a question, Rose?"

"Of course, Winter."

"Why did you hold me so deliberately while you were talking to Amaranth? I could only hear snippets of your thoughts, and I couldn't hear Amaranth at all, yet you... clutched me."

"I needed an anchor, and you were— you ARE— a good one."

"I don't understand."

"You're my friend, and we have a bond, and you're completely other from Amaranth. And the link to Amaranth is SO strong. I think that if I were to sit down there and fall asleep, I would merge into Amma's tree, and never get up again. Talking to her is an unsettling experience."

"Is it unpleasant?"

"No, just frightening. It's... Have you ever had GOOD sex? Sex that you really enjoyed?"

"No, Rose. It has occasionally been pleasant, but no more."

"That weakens the metaphor, but I don't have a better one. There's a feeling you get sometimes, after good sex, that the other person knows you better than you know yourself, that they love you, and that you can trust them infinitely, and that nothing could ever possibly go wrong between you. It's an amazing feeling."

"I have never had anything like that."

"It's a lie. It's a weird chemical thing that your body does to you to encourage you to make contra-survival choices. But DAMN does it feel good while it lasts."

"I would like to experience this lie sometime, I think."

"Yeah, you never really get enough of it. And not knowing that it's a lie can make you REALLY stupid. What happens with Amma is like that, except most of it's true. I really do know Amma almost as well as she knows herself, and she knows me the same. The edges blur. And we are so very, VERY different. So having my friend Winter, who has absolutely nothing to do with Amma, hold my hand while the link is open is REALLY good."

"I am glad that I could help, Rose."

"And now, if you don't mind, I am going to set you down, and go back to being a sorceress building a boat."

==)»> 21:7: Cherry Dryad's grove

“Good evening, Rose.”

“Good evening, Fid.”

“How was your day?”

“I issued the challenge; I talked to Winter; I did sword drills; I worked on my boat; I let Amaranth crawl around in my head some more, and the two of us did a compare and contrast on abortion and infantophagy.”

“Do I not want to know about that last one as much as I think I don’t want to know about it?”

“At least. Twice. Maybe three times.”

“Your ability to attract peculiarity continues to amaze me, Rose.”

“Yeah, if only I had had the sense to chase off that damned unicorn ghost, back in the day.”

“Ouch. But you left the beaten path before that, when you asked Auntie Moss for a favor, and she gave you a magic tattoo.”

“A custom designed and formulated magic tattoo.”

“That’s the one.”

“Nah, I was strange the moment I crawled out of the egg.”

“Weren’t you born human?”

“At least as much as you were born gullible.”

"What's wrong, Rose? Why the sharp tongue?"

"Other than facing a death duel and having to sleep with shields up to keep out the dreamspace torture monster and being forever away from everyone I care about and so touch starved that pretending a sword is a rag doll seems like a good idea? Other than that, I'm the happiest person on the planet."

"It won't be long, now, Rose."

"Tomorrow will be the longest day of my life."

"Fly."

"What?"

"Take Sister Wings out over the big lake and practice all of the stupid aerial tricks you learned from that crazy book of yours, and then come back and do the kind of useful things you've been doing all day."

"That sounds like a really good idea."

"Trying to be useful when your stomach is full of knots just ties them tighter. It you have to waste time, it's always best to waste it as flamboyantly as possible."

"Damn, Fid. That's...

"Don't say it. They might take away my 'Idiot' hat."

"And that would be tragic."

"It would. Also exhausting."

"Play me a lullaby?"

"Of course."

==)»> 21:8: Cherry Dryad's grove

"Shouldn't you be resting, Rose? That was quite a workout."

"Yes, Winter, but it's still morning, and I have more than 24 hours to recover from it. And I intend to be even more tired by nightfall."

"That does not seem wise."

"Neither does tying my brain in knots. Fiddler suggested that I do some stunt flying over the big lake, and I'm going to follow his advice."

"I repeat my concerns about fatigue."

"Funny thing about that and shape-shifting. I can fly until I'm exhausted, until my wings ache, and when I shift to a shape with no wings, the pain is gone. My heart and my lungs will still be tired, and I'll be HUNGRY, but pain in parts that don't exist in the new shape disappears with the parts."

"And when you bring your wings back?"

"They seem to recover at about the same rate whether I'm wearing them or not."

"Magic is strange and fascinating."

"Said the shape-shifting sword."

"That sounded like something you would say to Fiddler."

"It did, didn't it?"

"I am flattered, Rose. I know how much Fiddler means to you."

"Do you? I'm not sure I do. But you're welcome. And I think it's time for me to go wear out my wings."

==)»> 21:9: Cherry Dryad's grove

"And how was your day, Rose?"

"Not bad, Fid. Sword drills in the morning, aerobatics at midday, and boat building in the afternoon and evening. And the most amazing fresh fish for lunch."

"Fresh fish? Caught by hand and eaten raw?"

"Of course. Wings is a kobold, after all. Though Sister Croc actually did the honors."

"As it brings you joy. You may recall I was an herbivore, once upon a time."

"But not as a child."

"No, centaurs eat a LOT of meat. You can't funnel enough plants through a human mouth to keep an equine body going. But centaurs also COOK their meat. Even when it's fresh caught fish."

"Spoilsport."

"Whenever possible, it seems. Ready for tomorrow?"

"To the extent that it's possible. Which it isn't."

"No, I don't imagine it is. Please don't die, Rose."

"I intend to do the stupid thing as carefully and as intelligently as I can."

"Within the parameters of being hopelessly stupid."

"Naturally."

"Should I check in with you in the morning?"

"Hm. No. I'll be here, tomorrow night, just the way I always am."

"As you say. Would my Heart care for a lullaby?"

"Your Heart would like to hear a lullaby very much, Fid. But chase the luck for me, first."

"As my Lady wishes."

==)»> 21:10: Cherry Dryad's grove

"Good morning, Amma. I'm off to fight a duel with King Horns. Just thought you should know."

"Kill him, my sister. Come back to me."

"That's quite a change of heart."

"My heart has been touched by Corrosion."

"And apparently your sense of humor."

"Perhaps. Come back to me, my sister. Do what you must, and come back to me."

"I'll do all I can."

==)»> 21:11: The Threshold road at the treeline

"Winter?"

"Yes, Rose?"

"Tell me again that no one who has carried you into battle has ever lost."

"It is as you say, Rose. No one who has carried me into battle has ever lost."

"Then let's keep the streak going, shall we? The gates are open. It's showtime."

==)»> 21:12: The Threshold road

"Winter?"

"Yes, Rose?"

"Thank you. That was much, much too close."

"You're alive, and he is not."

"Not sure I believe that, yet. Give me a few minutes. In the meantime..."

"Yes, Rose?"

"Do you mind if I clean your blade with my tongue?"

"I belong to you, Rose. You may do what you will. But... Why?"

"It's how I learn new shapes."

"Is that why you took his ears?"

"Yes."

"You have never struck me as the sort to take that kind of trophy."

"I don't strike me as that sort, either, Winter. Do you mind when I use you as a rag doll?"

"Of course not, Rose. It flatters me."

"Because as soon as we get past the treeline, I am going to shift to Sister Wings and go back to Cherry's island, and then I am going to go for a swim to get this gunk off of me, and then I am going to wrap my arms around you and curl into a ball and whimper for a long time."

"You are safe, Rose. The monster is dead, and it is over."

"My head knows that. My body still doesn't know why it isn't dead."

"Your body will catch up, Rose."

"You're a good friend, Winter. Let's go home."

22: Cherry

Not everything that breathes has a soul; not everything that has a soul draws breath.

—Feldspar Greymantle, *Thaumatology*

==)»> 22:1: Cherry Dryad's grove

"Fid?"

"Rose!"

"Thought you might be looking for me. I'm fine, Badger is mostly fine, Horns is dead, and I'm going to go take a long swim and wash away the minotaur bits."

"I'm just... Thank you for checking in with me, Rose. I was... just a BIT worried."

"Winter saved me. Saved us. I'll tell you all about it tonight. I get to sleep without shields for the first time since Horns discovered me, and you and I can talk for as long as you have the energy. But I have GOT to get cleaned up."

"Understood, Rose. Until then."

"Until then, Fid."

==)»> 22:2: Cherry Dryad's grove

"Hello, Amma. Just wanted you to know that the fight is over, I'm alive, and Horns is dead."

"I am glad, Rose."

"This means that you need to make that decision SOON, Amma. We'll talk later, but I wanted you to know."

"Thank you, Rose."

==)»> 22:3: Cherry Dryad's grove

"Hello, Winter. I'm back."

"You seem much calmer, Rose."

"I took Sister Croc for a swim. I don't often think about it, but I seem to have more tolerance for carnage when I'm wearing that shape than when I'm Dragon or Emma."

"That is a good thing?"

"Today it is. It was. I'm more or less used to the idea that I'm still alive, now."

"That is definitely a good thing, then."

"I also don't really need to curl into a ball and whimper, anymore. But I am going to lie here and watch the clouds blow past and let you hold my hand, just because it makes me happy."

"Me, also, Rose."

==)»> 22:4: Darkness

"Good evening, Rose. How was your swim?"

"Pretty wonderful."

"Good. How much small talk do I have to make before you tell me what happened?"

"Have you been taking subtlety lessons?"

"What do you expect, Rose? I spent half a day fretting about your survival, and then, once I knew you were alive, I spent another six hours waiting for the DETAILS. Subtlety is for people who live in more exciting neighborhoods than I do."

"Point taken. You're still rude."

"That's congenital."

"Probably. I met Badger on a hill about a half mile south of the treeline, about an hour before noon. We wanted to be far enough back that it made us hard to ambush."

"You thought Horns might attack you?"

"Not really, but since WE were going to cheat HIM, it seemed prudent to consider the possibility."

"Understood."

"Once we could see the wall, we plugged our ears with beeswax and waited for noon. I put on my minotaur illusion about a quarter hour early, and Badger did his invisibility spell. At noon, I stepped out into the sunlight, and waited for the gate in the wall to open, and for Horns to appear, and then we started walking toward each other."

"This was all in the letter from the spear?"

"Yeah. Badger followed me about ten yards back, which wasn't in the letter..."

"Really?"

"I don't HAVE to tell you this."

"But you want to."

"Not sure. And less sure as you harass me."

"I shall endeavor to maintain a level of decorum that makes you question my authenticity."

"That... Whatever. Horns and I got within about five yards of each other, and I drew Winter and saluted him; Horns reached behind his shoulder and pulled out the most amazing sword I have ever seen and saluted me with it."

"And this is where I ask you about the sword, and any other equipment that seems relevant."

"I had Winter, and a pretty good steel buckler that Badger had found for me, and the baldric for Winter's scabbard. The minotaur image, which was as tall as I could make it, about seven feet, was wearing a simple tunic, plus what I carried. The illusion didn't overlay me perfectly, because of its size, and I hoped it would give me a bit of defense. It might have."

"And Horns?"

"Horns had this amazing suit of armor that seemed to fit him like skin, and had a greatsword that must have been seven feet long, almost as long as he was tall, and probably as good a sword as he knew how to make."

"And he was styling himself as the best smith in the world."

"Yep. The armor would have scared me if I had been planning to fight fair, but lightning doesn't care much. It mauls you differently when you're wearing metal armor than when you're not, but the key point is that it still mauls you."

"Say what?"

"Without the metal, the lightning passes through you, and makes things boil and occasionally explode. With the metal, the lightning passes through the metal, which welds itself together at the contact points, and tends to vaporize the body parts near the contact points."

"Where do you learn this stuff?"

"I spent a year studying with a necromancer. Bing LIVED for this kind of thing."

"Of course he did. What next?"

"We both went to guard, and I circled to my right, and he circled to his right, and when we were on opposite sides of the road, Badger hit Horns with a lightning bolt."

"Game over?"

"No, but we didn't expect that on the first hit. Horns knew which way the lightning had come from, turned his head, and bellowed."

"But you had remembered to block your ears."

"But had forgotten that my ability to deal with Horns' bellow was mostly based on my not being a mammal. Badger lost his invisibility spell, and stood there ten yards away, in plain sight, glassy eyed and drooling."

"Gods."

"So I sneezed a lightning bolt at Horns, and he hesitated a moment, and you could tell he was deciding which of us to kill first, and then he charged me, and suddenly that massive bar of steel with an edge that was only a rumor was swinging at my head as fast as Horns could swing it. And I... I don't remember deciding to duck, I think Winter might have made the decision for me. I fell to one knee, shielded my head with the buckler, with Winter braced against the front of it. The greatsword met Winter edge to edge, and the impact lifted me up and knocked me over backwards, and the flat of the greatsword slid all the way up Winter's edge to the point, and the sword just fell apart. I ended up flat on my back; I rolled away, scrambled to my feet, and found Horns staring at the foot long blade that was all that was left of his beautiful sword."

"Gods. Score one for Winter."

"He glared at me, and I happened to have another lightning bolt on tap, so I hit him with it, and he put his head down and CHARGED. And again, I think Winter made the decision for me, because I have NEVER been crazy brave enough for what I did next. I turned to the right, braced my left hand against Winter's spine, pointed Winter into the middle of Horns' skull, and stepped between the horns."

"YOU. DID. WHAT?"

"I set him up to impale himself on my sword, and I let him run over me."

"You are insane."

"I was alive, and he wasn't. He also weighed something more than 500 pounds, and was squarely on top of me, so I had to deal with that. And all the while I was wondering when the Sisterhood would decide that they really needed to get involved."

"But they didn't?"

"Not before I got loose, cut off Horns' ears, revived Badger, and got the hell out."

"You tell this so calmly."

"I wasn't. I'm not sure I managed to blink until after I had shifted back to Wings and was on my way back here."

"So now what?"

"I finish building my boat in any case. Other plans depend on Amma and the other tree girls, and whether or not I wake up tomorrow with the ability to shift into a minotaur."

"Why would that matter?"

"Because if I can actually take the shape, I'll feel safe enough to walk up to the gate and warn the Sisterhood that a storm is coming."

"Rose... I never used to have nightmares."

"If you ever actually met a nightmare you'd just seduce her anyway. Don't whine. I'm the one who actually took the beating."

"Fine. Would her Grace care for a lullaby?"

"Yes, but could you play me, 'Marching Homeward', first?"

"As my Lady wishes."

==)»> 22:5: Cherry Dryad's grove

"Good morning, Winter."

"Good morning, Rose. You're... HUGE."

"I know. Don't you love it? If Fiddler is to be believed, I may be the first female minotaur EVER."

"I... wonder if I will ever get over being amazed at the things you get into."

"Said the intelligent, shapeshifting sword."

"But I have always been me, and I don't really change. You... DO."

"Which raises the question: How often can you do your shapeshifting trick? Because, if it comes up, your current shape is a bit small for these hands."

"I am a one handed sword, Rose. Within the parameters of that fact, I can change every time you draw me forth."

"That's what I was hoping for. But why specify one-handed?"

"I wondered if you wanted to replicate the greatsword we killed yesterday."

"No, not really my style. Wait a moment... Killed? That sword was alive?"

"Not in the sense that I am alive; it was not intelligent. But it had a soul; any object that absorbs that much time, and skill, and pride is bound to have a soul. And that... was a VERY good sword, proud and noble and brave and beautiful and strong. And we killed it."

"That's... Do swords have an afterlife?"

"I have no idea, Rose. But if they do, that one deserved the best."

"Winter... You're not the only one around here who is regularly blindsided by wonder. Let's get on with the day."

==)»> 22:6: Darkness

"Good evening, Rose."

"Good evening, Fid."

"Well? What's the news?"

"There was a minotaur in my closet this morning."

"Oh?"

"You'd like her, I think. At a guess, she's eight feet tall, weighs about four hundred pounds, and is the color of autumn oak leaves."

"She sounds beautiful."

"I think she is. But mirrors are a bit scarce in this part of the world."

"So you visited the Sisterhood?"

"No, Cherry told me to give it a few days. I flew to Threshhold and talked to Badger; he hasn't told anyone that Horns is dead, and doesn't intend to. I think he doesn't want to be held responsible if things go sideways."

"Is that likely?"

"I have no idea, and I don't want to be here to learn the answer. Though Cherry seems to have something up her... um... sleeve. Which she doesn't actually have, since she doesn't really bother with clothing."

"You never take me to the good places."

"If I recall, your favorite place was always clothing optional."

"Yes, but there was no good way to parlay that into a lecherous comment."

"I take it you've forgiven me for yesterday's excesses?"

"Mostly. I have to, don't I?"

"Or dump me and try to find someone better."

"I'm already certain that there is no one better."

"So you're stuck with me?"

"And just that much more terrified when you insist on being yourself when there's blood on the wind."

"Until the day, Scorps."

"Until the day. Lullaby?"

"Always."

==)»> 22:7: Darkness

"Good evening, Rose."

"And to you, good Scorpion."

"So how was your day?"

"Routine. I finished the boat, and rowed her around the island. She needs a sail and a fair amount of rigging, but she does the things a boat really NEEDS to do tonight."

"Sounds good. Does she have a name, yet?"

"Still working on that. It will come."

"Any other news?"

"Amaranth is going to be decanted tomorrow. Apparently she told Cherry to start the process yesterday while I was in Threshold, and by the time I got back she had changed enough that our link was broken, at least for now. I'm kind of glad; that link was scary."

"You don't like to share?"

"Not that much. No one really needs to know about the fact that Sister Croc never stops wondering what the people around her will taste like."

"You just told me."

"Voluntarily, as an example, and I TRUST you. Amma doesn't know herself well enough to be trustworthy."

"You TRUST me? What is WRONG with you"

"I trust you to be you, and to behave accordingly. And since I like you pretty well, that's all I need. Amma... Amma has been uprooted and is still pretty much lost."

"That actually makes sense. And here I thought I was going to have to defend my reputation as a cad."

"No, that one's safe. I just don't care."

"You really are a spoilsport."

"Guilty. Please punish me by playing me a lullaby."

"As my Heart wishes."

==)»> 22:8: Darkness

"Good evening, Rose."

"Good evening, Fid."

"Why so unhappy?"

"I've been played, Fid. Cherry has been working on a plan to get rid of Horns and set herself up as a queen for decades, and I played right into it."

"Did Amma lie to you? Was Horns not eating babies?"

"No, that part was true."

"That's why you killed him. What's the problem?"

"Cherry is going to annex the whole peninsula into her grove, and take over the administration of the Sisterhood, using animated trees as enforcers. She's planning to magically lobotomize a couple of the male children, for breeding stock, and kill the rest."

"Again, this solves the problem of the long term survival of the Sisterhood, which you were worried about yesterday. What's bothering you?"

"Did I mention that by building a boat with her, I gave her a means to cross the water so that she CAN annex the peninsula?"

"You're tying yourself into a knot because Cherry used you in a long term plan without your consent or knowledge, even though you didn't do anything that you probably wouldn't have done anyway, and almost everyone— except the minotaur's sons, who were quite frankly dog meat in any case— gets to live happily ever after. You're just unhappy because you weren't the smartest person in the room."

"I hate it when you make sense. It's disturbing."

"Stop tying yourself in knots for irrational reasons, and I'll happily remain the comic relief forever."

"Hah!"

"Where does all of this leave Amaranth?"

"She's just been decanted, and wants to travel south with me."

"Is that a problem?"

"More of one since Cherry has commandeered the boat. I have to build a new one, without Cherry's help, or walk."

"And the problem with walking?"

"Two hundred miles of being out of Fiddler range."

"That's a problem."

"It is. It's probably a fifteen day walk, though there are a lot of variables. And if I can find a safe place to stash Amma for a day or two, I can fly ahead, check in with you, and then go back to her."

"You can fly two hundred miles in a day?"

"I can now. Apparently I made that Luck breakthrough I was hoping for in the process of killing Horns, and I can actually DO the spell extensions

I've been studying for so long. I can hold Sister Wings for eight solid hours if I need to."

"Or Sister Shark."

"Or Sister Shark. I have all the magic I need for the dive, Fid. All I need is a ship, and I'll have you."

"You knew this two days ago, didn't you? As soon as you tried on the minotaur."

"Maybe."

"And you waited TWO DAYS to give me the most important news in three years because?"

"It never came up?"

"And you call me an idiot."

"I'm sorry, Fid, but it wouldn't have made a difference. Telling you wouldn't have made me one second closer to rescuing you."

"So you say. I have a right to sulk, and I'm exercising it."

"Fid?"

==)»> 22:9: Darkness

"Rose?"

"Yes, Fid?"

"When are you going to go dark?"

"Probably the day after tomorrow."

"I didn't want to start that being angry with you."

"I didn't either, but you control the link."

"I'm sorry I got angry."

"I'm sorry I forgot to tell you about the spell extension. I know how much it matters to you. But you know that I want to rescue you almost as much as you want to be rescued, right?"

"I do know, Rose"

"Well, then. I should still be right here tomorrow night, and we can drive each other crazy with mutual frustration then."

"I look forward to it. Lullaby?"

"I think I've been sound asleep for several hours at this point, but... please."

==)»> 22:10: Darkness

"ROSE!?!"

"Hello, Fid. Sorry."

"WHAT THE HELL, ROSE?"

"I said I was sorry, Fid. Things got difficult."

"FOR FOUR DAYS?"

"Cherry made a grab for Winter, so Amma and I did three days of hard marching before I thought it was safe to leave Amma and Winter behind, and check in with you. And then the fourth day was spent flying down to a place I knew you could find me."

"I... Hmm. Fine. I guess I'll forgive you, this time."

"We still have a way to go before you can talk to me freely. Amma is camped on the lake shore about a hundred and eighty miles from here. One day to fly back, plus ten or more days to march down here."

"It takes ten days to march the distance?"

"At least. We covered ninety miles in three days getting away from Cherry, but Amma is a wreck and I would be just as bad if I didn't have a choice of forms to spread the fatigue over. Sister Wings is going to be mostly dead by the time I get back to Amma, though."

"So spend an extra day with me here and rest."

"It's tempting, but Amma needs me more than you do."

"I categorically deny the possibility of that. I hereby assert that I am infinitely needy."

"That's 'greedy', which rhymes, but isn't the same thing."

"I've been in the dark for four days."

"During which time you have made a nuisance of yourself to Bing and Dlef and Drellan, at least, and have probably visited Auntie Moss and

Maelstrom at least briefly."

"Maybe."

"On the other hand, Amma is most of a hundred miles away from everything she has ever known, camped next to a lake that she is sure is full of monsters, and is alone except for a talking sword. Though Winter actually is pretty good company."

"Fine. She needs you more than I do."

"That's delightfully rational of you."

"Wait a moment... Full of monsters?"

"Yeah, I wondered if you would catch that. It turns out that my plan to sail Amma south to the end of the lake wouldn't have worked anyway, because she is TERRIFIED of open water. Apparently Horns taught the Sisterhood that the lake is full of horrible monsters, EXCEPT for an area around Cherry's island that happens to include six or seven miles of the shoreline of the peninsula. The lake scares her stupid."

"And yet you camp on the shore."

"The beaches are a pretty good road and there's unlimited fresh water. Also, it's easy for Sister Croc to find food for both of us."

"So you're living on fish?"

"Until we get to the south end of the lake, yes."

"Raw?"

"No, wood is fairly abundant, and Amma has a tinder box."

"YOU need a tinder box?"

"Of course not. But Anna's alone at the moment."

"Oh."

"I've missed you, Fid."

"You should. I'm wonderful."

"I'll give you inimitable. And even irreplaceable."

"Those are not bad consolations. But I'm still holding out for wonderful."

"I think you'd have to earn that."

"Oh? How?"

"I'll think about it and let you know. In the mean time... Damn. I was going to ask for some music, but I can't hear it from here, can I?"

"No."

"Double damn."

"I'm fading a bit, Rose. The distance is hard."

"Go then, but look for me in the morning before I go back north."

"I will. Until the day, my Heart."

"Until the day, my Scorpion."

==)»> 22:11: Lakeshore

"Did you sleep well, Rose?"

"Well enough. I miss my rag doll."

"Say what?"

"I've taken to sleeping with Winter in my arms. It helps with the loneliness."

"Ah."

"Will it be as good as I remember it, Fid? Being in dreamspace with you?"

"I am inclined to say, 'Yes', but I honestly can't promise it. I hope so, and I believe so."

"I have hope. My belief is decaying."

"The day will come, Rose."

"Gods, I hope so. So... look for me in six days, I guess."

"SIX!?!"

"One to fly back, four to march, and one to fly down here again. That puts a third of our travel time into visiting you, and I really can't see giving you more than that."

“That’s a long time.”

“I know. For me too, and I have to walk or fly every day in the meantime. All you have to do is wait.”

“And whine. I’m good at whining.”

“That you are. I need to go. Until the day.”

“Until the day, my Heart.”

==)»> 22:12: Lakeshore

“Good evening, Winter. How did things go?”

“Good evening, Rose. I am very glad you are back. Amma is deeply unhappy.”

“I know.”

“She hides it well, but everything frightens her.”

“I’ve noticed that, too. How often did you have to tell her that no one who has carried you into battle has ever lost?”

“Every time she heard a noise she didn’t understand.”

“Which is almost all of them.”

“Which is almost all of them.”

“Did you get her to work on sword drills?”

"Yes. She is not without skill, and she is strong. She could be faster. Why are you giggling?"

"I am listening to a report from a talking sword about a woman who used to be a tree."

"Is that funny?"

"It's normal in my life. It would be insane for most people."

"But you ARE you."

"That I am, Winter. Gods help me, that I am."

23: Traveling

If you would be happy, you must learn to tell lies without malice, and to forgive lies without rancor.

—*The Book of the Blind King's Wisdom*

==)»> 23:1: Lakeshore

"Good evening, Rose."

"And to you, Fid."

" How was your journey?"

"Long, tiring, boring, but beautiful anyway."

"And how are your companions?"

"Winter is a bit unhappy about the amount of travel; she's concerned that we're making it harder for her sisters to find her."

"I can see that."

"And Amma... Amma is a pampered house cat who's been thrown into the wilderness. She's brave, she's game, she's fierce, but she's still coming apart."

"And how about you?"

"No one has played me a lullaby for several days, and I'm responsible for keeping the wheels on the wagon, but other than that, I'm fine. I'm ME."

"Which means that you want a hot bath and a day of aerobatics next to a reliable thermal with no responsibilities."

"You can feel that?"

"I can barely hear you, but I KNOW you."

"You would seem to. How have YOU been holding up though the longest blackout you and I have ever had?"

"I survived the first four years; I can handle six days. I'm not happy about it, but I understand, and I'm glad that you're here now. No, that's lame. I am... stupidly happy that you're here now, and I never want you to go away again, even though I know you will."

"I think, for everyone's sake, that once we all get to the end of the lake, and communications are more normal, we're going to find a good camp site and just rest for a few days. And then do it again when we get to Apple's grove."

"Ah, yes, Apple who wants to keep you forever."

"Apple, from whose grove I will be able to hear the music, and who will give Amma another kind person to talk to, and yes, a few other things as well. Which reminds me: I have a riddle for you."

"Should I be afraid?"

"No."

"Then proceed. Not that I could stop you."

"What happens when two lonely, touch-starved people camp on a warm, moonlit beach?"

"Does it involve monsters?"

"No."

"Damn. Monsters make for better stories."

"Not if you're in them."

"I'm on the bottom of the ocean, and we have already established that you, Amma, and Winter are fine, so I thought there might be room for one."

"No monsters."

"Well, in that case, I imagine that Amma got a really amusing lesson in the difference between knowledge and understanding."

"That's... kind of poetic. Also correct. I just thought that since you were grousing about Apple, I ought to let you know."

"Are you still coming for me?"

"Yes."

"Do I still get to keep you forever?"

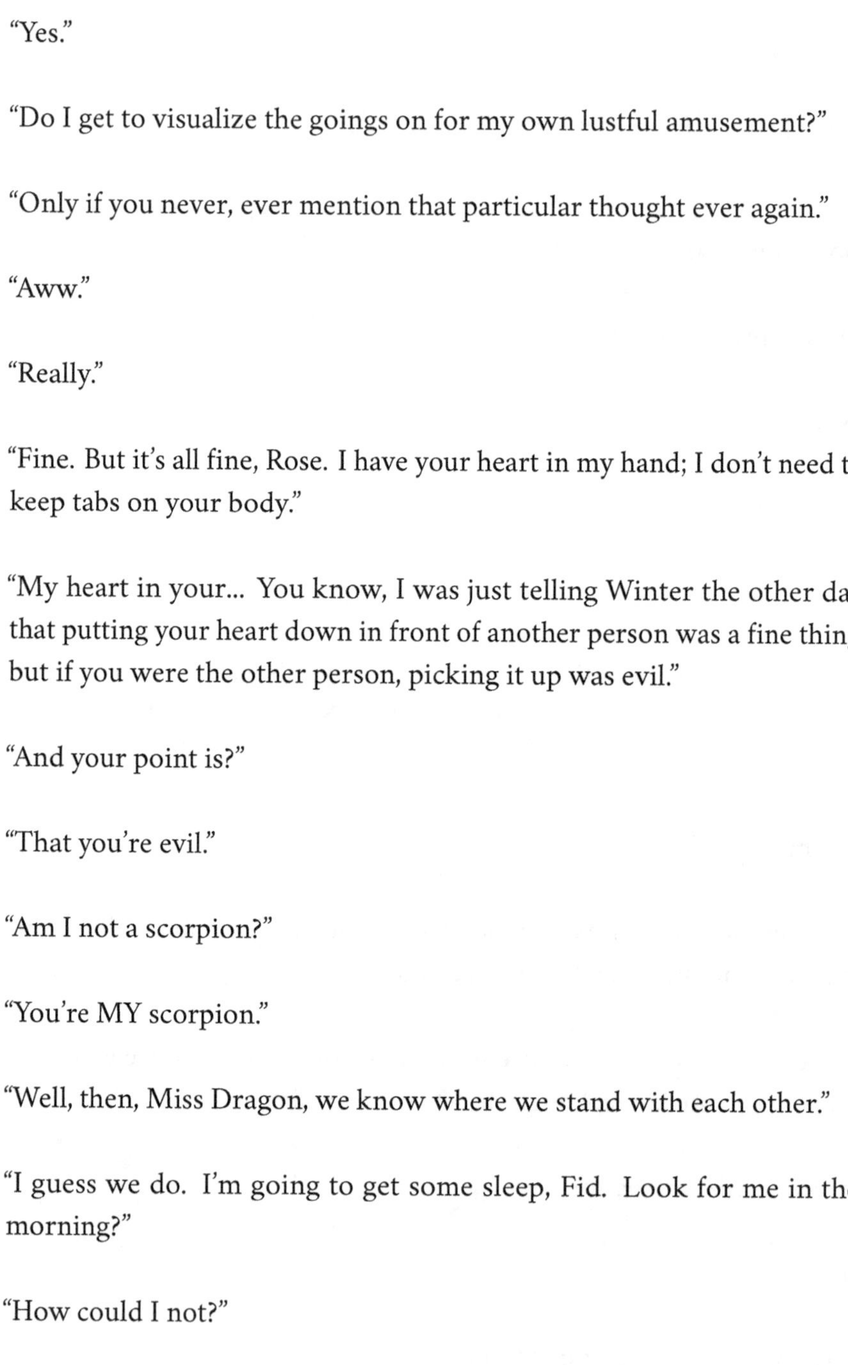

"Yes."

"Do I get to visualize the goings on for my own lustful amusement?"

"Only if you never, ever mention that particular thought ever again."

"Aww."

"Really."

"Fine. But it's all fine, Rose. I have your heart in my hand; I don't need to keep tabs on your body."

"My heart in your... You know, I was just telling Winter the other day that putting your heart down in front of another person was a fine thing, but if you were the other person, picking it up was evil."

"And your point is?"

"That you're evil."

"Am I not a scorpion?"

"You're MY scorpion."

"Well, then, Miss Dragon, we know where we stand with each other."

"I guess we do. I'm going to get some sleep, Fid. Look for me in the morning?"

"How could I not?"

==)»> 23:2: Lakeshore

“Good morning, Rose. How was your sleep?”

“Utterly unmemorable. I might as well have been dead. Which is kind of wonderful.”

“So back up the shore?”

“No other choice I’d consider.”

“And six more days to wait?”

“No. Let’s plan on four and a half, this time. Three more days of marching should get us close enough that I can get down here, and back again, in a day. That way I wouldn’t have to leave Amma alone overnight. So look for me at noon on the fifth day.”

“I like this plan.”

“I do too. See you then, my Scorpion.”

“Until the day, my Heart.”

==)»> 23:3: Lakeshore

“Hello, Winter.”

“Hello, Rose.”

“Does it help if I tell you that I won’t be gone overnight again, and that is the last time you’ll have to deal with Amma in the darkness?”

"It helps a great deal, Rose. I am a sword. I kill things. I am not equipped to deal with unbalanced humans."

"I know, Winter, and I'm grateful for your patience. In addition to owing you my life."

"That was just a matter of being a sword, Rose."

"A sword with an amazing volitional edge and the knowledge to direct my muscles when my brain froze up."

"Even so. I am a very GOOD sword."

"That you are. Maybe next time I'll be able to talk Amma into continuing to walk when I visit Fiddler. That will give her something to do, and make the trip shorter."

"We are still getting farther away from where my sisters expect me."

"But they WILL find you, won't they?"

"If I am not moving, yes. But you never stop moving, Rose."

"I'm working on it, Winter. I know I have a responsibility to you and your sisters, and I intend to keep it."

"Thank you for confirming that, Rose. I do not like to think I made a bad choice."

"You didn't, Winter. I swear to you, you didn't."

==)»> 23:4: Lakeshore

"Rose?"

"Yes, Winter?"

"What's wrong with Amma?"

"You mean other than being lonely and afraid of people at the same time?"

"That's part of it."

"She's broken, Winter. Horns hurt her, and tortured her, and then I poisoned her brain."

"You... On purpose?"

"No, of course not. But that crazy link Cherry set up for us, that I asked for, and that Amma volunteered for, messed her up badly."

"But not you?"

"It wasn't good for me, either, but I'm a different sort of person. I'm... Say that you have two bottles, one full of the purest water you can find, the other full of the purest alcohol you can find. Now you mix two drinks, one with one part alcohol and twenty parts water, and one with twenty parts alcohol and one part water. You have had alcohol somewhere along the line, haven't you?"

"Yes. All of my sisters liked it better than I did, though."

"Well, then... Will you notice the alcohol in the drink that is mostly water?"

"Yes, definitely."

"And will you notice the water in the drink that is mostly alcohol?"

"Probably not."

"I'm alcohol, and Amma is water. And the mix was more like two to one in either case. Being inside Amma's head has messed me up a bit, but I'm lot bigger and stronger than Amma is, so I can mostly shrug it off, except late at night, when things are quiet. But for Amma..."

"She gets lost."

"She certainly seems to. She's seen too much of my world to be happy with her sisters, but it is NOT her world, and she doesn't fit there. And right now we aren't really in either, because we're physically in the middle of nowhere."

"What are you going to do?"

"Make guesses and hope. Amma didn't do well in Threshold, so I'm afraid to take her into another town. And the isolation we have now isn't good either."

"But you leave her to talk to Fiddler."

"I leave Amma in a safe place, with food, and adequate shelter, in the company of my long-suffering friend Winter. Fid is all alone on the bottom of the ocean. And I am still giving Amma hours for every minute I actually have with Fiddler. And before too long we'll solve the range problem, and I won't have to leave Amma alone at all."

"And then what?"

"And then we keep marching until we get to the Garfish River and my friend Apple, who may be able to help get Amma straightened out."

"Why do you think Apple can help?"

"Because Apple is also lonely and afraid of people, but she lives with it much better than Amma does, and might be able to teach Amma a few things."

"Ah."

"And now, it's time for me to fly down and visit Fiddler. Encourage Amma to keep walking, if she seems bored; there are no towns on the next stretch of lake shore, so she can walk as far as she likes."

"Aren't you worried about losing us?"

"No. Even if Amma TRIED to hide, I'd find you. Though don't take that as a challenge; I don't want to come back from a day on the wing and have to play a game of 'find the fool'."

"I am sure that Amma will be disappointed by that."

"Gods. PLEASE don't suggest it. Just try to take care of her, and yourself. You're a good friend, Winter. I hope I deserve you."

"I think that you do, Rose. I know that you try."

==)»> 23:5: Lakeshore

"Hello, Rose."

"Hello, Fid."

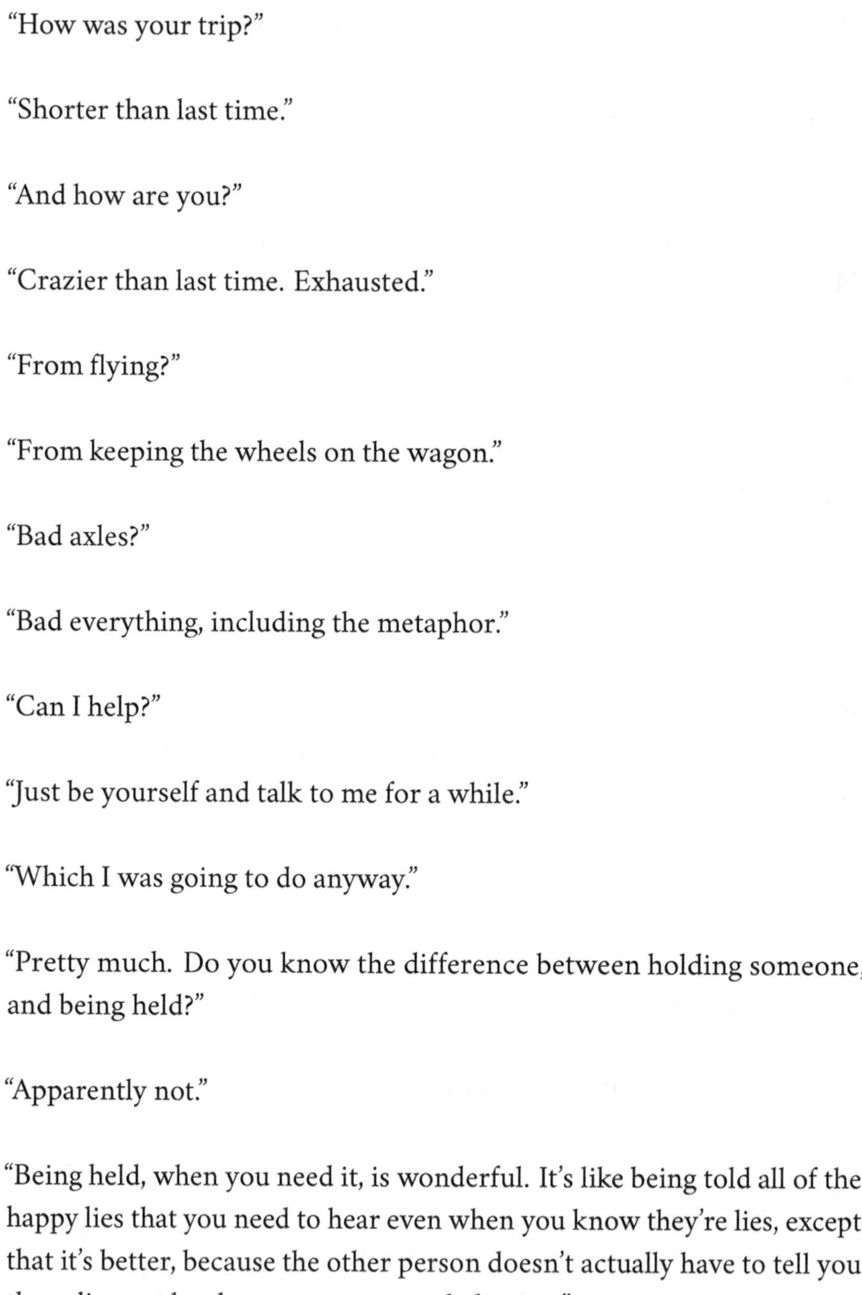

"How was your trip?"

"Shorter than last time."

"And how are you?"

"Crazier than last time. Exhausted."

"From flying?"

"From keeping the wheels on the wagon."

"Bad axles?"

"Bad everything, including the metaphor."

"Can I help?"

"Just be yourself and talk to me for a while."

"Which I was going to do anyway."

"Pretty much. Do you know the difference between holding someone, and being held?"

"Apparently not."

"Being held, when you need it, is wonderful. It's like being told all of the happy lies that you need to hear even when you know they're lies, except that it's better, because the other person doesn't actually have to tell you those lies out loud, so you can go on believing."

"That's grim."

"But when you hold someone who needs it, you KNOW that you're telling all of those happy lies anyway, even though you aren't saying them out loud, and if you have a soul, every second that you hold that person tears off another piece of it."

"That's REALLY grim. Are we talking about Amaranth?"

"Yeah. That's what's so wonderful about music, about your music in particular. Because it feels full of happy lies, too, except that with music it's all true. Even when it isn't exactly happy, it's always something you want."

"You get deep when you're exhausted and burned out."

"Maybe. Do you have any idea how much I need to be held?"

"As opposed to holding?"

"Yeah."

""Within the limits of my fundamental indifference and insensitivity, I think I do."

"Winter helps, but it's not the same. I hold the sword, and I know she would hold me if she could, but..."

"I'm never going to be able to give you that."

"Fid, if you hold me in dreamspace while my body is sleeping, I wake up with a memory of being held."

"Good to know."

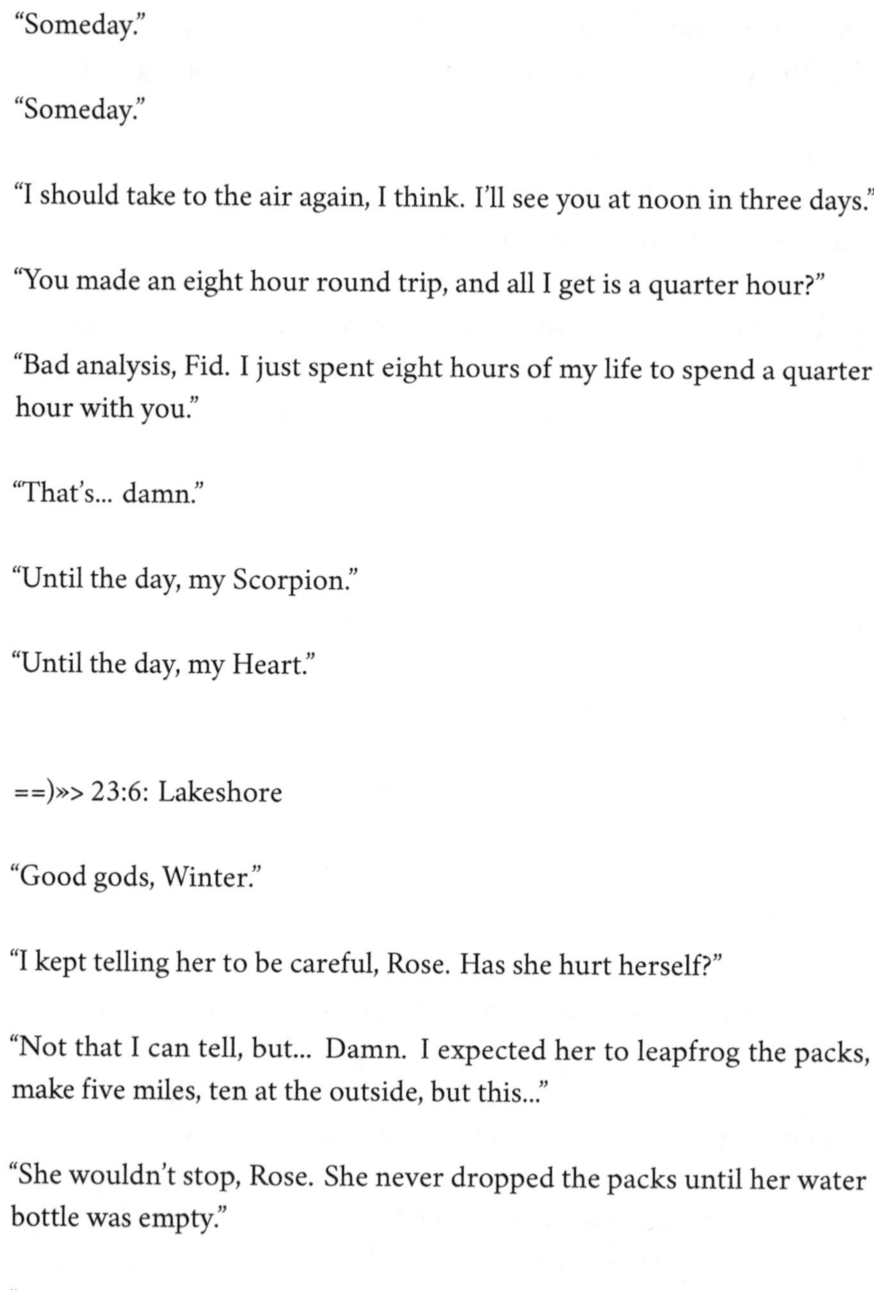

"Someday."

"Someday."

"I should take to the air again, I think. I'll see you at noon in three days."

"You made an eight hour round trip, and all I get is a quarter hour?"

"Bad analysis, Fid. I just spent eight hours of my life to spend a quarter hour with you."

"That's... damn."

"Until the day, my Scorpion."

"Until the day, my Heart."

==)»> 23:6: Lakeshore

"Good gods, Winter."

"I kept telling her to be careful, Rose. Has she hurt herself?"

"Not that I can tell, but... Damn. I expected her to leapfrog the packs, make five miles, ten at the outside, but this..."

"She wouldn't stop, Rose. She never dropped the packs until her water bottle was empty."

"Did she say what she was thinking?"

"She said that the more miles she covered, the sooner you would get to the end of the lake, and wouldn't keep leaving her. How far did she go?"

"About twenty-eight miles, with a double pack. It's insane."

"Are you going to reprimand her?"

"For working hard and trying to be helpful? Hell, no. I may give her a SMALL lecture on self-preservation, it she's really hurting tomorrow."

"She is trying so hard, Rose."

"I know. I just wish she wasn't so unhappy."

==)»> 23:7: Lakeshore

"Hello, Rose."

"Hello, Fid. I know I promised you more time today, but... Will you forgive me if I promise we can talk until you run out of energy tonight?"

"If you promise... Where are you?"

"About fifteen miles from the place I usually stop to contact you. We'll be THERE by sundown."

"That's... What happened?"

"Amma has turned into a marching machine. She did most of thirty miles the last time I visited you, and we've held that pace. She REALLY didn't want to be left alone again."

"I guess not. Get back to marching; I can wait. Just... damn."

"I know. We're that much closer to me being... Well, back in fiddle range. Among other things."

"Go. Until tonight."

"Until tonight."

==)»> 23:8: Darkness

"Good evening, Rose."

"Hello, Fid. How are we for feelings tonight?"

"Not much. Until you get back into music range, it's pretty much just words."

"That's a shame. I wish you could hear what I'm feeling right now. I'm in a secure place with all of my 'children' around me, and you in my ear, and I don't have to sleep with shields. I can think of a whole lot of ways things could be better..."

"So can I..."

"And even when we have only words, the lechery comes through clearly."

"It's a gift."

"The point is that I'm actually pretty close to being happy at the moment."

"Only close?"

"Not sure. I may have forgotten how."

"I can fix that. But you'll have to get a lot closer."

"Counting on it, and working on it. But it's a good night."

"It sounds like it. And I'll get to talk to you every night from now on."

"Gods, I hope so."

"So now what?"

"We take tomorrow off, since I haven't had a rest day since... I'm not sure. A long time."

"And then?"

"And then we have a hard last day on the lake shore, and then we start beating the bushes until we find the river that will lead us back to Ironbridge. The next major point is Apple's grove, and we're going to take a LONG rest, several days, there."

"How long will that take?"

"One day by air, but maybe twenty on foot. After we leave the lake shore, we'll be plowing through the undergrowth the whole way. That's slow going."

"How does Winter feel about becoming a brush cutter?"

"We haven't discussed it. I can sell the idea, but it won't make her any less unhappy than she already is."

"She wants you to stand still?"

"She does. As does Amma. And, for that matter, Apple when we get there."

"Are you tempted?"

"I might be if I had a certain dagger on my belt. As it stands, not at all. And really... I can stand still for a year or two, but the horizon is always calling. And it calls SO MUCH LOUDER when you see it from the air..."

"I can only imagine."

"We'll work on giving you a better impression."

"That would be good."

"I want a lullaby, Fid. But since that's not an option, I should probably just go."

"Sleep well, my Heart."

"Until the day, Fid."

==)»> 23:9: Darkness

"Good evening, Rose."

"Good evening, Fid."

"And how was the day?"

"We reached the river, so now we have a path to follow all the way to Ironbridge. It's still full of undergrowth, but it's there."

"Too bad you don't have a boat."

"I've thought about that. Between Winter, my magic, and a little judicious fire, we could make a dug out canoe in a day or two. It wouldn't be faster, but it would be easier."

"But you won't."

"No, Amma is terrified of boats. And being actually ON the river would open up new options for stupidity. Amma can't swim, and dumping the boat at a log jam might get her drowned. So no boat. But I love boats, and it hurts."

"I know, Rose."

"Until the day, Fid."

"Until the day, Rose."

==)»> 23:10: A river bank

"Winter, do you mind if we talk a bit? As long as you're in my hand anyway?"

"You are the one doing the work, Rose. I am only a tool."

"Right. A really fine, if somewhat inappropriate, tool."

"As you say."

"Though I'm glad you're you. We would have spent a quarter of every day re-sharpening steel blades."

"I am, as you say, a GOOD tool."

"I'm trying to work through this impasse that you and I have, and I thought you might help me with it."

"I will do what I can, Rose."

"I offered to accept ownership of the Panoply so that your sisters could come back, and I promised to do my best to see that you did not fall into the hands of an owner who would abuse you."

"Yes."

"And living my life the way I need to makes it difficult, and maybe impossible, for your sisters to find you, and for the Panoply to reform."

"Yes."

"Can I loan you out?"

"Excuse me?"

"When I get tired, Amma takes the lead, and you work just as well for her as you do for me. And when we were on the lake shore, and I left you behind with Amma, you would have worked just as well for her, if she had been attacked, as you would have for me. And you even taught her sword drills."

"Yes."

"Would it be legitimate if I were to leave you in the custody of someone that I trusted, who could be counted on to stay in a safe place, so that your sisters would be able to find you, and the Panoply could reform?"

"Yes, you could do that."

"I mean, I know I could just give you away, but if I made a mistake in choosing your new master, I would have no recourse. If I remain your master, and just loan you out, there's less risk if I choose a poor custodian."

"I imagine, Rose. This has never come up before."

"I didn't realize, at first, how much my responsibility to you would conflict with my responsibility to Fiddler."

"Or your heart."

"Or my heart, yes. Though I have stayed still for long periods in the past."

"I trust you, Rose. And I am very fond of you."

"And I, you, Winter. You're my rag doll. My rock hard, terrifyingly lethal rag doll."

"Is that a joke, Rose?"

"Sort of."

"But... Given who you are, I would be surprised if you would take comfort in any object that was NOT terrifying lethal."

"That's... I have no answer for that. But I like it. Thank you."

"You are welcome, Rose."

==)»> 23:11: Darkness

"Good evening, Rose. Rest day?"

"Hello, Fid. Why do you ask?"

"Because I can usually see that you've moved a bit, and you don't seem to have."

"We didn't move much. Amma fell down a hill and hurt her ankle. I don't think anything is broken, but I've done all I can, so we need to get her to Apple for proper healing, and to make sure it isn't serious."

"She can't walk?"

"Not well. So I'm building a canoe."

"Expediency outweighs caution?"

"Sometimes. Necessity outweighs caution always. And the river is wider here, so I'm not really worried about log jams, and the current is a bit faster. And no one is going to try to paddle the canoe, so it should be pretty stable."

"You're just going to drift?"

"No, Sister Croc is going to tow it. That seems the best use of resources. Between the current and Croc's ability to swim, we should move faster than we could on foot, even if Amma were healthy. And I'm REALLY tired of bushwhacking, anyway."

"So this is actually good news for certain impatient spectators."

"Yes."

"I'm fond of good news."

"Are you going to play me a concert when we get to Apple's grove?"

"If you wish."

"I wish very much."

"Then it will happen."

==)»> 23:12: Darkness

"Good evening, Rose."

"Hello, Fid."

"How's life on the river?"

"Better than expected. I'm SO MUCH happier being back in and on the water, and finally making good time, that I'm able to feed that back over the link to Amma, and SHE is almost calm about being in the boat."

"The link still works?"

"Sort of. That mark on Amma-the-tree showed up on Amma-the-human right between her shoulder blades, just like mine. If we sit back to back with the tattoos touching, we can... It's not like it used to be, crawling around inside each other, but we feel each other's emotions. And since I'm so much stronger than Amma is, I'm AWARE of what she's feeling, and she FEELS what I'm feeling."

"That doesn't sound like something you'd approve of."

"Circumstances dictate. I wouldn't open the link if I was unhappy or angry. But right now I'm relaxed and pretty happy, and Amma is stuck in self-perpetuating misery cycles, so if my happiness breaks her out of it, we're both better off."

"Slippery slope."

"I know. And since when do YOU get to lecture ME about the dangers of domination?"

"Since you're the one with opportunity, and I'm the one with experience."

"Yeah, but I have a conscience."

"I have a conscience. It's in a box in the attic, and I take it out and play with it every now and then."

"Gods, I miss you, Fid."

"I know. And I, you."

"Does knowing that there's only one wall left to climb make it worse or better?"

"Only one?"

"The money. I'm inclined to look at the dive itself as an afterthought at this point."

"The dive that you have taken more than three years to prepare for."

"If you do the prep right, the event itself is an anti-climax."

"I know I've always felt that way about sex."

"Damn. I walked into that one. I surrender abjectly, and request that we tear up the score book and start from scratch."

"First tell me a bit more about this 'abject surrender' thing."

"Good night, Fid."

"Good night, Rose."

24: Apple

Coffins are very safe. But they're coffins.
—*The Book of the Blind King's Wisdom*

==)»> 24:1: Apple Dryad's Grove

"Hello, Winter."

"Hello, Rose. You are meditating again. You have not done that in a while."

"It's earlier than my usual visit with Fiddler, and I'm not ready for sleep yet, and I wanted him to be able to find me. And I haven't talked to you for a few days, so I thought we could keep each other company while we wait for Fiddler to find us."

"I am glad of your company, Rose."

"I should probably be doing sword drills, but I've just been too tired after towing the canoe all day."

"I understand, Rose."

"Any news on Amma? I know she still clutches you all day when we're on the river."

"She is better since you have been re-linking with her. She is still very lost and lonely, and asks me to tell her stories about my sisters."

"Do you? Tell her stories?"

"All that I can remember. What is special about today? Why have we stopped here?"

"We're in another dryad's grove. This one belongs to my friend Apple. We're going to stay here for a few days."

"Are you thinking of leaving me here?"

"I'm thinking that you might want to stay here, but it's YOUR choice. I owe you a solution that YOU approve of."

"And you think that Apple might be that solution?"

"It's possible. I think a lot of things that I intend to keep to myself. Which I think might be the dragon in me asserting herself."

"Why do you think I might like it here?"

"Because Apple is a good and generous person who will live a VERY long time, and is not EVER going to go on the road."

"Those are good reasons."

"I thought so."

"Good evening, ladies," said Fiddler.

"Hello, Fid," answered Rose.

"Hello, Fiddler," said Winter.

"I take it you've reached Apple's grove?" asked Fiddler.

"We have," Rose answered.

"Is there news, or shall we start in on the music immediately?" asked Fiddler.

"The news," replied Rose, "Is that I can once again hear your music, and I have invited Winter along for your concert."

"Well, in that case," Fiddler said.

==)»> 24:2: Darkness

"Rose?"

"Yes, Fid."

"Are you really thinking of leaving Winter with Apple?"

"No. I'm thinking of leaving Amma with Apple, and then leaving Winter with Amma."

"That's devious. Also fairly complex."

"Just looking for chances. I have no intention of forcing anyone into anything. But Apple is looking for someone she can keep forever, Amma is looking for someone who will love her and keep her safe, and Winter is looking for someone who will have the sense to stand still while her sisters find her."

“So what are you going to do about it?”

“Wait.”

“I see a problem with that.”

“No you don’t.”

“Excuse me?”

“It’s about 800 miles from here to Ironbridge. That’s four days for me, alone, by air, or ninety days for Amma and I by land or about half of that by water. How long can I afford to wait here, where you and I can talk and I can hear your music, and we’re all safe, while Apple and Amma decide that they like each other better than they like me?”

“At least thirty days, as long as it works out.”

“It will.”

“Hmmm, I ended the concert with a lullaby, but I’m feeling generous, and will offer you a second one.”

“And I’ll take it.”

==)»> 24:3: Darkness

“Good evening, Rose.”

“And to you, Fid.”

“Any news of the day?”

"It was pleasant. I'm teaching Amma to swim..."

"That sounds fraught."

"It's not so bad. There's a small lake inside Apple's boundaries, and I've managed to convince Amma that there are no monsters in it, so she can ALMOST relax. I think she'll learn to like the water, eventually."

"And other than that?"

"Winter is giving Amma and me sword lessons, which is fun. And I've been able to get in some aerobatic time, which is always good."

"And Apple?"

"Apple is fascinated by the tattoos Cherry gave us, and is trying to duplicate the magic."

"The magic that hasn't worked properly since Amma came out of the tree."

"Yes, but Apple can merge with a tree at will, so she's going to mark one of her pet trees with an evolution of our tattoos, and we'll see what happens."

"Apple wants to get inside your head that badly?"

"Apple has discovered dryad magic that she doesn't understand, and NEEDS to fix that. Which is not to say she'll object to being inside my head, but that's not what drives her."

"If it works, how will it effect your evil scheme to abandon your friends?"

"If it works, Apple will know what I'm thinking, and will understand why, and will make her own decision, which will probably be to agree with me. And if Apple THEN links with Amma, it will follow the same pattern. I want what's best for everybody, and they'll know that."

"It only looks like you're leaving them in a heap to fend for themselves."

"Just stop. I want everyone to be happy, and this will help Apple and Amma figure that out. Winter..."

"Yes?"

"Winter-the-person is my friend, and I want what's best for her, and I'm convinced that that means leaving her here in Amma's custody. But I have a full-blown case of dragon lust for Winter-the-sword, and I'm just going to have to swallow that. It HURTS."

"There's room in the box in the attic for another conscience, if you're interested."

"You're evil. And I'm not. And I can handle a bit of pain if it helps my friend."

"Generations of dragons are ashamed of you."

"Do you really WANT to compete for my affections with another sentient blade?"

"If it comes with four female roommates, I'm pretty sure I could learn to adapt."

"Good night, Fid."

"You don't want your lullaby?"

"I want you to stop planning to roll my friends into bed."

"But you haven't even met three of them, yet."

"Not helping."

"No, but I'm having fun."

"Of course you are. This is always going to be a problem, isn't it?"

"What is?"

"Once I have the dagger, I'm going to have to assume that you will roll every female friend I ever make as part of the package. Even if you behave yourself and never coerce or frighten them."

"We've been over this."

"But my female friends never had names before."

"Rilla? Dzee?"

"Fine. But you were farther away, and they were only physically vulnerable. Rilla and Dzee have souls made of shoe leather."

"And Winter and Amma don't?"

"You know Dzee, and you've spoken to Winter."

"Point made."

"Just... Be kind, and be careful, and try not to give me the impression that you regard my friends as a tavern buffet."

“Even if I do?”

“Especially if you do. Here’s what I want to NEVER have to say to myself: ‘I like her but I can’t afford to become her friend because if I do Fiddler will roll her into bed and I can already tell that that will be bad for her so I’m leaving.’ Got it?”

“Got it. I can still make lustful comments about strangers, though, right?”

“I’m going to explode.”

“No you’re not.”

“Fine. Make all of the lustful comments you want about anyone you want, just as long as you never give ME the impression that you are being careless and are likely to hurt someone.”

“That’s a tall order.”

“It would be easier if you brought that box down from the attic.”

“That’s just crazy talk.”

“I suppose. So my poor, beleaguered conscience has to do double duty. Play me my lullaby, and let me sleep.”

“No ‘please’?”

“Five hundred miles and two thousand fathoms.”

“Yes, your Grace. As it please your Grace.”

“Damned straight.”

==)»> 24:4: Apple Dryad's Grove

"Rose?"

"Yes, Winter?"

"Why do the dryads avoid me?"

"They do?"

"When I first woke up, I could feel Cherry's magic all around me, though I did not notice that it was there until after I was no longer inside her grove. And now I can feel Apple's magic around me. And I can tell that there is a bit of... distance, almost distrust, there."

"I don't know, Winter. I could ask. My first guess is that you're a very alien thing to a dryad. You're a sword, a thing of air and death, and they are creatures of earth and life."

"You will ask? If I am to stay here, I would like to know that I was welcome."

"I'll probably know without asking tomorrow, if Apple's tattoo link works. If not, I'll ask."

"That would be good, Rose. I like this place. I wish that it felt like it liked me."

"I understand, Winter. That's a feeling I know fairly well."

"It is?"

"Wanting to belong? It's a proof of humanity, Winter. Even for a sword."

“That is... a very nice thing to hear, Rose.”

“And true. I’ll see what I can do.”

==)»> 24:5: Darkness

“Good evening, Rose. Are we friends again?”

“We’ll always be friends, Fid. You’re MINE. There are just some points of friction that we need to work out, or around.”

“I think I like the vehemence with which you say, ‘MINE.’”

“Heh. Remember what I said about having dragon lust for Winter?”

“Yes.”

“Which I said was manageable?”

“Yes?”

“You, Master Scorpion, and your dagger, are the objects of as much dragon lust as the world has ever seen, and I have not yet held the dagger in my hand and CLAIMED it. I am reasonably certain that walking away from this quest at this point would DESTROY me. You. Are. MINE.”

“Wow. Warm fuzzies and abject terror in the same package.”

“Damned straight.”

“I take it you’ve gotten over your qualms about owning sentient beings.”

"Not really. But the idea of you belonging to someone else makes me murderous, so I've decided to adapt."

"I'd say that was reasonable, but 'murderous' and 'reasonable' are not easy bedfellows."

"Tell me about it."

"Any other news?"

"Apple made some modifications to my tattoo, and then Amma's, this afternoon. Tomorrow I get to try out the link."

"You go first?"

"Of course. Amma's a... I was going to say, 'mouse', but maybe ,'cow' would be more appropriate, given her parentage. But whatever, she's passive and timid and kind of broken, and I'm most of a dragon. So which of us would you expect to lead?"

"The one I would mind losing the least if something goes wrong?"

"Nothing CAN go wrong that badly. On the weak side, if the link is weak or broken, there's no risk at all, and on the strong side... Worst case, we merge permanently. Which would not make me happy, but I swear to you that I would be dominant. Good enough?"

"If that's all the assurance you can give me, I'll be content with it."

"Well and good. And with that... Would Master Fiddler please deign to play a lullaby for a lowly supplicant?"

"Master Fiddler would be grateful for the opportunity."

==)»> 24:6: Apple Dryad's grove

"Greetings, Rose."

"Greetings, Apple."

"This is interesting magic."

"It's all yours, now."

"Not quite all mine, yet, but I am learning. Thank you for bringing it to me."

"I'm glad you like it, but all I really brought was myself."

"And your friend, and your talkative sword."

"Well, yes, those, too."

"I am intrigued by your optimism regarding your dominance if you and I should be locked together."

"Do you doubt my conclusion?"

"I am VERY resilient, Rose."

"You have much more endurance than I do. But I have a stronger will; you're a nurturer, and I'm a killer."

"These things are so. You may be right. I am glad it need not be tested."

"So am I, Apple, so am I."

"Your world is much bigger than mine, Rose."

"I'm aware, Apple."

"I still do not understand what drives you, Rose, but I do now believe you when you say you can not stay here."

"I'm glad. I'm sorry I can't share more of your happiness."

"As am I. But I will be here, and you will always be welcome."

"Good to know. Thank you."

"Do you think the minotaur's daughter can be happy here?"

"I believe so. You'll have to make your own judgment, as will she."

"You are a very complex creature, Rose Dragon-marked. I do not envy you your road."

"But you wouldn't, would you? You have a beautiful place here, Apple, and I wish I was able to share more of it with you."

"As am I. May I call you sister, Rose?"

"Of course, Apple. I'm flattered."

"You're welcome, my sister."

==)»> 24:7: Apple Dryad's grove

"Hello, Winter."

"Hello, Rose. You seem edgy this afternoon."

"I've been inside Apple's head."

"Is that good or bad?"

"It's confusing. I like her rather better than I did before, and I liked her a lot already, and she likes me somewhat less. Hell, I like me somewhat less."

"That sounds like a problem."

"It would be if I planned to stay here. As it is, it's just another reason to move on."

"What is the problem?"

"She's a creature of earth and life, and I'm a creature of air and water and death. We clash."

"Or complement each other. My sisters and I each have our own element, and have no trouble over it."

"It's not insurmountable, certainly. And she did call me, 'Sister'. That's quite a thing, from a dryad."

"It is quite a thing from any person with a heart."

"It is, isn't it? But whatever problems Apple may have with me, she has twice with you."

"Because I am also a creature of air and death, and she had no affection for me before she learned that."

"Pretty much."

"Where does that leave me? I do not wish to follow your road until I have gathered my sisters, and it seems I am not welcome here."

"It leaves you in need of a buffer, who would be Amma."

"You are a devious creature, Rose."

"I'll take that as a compliment."

"If you wish."

"You've been consorting with Fiddler and me FAR too much."

"I'll take that as a compliment."

"My sword just made me laugh. Deliberately, and with forethought. We are SUCH bad influences on you."

"I would beg to differ, Rose. There is joy in your banter, and I am pleased to share it."

"Fair enough."

"What will we do if Amaranth chooses to stay, and Apple will not have me?"

"I don't expect that. You're a sword, but you're also a person, and as such you're loyal and capable of friendship and kindness. Apple will see that, with a bit of coaching. And your sisters, when they arrive, are NOT death creatures. It'll work out."

“I hope so, Rose.”

“So do I. Care for some exercise?”

“It is hardly exercise for me, Rose. I only observe and comment.”

“Even so.”

==)»> 24:8: Darkness

“Good evening, Rose.”

“Good evening, Fid.”

“How was your day?”

“Productive. I linked with Apple, and Amma linked with Apple, and Apple FINALLY agreed to talk to Winter, which she’s been avoiding, and the end result is that tomorrow is going to be a party, and the day after I’m going to head downriver all by myself.”

“Which makes you sad.”

“I don’t have many friends, Fid, and I’m leaving three of them behind.”

“By your own design.”

“It’s what’s best for them, Fid. And what’s necessary for me.”

“So we’re stuck with another best bad plan.”

“Pretty much. Though this one doesn’t involve mortal danger, and actually leaves everyone but me in a pretty good place."

"So you're regretting the call of the horizon."

"A little bit, yeah."

"You need to stare that thought in the face for a few minutes."

"No, I don't."

"No?"

"No. I've already learned that lesson, Fid, learned it long ago. The only really safe place is a coffin, and I'm a long way from ready for mine. If it never hurts, how do you even know you're alive?"

"I was going to say..."

"You don't feel pain, but you're not alive either. And I know you felt pain when Osprey died, anyway. And Salsi."

"Yes."

"So for the purposes of this discussion, your peculiar state of existence is close enough to life to count."

"Yes. I was trying to find a joke in there, but you bit me instead."

"Sorry. I'm edgy."

"I think that calls for a lullaby."

"It so very much does. Please, and thank you."

"As my Lady wishes."

==)»> 24:9: Apple Dryad's grove

"You've been a very good rag doll, Winter."

"Thank you, Rose."

"And a very good sword. And a very, very good friend."

"I am very glad of your friendship, Rose."

"I really hate the idea of you being a chattel, Winter, but if you must belong to someone, I'm glad you belong to me."

"I understand, Rose."

"Let's do this formally, then. I know we've been over it already, but, well, it just doesn't hurt to make it all clear."

"As you say, Rose."

"I am Emerald Corrosion Flower Stonecrow, Dragon-marked, Twinbride, Minotaur-bane, Dryad-sister, and I claim ownership of the Panoply and all of its parts. I leave the sword, Winter, in the custody of Amaranth Minotaur-daughter, and, in the event of her death, in the custody of Apple the dryad, or whatever other custodian that Amaranth, with the consent of the Sisters of the Panoply, might choose. I charge Winter, and her sisters as they are available, to inform me of any change in the custody of the Panoply."

"I am Winter of the Panoply, and I acknowledge the things that have been stated."

"I'm getting weepy again."

"You were weepy all day yesterday, Rose."

"I was, wasn't I? Hazards of the course, I guess. It's odd to think that the next time I see you you'll be able to take human form."

"That seems likely, Rose."

"It'll be odd to have a face to put with the voice."

"And three sisters."

"And three sisters. And I'll have Fiddler's dagger, and won't THAT be an interesting experience?"

"Rose?"

"I'm getting ahead of the story, Winter. We'll deal with that circumstance when it comes up."

"If you say so."

"I do. Would you like to say goodbye to Fiddler?"

"May I ? CAN I?"

"If he's paying attention, and I'm sure he is, we should be able to call him. Let me get into a trance..."

"Hello, Ladies," said Fiddler.

“Hello, Fid. Winter would like to say goodbye,” Rose said.

“Hello, Fiddler,” said Winter.

“It has been my great pleasure to make the acquaintance of another sentient blade, Lady Winter,” Fiddler said.

“And mine also,” said Winter.

“And with that,” Rose said, “I think I need to find Amma and turn Winter over to her. Fid, we’ll speak this evening.”

“Rose? Is there time for one melody?” Winter asked.

“Of course,” Rose and Fiddler said in unison.

“Then could you please play ‘Chasing the Luck’ for me?” Winter asked.

“It would be my very great pleasure,” Fiddler said.

==)»> 24:10: Darkness

“And where are you tonight, Rose?”

“Halfway between Apple’s grove, and Auntie Willow’s.”

“And how far from there to Ironbridge?”

“Two easier days to Auntie Rowan’s grove, and one more day after that to Ironbridge.”

“And what then?”

"And then I go back to drinking green swill and trying to court the Jade Empress."

"And what has been the point of all of this?"

"I've been wondering that, myself. Horns is dead, which means he won't be eating a baby every day."

"That sounds good."

"The Sisterhood should be at least as stable under Aunt Cherry as they were under Horns, though I don't know if Cherry will be as clever as Horns was."

"Clever?"

"Horns set up a stable, isolated community that held its own for over a century. That's almost impossible. Cherry will have to work hard to sustain it, even after Horns did all of the hard work."

"So the Sisterhood broke even."

"I think so. I hope so."

"What else?"

"Amma isn't a tree any more. She's found someone who will love her and take care of her. Apple has someone to love and take care of."

"Even if Amma is pretty much going to be Apple's pet."

"The whole Sisterhood was raised to be sentient cattle. I don't know what's going to come of that in the long run. I really can't wrap my head around it."

"So if Amma is going to be someone's pet in any case, she's better off with Apple than with Cherry."

"No question there."

"Which leaves Winter and the Panoply."

"Which leaves Winter and her sisters. And Winter assured me that, as long as they weren't being abused by a corrupt master, they would all rather be sentient and together than dormant and separated."

"So that's a good thing, too."

"Yes."

"Even though you didn't get to keep the sword."

"Even though I didn't get to keep the thrice damned, beautiful, so sweet it HURT to let it go sword."

"Which was the original point of the quest."

"No, the original point of the quest was to help me find more luck, which I did, as evidenced by the fact that I can fly about twice as far in a day as I used to. Allowing that I've gotten into a lot better shape along the way."

"And you've made some friends."

"And I've made some very good friends, and I shouldn't have to worry about feeling touch-starved in quite a while, as long as nothing horrible happens along the way."

"So that's good."

"That's very good. But it reminds me. Someday, in the not too distant future, I am going to go back to Apple's grove with a certain dagger on my hip."

"Yes?"

"And there are three women there who are very dear to me, and there will be three others who are, at least, very dear to Winter, and if you hurt any of them even a tiny bit, I will make you wish you had never been born. Got it?"

"Yes, your Grace. Absolutely, your Grace."

"I just wanted to get that out. I am not going to give you a prohibition against being who you are, that I know won't hold, I am just saying that there will be NO casualties. Understood?"

"Yes, your Grace."

"I think that you and I are going to be together for a very long time, Fid. And I expect to be happy about that, and I want to make sure that YOU are happy about that. But there can't be collateral damage. Particularly among my friends."

"I understand."

"And having said all of that... Would Master Fiddler be so kind as to play me a lullaby?"

"Master Fiddler, whose somewhat illusory hands are still trembling with the vehemence with which he has recently been threatened, will do his best to comply."

25: Empress

All things of value are fated to dragon hoards.
—*The Book of the Blind King's Wisdom*

==)»> 25:1: Willow Dryad's grove

"Someone's been in the dryad brandy again."

"Maybe. Is it that obvious?"

"It's nuance, but a distinctive one. And I've had a lot of practice at reading your nuances."

"That you have."

"And how is Auntie Willow?"

"Lonely. Generous. Curious. I tend to think of Willow and Rowan as typical dryads, out of my sample of five. Apple is most human, Cherry is most devious, Moss is... different. More powerful, better at pretending to be human, probably least human in the end."

"Should I tell her you said that?"

"Your risk."

"That would be a no, then. Any actual news?"

"Auntie is REALLY curious about the link tattoo, and wants to try to duplicate it the way Apple did."

"Which means another day or two without moving, and another dryad crawling around in your head."

"And almost guarantees a repeat performance with Auntie Rowan when I get there."

"So what will you do?"

"Observe the customs of hospitality. If I'm going to claim the title of 'dryad-sister' I might as well earn it."

"While I continue to languish in my watery prison."

"Pretty much."

"Oh, cruel Fate, that bound me to such a callous and unfeeling Rescuer."

"If I laugh too hard it will break the trance."

"Oh, cruel Fate..."

"Just stop. We have good communication, and only one more wall to climb, and we can afford a few more days. And beyond THAT, I can probably talk Auntie into giving me a bottle of brandy to sell at the next town I come to."

"Because?"

"Because I could use some pocket money, and any innkeeper who doesn't empty the till to buy the rest of the bottle of dryad brandy after taking one taste is probably in the wrong line of work."

"Fine. Just don't turn into a dryad on me."

"No worries. If Apple didn't get to me, a less human dryad doesn't really have a chance."

"Says the bold voice of ignorance."

"Says the sorceress who has already played this game twice."

"Fine. But you owe me a taste of dryad brandy."

"Now, THAT is an interesting challenge. I'll put it on my list. In the meantime, might I have a lullaby?"

"I guess. If you insist."

"I don't. I ask, with affection, humility, and gratitude."

"Well, damn. Can't say no to that. As my Heart wishes."

==)»> 25:2: Darkness

"So did Willow get the link figured out?"

"She did."

"And how did it go?"

"Oddly."

"How so?"

"She's a bit afraid of me now. She doesn't dislike me, or want me to hurry away, but she's gotten a bit... deferential. Like she's suddenly realized that I'm royalty, or... Imagine how a child feels when it finds a box in the attic full of medals, and suddenly realizes that silly old Uncle Feltus is a war hero who has killed a LOT of people."

"That sounds unfortunate."

"I should have told her all about Horns before we opened the link. And Losty. And, well, I'm just a lot more dragon that she expected, even though she knows what my true form is. But she still LIKES me, and still enjoys my company, and I'm still going to leave here tomorrow with a bottle of her brandy that I can try to parlay into some coin."

"And you're still welcome to come back?"

"Definitely. She's another adopted sister, though that was odd, too. Apple offered me sisterhood as a gift, a thing that she had that she knew I would value. Willow WANTED me to offer HER sisterhood, but was too shy to ask."

"But you asked her."

"Of course I did. I cost me nothing, and would have been cruel not to. I'm just marveling at the surreality of being solicited for sisterhood by a dryad."

"That's near-the-edge weird, for you. Well over the edge for a normal person, of course."

"Which is to say that I'm over-the-edge weird for humanity at large."

"When was the last time you looked in a mirror?"

"Point made. Lullaby?"

"Of course."

==)»> 25:3: Darkness

"Good evening, Rose. Something is different..."

"I'm sleeping in a real bed for the first time since Ironbridge, courtesy of Willow's brandy."

"I thought you were going to trade that for coin."

"Bed, bath, two meals, AND a pocketful of coin, as it happens."

"Clever girl."

"Clever enough, anyway. Any news from the south?"

"Not much. I'm getting better at Territories, which is still not exactly good. Everyone is happy that you found the sword, and they're all eager to hear about killing the monster from you directly, and they're all mystified as to why you still don't have the sword. Well, I gave all the details to Bing and Auntie Moss, because of the distance, but Auntie Moss seemed to know a lot of it already."

"She's Auntie Moss. Did she say anything about the fact that I don't have the sword with me?"

“She seemed to expect it. I didn’t push. She’s Auntie Moss.”

“Exactly. I’ve been inside the heads of two dryads, now, and I still don’t have a clue about Auntie Moss. And she still scares me, to be honest.”

“That’s almost proof of sanity.”

“Almost.”

“Well, you’re still you. Not many people look at the horizon and wonder how big a piece they can bite off.”

“Their loss.”

“My gain.”

“If you say so.”

“Lullaby?”

“Please.”

==)»> 25:4: Darkness

“Good evening, Rose. How is Auntie Rowan?”

“As expected, mostly. Not interested in studying my tattoo, though.”

“Oh?”

“Been there, done that, regards it as a mistake. Won’t say why.”

"Is she hostile to you about it?"

"No, she's at least as friendly as she was on the outbound trip. AND taught me something interesting about this 'dryad-sister' thing."

"Which is?"

"It's not just a formality. She could sense it, on me. She looked at me, called me, 'Dryad-sister', and named both Apple and Willow. And then she offered me her hand and said that she had enough sisters, but could always use another friend."

"And you said yes."

"Of course. But then I asked if there was a limit, or a danger, to having too many sisters."

"You're getting prudent in your old age."

"Brat. She said that she'd heard of dryad-sisters becoming dryads themselves, but never involuntarily. She said it was usually a case of a woman who could feel death approaching wanting to change the game."

"Which doesn't apply to you. And may never, if I can do anything about it."

"Yup. If Death wants to come for me, he had better not try to slip through the bedroom window on a quiet night; he's going to need an army."

"I like the sound of that. The resistance, not the army."

"When have you ever known me to be meek and submissive?"

“I’d think about it, but I’m laughing too hard.”

“Exactly.”

“Where does Auntie Moss fit into this ‘dryad-sister’ thing? Rowan was the first dryad who recognized something special about you because of your tattoos.”

“I asked Rowan that. She said that my other tattoos marked me as a dryad FRIEND, and that was enough.”

“And the difference between that and what she offered you today?”

“I think it means that I arrived with an ASSUMPTION of trustworthiness, and now I’ve EARNED it. But it has magical teeth behind it, so it’s a bit deeper than that. Also subtle, and very much not human.”

“Better you than me, I think. Would my friend-of-vegetables care for a lullaby?”

“I’d love one.”

==)»> 25:5: Darkness

“Rose, what are you doing in Losthaven?”

“Sleeping, silly Fiddler.”

“But... I thought you were going to Ironbridge.”

“So did I, but I thought about it, and realized that Losthaven was closer, and I had friends there, and I don’t really know anyone in Ironbridge, and I can stage my journey into the Land of Jade equally well from either place."

"Are you at Drellan's place?"

"Yep. Got my own room back, too."

"Dzee moved into Drellan's room?"

"Yep. Not quite sure how that happened without intervention, but I'm glad it did."

"As if you were the only possible source of intervention."

"Someone from the town?"

"Or maybe someone who knows Dzee fairly well, and has been talking to Drellan regularly."

"You didn't!"

"Of course I did. I haven't been able to speak to Dzee since Osprey died, but she's still one of my girls, and I care about her."

"I did not see that coming. Should have, but didn't."

"It's still your plan. I just rushed it a little bit."

"You've gotten generous, lately."

"What, with Dzee? I never had a claim on her, or she on me. I just liked her, and want her to be happy. And I'm not inside her horizon."

“You used to save up hatred for anyone that I had sex with.”

“I’m currently inclined to jealous hatred for ANYONE who manages to have sex. Except I really CAN’T hate you, so I hate your partners. But celibate Rose is cranky Rose. and I can’t do anything about that at the moment, so I’d rather have you happy than chaste, at least most of the time. “

“And where will that leave me once I have the dagger, and we can be together again?”

“Free to sample other people’s cooking, but never, ever hungry, ever again.”

“No more jealousy?”

“What’s to be jealous of? I’m the best that’s ever been.”

“And a paragon of modesty.”

“It’s my nature.”

“Fair enough. Would Master Scorpion care to play me a lullaby?”

“Master Scorpion would be honored.”

==)»> 25:6: Darkness

“You’ve been in the green swill again.”

“A bit. I can’t avoid the stuff and continue to socialize with kobolds, so I’m trying to find a sweet spot between rejecting hospitality and wanting to die the next morning."

"Is it really that bad?"

"It's hard to explain to someone who's never been hung over. Imagine having a headache so bad that every footfall feels like someone is using your head as a drum, and then imagine having to GALLOP a significant distance in that state."

"Ouch."

"Every wing stroke is ALMOST as bad as one of the footfalls."

"Ouch, twice. But you're back to ingratiating yourself among the kobs?"

"It seems the best course. Though now I can get everywhere in the Land of Jade in a day, so I can sleep in my own bed every other day if I want to."

"It's back to being YOUR bed, is it?"

"Dzee has made it clear to both Drellan and me that she owes me too much for it to EVER not be my bed, if I want it."

"It's nice to have friends."

"It is, that. In the meantime, I'm making some progress with the kobs. I was pretty sure that the Empress had some kind of information network in place, and I got a little bit of proof of that tonight. Not sure of all of the details, but it's pretty clear that she knows everything significant that happens in her territory in three or four days, and she can then check it out herself the day after she gets the news. Her whole territory is a day trip for her."

"That's handy."

"It also means that however her communication system works, it's mostly one way; it brings information to her, and she deals with it in person. I imagine that news CAN travel outward, but not nearly as fast."

"All of which means?"

"If she decides she wants to see me, it'll probably be a summons to meet at a particular landmark some days in advance, to make sure I get the message and have time to travel."

"So no chance to actually see her home."

"I don't think she would want that, anyway. Not if she has anything like her rumored treasure there."

"Ah, well. It's never easy."

"I'm not planning to rob her anyway, Fid."

"But theft is so much faster than honesty."

"And getting eaten by an angry dragon is SO productive."

"Yes, it's much better to be eaten by a friendly dragon."

"Idiot."

""I'm a lot smarter when I'm not so impatient."

"Hah!"

"Fine. But I CAN play the fiddle."

"I've heard rumors."

==)»> 25:7: Darkness

"What are you doing in Skytower?"

"Sleeping. Visiting. Sleeping in my very own room in my very own bed that might even be better than the one that Bing loaned to me in Landfall. I had to shift into Emma just so that I could fully appreciate how wonderful it is."

"Come again?"

"Human skin is better at experiencing fabric texture than Sister Dragon's scales. Or anything else that my other forms offer, for that matter."

"Start the story at the beginning."

"Skytower is a day trip from Losthaven, these days, and I just wanted to fly down to say hello to Dlef and Turo and Ollie. And the twins were all excited to show me that they had remodeled their house, and that they had built a new bedroom just for me under the roof. It has a balcony that Sister Wings can fly from, and, since I occasionally rhapsodized about the bed I had had in Landfall, they hunted down the best bed maker in Skytower, and now I have THAT. So of course I had to stay the night."

"Do the brothers expect to participate in breaking in the new bed?"

"I don't think so. They've been exploring their legal options, and have figured out that if either of them found a female who was willing to become a secondary wife, after me, she'd still be legally married to both of them, and would have to have my consent, but in practice she could really be married to only one."

"I don't get headaches, but you're trying really hard to cure that."

"And, as it happens, they've BOTH found females who're willing to become legal secondary co-wives who are effectively primary wives, and they would all REALLY like it if I gave consent."

"Which you will."

"Of course. The five of us had a meal together this evening, and the girls seem very pleasant and polite. I terrify them."

"THAT sounds cozy."

"Well, Sister Dragon is STRANGE to them, and they're pretty much homebodies, so meeting someone with ten thousand miles behind her is just a bit intimidating."

"Particularly when she's you."

"Maybe."

"So when will this latest affront to the concept of marriage take place?"

"As soon as it can be arranged. A matter of months."

"Are you postponing your further adventures among the kobolds in the meantime?"

"Of course not. But I have a place to visit here, any time I want it, when I get tired of the swamp. Or of Losthaven."

"So that's good."

"I haven't lost sight of the prize, Fid. I want that dagger almost as much as you want me to have it."

"So you say."

"I do say, Silly Scorpion. Now play me my lullaby, and let me sleep."

"Yes, your Grace."

"And Fid? Thank you."

"For the lullaby?"

"For you, silly Scorpion. Just all of you."

==)»> 25:8: A kobold village

"You're not sleeping."

"Too agitated. I got my summons."

"From the Empress?"

"Yup. Noon, on an island just off the coast, six days from now."

"An island?"

"A recognizable mud flat. A place with no cover and long sight lines."

"So a difficult place to mount an ambush."

"Exactly."

"So what now?"

"Tomorrow, as soon as it's light, I fly by the meeting point and get it fixed in my head. Then I go back to Losthaven and try to figure out what to say. I'll talk to Drellan and see what he thinks. Maybe I'll fly down to Skytower and have a talk with Dlef, too."

"These are conversations you should have had long ago."

"They're conversations I DID have long ago, and didn't come to a conclusion. And probably won't this time, either, but I have to do something. Six days is a long time."

"Take 'Revenant' for a sail."

"That's... a really good idea, actually."

"Thank you. But why are you so nervous? The Empress isn't close to as terrifying as Maelstrom, is she?"

"No, Maelstrom could bite her in half. But Maelstrom came to ME, offered me friendship. I'm seeking the Empress out. And when you're a cockroach, it doesn't really matter if the foot that crushes you belonged to a small child or a minotaur."

"Ah. Time for a lullaby?"

"Almost. Chase the luck for me first, please?"

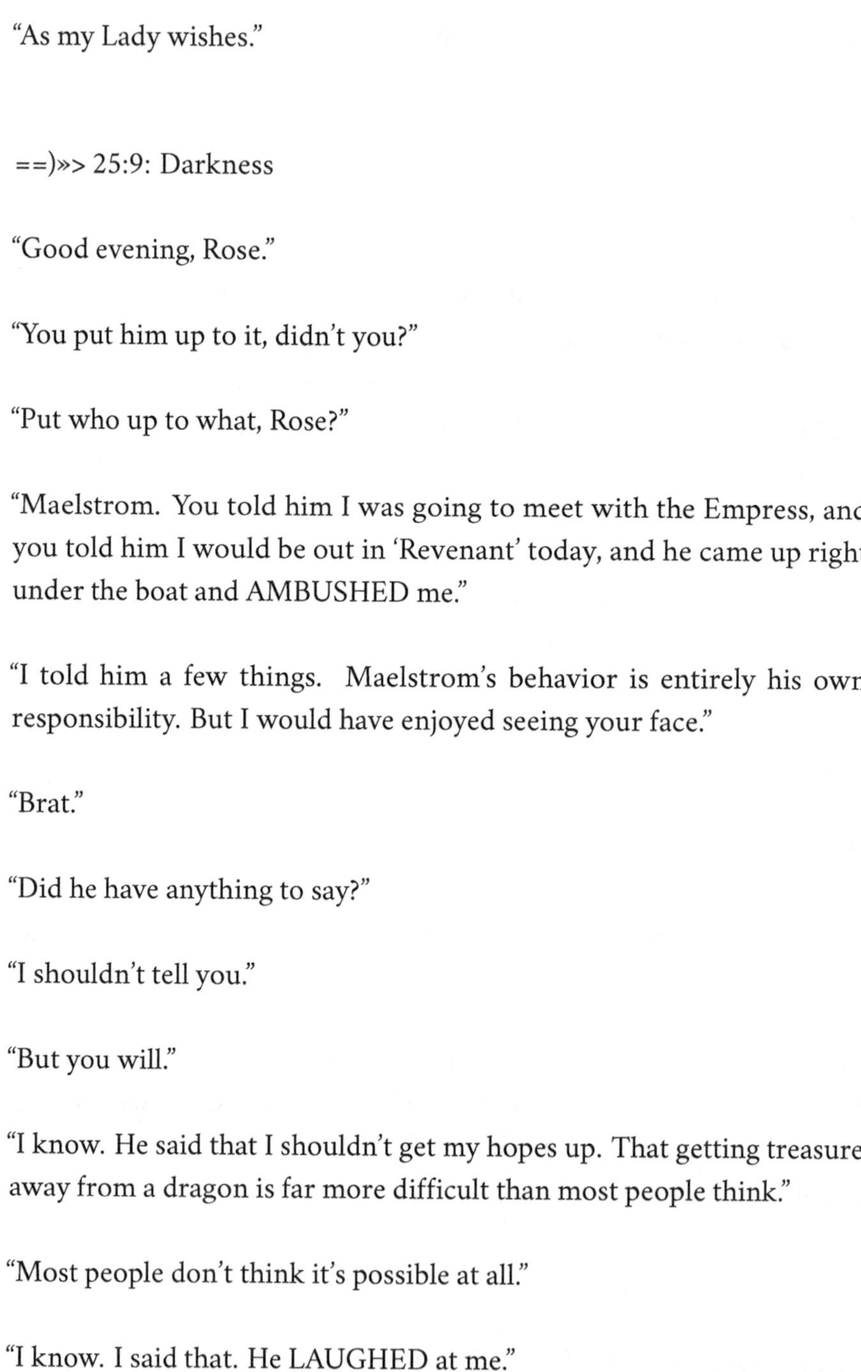

"As my Lady wishes."

==)»> 25:9: Darkness

"Good evening, Rose."

"You put him up to it, didn't you?"

"Put who up to what, Rose?"

"Maelstrom. You told him I was going to meet with the Empress, and you told him I would be out in 'Revenant' today, and he came up right under the boat and AMBUSHED me."

"I told him a few things. Maelstrom's behavior is entirely his own responsibility. But I would have enjoyed seeing your face."

"Brat."

"Did he have anything to say?"

"I shouldn't tell you."

"But you will."

"I know. He said that I shouldn't get my hopes up. That getting treasure away from a dragon is far more difficult than most people think."

"Most people don't think it's possible at all."

"I know. I said that. He LAUGHED at me."

"He laughs a lot."

"And it's always terrifying. But I'm glad I talked to him, and he offered to back me up, sort of."

"He what?"

"He said he would be in deep water straight off the island, and if things go sideways, and I can survive long enough to start heading out to sea, the Empress will know that I have friends."

"That's... kind of amazing. Hard to take advantage of, but amazing."

"That was my thought. Why does he care about me, Fid?"

"All he's ever told me is that you amuse him. And he seems to be proud of you, for some reason."

"That IS strange."

"I mean, I think you're pretty wonderful, given the fact that you take WAY too many risks on behalf people who aren't me, but I don't know what's in it for Maelstrom. Why haven't you ever asked him yourself?"

"Among other reasons, saying something like, 'Why bother with me?' to the Great Monster Turtle while you're riding on his back might prompt him to change his mind."

"I can see that. So what are you going to do tomorrow?"

"Aerobatics, I think. Something that doesn't leave me room to think."

"And then the meeting the day after."

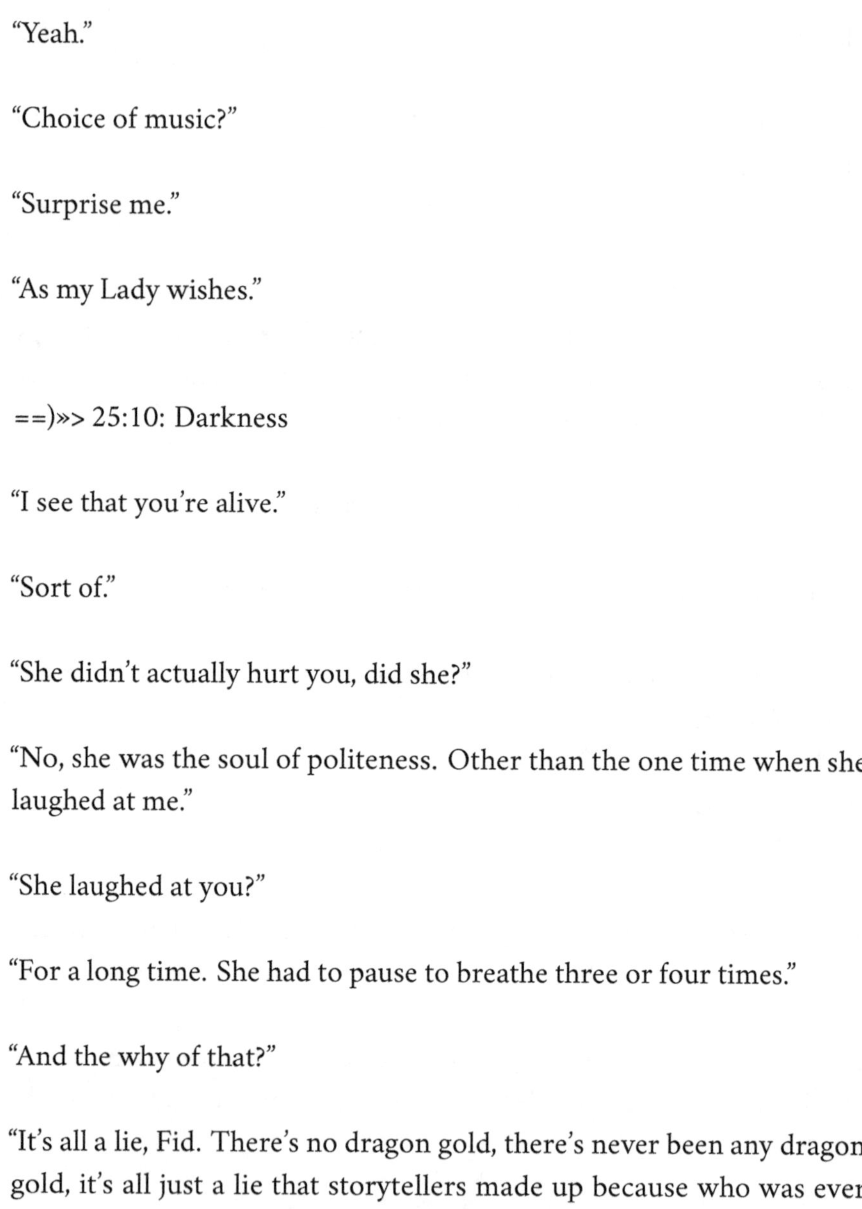

"Yeah."

"Choice of music?"

"Surprise me."

"As my Lady wishes."

==)»> 25:10: Darkness

"I see that you're alive."

"Sort of."

"She didn't actually hurt you, did she?"

"No, she was the soul of politeness. Other than the one time when she laughed at me."

"She laughed at you?"

"For a long time. She had to pause to breathe three or four times."

"And the why of that?"

"It's all a lie, Fid. There's no dragon gold, there's never been any dragon gold, it's all just a lie that storytellers made up because who was ever going to know better? No one would ever believe the kobs who have been there because they're just stupid kobs and no one ever believes them about anything.."

"No. Gold. At. All."

"None. No treasure of any kind. You know what the Empress cares about? Land. Start to clear cut a field on her land, and she will hunt you down and kill you and your bothers and your sisters and your parents and the girl that you almost married, just to prove a point. Civilization STOPS at her borders, because this land is HERS. But treasure? What would be the point?"

"Um.... You can use it to buy things?"

"Like the loyalty of kobolds who are so terrified that it amounts to worship? Or maybe the loyalty of a lieutenant who is just as happy with a platoon of those same kobolds for his or her own purposes, or maybe just the idea of being outside of civilization and PROTECTED?"

"Um..."

"Look at it this way. Suppose you had a friend who was a pixie, less than two feet tall, less than five pounds. He was a fiddler, too, and he gave you the best fiddle he had ever made FOR HIMSELF. What would you do with it? What would Fiddler-the-faun or Fiddler-the-centaur have done with it?"

"Put it on a shelf and gaze fondly at it from time to time?"

"Because?"

"Because it would be about the size of the palm of my hand."

"And what would a multi-ton dragon that was proportionally bigger than a human by that same margin do with ANYTHING that a human made for human use? If that dragon didn't happen to HAVE any shelves, or a good place to store otherwise useless keepsakes?"

"Throw it away?"

"And there is no dragon gold and there never has been any dragon gold, because keeping gold or really any kind of treasure that humans would care about would be just plain insane. Dragons live hundreds of years, and they sleep a LOT of that time, but every last one of them has better things to do than pile up things that are completely useless to themselves just for the sake of doing it."

"Bait?"

"Say what? Maybe. If they really liked the taste of humans, but... It still doesn't work. It's easier to just raid a village."

"So now what?"

"I have no idea. Maybe I'll visit Auntie Rowan and get stupid on dryad brandy."

"That's one day, maybe two..."

"Maybe I'll go visit Apple and work on, 'Never seen again,' for a while."

"I doubt that."

"So do I."

"Are you quitting?"

"What? Gods no. You. Are. Mine. And I am GOING to get my hands on that dagger, and you are going to pull me into dreamspace and we are going to forget all about this idiocy for a long time, and THEN I am going to go out and tear off a piece of the horizon with my teeth."

“I like the way that sounds better. But you still need a path.”

“I know. I suppose I could go visit Auntie Moss, and see if she has any ideas. Maybe she knows of another sword that needs rescuing. Or maybe a staff this time...”

“Yes? I can HEAR the wheels grinding.”

“Not yet, Fid. I have to do some research, first. And talk to the Empress again, and Maelstrom, and, well, do a lot of planning and thinking and you are SO not going to like it, but it’s a PATH and I am on it we are sure as hell going to tear that hole in the horizon.”

“Um... Good?”

“Damned straight.”

“Music?”

“Please.”

“If you ask me for a march I am going to refuse. Tonight, you get sleepy.”

“Spoilsport.”

“Every chance I get.”

26: Rotters

Flight is easy. A rock can fly, with a bit of help. A man on a clifftop can fly. It's at the other end, during the transition from airborne to earthbound, where bones break and life ends. Getting airborne is easy. The magic is in surviving the experience.

—Xart Windchaser, *Flight*

==)»> 26:1: Darkness

"Good morning, Rose. Are we more nearly sane this morning?"

"Morning?"

"Nearly dawn."

"Ah. What's that about my sanity?"

"Last night you shifted from depressed to manic so quickly I got dizzy."

"Really?"

"No. But I was and am concerned."

"Sorry."

"Does being sorry include letting me know what's going on?"

"Um... Yeah, I guess so. It was too crazy last night. But I just had an epiphany about dragon treasure, and you are SO not going to like it."

"Yes?"

"Think about Sulissa. And Winter."

"Artifacts made from dragon bone."

"Which is almost certainly very valuable in the right hands."

"I would assume so."

"And generally hard to get your hands on, but actually plentiful at the source, if you can get any at all."

"Hundreds of pounds are available once you have met the access conditions."

"Yes."

"Are you planning to murder the Empress?"

"No. But I realized that if I found a dragon that NEEDED killing, and killed it, I would have access to a fortune in dragon bone."

"If you can find a dragon that needs killing."

"Yes."

"And can then actually kill said dragon."

"Yes."

"You were right to say I'd hate this idea. Hatred isn't a strong enough word. This makes all of the craziness that you've dealt with in your life so far look stable and boring."

"I know. But I already have a dragon in mind."

"This does not comfort me."

"Sorry."

"No, you're not. Not in the least. But continue anyway."

"After I told the Empress what I wanted, and after she stopped laughing, she said that it was a shame that she couldn't hire me, because she DID have a problem that I MIGHT be able to help her with."

"A rival?"

"A rot dragon, with a pair of young concubines. He's set himself up on the northeast corner of her land, and is killing the local countryside, which is what rot dragons do. And in a couple of decades, when his playmates are old enough to start laying eggs, he is probably going to start building a colony of rot dragons. In a hundred and fifty years, the Empress will be dead and forgotten, all of her land will be toxic, and he'll start expanding into the surrounding human lands."

"In a hundred and fifty years?"

"When you have an unlimited lifespan, you tend to think in the long term. You should know that."

“Regular exposure to human mortality tends to mitigate that.”

“Have you been saving that line?”

“Maybe.”

“And you make noises about MY sanity. Anyway, it’s a stupid idea, because if this idiot manages to kill the Empress and capture her territory, humanity will NOTICE, and any effort to expand will be put down. But I kind of LIKE the Empress, and would love to have a few dead dragons to play with, so I can use this.”

“Why doesn’t the Empress handle it personally?”

“The big rotter is too close to being her match, and the presence of those concubines makes the fight unwinnable.”

“And the reason he doesn’t attack the Empress?”

“He doesn’t want to risk those same concubines. Dragons are rare. Dragons who are eager to breed are rarer.”

“And you think you can kill them.”

“I don’t need to KILL them, I just need to make sure that they die, and that I can collect the bodies.”

“So what insane thing are you going to do next?”

“Guess.”

“You are NOT.”

"I have to."

"You... 'Excuse me, Mister Dragon, Sir, I have been led to believe that you deserve to be killed out of hand. Would you be so kind as to confirm or deny that for the record?' Of course you're going to. You wouldn't be you if you didn't make SURE."

"You're good at that. Can you do an impression of a chicken next?"

"Rose..."

"You're right. I can't kill them unless I talk to them and confirm that they need to die, first."

"I hate you."

"No you don't."

"I hate the fact that you have a conscience that won't let you just kill them for profit."

"No you don't."

"I hate the fact that I actually admire you for being self-destructively ethical."

"That sounds closer."

"Please don't get killed."

"I'll do my best."

"Go. Get on with being insane. I'll still be here tonight."

"Until the day, Fid."

"Until the day."

==)»> 26:2: Darkness

"You're still alive, I see."

"So far."

"What stupid thing did you fail to do, and thereby make this conversation possible?"

"Your speech gets elliptical when you're cranky."

"When I'm worried."

"You're usually worried."

"Even so. I repeat the question."

"I just did some exploring. Rotters are NASTY. Their territory is really easy to spot from the air; all of the vegetation is sick. Or maybe different; it doesn't seem to actually DIE, just mutate. But it changes color, and is easy to find."

"So you know where they are?"

"Very roughly. The Empress claims about ten thousand square miles, and they're established inside about five hundred of that."

"Enough to make the Empress unhappy."

"Particularly if they start breeding."

"So now what?"

"Same deal as with the Empress. I start cultivating the local kobs and crocs and hope for an audience. And in the meantime I keep looking for the lair itself."

"Sounds unpleasant. And dangerous."

"Fortunately it's not the only thing on my agenda. I have to go down to Skytower and have a talk with Cinnabar about the price of dragon bone, and I really ought to have another conversation with Maelstrom, too."

"He's usually available, given a few days notice. Unless he gets bored with you, and adopts another pet."

"Does that seem likely?"

"I have no clue. I still haven't figured out why he keeps playing Territories with me."

"He thinks you might turn into a worthy opponent."

"In several hundred years, maybe."

"He's got the time, and so do you. He plays a LONG game."

"I suppose."

"In the meantime... Lullaby?"

"As my Lady wishes."

==)»> 26:3: Drellan's house

“Why aren't you sleeping? What's wrong?”

“Sleep? I don't do that any more. I've given it up.”

“That won't work. I repeat, what's wrong?”

“I met one of the rotters.”

“Big or small?”

“One ton as opposed to six ton. ‘Small’ doesn't work.”

“I take it things went badly.”

“I lived.”

“Alive is good. What happened?”

“She was stalking me. She must have taken to the sky at dawn, and been looking for me from very high. I was flying along, minding my own business, and suddenly a head as big as my torso was right next to me. She could have bitten me in half if she had wanted to.”

“It would seem that she didn't.”

“So far. She asked me why I was asking about her family, and I was so flustered I told her the truth.”

“That you wanted to kill her?”

“Well, some of the truth. That I had been tasked by the Empress to convince her family to leave the Land of Jade."

"That's not much truth."

"It's absolutely true. Just incomplete."

"Continuning..."

"She laughed at me, told me that it was their land, now, and that they had no intention of leaving. "

"Not surprising."

"And then she said that I looked tasty, and that she couldn't decide if she should let me carry the message back to the Empress, or just eat me."

"It would seem diplomacy won."

"After a fashion. She said that she COULD just burn me out of the sky immediately..."

"Rotters breathe fire?"

"Rotters spit acid. Burned is burned."

"Point made."

"She said she had been watching me, and that she was sure she could out run me, and out climb me, but that I almost certainly had an edge in maneuverability. So she said we would play tag. If she won, she got a snack, and if I won, I got to live."

"Generous of her."

"I asked what the end condition was, and she just laughed and bellowed, 'GO!' and I went."

"And how long did this go on"

"Almost two hours. I was going flat out the whole time, constantly looking over my shoulder, using every trick I knew to stay away from her claws and her mouth. And she would NOT stop talking, telling me what a stupid, arrogant little lizard I was, and how hopeless my situation was, and how good I was going to taste when she finally caught me..."

"But she didn't."

"I don't think she really wanted to; it was too much fun to torture me. She probably would have if she'd gotten bored, but I got away before then."

"And if one might ask how?"

"I found a decent sized lake, dove in, shifted to Sister Croc, and hid in the mud."

"And she didn't follow you? I though rotters were good in the water."

"I can only guess that she had had enough fun for one day, and wasn't really that hungry for kobold."

"Small favor."

"Damned straight."

"So now what?"

"Eventually, I am going to stop shaking, and then I will drink a distillery, and someday I will get some sleep."

"Would some music help?"

"Can I pretend that you're holding me?"

"Of course."

"Then play on, Master Fiddler. And Fid?"

"Yes?"

"Thank you."

==)»> 26:4: Darkness

"And how was Maelstrom?"

"He was Maelstom. He was worried about me, but also willing to talk. And willing to kill rotters for me, if I can work out the logistics."

"That would be difficult."

"Really tempting, though."

"And what did you talk about?"

"Rot dragons, mostly.."

"Did you learn anything useful?"

“The best bit was about their ability to spit acid. They don’t have much range with it at all.”

“Which is useful if you have occasion to fight a rot dragon with the appropriate combination of broken legs and wings.”

“Which is useful if I can figure out how to out-fly them.”

“Is that likely?”

“I don’t know. I do know that I’m going to have to start studying Crazy Xart again.”

“You’re going to study. A book. Under a roof.”

“Yes?”

“That would be comforting if I wasn’t sure something terrifying will come out of it.”

“Then take comfort in the idea that I’ll be absolutely safe as long as I’m studying.”

“I will. I do. But I know it won’t last.”

“Then play me a lullaby and enjoy the eye of the storm.”

“As my Lady wishes.”

==)»> 26:5: Drellan’s house

“You’re not sleeping.”

"Too excited."

"Because?"

"I got a secret message from Xart."

"Hasn't he been dead for a long time?"

"Maybe."

"So how are you getting messages?"

"I just noticed a line in one of his thaumatology passages that I hadn't considered before."

"Which was?"

"Something like, 'While the standard levitation spell can be modified in a similar way, and will produce significant thrust at a very low cost in magical energy, the spell includes no means of controlling the object's attitude, and has proved to be far too dangerous to be practical.' It's GREAT."

"Attitude?"

"Orientation in space. Which compass point you're facing, and whether you're looking at the ground or the sky."

"That sounds important."

"It is, but just because the SPELL doesn't control it doesn't mean you're out of control."

"And this is relevant because?"

"Because the flight spell is still over my head, but the levitation spell isn't."

"The levitation spell, which, when modified, was too dangerous for Xart, whom everyone thought was insane."

"Maybe."

"Which you are going to learn and modify at the first opportunity."

"Maybe."

"Explain to me, again, why I don't hate you."

"It gets better."

"I can hardly wait."

"The modified flight spell works off of body weight, and only has a surplus thrust of five percent of rest mass. The modified levitation spell has a thrust ceiling of five hundred pounds."

"Which means?"

"A human, or Sister Dragon, under the influence of the flight spell, is capable of about ninety miles per hour, and a maximum climb speed of about twenty-five miles per hour. The levitation spell, applied to Sister Dragon, is probably capable of two hundred and fifty, and can climb at about one fifty. Assuming Xart's math is any good."

"So you want to learn a spell that will let you spin and tumble uncontrollably at two hundred and fifty miles per hour."

"Absolutely. Though I really don't think I'll ever fly at that speed; I think it would peel my skin off."

"And what makes you think you'll survive this idiocy?"

"Xart and all of his fellows were sorcerers who STUDIED winged flight, but none of them ever actually DID it. Sorcerers with wings are rare, and, in the normal course of things, the ability to shift into a winged shape comes AFTER the ability to cast the flight spell. But I'm coming into this with a few hundred hours of winged flight behind me. Most of the things that Xart writes long warnings about are things that I already know how to do, and can do well."

"Please don't die."

"I have no intention of it."

"Do you have any news that a sane person might actually consider GOOD?"

"Maybe. Would you like it if I told you that this means I could out fly a dragon?"

"Slightly."

"So this isn't completely crazy?"

"You're going to try to learn a trick that was too dangerous for crazy-man Xart because it will be useful when you try your NEXT insanely dangerous trick."

"Maybe we should just stop talking to each other until I actually have the dagger in my hands."

"Maybe we... Good gods, Rose, NO. Just don't get killed."

"I'll do my best. In the meantime, I think that I might be able to get to sleep, if someone were to play me a lullaby."

"Someone might. Maybe."

==)»> 26:6: Darkness

"So how is Skytower?"

"Still Skytower. I found Cinnabar and talked to him about dragon bone, WITHOUT having sex with him, thank the gods, and then I visited Dlef, and found that he had a Standard Notation copy of the levitation spell..."

"Standard Notation?"

"Every sorcerer is different, so every sorcerer's spell book is different. Part of learning book magic is learning the notation that all sorcerers use to record spells. If you get your hands on another sorcerer's spell book, you have to work your way through each spell and find the common skeleton underneath the necessary personalizations."

"And the skeleton is the Standard Notation version."

"Right. Something that everyone needs, but no one can use directly."

"And then you went on to modify that with Xart's insane parameters."

"After I get the standard spell down. The modified version will be a DIFFERENT Standard Notation spell, which I'll then have to mark up to be functional."

"So how much longer are you going to be in Skytower?"

"A few days. I want to get the Xart version of the spell working. And then I need to practice flying with it a bit, but I think I'll do that in Losthaven. And THEN I go back to the swamp and start hunting for rotters."

"Hunting for them."

"Well, the one who terrorized me, anyway. I want a rematch."

"With a ton of rot dragon."

"Yes."

"I'm doomed."

"I can already out-maneuver her, I have a longer ranged weapon, and if I can out run her, and out climb her, it won't even be a fight. It'll be an execution."

"That doesn't sound like you."

"I'm going to get another audience with the Empress first, and I'll get a formal commission to banish or destroy the rotters."

"Which will make it legal, sort of. It still doesn't really sound like you."

"I'm going to tell them that they need to leave of die. And I'll give them that choice. And if they don't leave..."

"Which they won't..."

"... I'm going to kill them."

"Rose against several tons of dragon."

"They're violent thieves, Fid. They need to be stopped. I happen to be trying to make a profit on the deal, but I might do it anyway, because it needs to be done."

"Don't. Get. Killed."

"This is really all for you. You could be more grateful."

"Yes, your Grace. Certainly, your Grace."

"Just... stop. How did you survive four years of silence?"

"I used to just... not sleep, exactly, but fade out, and not pay attention to the time. Every now and then I would wake up and look around, and then fade away again. Sooner or later I would have just faded out forever."

"And now?"

"And now I have hope. And it's tearing me apart."

"I can see that. I can FEEL that. But the end is coming. I can feel that, too."

"Not soon enough."

"Never soon enough. But the music helps a lot."

"Ah. A song cue."

"I was hoping."

"Hope fulfilled."

==)»> 26:7: Drellan's house

"Good evening, Rose. You're... exhilarated and exhausted?"

"Good call. Yes to both."

"And the why?"

"Sister Dragon can fly."

"Which answers the exhilaration. And the exhaustion?"

"It took six hours of practice to learn how to land."

"That sounds like a story."

"I understand why Xart thought the unbound levitation spell was too dangerous to mess with. I came into the game with a ton of flight experience, AND a tail, and a ton of experience with water landings and the associated swimming skills. And I STILL nearly broke myself."

"This wasn't supposed to be a scary story."

"Sorry. Let's start with a little theory. The standard levitation spell provides variable thrust through the center of gravity of the object, along a line that goes through that center of mass, and the center of the earth. After stripping the safeties out of the spell, it still wasn't useful until the thrust vector was shifted to something useful, so I tied it to the average vector of the thoracic spine. This is boring you to tears, isn't it?"

"No."

"Why the hell not? I know you don't give a damn about thaumatology or anatomy or flight dynamics."

"I don't. But I love the joy that you radiate when you talk about those things, and I don't want you to stop."

"That's... damn you, Fid. That's just too sweet."

"The gobbledygook has stopped. I like the gobbledygook."

"Fine. So the center of thrust is somewhere around my breastbone, and my center of drag is somewhere between my hips, so if I just want to go straight and fast, everything takes care of itself. But when it comes time to land, I have to slow down, and get my feet underneath me, and that gets tricky."

"Because?"

"Directional control is entirely a matter of speed, and to land I need to either get speed to zero, or at least down to a running speed with my body in an attitude that allows running, A ten mile an hour pancake landing on my back is not an option."

"Did you by any chance think of any of this before you took off?"

"Most of it. I though that, worst case, I could get up a few thousand feet and shift to Sister Wings, and let HER land."

"You're being sane again. That makes me nervous."

"You wouldn't have thought so to see me. And you would love the braking maneuver: Tail straight behind me, legs tucked up tight, and hands high overhead. It looks silly, but it works."

"I can see that."

"I realized that trying to land dry would almost certainly break something, so I started practicing landings out in the middle of Dragon Lake."

"And how long until that became a public spectacle?"

"Not very."

"Was there a betting pool?"

"Two of them. One in Losthaven, and one in Kobtown. There were some pretty spectacular crashes, and a LOT of impressive rooster tails from near misses, and eventually I nailed several in a row, came into shore, and did a nice, soft, flat-footed landing on dry land."

"In front of half the town."

"At least. And no one knew quite what it was all about, because I was wearing an illusion of Sister Wings the whole time."

"Sister Wings, whose reputation for grandiose eccentricity has now reached new levels."

"Of course."

"So now what?"

"Now I get an audience with the Empress, and then I go hunting."

"Lullaby?"

"Oh, gods, yes."

==)»> 26:8: Darkness

"Good evening, Rose. How was the Empress?"

"Irritated at first. Frightened, by the end."

"That's an accomplishment."

"Not really one I'm proud of, but it was necessary."

"And the story?"

"She wasn't thrilled about meeting with me, but she had realized that I was looking for her lair, and decided that she would rather meet me on neutral ground, like last time. She said she didn't expect me to have anything worthwhile to say, and wanted to get the meeting over with."

"The soul of politeness."

"Pretty much. So I told her I was prepared to kill the rotters, and I wanted her commission to drive them off or kill them if necessary, and she laughed at that, and said that if I could pull that off, she would make me a real duchess to go with my nickname."

"Generous of her. Since it still won't really mean anything."

"Probably. Then I said that, since I would almost certainly have to kill at least one of the rotters, I wanted the bodies as payment. THAT got her attention."

"I don't imagine dragons enjoy dealing with dragon slayers."

"Nope. So I told her what I had in mind, and she was skeptical. She was pretty sure I would fail, and was afraid I would goad the rotters into attacking HER, so I suggested a demonstration."

"And she went for it."

"She did. I backed off half a mile, and then came straight at her; she had to take me down with poison gas before I could tag her with a mage bolt."

"You're here, so I assume you won."

"Yep."

"I don't imagine she liked that at all."

"I told you she was afraid of me by the end."

"I imagine."

"Fid... as I was leaving, I called her, 'Your Majesty,' and SHE called ME, "Your Grace.'"

"That's... Damn."

"Yeah."

"Would her Grace care for a lullaby?"

"ROSE would like a lullaby very much."

27: Dragonfall

Fearless, fierce, and foolish is an acceptable epitaph.
—Sessoria Terrorwind

==)»> 27:1: Darkness

“So how is Skytower?”

“Friendly. Comfy. Busier than I thought.”

“That was terse.”

“Sorry.”

“Not really.”

“I suppose not. Start over?

“Please.”

“I came down here to get a pair of goggles that FIT Sister Dragon. I’ve been wearing a pair made for Sister Wings, and they’re only marginal.”

“Understandable.”

"And being here means being able to sleep in the very best bed in the world, which is always a good thing."

"Best in the world?"

"Really, really good, and it BELONGS to ME."

"Ah."

"And since I'm here, and since I 'm going to go off on another insanely dangerous adventure, we're going to get all of the documentation for the twins' next marriages out of the way. And since we're doing THAT, I'm probably going to say horizontal goodbyes to the twins before I head back to Losthaven."

"That's both gratifying and disturbing."

"Horizontal goodbyes?"

"Yes."

"I'm not dropping out of their lives, and I'm not planning on dying. But life will be easier for THEM, and their new wives, if no one sees me as competition. So this will be a good time to say, 'This is the last time.'"

"That sounds like an excuse for a party."

"Brat."

"Always."

"And, assuming things go according to plan, by the time the weddings take place, I'll have somewhere else to be, anyway."

“Oh. Right.”

“That’s cute. Your jealousy actually interfered with your lechery.”

“I’m so embarrassed.”

“You should be.”

“One of the advantages of being shallow is that you tend to forget embarrassment in the time it takes to cross a room.”

“Brat.”

“Of course, I haven’t actually MOVED in seven years...”

“If Master Fiddler would be so kind as to play me a lullaby, I will probably be sufficiently distracted that I don’t laugh at him.”

“Done.”

==)»> 27:2: The top of the Skytower

“You’re late tonight, Rose. And melancholy. And not in your bed.”

“I’m on top of the Skytower, looking at the stars, and the ocean, and thinking sad thoughts.”

“And the why?”

“We did the wedding paperwork today, which was boring and kind of silly. But this evening the twins and I did the musical beds thing for the last time, probably, and while that was pleasant enough, it was also sad.

So I took my late bath, and considered just going to bed, but then I went out on the balcony, and looked up at the Tower, and, well, here I am. Looking out over the ocean at a very particular point on the horizon."

"What..."

"Don't you dare. Don't even think about asking me what I'm looking at. Just stop and think for a moment and don't say anything."

"Oh. That."

"Yes."

"Melancholy Rose makes me stupid."

"I can see that."

"Is there anything I can do?"

"Just talk to me. Provide some music, by and by. Listen to me yammer for a bit."

"Topic of yammer?"

"Milestones. It just landed on me that, as of a few days ago, I actually have a clear path to rescuing you. I'm not just knocking probable things out of the way, I actually know all of the steps that will put the dagger in my hands, and I just have to take them. After all this time, it's... terrifying."

"I can see that."

"And it also occurred to me, though it's a small thing, the next time I have sex it will be with you."

"I like the sound of that."

"I do too, in isolation. But it scares me that my life has become so linear."

"You DO have to kill a dragon or three in the meantime."

"I know. It's not exactly a short path, or an easy one. But it's so CLEAR."

"Is that a problem?"

"No. I don't think so. I think... I think that maybe I've spent my entire life seeing clear paths as traps and prisons, and I can't help but see this one the same way."

"How long is it going to take?"

"A month. Maybe two, if a lot of things go wrong."

"You've taken detours a lot longer than that already."

"I know."

"So just get there, for my sake, and then we'll have the WHOLE horizon to play with."

"Fine. You know what I'm going to do now?"

"I suspect that I'll regret the answer."

"I'm going to climb onto the parapet, dive off, and shift to Sister Wings on the way down."

"Gods."

"You can play me a lullaby— please— after I'm safe in my bed."

"As long as you get there."

"Until then!"

==)»> 27:3: Darkness

"And how was your day?"

"The same as the last few. Aerobatics, touch-and-goes, and target practice for Sister Dragon. It would be fun, if I wasn't doing it all day, every day."

"When do you decide you have had enough?"

"When I'm so bored I stop caring if I'm actually good enough to go dragon killing, and decide to do the deed."

"Which will be?"

"The day after tomorrow. Maybe the day after that."

"So soon?"

"Not really. After that, I am going to spend some time creeping around in the rotters' section of the swamp, and see if I can actually find their lair."

"That sounds suicidal."

"I hope not. I can disguise myself as Sister Kobold, and the dragons won't notice me. As long as I don't run into any dragon-worshiping kobold fanatics."

"Those exist?"

"Kobolds are amazingly imaginative when it comes to being stupid and self-destructive."

"Ah. So is this a real danger, or just something you suggest to torment me?"

"About half and half. I don't think it'll be a problem, and I'm pretty sure I can fake a conversion long enough to escape, if it comes to that."

"How long will this wonderful new activity take you?"

"A few days. There are five sites that I marked as likely from three miles up, and it will take that long to check them all. Then back here for another day of target practice, then a rest day, and then..."

"Things get bloody."

"Or not. They might actually be smart."

"You know they won't be."

"I know."

"Please don't die."

"Trying hard not to."

"I'd hate to have to explain to someone that my favorite partner was someone I never actually bonded with."

"Aww. I'd be more flattered if I had any idea who you would tell."

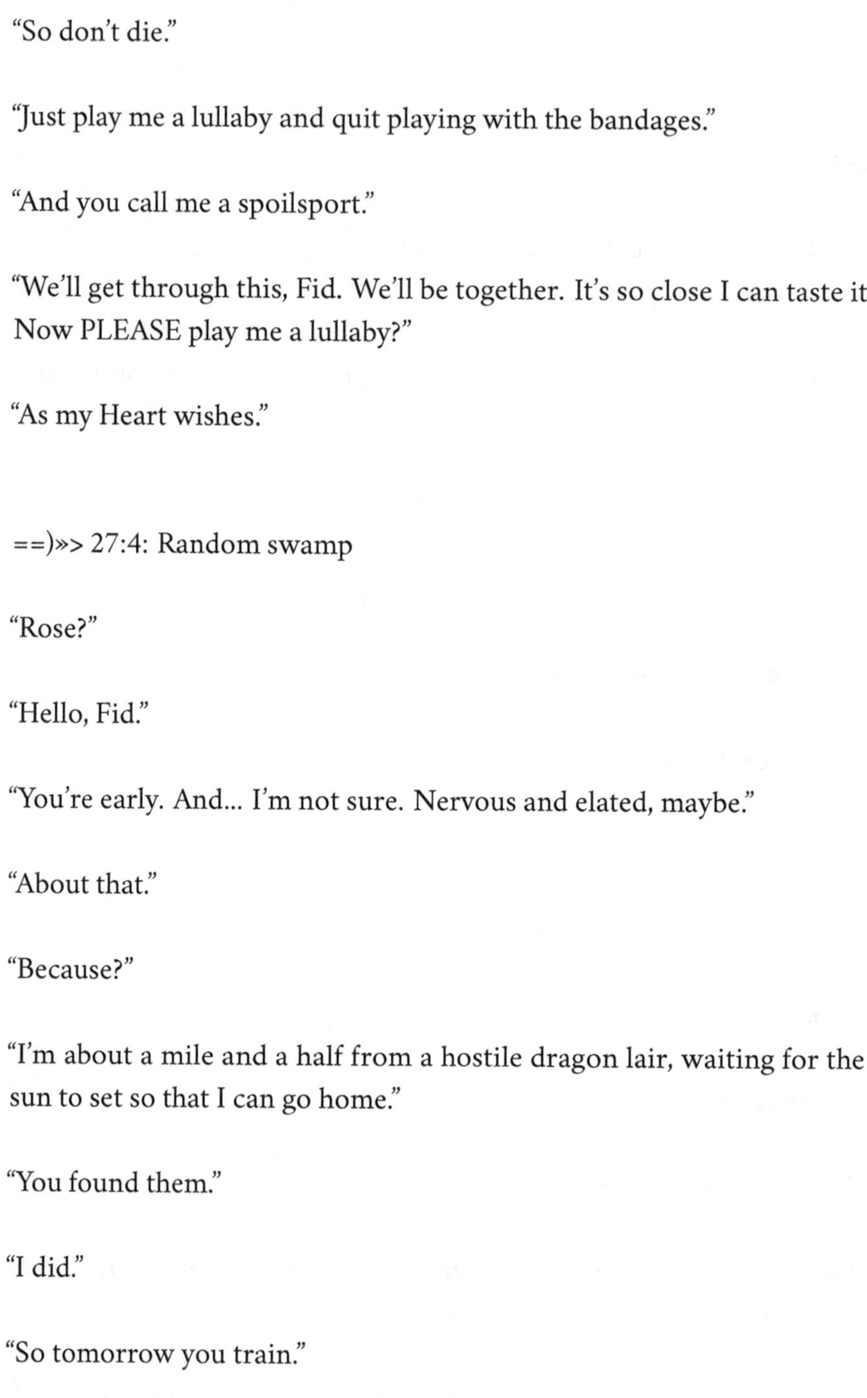

"So don't die."

"Just play me a lullaby and quit playing with the bandages."

"And you call me a spoilsport."

"We'll get through this, Fid. We'll be together. It's so close I can taste it. Now PLEASE play me a lullaby?"

"As my Heart wishes."

==)»> 27:4: Random swamp

"Rose?"

"Hello, Fid."

"You're early. And... I'm not sure. Nervous and elated, maybe."

"About that."

"Because?"

"I'm about a mile and a half from a hostile dragon lair, waiting for the sun to set so that I can go home."

"You found them."

"I did."

"So tomorrow you train."

“And the next day I rest.”

“And the day after that you fight.”

“Looks like it.”

“I don’t...”

“Just play me into the sunset, and don’t worry about it.”

“As my Lady wishes.”

==)»> 27:5: Aboard “Revenant”

“You went sailing today.”

“I did. And now I’m watching the stars come out over the docks.”

“And then home to bed?”

“No, home for some supplies, and then off to the swamp. I’m going to camp in a little hiding place I found, not too far from the rotters’ lair. That way I’ll be able to confront them with all of my reserves on hand.”

“So tomorrow.”

“Tomorrow. It amuses me that my indestructible pet monster is more frightened than I am.”

“Your indestructible pet monster is watching his all too vulnerable heart take absurd risks.”

"Large but necessary risks."

"If you say so."

"I do. And I'm following the rules, just like with the minotaur."

"Which was only saved from disaster by Winter, who's not with you."

"I played by the rules, and it was fine."

"What rules are these, again?"

"One, plan meticulously. Two, don't panic when the plan falls apart. Three, win."

"So if you follow the rules, you'll win, but if you don't win, you haven't followed the rules."

"Maybe."

"I hate you in so many ways."

"You keep saying that and I'll never believe it."

"I know. I wouldn't say it if I thought you might believe me."

"The honesty is getting thick in here. I think it's time I got moving. Look for me in an hour or two, and again just before dawn."

"Yes, your Grace. My Lady. My Heart."

"Aww."

==)»> 27:6: Darkness

"Good morning, my Heart."

"Good morning, my Scorpion. Is it dawn already?"

"Close. There should be light in the east."

"I need to wake up, then."

"Probably."

"I want two things from you, Fid."

"I will try."

"Second is to chase the luck for me, which will almost certainly wake me up."

"Done. What's the first thing?"

"Promise me you'll keep going if I die. Talk to Moss and Bing and Dlef and Drellan and find some other idiot who will rescue you. Don't just fade away. Keep playing Territories with Maelstrom until you can play him straight up. DO NOT QUIT."

"I'll do my best, Rose. I promise."

"Then play 'Chasing the Luck' for me, and let's get on with this."

==)»> 27:7: A dragon lair

"Rose! You're alive!"

"I guess that I am."

"I'd think you'd be happier about that."

"I just executed two people, Fid. Or rather hunted them down like deer."

"Very big deer with huge teeth and claws and toxic spittle who wanted to kill you."

"Even so. They were people with names, and now they're dead, and I killed them."

"Names?"

"That comes later, but yes. The big one was Sagalan Doomshadow, the one who tormented me the other day was Sessoria Terrorwind, and the one who's still alive is Sollamal Deathmoon."

"And now?"

"Sollamal is on her way to somewhere else to be someone else's problem, and I'm sitting in the middle of their awful and treasureless lair."

"Are you ready to tell the story?"

"I'll try. I may stop in the middle to relocate, though."

"Understood."

“I started by putting on an illusion of Sister Wings, then I went to the edge of their lair, which is really just a hilltop with a lot of big, sickly trees around it. I got there just before dawn, and waited for the sunlight to enter. Then I started hailing the dragons as loudly as I could, and they woke up, and laughed at me. Sessoria threatened to eat me again, and said I wouldn’t get away this time.”

“Charming.”

“I replied that I ‘d been commissioned by the the Jade Empress to see them removed from her territory, or destroyed, and they all laughed, and Sessoria claimed the right to kill me. Sagalan told her to go ahead, and as soon as she started to move, I took to the air.”

“As expected.”

“I just stayed in front of her until we were about ten miles from the lair, and then I started tagging her with mage bolts. She snarled at me, but kept coming. I was only hitting about half of the time, so it took her a while to realize that she was in trouble. She was pretty seriously hurt by then, and turned around and headed back to the lair as fast as she could go.”

“Sounds according to plan so far.”

“It was, except that part of me wanted to let her go, told me that my commission was for death or removal, and that I could probably convince the dragons to leave if I just let her go back to the lair.”

“But only part of you.”

“Part of me said that she was an enemy, that she wouldn’t turn into treasure if she wasn’t dead, and what was I waiting for?”

"And that's who you listened to."

"And that's who I listened to, even though, thinking about it now, I don't know why. I didn't HAVE to kill her; I did it for the money. That isn't who I am. Or, at least, it isn't who I want to be."

"She's dead, and you're alive, and there are worse outcomes."

"I know. But there will be nightmares. And I did enough mental vacillation that when Sessoria DID fall, Sagalan SAW it, and immediately took to the air himself looking for payback. So we started another chase."

"Which went the same way?"

"Not really. Sagalan never quit. He kept coming after me as fast and as hard as he could, right up until one of his wings collapsed, and he crashed into the ground. And when I landed to check on him, he went right on cursing me and trying to get in a hit until I put him down for good."

"Gods."

"Yeah."

"And then you went back to the lair."

"And then I went back to the lair, and Sollamal surrendered. She said that if Sagalan won, he would have been angry if she weren't waiting, and that if I won, after beating Sagalan, she didn't see any point in running. She told me her name, and the names of the other two, and I told her to leave the Land of Jade and to never return, and she took off into the north."

"So now what?"

"Now? I double check that Sessoria is dead, and then I head back to Losthaven to try to get my head back on straight. And THEN I start working on harvesting and storing a fortune in dragon bone."

"But you're alive. And you OWN a fortune in dragon bone."

"This is true."

"And all that stands between you and a certain dagger is a long list of relatively simple tasks."

"This is also true."

"I'm pretty happy about that."

"Yes, but you're a monster."

"But?"

"I'm not sure about myself. Or even what I want the answer to be."

"You're the Heart of the Unicorn. You're the Corrosion Flower. And you're a Dragon Slayer."

"Even so. I need to get to work, Fid. We'll talk tonight."

"Even so."

==)»> 27:8: Drellan's house

"You're not sleeping."

"No."

"You've had a long day, and are in a decent bed, aren't you? What's wrong."

"Sessoria wasn't dead."

"That's... bad?"

"Her neck was broken; she was dying, but it might have taken days if not for me."

"So you gave her a grace stroke?"

"Eventually. We talked, first."

"That sounds charming."

"It wasn't as unpleasant as you might imagine. She asked me if I had killed Sagalan, and was happy when I said I had, because that meant that there was no shame in dying by my hand."

"Interesting priority."

"I think it was all she had. I asked her if dragons had any funeral rites, and she laughed at that. Or more like wheezed; she wasn't breathing very well."

"Did she have an answer?"

"Only that she wanted to be remembered. She wanted someone to know that there had once been a dragon named Sessoria Terrorwind who had been killed by a sorceress whom she had no chance of defeating."

"And you said?"

"That I intended to live a very, very long time, and that I would always remember her, and she laughed and said she deserved that. And then I told her that I would also tell her story to the Turtle, and she was quiet for a while, and then asked me, in a kind of awe, if I really KNEW the Turtle, and I said that I did."

"Name dropper."

"It was the right name. She said that that was all that any dragon could ever hope for, and then she said that it was past her time, and asked me if I would cut her throat, because a proper dragon should die by tooth or claw or steel, not by crashing into the earth."

"Again, interesting priorities."

"Yeah. I told her I was sorry I hadn't just let her run, that I had kept hitting her until she crashed. She laughed again, and said that would have been stupid, that she would have followed Sagalan back into the fight, and that if both of them were fighting, Sollamal would have followed, and then I would have had THREE dragons to deal with at once."

"So Sister Dragon turns out to be a better tactician than Rose."

"Possibly. I told her that I had been expecting to fight three dragons at once. She was quiet for a while, and then she asked again for a grace stroke, so I conjured a mage-sword, and killed her."

"For the second time."

"Sort of."

"You care too much, Rose. It tears you apart."

"We can't all be blessed with pathological superficiality."

"You could cultivate it."

"I don't want to, Fid. One of us always has to be able to bleed or we really will be monsters."

"Which lets me off the hook in any case."

"Brat."

"So what IS bothering you?"

"Ambivalence. Uncertainty. My own carelessness."

"And if you push your internal arguments to their logical conclusion, how long will it take you?"

"Forever."

"In that case, just skip ahead a few pages, call it enough for one night, and get some sleep."

"That's... amazingly wise for an ethically challenged monster."

"I have my uses."

"You do. Promise to visit me with a lullaby as soon as I fall asleep, and I'll take your advice."

"Done."

==)»> 27:9: Darkness

“Good morning, Mistress Sorcerer. Or is it Master Sorceress?”

“My name is why the hell are you disturbing my dreams to yammer at me.”

“Look in the mirror, Rose. Or wherever it is that you look into to take stock of your power as a sorcerer.”

“Say what? I’m... Good gods, Fid, I broke third. How did I not know that?”

“You were distracted last night. Is this another ‘chasing the luck’ thing?”

“Pretty much. How did you know?”

“You’re larger and brighter, more substantial. You’re still you, I’d know you anywhere, but now you’re easier to see. Drellan used to be the most powerful sorcerer in Losthaven...”

“By some measure. He says that I scare him.”

“Have you talked to him since you’ve been a dragon-slayer?”

“He was intimidated enough by the fact that I was going to try.”

“Ah. Well, now you are at least as big and bright as he is. Maybe a little more.”

“Interesting. Now that I’m looking for it, it’s easy to see. I have more energy, and everything is just a little bit clearer than it was.”

"Didn't you once say that you had to break third circle in order to make the dive?"

"Yeah, I did, once. I thought so, then, but I found an alternate path. And now I've broken third, anyway. Who knew?"

"So what now?"

"Nothing has changed, really. I borrow some money from Drellan and put together a work party to haul two dead dragons from the places that they died to Hurricane Bay, and then I start butchering them and harvesting their skeletons."

"Sounds like a great deal of honest work."

"Doesn't it just. It's the path for the moment, and since I want to get to the end of the path, it's what I have to do."

"Well, then, sooner started, and things like that."

"YOU are telling ME to get to work?"

"Suggesting. Very deferentially. Along with offering you heartfelt congratulations on the magical milestone."

"Good enough. Until tonight, Fid."

"Until tonight, my Heart."

==)»> 27:10: Darkness

"You're still in Losthaven. I thought you'd be somewhere in the swamp with your kobolds by now."

"Nope. I asked Drellan for a loan, and he said he was willing, but didn't have a lot of cash, and then said that I probably ought to do some more planning, first. And he was right."

"Oh?"

"How many fifty pound kobolds does it take to drag a six ton dragon across soft, sticky ground?"

"A lot?"

"Too damned many. Probably a couple of hundred."

"So you cut the body up. You were going to to that anyway."

"There's a problem with that, too."

"Yes?"

"Given a creature that spits acid, what do you think its blood is like?'"

"More acid?"

"Close enough. You can pry up and pull out the scales, one at a time, and a first class steel blade will cut dragon flesh pretty well, but the blade starts to corrode as soon as it touches the flesh, so you have to clean and re-sharpen the blade after every cut. And that STILL destroys the blade in fewer than a dozen cuts."

"What about the mage-sword you used to kill Sessoria?"

"It's energy intensive, and has a short duration. Extending it as far as I can, I only have about half an hour a day with it."

"So what are you going to do?"

"I'm going to build a wall around Sagalan's body, build a kobold village next to it to keep watch, and then drag Sessoria's body down to keep it company. AND spend half an hour every day with the mage-sword, learning how to be a dragon butcher."

"This doesn't sound like a great deal of fun."

"No, it doesn't. And I really need to get permission from the Empress to proceed; it's all inside her territory."

"Is she likely to object?"

"No, I don't think she really cares much about what the kobs get up to. But it's still the right way to do things, and she should appreciate the courtesy."

"Makes sense."

"And there's one other thing. You can't really just be a generic duchess, you have to be the Duchess of Somewhere."

"And you haven't really had a Somewhere, and now you do."

"And now I do. Or I will, once my town is built. How does, 'Duchess of Dragonfall' sound to you?"

"I like it. I like it a LOT. Would her Grace, the Duchess of Dragonfall, care for a lullaby?"

“Her Grace would appreciate that a great deal.”

28: Harvest

The difference between nine-tenths done and finished is half the work.
—*The Book of the Blind King's Wisdom*

==)»> 28:1: Darkness

"Still in Losthaven?"

"Gathering the troops. We'll start marching tomorrow. Which will mean sleeping in the swamp with the kobs, when I could be back in my own bed in a quarter hour."

"Leadership requires sacrifice."

"Undead monsters should not recite platitudes."

"Feel free to hunt me down and stop me."

"Working on it. I don't actually have to do all of the marching, though I'm not sure all the flying I'll be doing will be much of an improvement."

"What flying?"

"Checking on the dragon bodies, and visiting kobold communities to leave requests for an audience with the Empress."

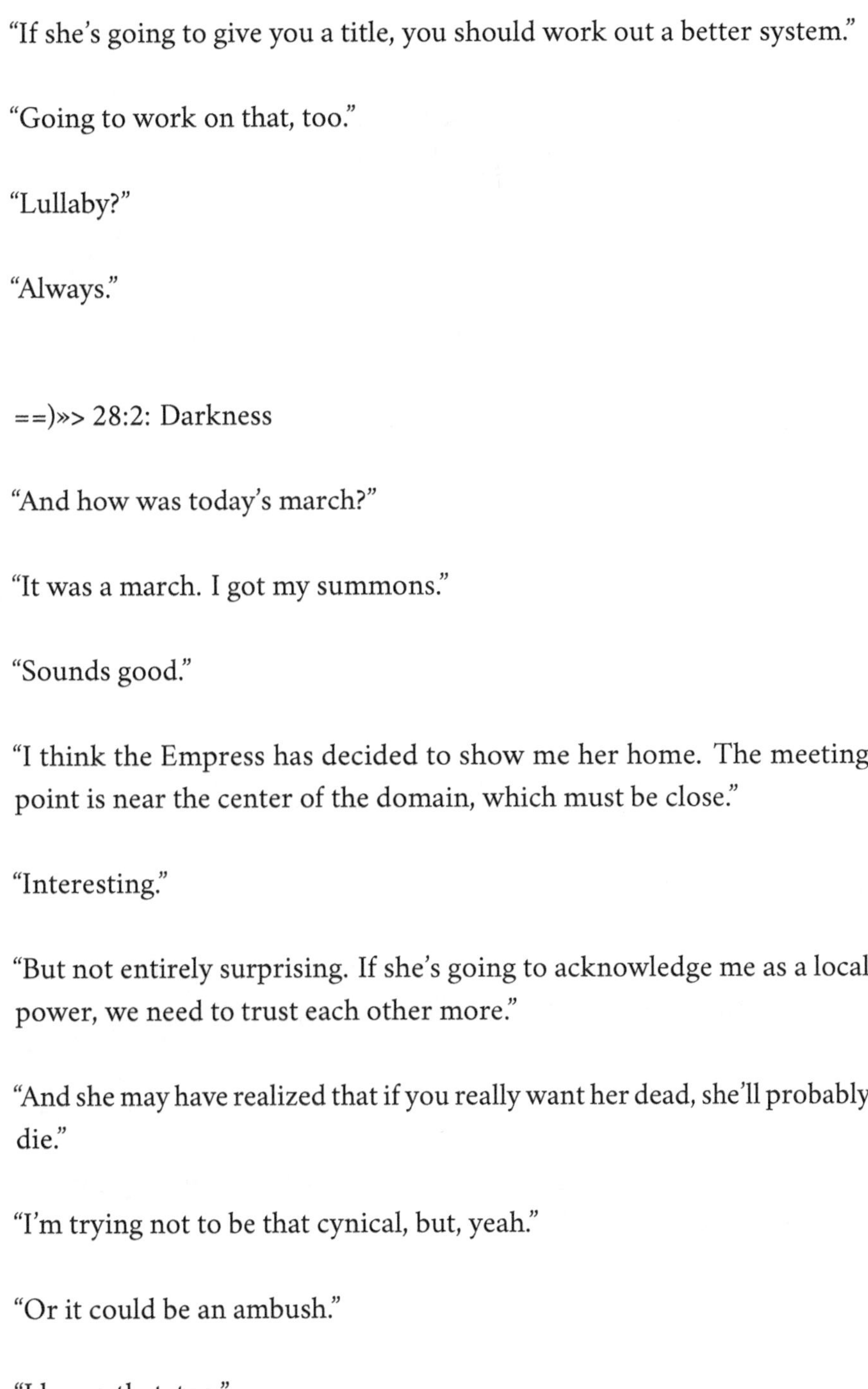

“If she’s going to give you a title, you should work out a better system.”

“Going to work on that, too.”

“Lullaby?”

“Always.”

==)»> 28:2: Darkness

“And how was today’s march?”

“It was a march. I got my summons.”

“Sounds good.”

“I think the Empress has decided to show me her home. The meeting point is near the center of the domain, which must be close.”

“Interesting.”

“But not entirely surprising. If she’s going to acknowledge me as a local power, we need to trust each other more.”

“And she may have realized that if you really want her dead, she’ll probably die.”

“I’m trying not to be that cynical, but, yeah.”

“Or it could be an ambush.”

“I know that, too.”

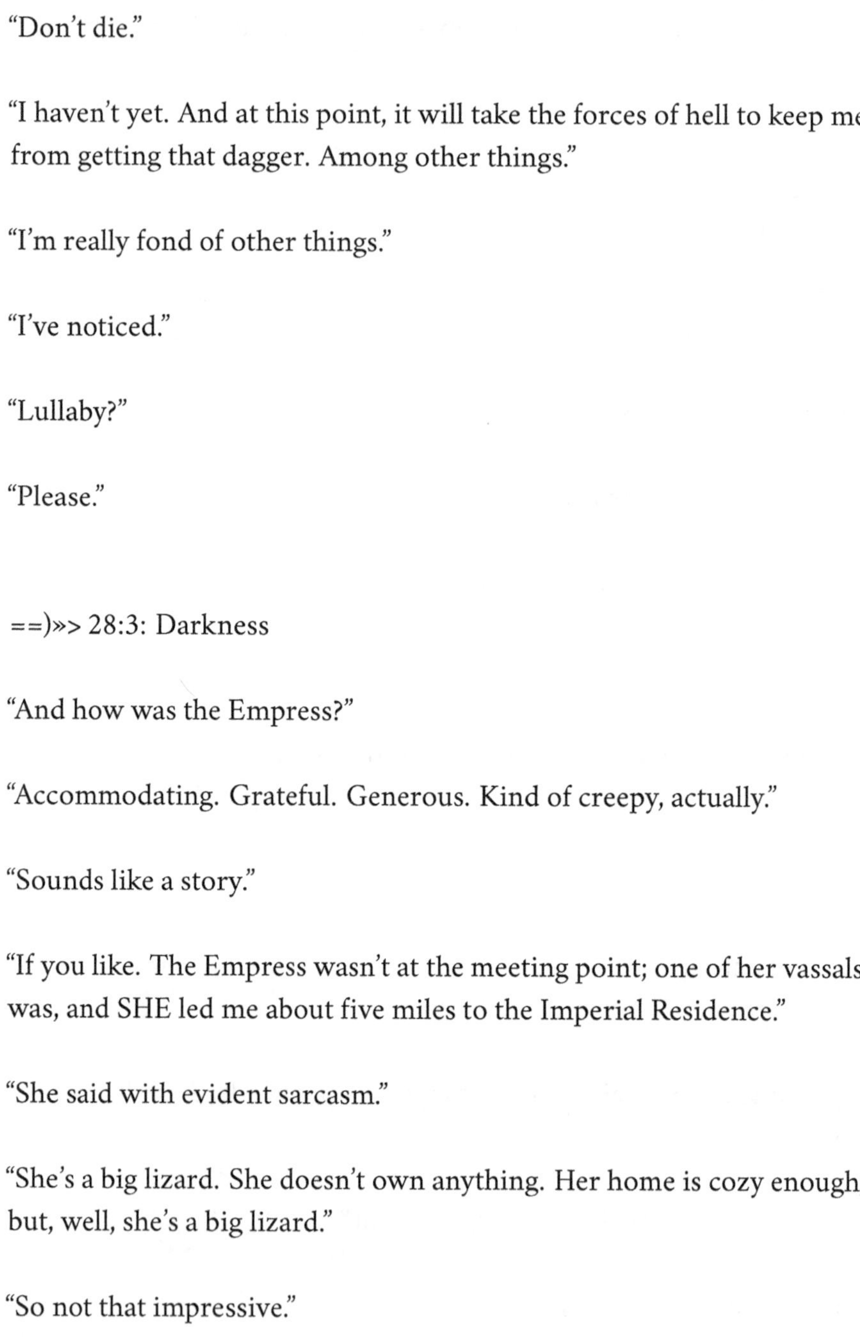

"Don't die."

"I haven't yet. And at this point, it will take the forces of hell to keep me from getting that dagger. Among other things."

"I'm really fond of other things."

"I've noticed."

"Lullaby?"

"Please."

==)»> 28:3: Darkness

"And how was the Empress?"

"Accommodating. Grateful. Generous. Kind of creepy, actually."

"Sounds like a story."

"If you like. The Empress wasn't at the meeting point; one of her vassals was, and SHE led me about five miles to the Imperial Residence."

"She said with evident sarcasm."

"She's a big lizard. She doesn't own anything. Her home is cozy enough, but, well, she's a big lizard."

"So not that impressive."

"It wouldn't have been, if it had been just the Empress and me, the way it was the last two times. But this time there were dozens of women in attendance, and they ALL reminded me of Auntie Moss. A LOT.'"

"Gods."

"You weren't there. Six tons of dragon is nothing to sneeze at, but I've met her twice before, and I've KILLED Sagalan. But a gallery full of terrifying magic women of unknown provenance? My knees almost melted."

"Any idea who they were?"

"In the short term, witnesses. They seem to be shapeshifters at some level, and I think they're actually the wise women of the kobold villages, which would explain the Empress' communication net."

"And you never caught on to this?"

"They avoided me, left me to talk to the war chiefs. I never quite realized that I was dealing with figureheads."

"So they've all outplayed you, so far."

"And that makes them even more scary."

"I imagine. Any idea on their nature?"

"Whatever Auntie Moss is. Very like dryads, but not focused as much on trees, and not bound nearly as closely to a place. But still very green, and still very territorial."

"That's clear as mud."

"It's what I have. I'll learn more. I'm going to hire one as a seneschal, and may have several of them as a sort of staff. But the Empress created me Duchess of Dragonfall, and accepted my fealty..."

"That sounds scary."

"I was worried about that, but the vows weren't terribly restrictive. She owns the land, and I'm its caretaker; the land doesn't own me. I owe her loyalty and support within reason. Any of the... gallery that claims land within my borders may choose to transfer their primary loyalty to me, or move. The ones whose lands were being destroyed by the rotters all seem inclined to come to me."

"Handy. So you'll pick your seneschal there?"

"That's the idea. We'll see how it goes. The good thing about having a staff, though, is that I won't have to DO very much to make things happen. I can concentrate on butchery, and expeditions into deep water."

"I like the sound of that."

"I thought you would."

==)»> 28:4: Darkness

"And how did today go?"

"Sessoria is stretched out next to Sagalan, and I hired a seneschal."

"Gossip first. Tell me about..."

"Chelonia? She was the wise woman for the kob village that the rotters demolished to make their lair. Since there's nothing left there to rebuild, and since she feels that she owes me, she's going to build my village instead of rebuilding her own."

"And her name is Chelonia? That's auspicious."

"I thought so. I like her. She spends most of her time looking like an elderly kobold, which takes some of the edge off of the Auntie Moss strangeness."

"But not all."

"By no means all. I need to come up with a term for them, though. 'Scary nature spirit women' isn't functional."

"I'll second that."

"And Chelonia isn't the only one in the area, though they seem to be falling into some kind of organization that acknowledges me pretty easily. It's all a little creepy. I'd be worried, maybe, if I was going to make a permanent home here. As it is, I'll have a house here, and will check in from time to time, and leave the day to day with Chelonia and her sisters, which will be fine with them."

"So where does that leave you?"

"Now that the dragons are together, we are going to build a palisade around the bodies, with enough extra space inside for a small camp. Chelonia is going to scout for a better town site that's close enough to the dragons to make guarding them practical, at least until I've finished harvesting bones. And then the palisade will get cannibalized for building materials."

"Sounds tidy."

"We are talking about kobolds, though."

"Given that."

"In other news... It seems that the kobs have decided that Duchess Rose is a kobold with wings, and they're disinclined to acknowledge my other forms. Also, the Losthaven kobtown has announced a desire to swear fealty to me."

"Is that likely to be a problem?"

"I don't think so, as long as Losthaven has a civilian government. They'll be happy with the illusion that SOMEONE is actually in charge of kobtown. If things shift, and Losthaven ends up with a grumpy military government, things could get strange. I can imagine circumstances under which Jade would annex Losthaven, but I REALLY don't want to look for that."

"I can see that. The desire to avoid that, I mean."

"In the meantime, I'm still sleeping on turf when I have a perfectly good bed less than an hour away."

"Which sounds like a request for a lullaby."

"Please."

==)»> 28:5: Darkness

"Skytower, tonight?"

"Yeah, it's time to start actually turning dragon bone into money, and to start shopping for a ship to charter. And to spend a night or two in the world's best bed."

"How did that go?"

"Well enough. Cinnabar seemed... off balance that I had broken third circle. I made him nervous. I never used to make him nervous."

"And no sex."

"Not even a hint. It was never about the sex, anyway. I was swindling him, and he was swindling me, and there was mutual nudity involved. I'm done with the swindle, and I think he just knows the window has closed. I wish I knew what it was he was going for, though. I don't think he ever quite got it."

"Which might account for his nervousness."

"It might. He might even be a bit afraid of me, now."

"Has HE ever killed a dragon?"

"I very much doubt it."

"Well, then."

"So I should expect people to be afraid of me now?"

"It comes with the territory."

"Are you afraid of me?"

"More than I already was? No."

"You've BEEN afraid of me?"

"You're reckless and fragile and beautiful and wonderful and no creature in the history of the world has been more able to hurt me that you can. OF COURSE I'm afraid of you."

"Ah. Um... I have no follow up for that. I just... Um..."

"Music?"

"Gods. Please, yes."

==)»> 28:6: Darkness

"You're back in the swamp. I didn't expect that."

"I finished my business in Skytower, and had both daylight and magic left, so I came back. This way I'll have a few more minutes with the mage-sword. I really miss that bed, though. Any bed, actually."

"You have no one to blame..."

"I know."

"So what business did you have?"

"I talked to a few more shipping agents, and I found someone who seemed competent to make my descender for me."

"Descender?"

"The idea of swimming straight down into darkness for two miles made me kind of crazy, and I worked out a way to get gravity to do the work for me."

"Say what?"

"Two twenty gallon copper barrels filled with the purest alcohol I can get, a metal frame to hold them together, and some detachable ballast weights. Each gallon of alcohol gives about two pounds of flotation, so the whole gadget should have thirty or forty pounds worth. I add enough ballast so that it's neutral, for when I'm on the bottom, and then add a thirty pound weight for the descent. When it comes time to surface, I dump ALL the ballast, and come back up. And once I'm on the surface, I can dump the alcohol, and have enough flotation to climb completely out of the water."

"Why the alcohol?"

"Because anything with air in it would be crushed."

"Ah. And why worry about floating at the end? Won't there be a ship there?"

"After at least two hours of drift for both me and the ship? I want a safe space to rest if I need it."

"Prudent."

"It even has a built in flooded box to put valuable things in. You know, like daggers. Since I don't know how leather or fabric will take the pressure. Better to just make everything metal, and not have anything turn to dust at depth."

"That's...detailed."

"I've had three years to think about it."

"I love the joy you take in this kind of thing."

"It's who I am. I like gadgets. I like learning things."

"I've noticed."

"In other news, I gave Chelonia a badge of office today, two of Sagalan's heel spurs. Spurs and claws are more visually impressive that small bits of bone, I think."

"Not the teeth?"

"I'm going to leave the teeth in the skulls, for now. I may offer Sagalan's skull to the Empress. And I'm kind of inclined to keep Sessoria for myself, at the moment, though that may change."

"What's that about?"

"I don't have a problem with selling off Sagalan; he was toxic, and he tried to kill me, and I killed him in self defense."

"Allowing for some provocation."

"Don't step on my rationalizations. It won't end well."

"Yes, your Grace."

"But Sessoria... I still haven't gotten past the idea that I killed her for the money, and until I resolve that, I'm not going to let myself make any money from her."

"That's twisted."

"Isn't it just? And I keep thinking that I haven't kept my promise to tell the Turtle, yet."

"Should I tell him you want to talk to him?"

"Please. I need to take care of that before the dive."

"You carry too much guilt, Rose."

"Possibly. But holding onto it is the best way I know to avoid picking up more."

"I keep telling you to cultivate superficiality."

"Fraudulent superficiality? Like yours?"

"That's just cruel."

"Not really. I need a hug, Fid."

"I would love to provide one, but..."

"I know. Until the day."

"Until the day, which draws palpably nearer."

"Damned straight."

==)»> 28:7: Darkness

"I've been in touch with Dlef, the way you asked me to. He said that Cinnabar came by this afternoon and said that he could get, quoting, 'An obscene amount of money', for a long bone, a femur or a tibia or a humerus, if you could get one."

"I ought to offer him a radius just to mess with him. He'll probably be grateful for it."

"Why 'if'? Doesn't he know you have a whole dragon?"

"I've been vague. He doesn't know if I actually HAVE the bones, or if I'm getting them from a third party. And he doesn't know how much I actually have access to. And since he's Cinnabar, I like it that way."

"And?"

"And I guess I'll clean up a radius tomorrow and take it down to Skytower."

"Is it as creepy for you to talk about selling parts of creatures you've spoken to as it seems to be?"

"At least. Why do you think I've stayed away from Sessoria? We actually had a conversation, and every time I look at her body— which, by the way, seems to be too toxic to rot— I can hear her voice, and I go back to working on Sagalan. All HE ever did was swear at me."

"How much of the bodies are you going to harvest?"

"As much as it takes to pay for the charter. After that, well, I'll see. I don't really need to be rich, and I'm not sure that the sort of people who can afford to buy dragon bone should be allowed access to it."

"Not sure I follow that."

"No? Wealth is power. Beyond a certain point, power DEFINES monsters. Anyone who can afford to buy a dragon bone toy is absolutely a latent monster, and very likely one in fact."

"Including you?"

"Of course. But I do my best to minimize the collateral damage, and am prepared to do penance as necessary."

"Sounds unpleasant."

"Maybe. But I get to pull my best friend out of prison FIRST, and then I'll worry about paying off the butcher."

"I approve of that sequence."

"I thought you might. And you owe me another lullaby for disturbing me in the middle of the night."

"Am I less of a monster if I pay my debts?"

"Less of one? Yes. I don't know if that makes you actually redeemable, though. And I'm not sure that's desirable, either."

"Being ethical makes my head hurt."

"Then let it go, be a good monster, and play the lullaby."

"As my Lady wishes."

==)»> 28:8: Darkness

"So do you know exactly what Cinnabar means by, 'An obscene amount of money'?"

"Yes, and his version of obscene is... a lot more vulgar than mine."

"That sounds good."

"I can pay for the charter without having to haggle, AND still have to worry about the amount of money I'm leaving with the twins."

"You don't trust the twins?"

"I trust them absolutely. I don't trust the rest of the world to leave them alone if word gets out."

"Ah."

"I'm going to stash some of it with Dlef, and some of it with Drellan and Dzee, and even some of it with Chelonia, I think. And all of this from ONE decent sized bone. And Cinnabar REALLY wants more."

"Of course he does."

"I told him I'd see what I could arrange."

"Which is probably nothing?"

"In the short term. In the longer term... it depends on what uses I come up with for disgusting quantities of money."

"So what now?"

"I fly a ferry flight or two back to Losthaven and Dragonfall, make sure that Chelonia is prepared to be without me for a month, and then head back to Skytower to find a ship."

"It sounds like 'the day' is getting very close."

"I can taste it, Fid. It's... amazing."

"That it is. Lullaby?"

"Absolutely."

==)»> 28:9: Darkness

"Good evening, Rose. How was your day?"

"Fabulous. The descender is ready to go, and I'm pretty sure I found a ship."

"Only pretty sure?"

"The captain is pretending hesitancy, looking for a little bit more money, I think. I have it, so he'll get it, but I don't want to make it too easy for him. Which means there is still time for the deal to fall apart."

"Does this ship have a name?"

"'Barracuda Dream'."

"Odd name."

"She's pretty enough, though. Two masts, a little too lean to be practical, so probably a smuggler. But well maintained, and with a cheerful crew, so a SUCCESSFUL smuggler."

"That's... good?"

"Good enough, I think. Disrespect for the law is usually just a matter of KNOWING the law, but you can't keep a competent crew loyal unless you're competent yourself."

"Just..."

"I know. Don't die. But do you really think a couple of dozen sailors can take me down?"

"Face to face, no. But you'll be alone, and you have to sleep."

"And a fair chunk of their fee is waiting to be collected AFTER they've brought me home safely."

"Much better. Greed is so much more reliable a motivator than decency."

"Well, then."

"So what's the schedule?"

"It'll be a few days. We have to finalize terms, and then they'll have to provision the ship. And I'll make one more trip back to Dragonfall, just to check on Chelonia."

"And then..."

"And then about four hundred and fifty miles of open water, somewhere between four and six days, and then I make the dive, and bring you home."

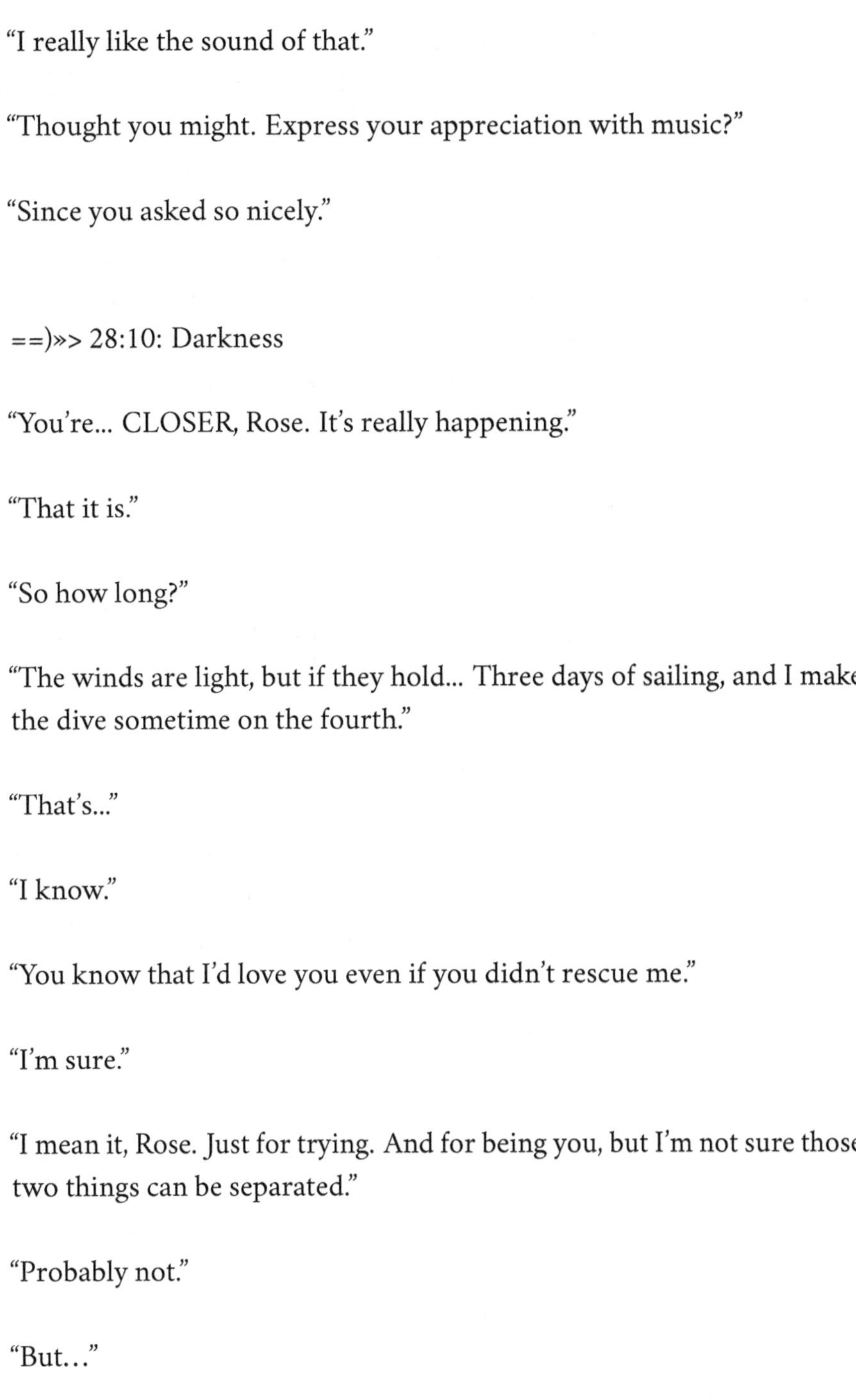

"I really like the sound of that."

"Thought you might. Express your appreciation with music?"

"Since you asked so nicely."

==)»> 28:10: Darkness

"You're... CLOSER, Rose. It's really happening."

"That it is."

"So how long?"

"The winds are light, but if they hold... Three days of sailing, and I make the dive sometime on the fourth."

"That's..."

"I know."

"You know that I'd love you even if you didn't rescue me."

"I'm sure."

"I mean it, Rose. Just for trying. And for being you, but I'm not sure those two things can be separated."

"Probably not."

"But..."

"I know, Fid. Don't boil your brain. Less than a hundred hours, and then we can say as many stupid things to each other as we want."

"That sounds really good."

"Doesn't it just. Before I forget: I want you to look for me at dawn and noon, and in the evening, from now on. I'll need you to give me a bearing, so I can give the ship a bearing. I want to make the dive from as nearly dead on top of you as I can. Finding you will be hard enough if you're in arm's reach."

"I thought you had locator spells."

"I do. But they're all foreground spells, and my foreground is going to be occupied with being Sister Shark, so all I can do with the others is momentary flashes."

"That's what you did to find Winter, isn't it?"

"Yeah, and this might actually be easier, since I won't be fighting the burn from fresh water. But then, I was just WORRIED that I might die if I lost Sister Shark at depth. If I lose Sister Shark in your neighborhood, I'm DEAD."

"Sorry."

"It's the job, Fid. And the prize is worth the risk."

"I'm glad you think so."

"Consider my eyes rolled, and play me a lullaby."

"Yes, your Grace."

“Eyes rolled. Again.”

==)»> 28:11: Aboard “Barracuda Dream”

“Good morning, Rose.”

“Hello, Fid. Do you have a bearing for me?”

“You’re north northeast, and have been since you started.”

“I’ll tell them to keep holding south southwest, then. See you at noon. And Fid?”

“Yes?”

“Soon. But not nearly soon enough.”

“Never soon enough.”

==)»> 28:12: Aboard “Barracuda Dream”

“Hello, Rose.”

“Hello, Fid.”

“You’ve drifted east by about half a point.”

“We’ll correct, thank you very much. Are you going crazy, Fid? I’m going crazy.”

“Compared to what?”

"Brat. I'm BORED, Fid. I don't have anything to do."

"Can't you fly?"

"I would, but the crew might mutiny."

"Say what?"

"Someone noticed that my shadow has a tail..."

"Don't you always have a tail?"

"I've been wearing illusory Emma. I thought that would make things easier, but maybe not. This crew seems to be more superstitious than most sailors, and ALL sailors are fairly superstitious."

"Is it a problem?"

"I don't think so. I've talked to the captain about it, and he assures me that everything is under control. He did advise me to stay in my cabin as much as possible, though."

"I repeat..."

"We're still following the course I tell them to follow, and no one has actually approached me in hostility, so it's probably fine. Probably."

"Unless it's not."

"You're borrowing trouble, Fid. It'll be fine."

"Your situation, your choice. But I reserve the right to worry."

“You’d do that anyway.”

“Probably. Until next time?”

“Until then.”

==)»> 28:13: Aboard “Barracuda Dream”

“Not sleeping, Rose?”

“Can’t. Too excited.”

“So tomorrow?”

“It’s my best guess.”

“So what are the rules?”

“I need you to keep an eye on me, starting now. If I start to rise above your horizon, wake me up. At 30 degrees, we’ll be about four miles from you; at forty five degrees, only two. We need to heave the ship to at that point and get the descender in the water.”

“Any idea when?”

“Best guess is early afternoon, but that’s only a guess. It happens when it happens.”

“And then?”

“And then we advance by longboat until we’re on top of you, to your best guess, and then I go over the side, cut the descender loose, and start down into the darkness."

"That sounds scary, but it's just too GOOD."

"I know."

"How are your crew problems?"

"Quiescent, I guess. They haven't gotten any worse, but I know that they're still making warding signs when they think I can't see."

"But they're willing to row you and your contraption away from the ship?"

"They think I'm probably evil, but I don't think they see me as a physical threat. It should be fine."

"They're not very bright, are they?"

"They're sailors. I haven't told them about taking out Sagalan."

"THAT would be amusing."

"They'd probably try to swim home. I may have to offer them bonuses at the end, anyway, just to shut up my conscience."

"You really need to..."

"Stop."

"...get rid of that thing. It's more trouble than it's worth."

"Just stop. Tonight is not the time."

“Yes, your Grace.”

“Well, if it’s like that, I might as well order you to provide music while I try to sleep.”

“With pleasure, your Grace.”

29: Dagger

The most crippling limits are those set upon us by our detractors, and we are ever our own greatest detractors. There are limits everywhere, but WHERE? How do we know a thing is impossible until we have attempted it, and failed? And even then, how do we know that if we had only done things a tiny bit differently, we might have succeeded? To be truly alive is to be constantly hurling ourselves at the barriers which our perception has placed before us, and the only way to truly know if a barrier is real or not is to break it.

—Xart Windchaser, *Flight*

==)»> 29:1: Darkness

"It's dawn, Rose. You're still on the horizon, and you're half a point west."

"Got it, Fid. How's your energy?"

"Good. I spent the night losing three games of Territories to Maelstrom."

"Sounds good. Where is Grandfather Turtle this morning?"

"Off Ironbridge. I suggested that he might want to be closer to you today, and he said it wasn't his part to interfere with today's business."

"That's ominous."

"Something about letting children stand on their own."

"And how did you respond to that?"

"Dishonestly. I'm not THAT stupid."

"You aren't, unless you're talking to me about doing something you don't like."

"Guilty."

"I should go. I'm going to be in trance almost continuously all day, so tell me if you have anything to say about our position."

"Only our position?"

"For now, yeah. Tomorrow, we can talk all we want about anything and everything. Today, I would hate to miss finding you because you ran out of energy when I needed to talk to you."

"Understood."

"Soon, Fid."

"Not soon enough."

==)»> 29:2: Aboard "Barracuda Dream"

"Forty-five degrees above the horizon, Rose. Still solid on north northeast."

"Got it. We're going to heave to, now, and continue to approach by longboat. I'll be out of trance for a bit, and then back in. Let me know if we get off course, and as soon as we're dead overhead."

"Understood, Rose. Hurry, but no mistakes."

"Absolutely no mistakes. Soon!"

==)»> 29:3: A longboat in open water

"You're overhead, Rose. Or as near as I can tell."

"I'm still two miles away. It'll be vague. I'll be busy for a few minutes, and then will get back into trance once the descent has started."

"And then how long to the bottom?"

"An hour, with a LOT of leeway. I need to go NOW. Look for me soon."

==)»> 29:4: Deep water

"Well?"

"Coming down, Fid. The last of the light just went away, and I'm falling at three or four feet per scorpion."

"Scorpion?"

"Quick and dirty time keeping, remember?. Count 'one scorpion, two scorpion, three scorpion,' and try to keep the tempo even. Assuming our information on depth is good, and it seems to be, I should be down in about an hour. How's your energy?"

"Good. We've only really burned a tiny bit so far today, and I think that the cost is less than we're used to."

"The difference between two miles and five hundred?"

"Probably."

"Well, let's assume we have a good margin for error, and if you would be so kind, do you have any music ready for a slow descent into infinite darkness?"

"I have a new arrangement for 'Marching Homeward.'"

"That would be WONDERFUL."

"As my Lady wishes."

==)»> 29:5: Deep water

"Hello, Fid."

"ROSE?"

"Yep. I've got the dagger in my hand, Fid. We're together."

"Damn."

"Exactly."

"Just..."

"I know, Fid. I'm going to put the dagger in the carry box on the descender, and start us up, then go back into trance. We can talk on the way. I think I'll leave the dagger in the box, though, because I do NOT want to drop it..."

"No. Don't drop."

"We'll talk shortly."

==)»> 29:6: Deep water

"Rose? What's wrong?"

"I'm an idiot."

"I doubt that. I repeat, what's wrong?"

"What happens when a second circle sorcerer who has NOT made a specialty out of dominating people takes on a third circle sorcerer who HAS?"

"The second circle loses?"

"The second circle loses so badly that she comes away thinking that she broke even, or maybe even came out a tiny bit on top."

"Cinnabar?"

"Yes."

"Who did what, exactly?"

"I'm still not sure of all of the details, but it looks like he figured out that I was on a quest for an object, but he didn't know what it was. So he bound me up in this gargantuan compulsion, so that if I ever managed to get my hands on the thing, whatever it was, I would NOT bond with it in any way, I would handle it as little as possible, and I would bring it to him as quickly as I could."

"That's BAD. Is there anything you can do about it?"

"I don't think so. I'm forbidden from trying to dispel the compulsion directly, or from asking for help to dispel it. The only loophole is that, since he didn't now what I was looking for, or that I was already talking to you on a regular basis, there's no ban on me talking to you."

"Those aren't affirmative. They'll break, given time."

"They'll hold long enough for me to give Nab the dagger."

"Damn."

"Yes."

"Do you know the end conditions?"

"As soon as he takes custody of the dagger."

"And we can start trying to kill him."

"Yes, I guess so."

"Do you have a problem with that?"

"Maybe a twinge. It will be gone by the time we get to Skytower, though. I don't imagine that time will make me any LESS angry."

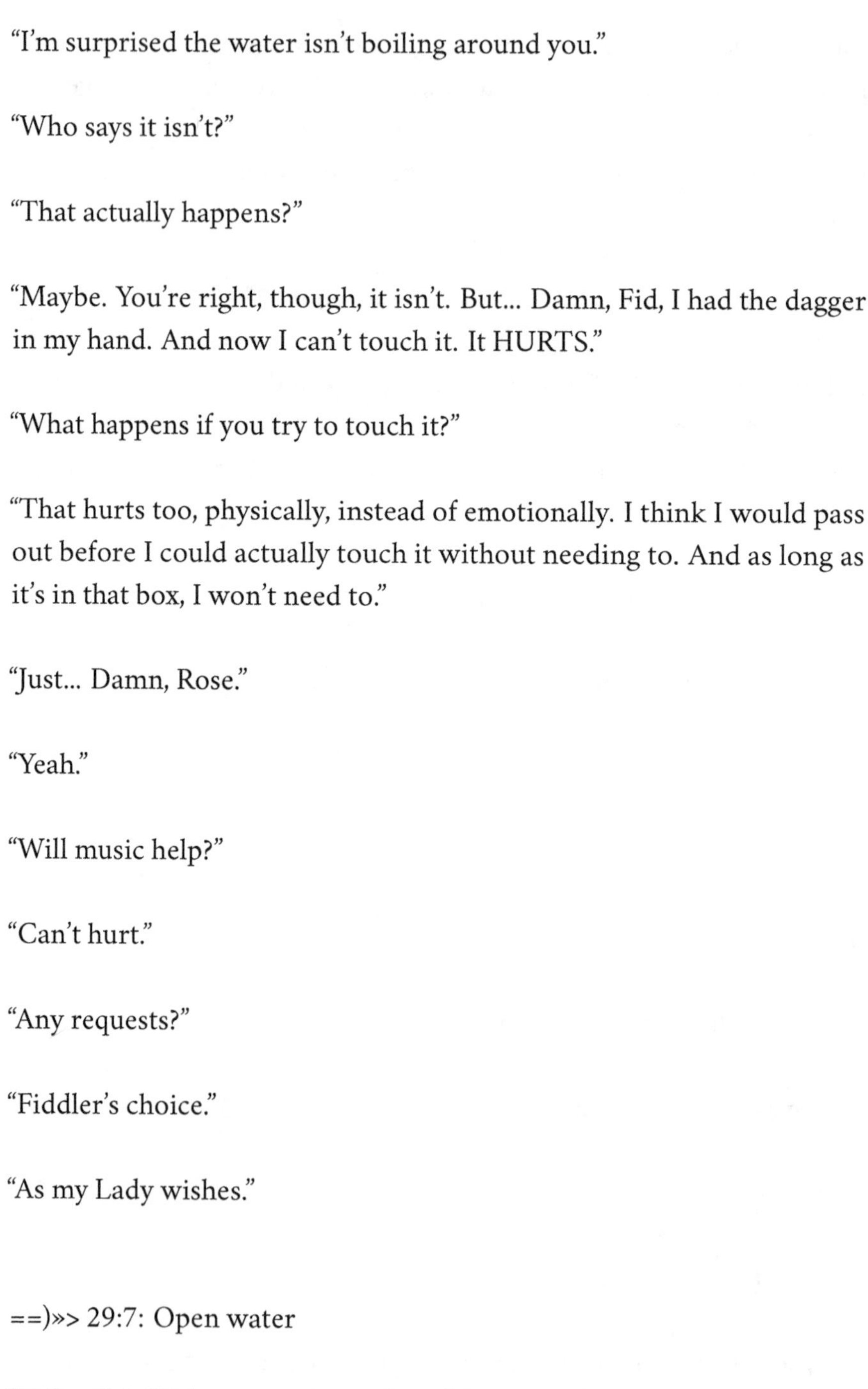

“I'm surprised the water isn't boiling around you.”

“Who says it isn't?”

“That actually happens?”

“Maybe. You're right, though, it isn't. But... Damn, Fid, I had the dagger in my hand. And now I can't touch it. It HURTS.”

“What happens if you try to touch it?”

“That hurts too, physically, instead of emotionally. I think I would pass out before I could actually touch it without needing to. And as long as it's in that box, I won't need to.”

“Just... Damn, Rose.”

“Yeah.”

“Will music help?”

“Can't hurt.”

“Any requests?”

“Fiddler's choice.”

“As my Lady wishes.”

==)»> 29:7: Open water

“Hello, Fid. Welcome to the surface. I know you're still in the box, but I think you can hear me, so I'm just going to assume that you can, and if you can't, you can tell me about it the next time we talk in trance or dream. But right now I HAVE to talk, because I've already turned enough of the local air blue, and there's nothing handy that I'm willing to punch. So the situation is that the idiots in the 'Barracuda Dream' have abandoned me. We were gone for a bit more than three hours, and they're over the horizon, which means that they pretty much had to set every sail they had and run as soon as I was under the water. But that also means that they'll be easy to catch. So I've disconnected your box from the descender, and slung it across my chest, and I'm going to hunt the 'Dream' down, and explain to them what a bad idea it is to anger a third circle sorcerer who was already so angry she thought she would explode. It's time to go flying. Sorry you can't see."

==)»> 29:8: Near "Barracuda Dream"

"HEAVE TO! HEAVE TO NOW, OR I WILL BURN YOU TO THE WATERLINE."

==)»> 29:9: Aboard "Barracuda Dream"

"What were you thinking?" Rose demanded.

"You were gone," the captain stammered. "And the men were— are— terrified of you. We had all been talking about it for days. We decided we didn't care if we never saw the last third of the payment, we just wanted to be away from you."

"You were terrified of me," Rose answered. "Because my shadow wasn't human, and what I wanted didn't make sense."

"Yes."

"You had no idea, did you?" Rose growled. "And now I am so angry, at someone else, who has nothing whatsoever to do with you, that I just want to DESTROY something, and you idiots go and give me an excuse to vent my anger at you."

"I'm... We're all... sorry..."

"I don't care. I'm not going to hurt you, unless you do something ELSE stupid. But any man who raises a weapon against me is DEAD, you understand?"

"Yes, Ma'am..."

"I am the Duchess of Dragonfall, and you will address me properly."

"Yes, your Grace. Certainly, your Grace."

"Now go. Best possible speed back to Skytower, and full sail in the darkness. I'll let you know if you can shorten sail. And stay out of my way."

"Yes, your Grace."

==)»> 29:10: Darkness

"Hello, Rose."

"Hello, Fid."

"I would like to apologize, on behalf of an uncaring universe, for the things that have happened to you in the last twelve hours."

"That's sweet of you. The universe can burn."

"It probably won't. Sorry."

"I can SEE the dagger, Fid. It's sitting right in front me, and the box is open. All I have to do is take it in my hand and claim the bond and you could pull me into dreamspace and... But if I tell my hand to pick up the dagger it feels like a bomb is going off inside my head. It's so CLOSE. YOU are so close. And I can't do it."

"We'll get through this."

"Maybe."

"We WILL, Rose. Cinnabar probably won't, but you and I will."

"We were so close, Fid. It was supposed to be easy. There wasn't supposed to be a duel with another third circle between us and being together."

"To say nothing of a mutiny."

"That's just a bad joke. I'm glad I didn't kill any of them. I wanted to sink the ship."

"Probably good you didn't."

"It would have made getting back to Skytower unpleasant."

"At least."

"And I would have felt guilty about it for YEARS."

"I know. I was proud of you for not killing any of them."

"As long as they stay out of my way. My reserves of self-control are low."

"I imagine."

"Music, Fid? Fiddler's choice?"

"As my Lady wishes."

==)»> 29:11: Darkness

"Good evening, Rose."

"Hello, Fid. Ready for the next stage of the trip?"

"Say what?"

"By morning we'll be close enough to Skytower that I can fly the rest of the way, so we're going to."

"Do I have a say?"

"Not really."

"Then I guess that that's what we're going to do."

"It'll be fun. You'll get to ride along while I re-energize the spell in free fall."

"Oh, joy."

“You know that I’ve practiced it. It’s routine.”

“Falling a thousand feet is NOT routine.”

“Well, it’s FUN...”

“I have bound my existence to a maniac.”

“Not yet, but you will.”

“I find that strangely comforting.”

==)»> 29:12: The streets of Skytower

“We’re at his door, Fid, and he had damned well better be home,” Rose said, and knocked.

“Rose?” a surprised male voice said shortly. “I wasn’t expecting you...”

“You should have been, Nab. You’ve been waiting for this day for two years.”

“You mean... You got it? You’re bringing it to me?”

“You didn’t leave me a choice, did you? But you bound a second circle sorcerer, and you CAUGHT a third circle. You should worry about that.”

“It’s just business, Rose, it’s not...”

“Personal? How many times did we have sex so that you could get this damned spell further into my head? A hundred? And it’s not PERSONAL?”

"Fine. Be angry. I still win. What is it?"

Rose set the box on something and flipped open the lid. "It's the horn of a unicorn. The ghost of the unicorn that grew the horn is bound to it."

"What's it good for?"

"I don't have to tell you. I will tell you, though, that that ghost has had five bound partners since he was killed, and HE has killed two of those himself."

"But..."

"And I will also tell you that, because of this little trick, I consider that you and I will be in a state of blood feud the moment you pick up that dagger and set me free from this compulsion."

"Rose..."

"You're better at mind tricks than I am; I'll grant you that. But I'm not going to be trying to beat you at your own game, this time. This time I'll be trying to make you dead. I'm GOOD at making people dead, Nab. I've killed a crocodilian and a minotaur with a blade, and two dragons, one of them third stage, with magic. Are you a killer, Nab? Or just a swindler and a thief?"

"Rose, I... What...?"

"Let us go, Nab. Pick up the dagger and hand it back to me, release me from all compulsions, swear to me that you will leave me and mine alone on pain of death, and I won't declare the blood feud, and my friend the ghost will have no cause to try to kill you."

"I have to pick up the dagger to release you."

"I know. Be quick. Stay away from the blade for your own sake."

"I accept delivery of this object from Rose Stonecrow, and free her from all obligation to me, either legal or magical, and I return this dagger to her of my own free will."

"Put it back in the box, and stay out of my way. Consider relocating to another continent." Rose closed the box and slung it over her shoulder. "I'm serious, Nab. Move far away."

On the street a few minutes later, Rose hugged the box to her chest and said, "I think we won, Fid. Sit tight for just a little longer."

==)»> 29:13: Rose's room

"Welcome home, Fid."

"What the hell, Rose? You put me back in that thrice-damned box!"

"What was I going to do, Fid? Walk down the street with a dagger in my hand?"

"Well..."

"Besides, I wanted to get to this moment with as few distractions as possible."

"This moment?"

"One of us has a physical body, which has now been bathed, and fed, and wrapped in silk, and is in fact ever so slightly drunk. And I wanted to get all of that out of the way before we did the binding, because I'm pretty sure that after we do the binding we're going to want to be off in dreamspace for a long time."

"I won't argue with that."

"And if I'm going to be abandoning my physical body for several hours, I want it to be comfortable. And trying to get ready while juggling an impatient dagger would have made me crazy."

"I guess."

"BUT... I am, as has been said, bathed and fed and sitting on the best bed in the world, with the aforementioned dagger in my hand, and Osprey has been dead for eight years, and I've been chasing you for four, and it's just plain time."

"I... Yeah, it is."

"So... I am Duchess Emerald Corrosion Flower Stonecrow of Dragonfall, Dragon-marked, Dragon Slayer, Twin-bride, Dryad-sister, and by my will, and by my blood... You need to let me make the cut, Fid. Really, you do."

"Fine."

"And by my will, and by my blood, and with your consent, I bind you, Fiddler Centaurson, to me at least as long as I draw breath, and as long thereafter as I can manage it."

"And I, Fiddler Centaurson, accept this binding gleefully and wholeheartedly."

"What? WOW, Fid, what was that?"

"Your will feeding me, and me feeding it back to you."

"I feel like I could do one-handed handsprings."

"You probably can. But you're going to want to wipe the flat of the blade across that cut before you get blood on your gown."

"It's healed. There's a scar, but it's healed."

"It's a binding ritual cut, so it's bound to leave a scar, but, yeah. You can heal ANYTHING with a unicorn's horn."

"Damn."

"Now clean up the blood, douse the light, and fall asleep already. I've been planning this night for... nine years, I think."

"NINE?"

"Ever since you left the 'Sufferance'. Contingency plans, just in case we ever saw each other again."

"Just in case..."

"And there's the blush. I've still got it."

==)»> 29:14: Waterfall glade

Rose put her hands behind her head, looked up at the stars— which perfectly matched her memory of the stars from the previous night—

sighed, closed her eyes, and for just that moment, was utterly content.

"Given the admittedly questionable assumption that we ever leave this place again, what does her Grace have in mind for the future?" Fiddler asked.

Rose opened her eyes and turned her head to look at him; he was lying on his side, his head propped on one fist. "With a certain amount of schedule juggling, we have to visit Maelstrom so I can get that fifth dragon mark; we need to see Turo and Ollie married to their new wives; we need to visit with Drellan and Dzee at least briefly; we need to visit Auntie Moss, and we really should pay a visit to Bing and Rilla. I need to make sure that Dragonfall is up and running, and I need to hire another one of the Weird Sisters..."

"Is that what they're called?"

"That's what I've decided to call them. But I need to get one of them installed as my castellan in the Losthaven kobtown. We should visit Ironbridge, so that you can say hello to your surviving fans, and yes, you can start some new legends with Granddaughter the barmaid if she's willing. And we need to visit Apple and Amaranth and Winter. And then, after we have given reasonable thanks to everyone who helped us get to this point..."

"Which is already sounding like a major quest in itself..."

"And then, we go looking for Salsi's bones, and make sure that they've been properly laid to rest."

"Why do you care about Salsi?"

"Because you loved her, silly Fiddler."

"Oh."

"And while I'm at it... Fiddler Centaurson, I love you. I promised not to let myself say that out loud until I could say it to your face, and now I have."

"You're a little late with that."

"When have I said that before? I've wanted to, but... I just wouldn't. I got it in my head that it would jinx things if I said it out loud."

"You said it. You just never said it in Kzanti."

"So what, Dragontongue? I haven't said it that way, either."

"No, not Dragontongue."

"Then what?"

"Not any particular language. But it means that you love me, and I defy you to deny that it means that you love me."

"You're probably delusional, and I'm definitely confused. Just say it, so I can laugh at you, and we can move on."

"Five hundred miles..."

"And two thousand fathoms. Well played, Master Fiddler. I think you get to claim a forfeit."

"Give me a moment. I'll probably think of something."

About the Author

Many, many years ago, P.D. Haynie, who is usually known as "Paul", decided to try his hand at writing as an alternative to jumping off a tall building. He has been studying the craft of story-telling, and trying to create a story worth telling, ever since. "Fiddler's Rose" is his first completed novel.

He claims to be human by Robert A. Heinlein's definition. In addition to being a writer, he has by turns described himself as a wastrel, a dilettante, an errantrist, an ethicist, a curmudgeon, a game freak, a math head, a history buff, a fan of science fiction and fantasy, a reluctant pagan, and a low-rent yachtsman.

Paul lives in Waukegan, Illinois, with his wife Julia and an embarrassing number of disturbingly personalized plush toys. He is currently vacillating between careers as a full time writer and a poverty-stricken, homeless wretch. He has not actually gone by "P.D." in the real world since shortly after he learned to talk.

E-mail: pauldavidhaynie@gmail.com

You can connect with me on:
https://www.facebook.com/SpiralPathPublications

Also by P.D. Haynie

Unicorns & Other Monsters
Nine medieval fantasy short stories will take the reader from twilight to darkness and back into the light. Some monsters are people; some people are monsters. Strange forces like courage, honor, friendship, and love can drive all of them– and all of us.

Available in print from Amazon.com, and as an e-book from most e-book vendors.

E-mail spiralpathpublications@.gmail.com for more information!

www.ingramcontent.com/pod-product-compliance
Lightning Source LLC
Chambersburg PA
CBHW052339020726
47503CB00001B/33

9781950237036